THE SWORD OF MARY

by Esther M. Friesner

THE SWORD OF MARY
Esther M. Friesner

Borealis is an imprint of White Wolf Publishing.

White Wolf Publishing
780 Park North Boulevard, Suite 100
Clarkston, GA 30021

World Wide Web Page: www.white-wolf.com

Cover Photograph by Pamela Dawn
Cover Design by Michelle Prahler

Printed in Canada

Chapter One

Maiden sleeping, speak your dreams.
I see a city far away,
Gold and silver, pearl and rose,
Vanished with the break of day.
Maiden waking, speak your heart.
Still I behold the city clear,
Safely pent within my soul,
Free of ruin, free of fear.

"Becca, wake up! The rain's done. We can be on the road."

Becca sat up and rubbed her eyes once, then again. Since she had lain down to sleep last night, her world had wrapped itself in a shroud of fog that pierced her, flesh and bone. She couldn't remember ever having been so cold.

Gilber Livvy looked up from where he squatted by the small, dead ashes of their campfire, packing away the last few bits of his gear. He traveled light, Becca's sweet man from the mountains, because he owned the lore to use the findings of the trail. Unlike any stead-raised man, Gilber could step into a wilderness and see a full-stocked storeplace. Sometimes Becca asked herself whether it was so for all his tribe, and if it was a thing they gained through lessoning or had at birth. You couldn't tell with Jews.

"What's wrong, love? The damp?" Gilber was with her at once, his arms around her, driving out the chill. When he pressed his face to her hair she could smell the good woodsy scent of him. She closed her eyes and sighed.

"That," she answered. "That and then some." She made a short, impatient sound, riled at no one but herself. "How could I have been so *wrong?*"

"Wrong over what?" He settled her more snugly in his embrace and leaned back. There was a rough, half-ruined wall behind them, one of three left partly standing to hold up a scrap of roof. It was all that had kept the rain off them last night and spared their campfire. Such shelter in the heart of wasteland was a miracle; finding it another. Gilber Livvy believed in miracles.

And Becca believed in Gilber Livvy. All he'd saved her from, all he'd done for her, added to how heartily she longed after him. So much yearning was a frightsome thing. Even the touch of his breath over her cheek had the art to kindle her desire. She closed her eyes tight, driving out the demons.

What's the use to go aching after him when you know—

"I thought we'd be there by now," she said. She made the words come out angry. Maybe if she riled herself enough, she could think on something less contrary than this peculiar man. "The city didn't look so far off as this when I saw it, but here we've been two days on the road and still—"

"You weren't bred to have an eye for gauging distance," Gilber soothed. " 'Sides, I don't think you had a clear seeing."

"How can you say that?" Becca snapped, pushing away from him and scrambling to her feet. Anger could burn away desire, give her back some measure of mastery over herself. She pointed a trembling finger in his face and shouted, "I know what I saw, Gilber Livvy! You saw it too, so don't try talking smart about it. I swear by the Lord Himself and Mary Mother, I saw the city waiting for us, calling, welcoming us to the gates!"

Gilber folded his long legs under him and shook his head. "I know what you saw too, love, and I know what you showed Virgie and me. Only thing is, we saw it with our eyes; you had a seeing from the soul."

"So what if I did?" She spoke a challenge. Since that twilit hour two days past, Becca wore her vision of the city like a crown, the shining crown that saints claim when they reach the Lord's own celestial home. Waking, it was all she spoke of; sleeping, it was all she dreamed. It had come to her at a ghost's summoning, sailing forth to meet her on the hour of brightness and shadows between night and dawn. Seeing it, she understood what the women of lost

Wiserways Stead meant when they spoke so breathless of Elijah's rapture into heaven. All the horrors she had passed through, all the evils she had borne were healed by the sight of the city alone. "So what if it was a soul-seeing? Does that steal the truth of it?"

Her man raised his hands and smiled surrender, though he didn't know the half of the war between them. "Easy, Becca, easy. I never meant it to sound like it was a lacking thing. My oath on it, our scrolls vouch for the holiness of visions. I just never quite expected to find myself yoked to a prophetess."

"You're making fun of me." Becca turned from him and hugged herself in misery.

She felt his hands on her shoulders, though she'd never heard so much as the whisper of a footstep to warn her that he'd stood up and come after her. The mist surrounding them was no more silent in its comings and goings than Gilber Livvy. "I couldn't do so, Becca. You know that." And without another word, his touch fell from her. She spun to face him in time to hear him say, "How can I mock what I love?"

You've a fine way of showing it. The thought came up out of her, fierce, but not fierce enough to let her speak it out loud. There was still some little scrap of Becca's stead-reared ways clinging to her, a fluttery warning flag that cautioned a wise woman from speaking her mind too bold, too often to a man.

She did find enough bone in her to say, "If that's so, you'd best tell me how your folk treat their Deborahs."

"Deborahs?" Gilber echoed.

"That's how we name women who can see beyond."

"Ah." Gilber nodded. "A fine name for a sight-singer *and* a fighter. My mother told me the tale of Deborah often enough when I was young. There was a woman for you! She was set up to judge all Israel, the same as any man, and all her words were wisdom."

Becca's brows knit. "A *woman* to rule?" Despite herself, the words came out robed in all her mother's tight, querulous disapproval of females who overstepped their natural place.

Now Gilber was mocking her, she could see it in the way his dark eyes twinkled when he said, "I thought you steadfolk knew all the tales we do. Don't tell me you've never read Deborah's story!"

"It's not for us to read Scripture freely," she replied, drawing herself up so that formality pushed him away from her even though their bodies stayed the same distance apart. "We're given the women's Scripture for our lessoning and Pa—" There was still a dull pain in her throat when she mentioned her murdered sire. "—Pa would read to us all from the full Scripture when it was fitting."

Gilber whistled low, marveling over her words. Then he shrugged and said, "Well, this is no place to fix your education. We've got a road to walk, and where's that Virgie?"

Becca shook her head. "You'd know that more than me, Gilber Livvy."

"I gave her a chore to do. You were sleeping so sound, I didn't care to trouble you," he said.

You never trouble me with chores at all, now, Becca

thought, and her mouth filled with the taste of sickness.

"I sent her with the gourds to fetch water for the march, but in this fog—" His eyes were keen enough to mark a moonlit target racing at full pace, but the twisting curls of mist baffled them. "She should've been back by now." For once, he looked as frighted by the fog-draped wilderness around them as any steadman. Cupping one hand to his mouth, he called the girl's name. Only silence answered.

He called again, and again there was no reply. Becca tried, adding her voice to his, to no effect. The emptiness turned weighty, hung heavy on Becca's shoulders. She forgot all her little grievances against Gilber as her concern for the lost girl grew. She stole nearer to him and slid herself under his arm, wanting comfort. "Maybe we should go after her? You know the way she took?"

Gilber's face was set tight. He only nodded once, short, and plunged into the fog. For once Becca had no trouble keeping up with his pace. He'd suffered a harsh wound not so long since, and it had taken some of the edge off his vigor. It was a miracle that it hadn't killed him. Becca shuddered at the very thought of losing Gilber, even now when all threat of it seemed gone. She pressed herself more closely to his side as they walked on, seeking Virgie.

A salt breeze began to blow in, thinning the mist with the scent of the sea. Gilber called out Virgie's name every few steps, but got no answer. A cold rain came drizzling down, little sister to what had fallen the night before, laying the fog to rest. Gray skies overhead mirrored the desolation of the land under their feet. Gilber stopped short at the verge of a shallow pond that was more of a puddle, stopped so short that Becca's foot went in up to the ankle.

"See here," he said, trying to keep the fear from his voice. He hunkered down and pointed to the two big gourds abandoned beside the water. They were Virgie's, brought with her when she joined her lot to theirs.

Becca felt a rock lodge in her throat. "Why would she—?"

Gilber's gaze swept the verge of the pond, his eyes narrowed. "They took her that way," was all he said, and stood up with his hands going to fists for battle.

"They—?" Becca stared hard at the earth where Virgie's gourds still lay. Gilber was trained to the trail and the wilderness, but even a stead-reared girl like Becca could see the story trampled out at the waterside. It was plain as hunger: Though Virgie was a tall girl, almost woman-grown, she'd never leave prints so broad, so big as these. Besides, here were the marks of her own feet beside the bigger ones. "How many?" Becca asked.

"I figure two." Gilber started off across the cold ground, rain caping his shoulders. He paused only long enough to say, "Take the gourds back to camp, Becca, and keep under cover until I come."

She left the gourds where they were and left his words to the air. Holding her skirts high, she pelted to his side and laid hold of his arm. "I'm not leaving you."

For an instant she thought she saw the

unthinkable: Gilber Livvy's eyes going hard as any alph's when faced with a headstrong woman. But then he said, "All right. We'll track this together. Best to take up arms first anyhow. No use in walking down a wolf's throat without a spike to stake open his jaws."

It took them only moments to fetch what was needful from their camp. Gilber cradled his rifle easily in the crook of one arm, but Becca held the gun that was her sire's legacy in a grip so tight it made her knuckles ache. The weapon itself she kept hid under her skirts, which made the footing awkward. At one point Gilber looked up from Virgie's trail, glanced over at grim-faced Becca, and couldn't hold back an almost soundless chuckle. Becca followed where his eyes rested, to the outline the hidden gun gave to her skirts, and turned red as apples.

If ever any man wanted proof that I'm no natural woman—she thought, shamed. She shifted the heavy weapon to one hand and carried it still wrapped from the rain but over to one side.

Gilber's free hand flickered up suddenly before her face, then made a gesture that bid her keep silence and hark. She froze where she stood, straining all her senses to learn what had set her man tensed to spring. The mist was almost gone by now, though bolls of it lingered in the hollow places. She and Gilber stood in such a scooped-out part of the earth, a shallow pocket of land in the midst of many low mounds. Gilber laid himself flat against the nearest one, crept up the slope on his belly, motioning her to wait.

She wasn't made for waiting any more. To bide and

to obey were womanly virtues long lost to her. They belonged to the life she'd left behind. She'd turned her back on the ways of the steads, the hard rule of alphs, the iron decrees of manlore and womanlore. Somewhere to the west lay Wiserways and all its sister steads, the farmland daughters of Verity Grange. They might as well have been on the moon.

Calmly Becca knotted the gun in one underskirt, then bound up the rest of them to free her legs. Miming Gilber's silent ways, she too sprawled down to hug the ground, to shimmy up the flank of the mound and see what it was Gilber had heard from the far side.

He was only a little surprised to see her beside him. Was that a smile he gave her? Her heart said it was because it had to be. Then his face darkened, all business, and he jerked his chin at the crest of the mound, no more than three fingers' span above them. Little by little they took the top and looked down.

Becca's jaw fell open so wide, she bruised her chin on gravel. There sat a beaming Virgie, queening it from a throne made of travelers' packs, while two men—one as black as she, the other almost sunbrowned so—filled her hands with bread and the cup at her feet with drink.

"Well, I'll be. . ." Gilber's voice didn't rise above an astonished whisper, but it was enough. Virgie's hosts had ears as trail-sharp as Gilber's own, it seemed. They were instantly on guard, whirling to a crouch that promised battle, hands clapped to their belt sheaths. Whether these held blades or better, Becca couldn't see.

"Who's there?" the black man shouted. "Show yourself!" Something silver-bright glittered in his hand.

"Wait, Matt!" Virgie cried, slipping from the pile of packs to seize his arm. "That'll be them, my friends I told you 'bout."

"You hope, girlie," the other man said. His weapon was out, a gun, but sleeker than the one Becca owned. Even at this distance, she could see he had eyes the same sickly green color as Adonijah's. Not knowing more than that, she felt mistrust tie her bowels in knots.

"Becca!" Virgie called. "Gilber, come on, come out! These are friends. They're from the city, they'll help us."

Becca hugged the hillside, partly unwilling to move, partly unable. As for Gilber, the tension ebbed from his limbs. By little and little he raised his body from the earth until he was standing in the clear atop the mound, his rifle down at his side, no threat to any man.

"Where's the other?" Matt demanded, his own gun still hovering between peace and death.

"*Becca!*" Virgie's voice sharpened with the impatience of the very young. "Where are you? Show your face! I tell you, these are *friends*."

Becca levered herself up, first making haste to undo the immodest set of her skirts. The gun knocked against her thigh when she stood, safe in its hidden hammock. She clasped her hands before her and lowered her eyes, a proper woman waiting on the judgment of men.

Chapter Two

*I've got a riddle for you: What's the most
dangerous part of a man?*
No, not that.
*It's his nose, if he always goes sticking it
into business where it never did belong.*

"Did you ever," Gilber breathed, standing with
Becca and Virgie, Matt and Solomon beside the
highway that led straight to the gates of the bastioned
city. Stock still he stood by the side of the road and
let his amazement steal all power from his legs. "Did
you ever."

Virgie quailed and pressed her lean body against
Gilber's, awestruck by the sight. Becca tried to
maintain some calm, though it didn't come

untouched by hard feelings. *They weren't this taken when I shared my vision of the city with them*, she thought, lower lip stealing out into an unbecoming pout. *Sometimes I wonder did they truly see it at all.*

Still, she knew this daylight seeing owned things her vision couldn't hope to contain. She'd done her best to give them all she'd seen of the city, luminous with distance, shining with all the lights of heaven, but how could she? Gilber himself had said that her vision hadn't come from the eyes, but the soul. How could she open up that hiddenmost part of her, even to the man she loved better than breath? No matter how much she wanted to, such a power lay beyond her.

Maybe it wouldn't, if he loved me the same as I love him, Becca thought. *But he can't; not anymore. In his eyes, I'm no longer just another woman. He thinks my secret's made me greater, but I know the truth: It's lessened me. If it's drawn me from him, Mary Mother witness how dear it's lessened me.*

It was a sharp-toothed revelation, the sort that Hattie would disapprove. Becca's ma believed that proper women governed themselves perfectly outside and in. Times past, when Wiserways breeding was still rooted fast in her blood, Becca might have put such thoughts down to the whisperings of the worm, Satan's own creature that slithered into a woman's mind like the Serpent himself, words dripping the poison of doubt, seeding questions like tares. These days, she knew different. The worm was gone from her mind, but not the words or the doubts: They were hers, and she admitted to them no matter what sort of a monster that made her. *In a world of monsters, I'll survive.*

She felt Gilber give her hand a gentle squeeze. "Look there, love," he said, voice newborn to wonder. He nodded toward the highway and all its seaward-running tide, human and machine.

Becca looked, and though the road itself was a marvel, she couldn't find it in her to be awed by its freight. *Why—why, this isn't such a much,* she thought, and the realization startled her more than anything. *There was more than this to see when we went up to Verity for harvest home.* That was so; she couldn't borrow any of Gilber's exaltation nor Virgie's fear any more than she could lend them the heart-high joy of her vision. All at once, she felt alone.

"It's something," she managed to say, and squeezed his hand back. And yes, it *was* something, that road leading straight and true to the Coop gates. Like Matt and Solomon, all the city-bound travelers wore the same wondrous, bizarre clothes Becca recalled from Verity Grange—breeches and boots, tunic and hood in their prismed brilliance—and all went mounted in chariots fit to lift a dozen souls at once into the sight of God. None of the passers-by spared the five companions by the roadside a glance.

At least they won't ask the reason for our coming until we reach the Coop. Becca gathered comfort from the thought. Her greatest fear, since they'd encountered Matt and Solomon, was that she and Gilber and Virgie would be questioned about what business brought them to the city.

She knew that Virgie would keep mum. The black

girl saw silence as her one salvation. She'd left kin behind her, little sibs hostage in the hands of the uncanny boy-alph, Mark. Becca and Gilber too had been his unwelcome "guests" and knew how he ruled his eerie stead in the ruins. The knowledge still troubled Becca's mind in the shivery time just before sleep. Virgie meant to go into the city, gather up as many goods as might make life on Mark's stead a measure easier, and steal off with her haul quick, undetected.

Or she meant so before, Becca thought. *As for now—* She stole a glance at the girl's wide-eyed face. Virgie had a fighter's heart, even though she was still little more than a child. She'd soon break the grip of this fear that had laid hold of her. That was good; Becca wanted Virgie strong beside her for what the two of them had to do when they reached the city.

For the children. And she thought about Mark's feral eyes, free of any mercy, and trembled.

Gilber? He wouldn't hold back an instant with the truth, if someone asked him—it was what had driven him so far, so desperately fast to the Coop, seeking answers for his tribe. There was no telling how Matt and Solomon would react once they heard that here stood a Jew, a creature out of legend, come begging aid for other Jews who'd holed up in the mountains since the Hungering Times. In all the years that had passed since then, they'd held off their enemies, lived their lives by their own peculiar teachings, scorned the ways of stead, grange and city. They had survived.

But Gilber'd told her how things were with his people now: how there were more and more babies born in that mountain isolation who came into this world flawed in mind and body. Mouths to feed, all of them, no matter if they could never earn their keep. Every life born into Gilber's tribe was a life to be sustained. His tribe had no slope where the Lord King Herod might gather in the souls of His children, no place like Prayerful Hill, built of the bones of the chosen.

As for herself, Becca knew she'd speak the truth willingly. Only thing was, not here, not now, not until she was well within the city gates. *Not until I'm face to face with Eleazar*, she thought. *He'll hear me out, my brother. He'll stand with me to get justice for Pa's murder. And even before I plead for that, he'll stand with me to save Virgie's sibs and all the other children.*

Now the city gates were well and truly within sight, within reach. Becca's heart beat high. "I wish we could ride," she said, eyeing the passing chariots. "We'd get there faster, sure."

She heard the Coop folk chuckling behind her. She couldn't tell whether they meant it kindly or thought less of her and Gilber and Virgie for gawking so at what must be commonplace to them. Solomon adjusted the fit of his hood more closely, to keep the dust and dirt of the road out of his bright gold hair, and said, "Sure you wouldn't be scared to be up so high, girlie?"

"I doubt it," Becca replied, holding back her temper. It would never do to lash out at this man for speaking down to her so. Gilber Livvy bore with such outbursts, but Gilber wasn't a man like other men. Becca knew she'd have to mount sterner guard over her own tongue now that they'd come out of the wilderness and back into the settled lands. Very softly, very maidenly she said, "On our stead, we had leave from the Coop to work our land with such engines, some even bigger than those." She gestured at the procession of fabulous carts and chariots the cityfolk rode. "They gave us leave to trade for the fuel to run 'em, too, and in the fitting season my sire even let some of us older girls ride 'em."

"And I suppose you were one of the chosen ones?"

"*Chosen?*" Becca's eyes shot sparks. This went beyond funning; she'd risk the consequences for it but she *would* speak. Lips taut, she told him, "I don't know where you were bred, mister, but where I'm from—stead, grange and Coop—the only ones fit to be named *chosen* are the Lord King's own."

Solomon's face flushed red beneath the tan. He looked away from Becca's fury for shame. Matt scowled and thumped his shoulder hard, saying, "You idiot! That tongue of yours is going to get you killed one day. Apologize to the lady!"

Solomon did, all trace of condescension vanished. "I beg your pardon, miss, I'm half the fools in the dictionary and then a few. It's just that Matt and I have been on the road for a long time, just the two of us on last-minute Coop business that our web wants wrapped away before winter. All the vehicles were assigned, we had to go on foot, so we're tired, and being tired always makes me careless of the courtesies. If you see fit to report this, I hope you won't lay any of the blame for it on Matt. He can't help who he travels with. The blame's all mine."

Becca no more liked to see a soul so humbled before her than she liked being humbled herself. The apology had come readily; forgiveness should come readily too. She smiled at Solomon and said, "You've made amends. There's no need to speak of this again that I can see, here or in the city."

His face transformed with a smile. "Well, bless you! You've got a decent heart. I'll tell you what, you're right: It *would* make your journey easier if you were to ride the rest of the way. Why don't I see what I can do to arrange that?"

He darted for the road, but Matt grabbed his arm and yanked him back. "What do you think you're doing?"

"What does it look like? I'm going to flag them a ride. We'd have to split up sooner or later anyhow." He shrugged off Matt's hand and waded into the traffic.

Becca watched him go, this time just as astonished as Gilber and Virgie to see the way the city man danced and dodged around the unrelenting parade of vehicles. She'd stretched the truth more than a handspan when she claimed to be used to machines like these. On Wiserways there were none to compare for size with the monsters now lumbering along before her eyes.

Only a few of the passing conveyances were small; these hewed to the left side of the road, nearest to where Becca and her party stood. Most of the vehicles, the giants, went in double file in the middle of the highway, which was all of beaten earth. If Becca strained her eyes to the east, where the city waited, she thought she saw the point where the road's surface turned to pave. The middle-road trams were made of several huge oblong compartments, linked together and mounted on treads, the whole chain conducted by the lone Coop-trader mounted on the head car.

Oh, you woeful liar! Becca chided herself. The fact was, she'd never before seen anything quite so impressive as these midroad trams, not even when she'd gone to harvest home.

She'd also never seen any daring to match the Coopman's as he bobbed in and out amid the trams, like a flight-drunk littlesinger in a summer sky. It was a mercy he wasn't run down more than once. Becca couldn't understand how the drivers were able to spy him in time to avoid hitting him. In spite of the recent rain, the churning of so many wheels and treads had already transformed the unpaved roadway back to sight-obscuring dust. Becca caught a lungful and coughed like to choke. Gilber and Virgie gathered around her, pounding her back and offering her a sip from their gourds. These were almost empty, and she drank what little liquid was left with no noticeable relief. Matt stood to one side, arms folded, making no move to offer her any of his own water.

Though her eyes were clouded with tears from the coughing fit, Becca still caught a glimpse of his expression and a sliver of dread passed over her heart. She knew hate when she saw it. *Mary Mother, more borrowed trouble? Now what've I done?*

Before she could seek an answer, she felt Gilber's strong hands on her, pulling her away from the roadside just as a single-car chariot lumbered up onto the shoulder almost on top of them. She gasped as she lurched backward into his arms, and that set her off choking again.

A voice steeped deep in disgust came down from on high. "Fine, what's this lot? More recruits? I thought the season was done. Show me your papers and— Oh, *here*, girl! Drink this and stop your damned coughing." A smooth, cool cylinder was put into Becca's hands and she drank a tart-sweet brew that settled the dust in her throat at once.

"Thank you, sir," she said, giving it back and wiping her eyes. The trader scowled, cold to her courtesy, eyes the only feature visible with that cowl pulled down low over brow and high enough to veil nose and mouth from the roadway dust.

"I told you to show me your recruitment papers." The driver shifted on the high seat and over one shoulder said, "They *do* have them, don't they?"

Becca saw Solomon's head pop into sight from the far side of the driver's seat. "I don't know. We met them sort of by-the-way the other night. Actually, you could say they met us. See that tall girl, there?" He pointed at Virgie. "We came on her just as she was going to draw water from a seeper."

"A seeper!" The trader whistled. "So how much did you charge them for the saving of their lives?"

Solomon shrugged. "You know that's not how we do things."

"Oh, maybe not how *you* two do things. If you lived any further by-the-way instead of by-the-book, you'd make your own web. Not one likely to last, but—"

"Anyone ever tell you you've got a big mouth?" Solomon grumbled.

"Everyone, always. That's why they don't expect me to hold any secrets." The driver's chuckle had a nasty bite to it. "Which still doesn't explain why you didn't ask for their papers. Other things on your mind, I'll bet, the freedom of the road for one last glorious time before— Never mind, I'm with you. I can give them a lift, as a favor to you and Matt, but I'm in a hurry." The driver's stare swung back to transfix Gilber. "Well, where are they?"

"Where are—?"

"Your recruitment papers. I'm no featherhead like these two boys. You might as well show them to me now, so we're not held up too long at the gates. Come on, come on, you've put me behind as it is."

"Papers," Gilber repeated. "I don't have—"

"My brother had them," Becca spoke up.

The driver nodded slowly. "And where would he be, this brother of yours?"

"In the city. He went there years ago."

"*In* the city. The other side of the walls, is that right?" The corners of the driver's eyes crinkled with mirth.

If a jest hung in the air between them, Becca missed it. Solemn as a winnowing she bobbed her head and said, "Yes, that's so. That's who we're going to see in the city, sir, my brother Eleazar."

"'Sir' again?" The trader laughed outright. "You *have* come fresh-cut from the fields! No one with an inch of entry-right would come this far without knowing how to tell *sir* from— What *do* you seedgrubs call your women? Marm? Ma'am? Missy?" High-pitched laughter filtered out through the cowl.

Gilber's eyes turned hard. "Sorry to have held you up this long…*ma'am*. Sorry to have troubled you. We've come this far afoot, we'll finish our journey the same." He stepped up to shepherd Becca and Virgie away from this strange creature, but a gloved hand shot down to light gently on the top of Becca's head.

"Oh no, pretty! You mustn't let your skins be made of tissue here or you're good and lost. Come up, come up, ride with me to the gates. You'll make better time—you'll need it—and I owe you for that laugh. Come on, don't be scared, I won't let you fall."

"Becca, I don't think—" Gilber began, but Becca had made up her own mind. A boost of her foot and a heave of the trader's arm and she was seated beside the still-chuckling driver. With a sigh of surrender, Gilber helped Virgie aboard, then scrambled after just as Solomon slid down.

"This is kind of you, uh, miss," Gilber said to the trader. He'd seated himself farthest from her on the narrow, padded bench, with Becca nearest and Virgie squeezed between them.

"Kind? Yes, very kind. And it'll be kind of you to call me by my given name: It's Sela." The trader spoke absently, not even bothering to meet Gilber's eyes. Instead she leaned over the side of the vehicle and hollered down to Matt and Solomon, "So long, boys! I'll see you before it's healthy!"

"If it's ever been healthy to see you at all, Sela," Matt shouted back over the noise of the slowly accelerating engine. The chariot slid back into the traffic stream, leaving the Coopmen to their own means for reaching the city.

Virgie sat twisted around in her seat, her eyes on the two slowly dwindling figures they'd left behind. "Couldn't we have given them a ride too?" she asked, all wistful. "I'd give 'em my place, crouch down behind this bench here and hold on good. Wouldn't you do the same, Gilber?"

"Gladly," Gilber replied. "But I don't think that was their pleasure."

"You think you know their pleasure then, little seedgrub?" The driver sounded amused. "Oh, you'd be a fun one to feed tales to on a winter's night! I'd love to watch those dark eyes of yours get rounder than round. They'd pop right out of your head before I was through."

"Is that so." Gilber kept his voice level, denying there was any bait meant to make him rise. "Could be you'll have the chance yet. Our paths might cross again if that city's not too big a place."

"What would you know of cities?" Sela's gloved hands played over two long, metal sticks, her booted feet spun a pebble-finished gray ball set into the top deck of the chariot. Between these three contrivances, the vehicle kept up speed and was smoothly steered. A lock of hair a few shades paler than Becca's own tumbled out from the edge of the cowl. Gray eyes nearly silver rested by turns on Gilber, Virgie, and last of all Becca.

"Just the little I've heard tell," Gilber answered. Virgie only shrugged thin shoulders.

"Some," Becca said. And then, "Not much. What's it like in there, beyond the gates?"

"Magical," Sela replied. "Enchanted. We're all kings and princes and princesses inside those walls. Only no queens. So sad, not to have a queen, but a princess is the tamer of the two. The towers are carved of gems, the gates are cast of gold. Can't you see it from here? The reflection is positively blinding." This time her laugh sounded like a cackle.

Becca did see. The trader's conveyance had eaten up enough distance to take them off the dirt road, onto a broad track made of closely inset stones of different sizes. The passage of so many vehicles over time had all but worn away the jagged borderlines between them. With nothing underfoot to joggle her sight and a high vantage to lend her eyes distance, Becca could see the Coop city plain.

Plain...

Too plain. The city walls which she'd dreamed so glorious were only built of stone, the pieces as irregular as the roadway paving, trimmed to the same perfect, interlocking fit. They were tall, yet nowhere near the soaring constructs of her vision. What lay beyond the walls was also rock and metal, not hope and dream. Becca folded her hands in her lap and bowed her head, refusing to see more.

She didn't lift up her eyes again until the walls were almost upon them. Becca felt the chariot slowing its pace. The closer they came to the city, the narrower the road grew until its many lanes were down to a track just wide enough to pass through the gate ahead. Sela wedged her chariot into line behind one of the long trams and brought it to a stop.

"Easier to breathe behind the big ones," the trader said over the sound of the idling engine. "It's only the first car that throws off any fumes. Be grateful we don't have to inhale that exhaust. It'd finish you off right away, little seedgrub." One sleekly sheathed finger stroked Becca's left cheek. "You should've waited a month or two; you'd've had the roads and the air to yourself. This is the tail end of the harvest traffic, but afterward there's nothing on the roads to speak of until spring. Ah! There's some luck; the guards finally got their asses moving and that big bastard too." At her words, the tram ahead of them trundled forward, through the gates. "We're next. You'd better get down. I have some slips to show these fine servants of the netherweb, and they don't mention you. Your business isn't mine any longer. What a shame." The gloved hand tugged at Becca's plait. "What a waste."

Becca was more than glad to leap down from the seat and find a place in the line of foot travelers behind Sela's chariot. To judge by their faces, Gilber and Virgie shared her relief.

"That was nothing human," Virgie declared, keeping an uneasy eye on Sela's vehicle.

"That was just one of the city folk," Gilber said, trying to smooth things over. "Their ways aren't yours or mine, but they're as human as we are. Even her."

"Her! That wasn't any kind of female I ever knew," Virgie maintained.

"Well, you know her now," Becca said, doing what

she could to shake the wrinkles and dust of travel from her skirts and make her whole appearance more presentable to the gate guards. The harsh sound of an engine regaining speed startled her. As she watched Sela's chariot rumble on into the city she added, "And with luck we may not have to know her any more."

Chapter Three

I met a man in the street the other day—
no one you'd know—and he looks to me
like he's fresh off the land so I think I'll have
a little fun with him. So I say to him,
"Friend, I can tell just by looking at you
that you're new to the city. It can be a bad
place for someone who doesn't know his
way around. What brings you here? Maybe
I can help you." And the seedgrub says to
me, "I've got business with Webmaster
Ignatius over something I discovered on my
land." (See, he was one of those stead
alphs. I should've known by the smell.)

Now I figure to myself What could it
be? And then I decide it's got to be
something worthwhile, worth a whole lot of
while, if you follow me. You never know
what these seedgrubs are going to dig out

of the dirt. Even a pig can root up gold, like they say. So I think maybe I'll save this fellow the bother of handing his treasure over to Webmaster Ignatius, and I start spinning him a story about how we've got all these rites and rituals for approaching the webmasters in this city, and how Webmaster Ignatius is real touchy about people doing them just so, and how it's worth a man's life if he stumbles over one word or gets one gesture wrong. Seedgrubs don't know; you can tell them anything you like about city ways and they'll believe you. "Maybe you better let me take your place," I tell him. "I know how to do things around here. I'd hate to see a nice strong man like you killed just because you're ignorant."

Then the seedgrub just looks me right in the eye and he says, "Where I come from, a strong man doesn't need to fear anything but a man who's stronger. Just how strong are these webmasters of yours?"

"Strong?" I reply, like it's the most foolish question anyone's ever asked. "Strong? Why, Webmaster Ignatius can destroy a man with a look!"

"Only one man?" the seedgrub asks. "I'm stronger than that. I can destroy a world." And then he reaches into this pouch he's carrying and pulls out a sheaf of papers. I can see writing on them, but it's peculiar stuff. There's words, sure, and there's also *all these lines like wire fencing running across the page, and dots scattered up and down the lines. I'm trying to spell out the words, but they don't make sense. Watch-tet something...Well, anyhow, before I can figure it through, he's got that one sheet in his hand and a match in the other—so I knew he must be one of the top alphs, to own such a thing—and he's struck it all on fire and he holds it, watching it flame, until he had to drop it and it burned to black ash in the street between us.*

So I let him go his ways. Oh, I sent word on ahead to Webmaster Ignatius of what he'd done, burning up that paper and all. Webmaster Ignatius really is touchy about such things, though why— Maybe Webmaster Ignatius had him killed for doing that and maybe not. I think not. Part of me hopes not. He wasn't just strong, that seedgrub, and he sure wasn't ignorant: He was cunning. Maybe even sharp enough to be tamed into a man we could use. See, what I'm saying is, never underestimate the seedgrubs.

Wait, I remember now: Watch-tet owf, that was it. Watch-tet owf. Damned if I know what it means.

The guards at the gate wore green suits, all of a piece, and visored headgear that looked slick as glass, hard as stone. There were about twenty of them at the gateway post, ten to a side. The weapons in their hands made Gilber's rifle look like no more protection than a dry twig.

"Returnees?" It was impossible to fix a sex to the voice of the guard who confronted them. With shining visor down and suit too shapeless to give any clues away, this person left Becca feeling worse thrown off than with Sela.

"No, sirrrmmm—no," she replied. She didn't want a repeat of that shaming scene with the trader woman. Best to give over *sir* and *ma'am* until you could tell such things for certain. "I've come to find my—"

"I didn't think so," the guard said, brisk to get on with business. "Not how you're dressed. And you're on the wrong side of Steadway Gate for unmounted reentry anyhow."

The helmet bobbed to Becca's right where the other decade of guards was questioning a crowd of five travelers afoot. All the way up the road the trams had kept the few walkers hidden from view. Now that she was on ground level again, Becca could see the separate, fenced-off footpath to the far right of the road, paralleling the highway. "If you were returnees, you'd know that."

"We had a ride here," Becca said. "We got down on this side the road. We didn't—"

"At least you're no liars." The guard's visor gave back a flash of light and the fleeting reflection of Becca's eyes. "Recruits, then? Cross over and show them your papers, on the proper side."

"We've got none," Gilber said.

For some reason this response made the guard snicker. "Of course you don't. Not *paper* papers! The pass our agents left with your folks—you know, those little cards? Where are they?"

Gilber only gave the guard a look full of puzzlement.

"Don't tell me you lost them on the road." The guard sighed as if burdened with the world's full weight. "Jesus Christ, this happens all the time! Give you people a freepass and ten to one the first thing you do's try to eat it. Then you go and lose it on the way here. Why couldn't you just wait to be brought here with the regular incoming, next spring? Things can't be that bad on your stead or we'd have heard. There's been a few more changeovers than projected this year, but you all look old enough to live through something like that."

"Changeovers?" Becca repeated, as bewildered as Gilber. Virgie just stood by, head bent, interlocked fingers twisting so hard they seemed like to snap themselves off short.

"Sure, you know— What do you folks call them?" The first guard turned to another and called, "Hey, Ree! You're from the outs. What do they call changeovers on-stead?"

The second guard didn't answer right off, and when she did the lone word came ripe with gall: "Winnowings."

The first guard snapped gloved fingers. *Winnowing* was only a word like so many others to this one. "Yeah, that's it. Right." The visor showed Becca her own face, caught halfway between shock and dead-heart anger. This too was nothing to the guard. "Any of that go on at your stead, then? Where are you three from?"

"We're not recruits," Becca said firmly, sidestepping the questions. "My brother Eleazar was, years back, and we've come to see him because—"

"Then why didn't you say so, damn it?" the guard roared, transformed in one harsh instant as if Becca's speech was spellcraft. "Not returnees, not recruits, waste my time like this when you're just a bunch of runoff trash? Get out of here!"

"But my brother's Coop now!" Becca implored. "Send word to him that I've come, he'll tell you—"

"*I'm* telling you to get the fuck out of here," the guard shot back. "Steadway Gate's for returnees only, and unaccompanied recruits who don't know any better. You want to try someone's patience, you get your butts around north to Old Gate, tell them your story, let them do something about it."

"Please, you have to listen—"

"*Move!*" The unknown weapon swung up to kiss Becca's cheek in the selfsame spot the trader woman's glove had so lately caressed. The three travelers fell back at once, retreating up along the north-running city wall. Behind them came the guard's voice, condemning them all to Hell.

"Well, one thing good's come of this," Gilber remarked as they made their retreat.

"I'd give enough to know what it is," Becca huffed, doggedly following his trail. Away from the great road, the earth around the city was overgrown with weeds and profitless grasses, though not a speck of refuse lay among the thickly teeming stems. Up close to the wall, Gilber was breaking them a path through the thigh-high growth. It was more than sufficient accommodation for a man in breeches, but still left some hard going for a steadwoman in her flowing skirts. Becca had to work hard to make her way, and it was putting her even more out of temper than that twice-cursed guard.

"At least we know you won't hang us all up by that tongue of yours," Gilber said as if it were A-B-C.

"What?" In the shadow of the city, Becca stopped short, hands on hips. "Gilber Livvy—"

Behind her, Virgie giggled. "He's right. The way you spoke up at the gate, oh my! On my old stead, any woman talked like that to a man and my daddy heard tell of it, she'd be gone before her teeth could cool."

"Oh." Becca's hands darted to her mouth, tucking back words already flown. "I never thought—I have been in wilderness too long."

"Forty years, that's the usual stay," Gilber replied. A bit of his old easy, funning way with her had crept back over him. "No, don't fret, love. Now I think of it—really think—we weren't ever in much danger from you talking so bold. Things are different here, that's so."

"Not even inside the city and you're an expert?" Becca challenged him.

He took it in stride. "Enough for what I've seen, what we've all seen. Or will you tell me that someone like that trader Sela'd fit in among your steadwomen?"

"He's struck it there, Becca." Virgie was always quick to back Gilber. "That Sela—" The girl's grin was untainted admiration. "She's a one! Not like nothing I ever saw in skirts before this."

"If she wears skirts at all," Becca said dryly. "Any road, I'll still bridle my tongue. We know what happens to women who talk too pert to men, but there's no rule—stead or grange—to keep women civil among their own kind."

"I don't see how—" Gilber began.

"The guard," Becca replied. "What was the guard?"

"You mean besides a suet-brain?" Gilber's teeth were very white.

"I mean man or woman? For all we know, Coop ways could be the same as stead when it comes to one woman speaking her mind plain to another. If the guard was female too, I didn't offend."

"But the next guard might be male, and if you speak up smart to him like that and the rules here are the same as where you come from—" Gilber clucked his tongue. "Yes, I see what you're after, angel. Guess I was right to start with. Best a cautious tread from here on."

The sun declined as they went along, following the wall. It sank over the scrublands they'd left far behind, yet still they didn't reach another gate.

"Now we know what that trader woman meant when she said we'd need time," Gilber remarked at day's end. "She knew the welcome we'd get. Did you ever hear language like that guard used? If she is a woman, she ought to be shamed."

"And if she's a man?" Becca teased.

"I say he's a man *and* a liar, that shell-head." Virgie sounded tired fit to drop. "There's no Old Gate to this city. He wants us to go all 'round this place until we come back to where we started so he can have a big ol' laugh."

"I don't think so, Virgie," Gilber said. "Simple good sense wouldn't let any man build up a city with just one gateway; not when they've got the manpower to defend more than one. Up in the mountains, even burrowing animals keep a back door for escaping unwanted company."

Virgie leaned against the city wall and slowly sank down in the crackly grass. "I'd rather have the company of those animals than that guard," she said, hugging her knees. "Or that trader, either."

Becca cocked her head. "I thought you took a liking to Sela."

"Partly," the girl admitted. "Just don't know how far I trust her, is all. She dropped us pretty quick when we reached the gate; *she* knew what'd happen when the guard questioned us, and she didn't give us so much as a warning."

"But she did give us a ride," Becca pointed out.

"I wonder if that was willing?" Gilber mused. "There was something between her and Solomon, I think. Times are you can smell secrets."

"Maybe you can," Virgie replied. "Not me. I just know how I feel, and I don't feel right in my skin about those city people. Either the trader or that

guard asked me into their house right this instant, I
wouldn't go."

Gilber scratched his head and looked around into
the gathering dark. "Not much chance of that
happening. We'd better make camp and go ahead
come morning." He set down his gear and started
scraping together what he could find for their fire.

"Huh!" Virgie watched his labors and for once
didn't try to bustle in with help. "I'm cold and there's
nothing decent to burn, and I'm thirsty and our
gourds are good as dry. Even if there is an Old Gate
to find come morning, what makes you think they'll
let us in? Or so much as give us the filling of our water
gourds before they send us back into the wilds?"

"We're not going back." Becca spoke so that no one
had better try arguing with her. "We've come too far.
What can I go back to, any road? 'Til I get justice
for Pa's death, it's worth my own life if I see
Wiserways Stead again."

"Me too," Virgie said, curling herself into a tighter
ball of sorrow. "If I go back to Mark's stead without
something to help us through the winter, I can't think
what he'll do to me. Or the little ones." She shivered.

Becca settled herself beside the girl and took her
in her arms, sisterly. "We came here seeking help and
we're not going back unless we find it. If I have to
climb these walls, I'll get to Eleazar."

Virgie's laugh was a half-hearted thing, made more
of bitterness than joy. "Climb these walls? You? And
I'll grow wings and fly over!"

"Wings, Virgie?" In the dark a stroke of flame
flickered up, caught dry grass to its bosom, flared into

strength and brightness. Gilber knelt by the seed of their campfire, feeding more stems to the little blaze. "Then I'll know you for an angel, sure."

"Some angel I make," the girl said, mouth muffled in her crossed arms. "Angels are pretty things, all white and gold. My mama had some picture books, so I know." She stretched out her arm, dark brown and shining in the firelight, and repeated, "White and gold. Huh."

"Little girl, I know what I've seen of you. Pretty's not a matter of what the Almighty's left done or undone on a person's face, nor the colors He's picked to paint them." His gentle smile sought to coax one from her in answer. "Anyway, I've seen angels, and not just in some old book. White and gold?" He snorted derision.

"You bald-faced liar, you never saw no angels." Virgie got back a scrap of her old spirit.

"Didn't I? Oh, yes I did! The first night I came down out of the mountains to the open lands, I lay me down to sleep with a stone for a pillow, and in the dark I saw a ladder spring between heaven and earth, blossomy as a spring branch with angels! I saw them go up and I saw them come down, and they were the colors of song, of prayer, of fresh water running through your fingers, of a healthy babe's first cry to the world. But *white* and *gold*?" Once more he made that scornful sound. "Colors like those, they're commonplace, fit for things of earth, not heaven. White and gold…"

Virgie gave him a peculiar look, but didn't say another word. Instead she turned to Becca and merely shrugged. Becca laughed. "Let it go, child. Best just take the honey and don't question the flower. If you argue with him, Mary Mother only knows what more crazy gabble he'll spin for us. Angels!"

"I do tread with angels, Becca," Gilber said, and now he wasn't jesting. "If you two don't have souls fit to soar with the seraphim, I don't know who—"

"That's plenty, Gilber." Becca cut him off. "That's worse than plenty; I won't hear more. Bad enough you've turned me into—into your miracle creature— now you're dragging Virgie off into worse craziness."

"But you are a miracle." He spoke softly, the way steadwomen traded the breath of love and wonder over the head of a sleeping infant. "And *creature*? You make it sound like I've made a monster of you."

"That's how it feels, sometimes." Becca found herself aping Virgie, hugging herself in closer, tighter, as if she was trying to shrink into her own bones.

Gilber shook his head. "I don't understand."

"When's the last time you touched me?" The accusation burst out with more force than she wanted. She was as bone-weary as Virgie, and fatigue loosed things from her tongue she'd been guarding. Still she was glad it had come out into the open. She wouldn't take it back into silence again for the world. "When's the last time you and I—?"

"How could we?" He nodded once, briefly, toward Virgie.

It was Becca's turn to blow a short, contemptuous breath that flared her nostrils. "You sent her off for water easy enough. You could've sent her off a time or two on the march as well. She's smart and she's stead; she'd've taken your meaning. Isn't that right, Virgie?"

"I guess so." The girl sounded reluctant to speak. She looked at Gilber, feared of bringing him trouble. "Sometimes on-stead—the stead where I was born, not Mark's, I mean—sometimes my daddy gave his men holiday if their work was good. 'Why make the boys wait on harvest home?' that's what he'd say, and he'd let 'em ask the kiss or the sign from any woman they liked, maiden or mother. My mama hated those times. She said she thought she'd given up all that once she became one man's bride, but Daddy'd have it so." Her thin shoulders shifted slightly under her tattered dress. "Those times, any of us kids happened on a man and a woman together, we knew how to get gone, fast and quiet."

Gilber stared into the fire. "Even so," he said. "Even so, I couldn't touch you. I was taught—"

"No." Becca felt her face grow hotter than the paltry fire could account for. "Don't spin me any tales of your laws, about how I'm impure, tainted by my own blood. I was cleansed of it, remember? Virgie tossed me in that lake and you said it'd do, but still you haven't been with me since. I know why: A man can only bed a natural woman."

"Becca—" It hurt her to hear how piteously he turned her name into a supplication. It hurt worse to pull herself away from the hand he extended to her, like a beggar seeking alms. "Becca, love, haven't I said you're more than any natural woman to me?"

"I don't *want* that!" She pounded her fists on her knees. "Curses take me, I don't *want* to be more than what I am! Not to you, not to anyone! Sweet Mary, why me?" She turned her face to the sky and starlight silvered her tears. "Not like a natural woman any more, no, but every moon, every moon—!" A sob dug free of her chest. She thrust away Gilber's offered embrace. "What's the use of it? What's it matter if I can be a taking woman any day, not have to wait out half a year to be in my times? You won't have me. Oh God!"

"Hey there!" A strong voice boomed out of the shadows. A party of three tall men stepped into the firelight. There was no questioning that they were men, for though they wore the same loose uniforms as the gate guards and were armed the same, their bearded faces were plain to see. Instead of visored helmets, they wore hoods like the tram drivers.

"Where's the trouble?" one red-whiskered giant demanded, holding his weapon on Gilber. "We heard shouting, cries. Who the hell are you, mister, and what are you doing to these women?"

They heard—! Becca's heart slammed wildly. How much did they hear? Not about me, the blood, oh please, precious Lord, not that!

Gilber Livvy looked up at the men, his face serene. "I'll be glad to tell you, but you'd do best to ask them yourself first, steal the lie from me."

The redbeard considered this offer and found it good. He turned to Virgie and asked, "Is this man bringing you grief, girl?"

"No, sir." Virgie's tone was as biddable and modest as any fitly bred maiden might use. There was no telling from it that she'd fled the horrors of a winnowing on her home stead and taken refuge in a place whose abominations harked back to the worst of the hungering times. "This man's been our mainstay and our help on the road. He's one of our sire's most trusted men. Me and my sib here—" she nodded at Becca "—we've come to the city to bring our brother word from home. Could be you know him? Take us to him tonight, maybe?"

The man ignored Virgie's questions, gave his face to Becca next. "Your sire trusted this one? Then why all the shouting? Who was doing it? Was it you?"

"Yes, sir." Becca took a leaf from Virgie's book on how a maiden ought to behave before a man. "It was my fault and I'm shamed by it. We've been traveling long, and when we reached the city gate yonder they told us it's Old Gate we want. I'm footsore and—well, how could this good man know which gate it was we wanted? So I flew out of temper."

"Did you, now?" The redbeard frowned, then looked back at his companions and said, "An honest woman." Only one of them shared the laugh with him before he returned his attention to Gilber. "You must be as trustworthy as the girl paints you, to let her yap at you that way and no correcting her. I know I wouldn't put up with half of what I heard."

"Just what did you hear?" Gilber asked.

"Mostly plain caterwaul. I don't make it a rule to waste my time listening to a woman's words, but it's the voice that can skin a man raw."

"If you'd've come on us a little later, you'd've heard her squawking another tune." Gilber relaxed and gave the men one of his wide grins. "Just because her sire trusts me doesn't mean a man can't teach manners. Nothing to do the girl harm, you know; just enough to make her recall herself. It's the traveling that unsettles them, you want my opinion."

One of the other men nodded his approval. "I know what you're saying, friend. Women turn flighty at any shift in the wind. Coming far afoot, it's no wonder she's gone snappish. Where've you come from, anyway?"

"Wiserways," Gilber replied.

"Wiserways…" This man's eyes were of such a piercing blue that the color shone true even in the faint firelight. They were soul-mirrors, those eyes, and a great upwelling of pity flooded them now. "Been on the road long, then?"

"Long enough." Gilber's face showed no hint of change. Becca thought she read his game rightly, and she felt her heartbeat rise with admiration over how serenely he played it out. "The young one there was taken ill for a time and we had to put up in wasteland. We should've been at the city gates long ago, but for that."

"Oh." The man sucked in his lower lip, reluctant to say more, but in the end compelled to speak. "Then I don't expect you've heard."

"Heard what?"

He looked at Becca and Virgie. "Your sire's name Paul?"

"Paul of Wiserways, yes sir," Becca answered, knowing what was to come.

The blue-eyed man laid one hand on her shoulder. "God's peace be with him, children."

"God's—" It was old news to her, Paul's death. She had built a wall round about it in her heart, every stone crying out for the blood of the traitor Adonijah. Now she tore it down, groping back in time for the first raw hurt of it. If she wasn't quick to make her sire's death into a freshly bleeding grief before these city men, there'd be a hard reckoning.

"*Daddy!*" Virgie's howl split the night. She folded up and fell to the ground like a bundle of sticks, hands clawing a face already wet with tears. "Lord King save us, our daddy's dead!"

The men clustered around Virgie, offering the sobbing girl comfort, leaving Becca to herself. *Mary Mother, that child's a wonder for cunning! She shames me with how true she wails for my sire's death. When she grows up, she'll be the saving of us all. What might've come to pass if she wasn't sharp enough to play along—* She pressed a fist to her breast, as if that were weight enough to keep her heart from leaping clear. She got hold of herself and hastened to take the part of elder sib trying to soothe the younger's misery.

Over to one side, Gilber was in earnest conversation with the redbearded man, who was telling him all he knew of the matter. Pricking up her ears, Becca heard the bare bones of the story the Coopman told: How word of the changeover on Wiserways Stead had reached the city; how the right folk knew that Paul had fallen in fair fight to Adonijah of Makepeace; how there'd been the usual time of winnowing after, with the new alph ridding the stead of those of his dead rival's children too young or too slow to escape. The empty cradles would be filled soon enough with babes of the new alph's begetting. Lore taught that women stricken childless—especially those still in milk—came back into their times all the sooner, out of the natural order of things.

"A new man, a new order, and new babies to stand proof of it," Gilber said as if he were discussing nothing more than which fruit to pick from a laden tree. "It always did make sense to me."

"Well, I expect it should." The redbeard unstrapped a glimmering metal flask from his belt and passed it to Gilber. He drank off a cautious measure and passed it back to his host who took a longer pull at the shiny neck, then wiped his mouth and smacked his lips with satisfaction. "Still, it can't be easy for you, finding out this way."

"Harder on them." Gilber nodded to where Virgie still kept up her loud pretense of weeping and where Becca knelt beside her, feigning sisterly comfort, the men hovering near.

"Oh, they're females, they get over it fast enough if you let them." Redbeard took another pull, then called to his men, "Hey! Let those girls alone. If you keep paying attention to them, they'll never shut up." To Gilber he added, "More to the point, friend, is what's to become of you? The word said that Adonijah of was-Makepeace-now-Wiserways came calling with a band of his own picked men. Sure, he kept Paul's old crew—he needs hands to work the land. But they were all there when he took over, on the spot. He could see with his own eyes how they kept the peace during the changeover, even how they helped out when the winnowing came. You're something unknown to him. You go back and first thing he'll wonder is how far he can trust you. If he can trust you. *If* he wastes any time at all asking."

He could see with his own eyes... Becca held back the crazy laughter. So word had come of the winnowing of Wiserways, but not of all that had happened after. This man didn't know that though Adonijah now ruled Becca's old stead, the new alph's eyes were dead as pebbles in his head, dead as all the helpless babes he'd slaughtered. It had been Becca's parting gift to him, the blindness.

She heard Gilber say, "I see your point. Of course I'm a good hand for the land—"

"So are plenty of other men. But you were the only one Paul chose to bring his daughters all this way. That's trust, solid trust, and would a man as sharp as Adonijah wait to learn how deep that trust's foundation's dug, or if it's bedded on loyalty?" Redbeard shook his head ponderously. "I wouldn't go back there, if I were you."

"Easy for you to say," Gilber countered. "It's not like I've got so many choices in the matter."

"You've got one, anyhow." The man patted him on the shoulder. "I can always use another trustworthy man, and loyalty's a plus with me. Once you're quit of these girls, come see me. My name's Galen; ask at any guard post and they know me."

"By no more name than that? Huh! City ways sure are different. Even I'm called Gilber of Wiserways, and I'm just stead; nothing so grand as you, all armed and outfitted so fine."

His flattery was subtle enough to make the big man beam with pleasure. "Well, it *is* different for the dwellers than it is for us guards when it comes to naming names. That one there doesn't even answer to more than You!" He waved at the third man, big-boned but carrying less meat than his companions, with whiskery patches of brown beard on a moon face. "But you just ask for Red Galen and you're safe."

"Red Galen," Gilber repeated. "Plain to see why." His pleasant ways set the new-made bond firm. "All right, friend, I'll take your word and your offer. But why don't we make for the gate now, together? My gut's churned up. The sooner I'm shut of these girls and find a new place for myself in this world, the easier it'll sit with me."

"I wish I could," Galen said. "I can't, though: Rules. We've got our rounds to make, and the only folks we're supposed to bring up to the gates wish they never met us. But you come on after, in the morning, and do what I told you. I've taken a liking to you, Gilber, and my men will tell you I don't like easy."

"That's for sure!" the blue-eyed one called. He and his still-silent comrade rejoined Galen, acting as if Virgie and her weeping had vanished from the earth. "We'd best press on. We've spent too much time with this lot, and if we're late reporting—"

"You worry too much, Toby," Galen chaffed him, amiable as a full-fed ox. "You know as well as I do that we could come in from patrol hours late, so long as I turn in a report fat enough to choke seven webmasters. Which reminds me," Gilber had all his attention once more, "I'll need to know what business it is that's bringing you and these girls to our city. For the report, you know."

Becca opened her mouth to speak, ready to drop Eleazar's name like a magic seed that would grow them all freepasses into the city. But Gilber spoke first, even shooting her a poisonous look that was so unlike him it scared all speech from her lips.

"I was ordered to bring them to their brother, Eleazar. He's been Coop some time now—more than ten years, how I figure."

"That's not something done every day. Why? What for?"

"Well, there's what I was *told* and what I *know*, if you follow me," Gilber said. He leaned his head nearer Galen's and dropped his voice so low that Becca couldn't hear a word he said. Whatever passed between the two men, it seemed to satisfy the redbeard, for when Gilber was done they shook hands and Galen commanded his patrol to move out. Becca held Virgie close as they watched the city men disappear into the night.

"What was that all about?" Becca demanded as soon as she was certain it was safe to speak freely.

"That was about pledging my soul to Gehinnom for a year," Gilber replied. "My mother used to scare the truth into us by telling about how that's the place where liars get their punishment: hot irons on the tongue and a throat stuffed full of burning coals. But it was that or have us all die now, so I lied like a go-between, with all my heart."

"You didn't lie, not so it'd count." Virgie was there

to defend Gilber, staunchly loyal, even when it meant shielding him from his own harsh judgment.

If that girl were older, I'd say there was more to it, Becca thought. *And how much older than that was I when I first took heed of Jamie?* The remembrance of her lost love ached, but beneath the pain came a prickling notion: *Is that how she thinks on Gilber? With love?* It chafed her until there was a nasty sneer to her voice when she asked, "How can you be so sure? Did you even hear what he told that man?"

"No." Virgie faced her down. "But I know what made him say whatever it was. If it saved us, it won't count against him as a lie. The Lord knows forgiveness better than we do."

"That's a comforting thought," Gilber said, laying a hand on Virgie's shoulder. "I'm grateful for it."

"But what *did* you tell him?" Becca wanted to know. "If we run into him again once we get through the gates—"

"How, unless we go seeking him? I've been marking out the space this wall circles, and unless it's hollow as a blown egg inside, I doubt people just happen onto one another that much." Gilber was teasing, but he cut it off, short and cold, when he saw the concern on Becca's face. "Look, I only said what you'd've told him yourself: That it's your sire's will we're here, seeking your brother Eleazar. I said how it wasn't safe for you back home anymore, and I left it at that. So I guess you could say I spoke truth, and what I gave over to Galen's imagination was the lie."

"What do you reckon he thought?"

"I can't say. I don't know what the possibilities

might be with you people, stead or city. It's good enough for me that he did."

Becca pondered this. "You could say that Paul saw something in Virgie and me worth sending us here, the way that man from Coop saw something in Eleazar. Only—only because we're girls he thought maybe no agent'd notice us, so he took it on himself, and he hopes Eleazar'll put us forward with the right people."

"Yes, that's a fine notion!" Virgie was as ready to throw her enthusiasm behind Becca's tale as she was to champion Gilber. "And the reason he sent us now was—was—was—" The girl groped for a reason that wouldn't come.

"Was because some of the other women were starting to notice how we're different, and maybe go about laying snares for us, out of envy," Becca provided. "The only way to keep the peace was to send us on quick."

"Becca, what's the use of spinning moonbeams this way?" Gilber asked. "Galen and his patrol took my words at fair weight. We don't need more explanation than what I gave."

"We might," Becca said. "What if there's more patrols? What if they're not as easygoing as that Galen? We need a full tale to tell them, if they ask, and one we're all agreed on."

Gilber yawned. "What we *need* is sleep. You two can stay up yarning if you like, just wake me when you're ready to shut your eyes." He stretched himself out beside the little fire and was snoring before Becca or Virgie could reply.

The night passed with no more meetings. Virgie took first watch, then gave over to Becca when the stars had turned a third of the way toward morning. Becca sat up with silence and darkness settled over the land, from the city wall at her back to the world that stretched out beyond the firelight. It was eerie, the way not a single sound broke the peace. She figured that the cold stone of the city wall must lie very thick, to hold back any rumor of human presence. Only once she thought she heard a rustling in the night, but it didn't come from inside the wall and before she could be certain of it, Gilber was awake, greeting her, bidding her get some sleep. She closed her eyes and didn't open them again until just before dawn.

They resumed their trek without waiting for full light. Gilber took the lead, making a way through the rough grasses. They hadn't gone too far before he paused in his tracks and remarked, "Now that's strange."

"What?" Becca came up behind him and edged herself close.

He let his lips brush her hair with a kiss casual enough to be a handclasp, then said, "The grass ahead. It looks like we're the first ones to come this way."

"I don't—"

"Galen's patrol," he reminded her. "Three big men go marching along and not a single stalk trampled down? Not even one bent?" He knelt and felt the parched growth that ringed the city. "So dry, too, although…"

"Think they were ghosts?" Virgie crouched beside him, trembling. Becca said nothing; she'd walked too long with her own phantoms to mouth off a pat answer. She crept up on Gilber's other side, trying to see what it was about a lone stalk of grass that held him so rapt.

"They were living men. Else ghosts have got themselves a new taste for brewed liquor." Gilber continued to stare down at the stems. He cradled a pale yellow seed head in the fingers of his left hand, his thumb stroking its bristly beard. "Becca, this like anything you've ever seen, back home?"

He didn't give her the chance to answer. Suddenly his eyes flew up from the seed head. "Look there." He pointed to a curve in the great wall just ahead of them. Something long snaked against the stones. Gilber sprang to his feet and dashed forward to see, the girls scrambling after.

Becca reached him first and saw him staring up at the crudely knotted length of rope and twisted cloth dangling from a point somewhere high above. If there were any openings in the rocky face, she couldn't see them from where she stood, yet she knew there must be: The rope didn't begin its descent from the very top.

"I guess climbing the city walls isn't so far-fetched," she told Virgie, smiling.

"Climbing down 'em, anyway," the girl commented.

Gilber stretched one arm straight up. The rope ended just short of his wiggling fingers and the weeds at the base of the wall were crushed. He knelt to study the signs. "A bad landing," he opined, touching the broken stems. "And a recent one. If this growth only wants some hours to recover from being trodden down, this is all fresh doings. So's this." He pointed out a bright red stain smearing the grasses. "Looks like getting out of here's nigh as rough a job as getting in."

"Why would anyone want to escape Coop?" It was unthinkable to Becca, whose childhood had been filled with wonder-tales of the high life her brother Eleazar enjoyed.

"Who's to say? It doesn't matter; we've got our own concerns. We need food and water we won't get until we make Old Gate. Let's make the most of the light." He straightened up and took back the lead.

Little more than an hour's walk proved that the Steadway Gate guard hadn't lied; there was another way into the city. The tall weeds broke at a highway not so wide or fine as the traders' route, but better than any road connecting stead to stead. It ended at a gate that was smaller sister to Steadway, an arch too narrow by half for tram or chariot.

There were guards here too, poorer cousins to the splendidly appointed wardens of Steadway Gate. No one with a working eye could mistake those of one sex for those of another: Their motley helmets wanted visors, and the females among them were clearly distinguished by the curve of hip and breast against the fabric of shirts and breeches.

Unfortunately, their unwillingness to let the travelers in was identical to that of their better-equipped brethren.

"I'm just doing my work," said the woman who took

it upon herself to turn them away. "Does your stead let just anybody in?"

"We can't." Becca begrudged admitting it.

"Aha! And why not? Don't tell me, anyone with half a brain knows: You can only support so many mouths. That's the way it's always been, the way it'll always be. Who told you it's any different in the Coops? We've got to feed ourselves, same as you. How'd we do that if we just left our gates wide open? Hell, we'd have things back like they were in the hungry years before you know it. No thanks."

"But my brother—"

This guard's kindness was more sincere, and she didn't seem to see anything peculiar about Becca being the one to speak up for the rest. "Listen girlie, if you'd been sent for, I'd have the right—shit, the duty—to call up your brother and have him down to decide what to do with you. But you showed up on your own."

"Their sire sent us," Gilber put in.

The guard eyed him coolly, then spat. "You told me so already, seedgrub. I'm capable of remembering more than that. Like your face, for one thing. It *looks* like you've got some intelligence hiding behind it; maybe you can be educated. God, I hope so. If there's the skinniest chance in hell that you lot get inside, I don't ever want to see that face bleating at me *But that's always how we treat the women on-stead!*"

"Yes ma'am," Gilber said, without so much as a hint of funning.

The guard got back to Becca's case. "The best I can do for you is pass along your message as a favor, from me to some other guard to someone else until maybe—just *maybe*, I say—maybe it gets into the webs and reaches him. If no one forgets to pass it on and if your brother decides he still wants to know anyone from his old stead. Some of the webwalkers get like that, you know. Fucking snobs."

"Eleazar will want to know me." Becca struggled to stay master of her voice, but it quavered a little. "Virgie here and him are just sibs, but he's my true, full brother."

The guard cocked her head. "Means nothing to me, even if it sounds like it means plenty to you. I've told you all I can do and I'll do it, but no promises. You'll have to stay outside if you're bound to wait. Or you could take some good advice."

"We are *not* going back."

"No, that'd be the smart thing to do." She didn't say it nastily. "If you like, you can go around the wall a ways farther until you reach Black Gate. There's been a lot more activity for this late in the year than I remember, so maybe they'll take you on one of the outworker crews. You'll still have to make camp outside the walls, but they'll see to it you're fed. *If* they're hiring, you know. We've got so many hobays coming into the force that— Well, like I said, no promises, but you can tell them Melanie of Old Gate Thirdwatch sent—"

A thunder of elite guards saved Becca the trouble of repeating her plea. About thirty of them came charging up to the guard post, visored helmets blinding. They were led by a man in plain black blouse and trousers, five tiny silver flowers blooming in the shape of a cross over his heart. When Melanie got a look at him, everything slack and soft about the way she manned her post vanished. The weapon she carried at her hip came out at the ready. Holstered, it had looked a bit like Becca's gun, but in the waxing sunlight anyone could see how much more art and ingenuity had gone into the molding of this death done small.

"Out of the way!" she barked at Becca and the others.

"What's going—?"

"Fine, stay there and die, I don't give a shit." She motioned for one of her comrades to take her place at the gate proper and ran to present herself before the man in black. Words were exchanged—short, sharp, fiery. Becca could just catch some of what was said, but it sufficed. A look at Gilber's face told her that his ears were leastways as sharp as hers, and likely sharper.

"Seems our wall-climbers are in for it," he remarked.

"More than one?" Virgie asked.

He nodded. "Signs said so, and that happy man over there confirmed it: two of them."

"I hope they get away," Becca said. "Far away. They'll be killed if they're caught."

"Not from what I just heard." Gilber's eyes flickered toward the man in black. His thin face was the sallow color of top cream, with blue veins webbing a nearly hairless head. "He wants them back alive. You wouldn't know to look at him, but he sounds frightened for what'll become of them out there.

They haven't got any more idea of how to live outside the city walls than fly."

From the center of the clustered guards the man's voice rose in volume until they could all hear him saying, "—gone sometime last night. We discovered it and sent out a search party, but they left by the wrong gate and in the dark they were worse than blind. The patrols had nothing useful to report either, worthless turds. Maybe this squad will have better luck by daylight. How could two children do such a thing? How could Van even *think* of something so insane? How—?"

While the man in black ranted on, Gilber handed his rifle to Becca and stepped over the threshold of Old Gate. A guard moved to block his path. He gave the man an apologetic smile and followed it with a knee to the groin and an elbow to the center of his chest. Becca cried out as every weapon in the gateway area leaped up to center on Gilber Livvy.

"If you want me to find your runaways for you," he said calmly, "put those things down."

Chapter Four

"We cannot go on like this, living like animals, fighting over any sexually receptive woman as if we were those benighted souls out there in the country. Certainly our young men have drives—we all do! Contrary to what my esteemed opponents say, even I have been known to appreciate the, ah, benefits of female companionship on occasion. Say, once every six months." (Laughter from the general meeting.) "But will we master our drives or be mastered by them? Each one of us is here precisely because we do have the foresight and the strength of purpose to look beyond the needs and demands of the moment. It is too late to civilize the country; that we all know. All the more reason for us, in the name of civilization, to find a solution that

transcends the current system. Which is, might I add, no system at all. To those of you who blindly cling to the notion that such urges by their very nature defy systematization, I say: What next? A full reversion to the old days? Hunger and thirst are drives as natural and imperative as sex, yet have we not found the means to govern them so that there is plenty for all present? Gentlemen, I don't know about you, but when someone asks me to join him for lunch, I take a certain comfort in knowing that the invitation begs my attendance as a companion and not as the main course!"
(General laughter and applause.)

"Well, Becca, is it still all that you dreamed?" Eleazar's hands closed on her shoulders as he guided her eyes over a panorama of the city. From the semicircular balcony attached to his chambers, she could see almost a quarter of the world behind the walls. There were her glimmering spires—not quite so tall as her vision had painted them, but still there. Below, the people passed in a multicolored weaving of bright colors, their steps made light and fearless by knowing who they were and in what happy state they dwelled.

"It's wonderful," she said, again feeling the tears coming over her. "It's more wonderful every time I see it. I don't think I'll ever get used to it." They trickled freely from her eyes.

"Why do you cry, little sister?" Eleazar turned her to face him. For her, it was like seeing a younger copy of Pa's face, unseamed by work and worry, unburdened by the weight of so many dead children. "Is it for your friends?"

"Yes." That answer was safer than the truth. "I miss them."

"You would, after all you three went through together. Such trials...tsk. But you're a grown woman, Becca; you understand what's necessary. That little girl with you was terribly malnourished. She might not have looked it, but she wants special care."

"Virgie's not the only one needs help." One of the first things Becca had done when they brought her to her brother was to tell him of Mark's stead and its barbarities. How Eleazar's face had gone strained and white when she described all she'd seen there! "Have you heard any more from the others about sending an expedition out after the little ones?"

"Of course, of course, all in good time. You know I'd do it at once, if I could; it's not so simple. We have to make provision to receive those unhappy children here. Planning is everything. Besides, I'd think you'd want us to take care of your companions first. Virgie must have proper medical attention until she's well enough to take her rightful place. I saw a lot of promise in her, even though we met only for a brief while. And that other friend of yours, Gilber Livvy—sweet Jesus, Becca, I still can't get over how my own little sister managed to find a Jew alive in this world!" He laughed.

She didn't share the humor. "Did Gilber tell you

what his folk suffered? Did he say anything about that pretty rite *our* folk had when they caught one of his kin, called Going to Moriah?"

Eleazar's laughter ended in a rueful sigh. "He did, and I'm sorry you were excluded from the interview. No, on second thought I'm glad. You should be sheltered from such things."

"There's no use protecting me from what I already know."

"True, too true." Eleazar eyed her sorrowfully. "The things we've done…I wish you could've been there to see how Thirdweb Council reacted to Gilber Livvy's words. He may be a Jew, but he's well-spoken. We aren't beasts here, Becca; we're responsible, accountable, civilized beings. In simple charity we owe that young man and his people all the help we can give them. Double that, to make up for all the evils our so-called Christian brothers visited on them. It was a long time ago, I know, but still that's no excuse for—" He shuddered off any further words.

Becca followed him as he moved from the balcony back into the room. A bottle of honey-colored liquid and four goblets rested on a shiny blue pedestal table, each bubble of pale pink glass balancing light as breath on its gilded base. Becca had never seen anything so finely wrought. Eleazar poured for himself and Becca. In the days since she'd gained admittance to the city, she had grown accustomed to the taste of wine.

"Then there's the straight debt Thirdweb itself owes him for bringing Van back to us," Eleazar added, after they had drunk. "Amazing. I know those

Highlandweb security people trampled most of the trail into mush—what the springweed hadn't already covered—yet he still managed to track Van and find him."

"And the girl," Becca prompted. "How's she called?" It wasn't the first time she'd tried to learn the fugitive's name.

All her brother said was, "Mm," and then: "This wine tastes odd. Wait here, I'll bring us a fresh bottle." He was gone, leaving her alone with questions he never meant to answer.

Just as if she never was, Becca thought, studying the way sunlight swirled through the lees at the bottom of her glass. The way Eleazar had dodged her question was nothing new. In all the time since Becca had come into her brother's house, he'd never once spoken willingly of the young woman who'd run off with the boy Van. When Becca did so herself, he changed the subject or abruptly recalled some urgent errand demanding his immediate care.

Is this some city way I don't know? Is it how they mete out shaming, shunning mention of a person's name? Does she bear full blame for what happened? When she and Van ran off, was that escapade all the girl's doing?

Hard to believe. Becca had been there when Gilber Livvy led the baffled party of guards right up to the couple's hidey-hole. A tired Virgie stayed behind, given over to the care of the Old Gate guard called Melanie. That was the last Becca had seen of the child. At the time, she hadn't given it much thought, so avid was she to see how Gilber fared on the trail.

She might have foreseen how it would turn out,

knowing Gilber's skills the way she did: He found them with no more bother than if they'd scattered handfuls of new-hulled grain in their wake. They had taken refuge among that long, low chain of hills well beyond the city. Becca and her party had come through that way, and little Virgie had even ventured to explore there. The hills were no natural part of the land, but mounds of earth cast up to cover a series of time-ravaged shelters. Under the sod, each was little more than a hollow shell, stripped ages past of all usable material by the cityfolk, though from one Virgie'd turned herself up a doll-baby made of some queer hard stuff. (Becca didn't like thinking how glad she was when the girl lost interest in that cracked, filthy monstrosity and let it drop by the wayside.)

It didn't matter how thoroughly plundered those ruins were: A person could still lose his pursuers pretty well just by banking on the sheer number of hiding places. At the time, Becca thought how smart that pair was to flee there. If they truly want to escape, it's wise to find a safe place to recoup their strength. That climb down from the walls must've been exhausting. Even city souls know better than to take to the wilds tired. They want a chance to rest.

They didn't get that chance, not with an expert tracker like Gilber Livvy set on their trail. Eyes on the earth, he led the guards and their black-garbed commander straight and true to their goal.

When they found the couple, the girl hadn't looked like much more than a rag of a person: Chalky skin, skinny arms sticking out of flimsy, tattered draperies, the biggest, brownest eyes Becca had ever seen. She remembered thinking, It's a mercy we've found them. That child would perish, else. And where'd these two think to run for, any road? What stead would have them, even if they could live off the land until they reached one? Just look at her eyes! She's knows they never had a hope.

Still the girl clung to Van as if he were her last breath of life, even while the boy tried to fight off the invaders. Becca still marveled over the softhand way the guards treated him in the struggle, taking such care not to do him any real hurt that he managed to down three of them barehanded. And what good did it do him? It ended, inevitably, in capture. The girl whimpered when they overcame him and yanked her out into the light, but she did not resist at all.

No, that nameless girl hardly had the bearing or the bone to be an adventuress. The notion for the couple's flight hadn't come from her, yet as far as Eleazar and the rest were concerned, she bore all the blame.

"Here we are!" Eleazar was back, another flask of wine held high. He snatched Becca's old glass away and gave her a clean one, filling it to within a fingerspan of the brim. "Try this and tell me what you think."

Becca sipped her second glass charily. It was sweet and potent. "Nice," she said. If Eleazar was bound not to speak of Van's girl, she'd let it go for now. There were too many other things she needed to learn from him. Ever since they'd separated her from Gilber and Virgie, she'd done her best to adapt to life in Eleazar's new family—his "elic," he called it, though he spoke of "webs" too. Try as she might, she still had no notion of who his alph was or if she'd be required to show him gratitude once they met. Her heart prayed not, for Gilber's sake.

So faithful to him? Her wayward thoughts pricked. Does he know what a steadfast heart he owns in you? Does he even care?

She wondered mightily over that as well. All the things he'd told her that night outside the walls had the ring of emptiness to them. *He's a fine one to speak of the liar's punishment hereafter, as if he truly feared it! What's all he said to me but lies? If he wants to be shut of me, there's nothing I can do. I only wish I knew what it is I've done to earn this pain.* She gazed into her glass; a falling teardrop spread its ripples over the surface of the wine.

"Little sister, what's wrong?" Eleazar's arm threaded around her waist. One thing Becca had learned of city ways: Touch like this was no sin, even between man and woman.

"Nothing." If Gilber would burn in his liars' Gehinnom, she'd burn with him. *With him…or for him?* She could lie to anyone but herself. She yearned for Gilber and she knew it—if not as lover, then as friend. The days had flown since they'd made the city. Soon enough the moon would be turning 'round to the same face it had worn the last time her difference manifested. Women who were different were dead. City wasn't stead, but where did they make the distinctions? Gilber was clever: His help, his protection were what she needed to keep her from detection until she could know for sure how safe she was.

"When do you think I can visit Gilber and Virgie?" Becca asked with pretended nonchalance. "I miss them."

Eleazar looked surprised. "Any time you like. Haven't you been given the freedom of the city?"

"Well, you said I could go where I liked, but—"

"And you've stayed here. Listen, you can't see Virgie yet because she's still being brought along through recovery, but you can seek out Gilber whenever it pleases you. I told you, he's been living over with the Greenwoodweb people. They checked him out first—you'll be glad to hear his head's healing nicely, and one of their dental surgeons took care of his missing teeth—and now they're working with him to find a practical way of dealing with his other problems. Just get yourself over to Greenwoodweb and ask around. I guarantee that everybody over there will know where to find him. He does stand out in a crowd."

"But Eleazar—"

"I have to go. You know how busy I am. Be back in time for dinner. Have you got your pass?" She nodded. "Good. Have fun, darling. I hope to have some good news for you tonight." He kissed her cheek and was gone.

Becca put back her wine glass and wandered from her brother's chambers back into her own. She could almost feel the weight of the towering building all around her, floor after floor of lives belonging to a single web. The entire suite of rooms set aside for

Carsonelic appeared to be deserted at this hour. She
didn't like being alone in so much space, even in the
portion of it reserved for her alone. She was used to
dormitories and spaces holding more than a single,
lonesome soul. Her room felt like a cage, and the
wide windows could not take away that feeling. What
did it matter how many lives surrounded her if there
were walls between? To sleep in solitude, beyond the
sound of another human's breath, was not to sleep
at all.

Well, if you don't like solitude, why not go out? she
asked herself. *Find Gilber. You do have the freedom of
the city. If anyone stops you, just say "I am Becca of
Carsonelic, Thirdweb," just the way you used to be
Paul's get of Wiserways. You can remember that much,
can't you?*

She lay down on her bed and jammed a pillow over
her head to muffle the teasing whisper. Go out? Oh
no, not again. She'd done it once, soon after the first
time Eleazar told her she could. He was too busy to
escort her personally—she did understand?—but
being in the city was different from being out there,
in the untamed land beyond the walls. Here a woman
alone was safe to travel anywhere she liked. Why
didn't she take advantage of it?

Why didn't she?

"They won't eat you," said a voice from the open
doorway.

Becca pushed the pillow aside and lifted her head.
A young man with hair as dark as Gilber's, eyes as
blue as her own, slouched against the jamb. His face
was vaguely familiar. The first time she'd seen him,

that same face had been twisted into a mask of rage, the mouth contorted with blasphemies as the elite guards dragged him and the girl from hiding: Van.

"May I come in?" He didn't wait for her answer, but entered the room as if he owned it and sat down in the chair nearest the bed. "That *is* what you're afraid of, isn't it?" he went on. "That someone's going to eat you? One time Auntie Salome brought back a stead girl who was sure we only took in people like her because cityfolk ate human flesh. Auntie must've slipped up and picked her just for her looks. Either that or the girl was bright enough, but she made the mistake of holding onto stupid country tales *and* believing them. In any case, with an attitude like that she didn't exactly shine at the evaluation. You know, the test?"

"I know what an evaluation is," Becca replied, not liking Van's own attitude much. "So that's what you do with the steadfolk you bring here—evaluate them?"

"We have to. First, to check on whether the recruiter had the right idea, choosing them. Second, to see if their aptitudes fit them for one web more than another. That girl wasn't good for anything by the time we got her. Too bad." He smiled coldly. "But she *was* tasty."

"Get out." Becca stood and pointed at the door.

"Can't you take a joke?" He stayed where he was.

"Well enough to know one when I hear it, and that wasn't it. My brother told me that this room's mine, and I can have it the way I fancy. I don't fancy you, so get out."

"Sorry." He stood up too and stretched. Like most cityfolk she'd seen, he wore clothing akin to what they wore on stead, only cut from fabric finer to the touch and brighter to the eye. She couldn't put an age to him—he acted spoiled enough to be a stripling scarcely old enough to run the fieldwork machines, but he was almost as tall as her Pa. She didn't like the way he seemed to be looking down at her from more than just his height. His words were dry when he added, "My mistake."

"Don't you have something to do, somewhere else to be?" she snapped at him. "Everyone else around here does."

"I'm the exception. Webmaster Steven said I've done too much already, and the others all agree. You met Webmaster Steven, didn't you? Tall, sharp-faced, hardly any hair to mention? He was right there when your trained wildman nosed us out of our burrow."

"You don't talk like that about Gilber! If you could've seen yourself when they got you out, you'd know who the real wildman is!"

Her fierce words didn't have much visible impact. All he said was, "Sorry." This time too there was no real apology behind it. Then: "I've made a bad hash of this. I came here to offer you some assistance. I'm bored with having my regular tasks taken from me. All Webmaster Steven says I should do is go for counseling twice daily and use the rest of my time to meditate on my sins. Not that he'd use a term that countrified, but they're still sins in his mind. My failures of judgment, he said. Anyhow, if you're willing, I'd be happy to be your guide."

"Why should I want you?" Becca didn't trust him and didn't care if it showed. "Why should I want any guide? I may be from—from the *outs*—" She used the city term for the land beyond the walls. "—but we all do speak the same tongue, stead and Coop. I can ask my way if need be."

"Sure, and if you can get the words out." He was lounging against the doorjamb again. "You tried, the last time you went out. The only time. For a while there I thought you were going to make it. But then the way you stood goggling at that man on the street, your lips moving, not a whisper coming out—"

"You spied on me!" Becca's hand rose up to slap his blandly smiling face. All that stayed her was the thought of what might happen if Eleazar and the rest of the elic found out. Touch between man and woman was no sin, but a slap wasn't just *touch*. She curled her fingers closed and let the hand drop to her side. "You're hateful."

"I told you, I'm just bored. I did spy on you, I confess it. Smack me if it makes you feel better; I won't say a word about it. At this point I'd even relish pain for a change."

Slowly she let go of her blind anger. "All right. I can make confession too: I am frighted by this place. I could ask the way, but I don't know the proper manner of asking. I'm feared I'll trespass against what's done and what's forbidden, that's why I won't go roving the city on my own."

"The custom of the country, hm?" He smiled, and for a moment he looked free of all pretense. "I guess I'd feel the same in strange territory."

"Will you take me to Greenwoodweb? And back?"

"And not just leave you there?" He cocked an eyebrow. "Yes, I'll take you to visit the meddies, and I'll even help you look up that wi—friend of yours. It'll do us both good to get out. There will be a price, though."

"What?" Her mouth hardened.

"Good Lord, not that! If you're thinking what you must be. You don't really know where you are, if you're afraid I'll ask for any of your precious country gratitude." He actually shook with revulsion at the thought.

"Afraid?" A mischief sneaked over her tongue and spoke aloud. "Don't worry, I won't *eat* you."

❧ ❧

The truce they declared was heavily armed with silence on both sides as Van conducted Becca through the city streets. There were crowds and crowds of people afoot, more on horseback, some in small beast-drawn carts on the wider ways, and no sign at all of the motor-driven chariots and trams that had come in by Steadway Gate.

"They're for trade only, over long distance," Van explained when Becca asked. "Or emergencies like the one you stirred up. I don't envy the alph of Wiserways when they bring him back here for judgment."

"When do you think that will be?" Becca asked.

"Webmaster Steven made that his first order of business, even dispatched some of the

Highlandwebbers to escort the traders who'll fetch the poor bastard. Just in case of a fight, you know."

Becca disliked asking Van anything. His tongue seemed to be barbed on both ends, but she had to know: "What do you think will happen on Wiserways when they remove Adonijah?"

"Who cares?"

"*I* do, damn you!" The curse was out of her mouth before she knew it. She lost all color at the realization of what she'd done. Language like that, from a woman's lips in a public place, was good for any punishment a stead's alph could offer.

But in the thick of the city crowd, where everyone couldn't help but hear, no one so much as paused or turned a head to see the sinner's ashen face. Like Van, each passer-by seemed to say by his detachment, Who cares?

"Are you all right?" Van asked, steadying her by one elbow. "You look ready to faint."

"I'm sorry, it was what I said—I—I apologize for—" She looked around, still not daring to believe that she had spoken so plain and gone unpunished. "I guess things really are different in the city," she said sheepishly.

"You *won't* faint on me, will you? I heard that meddies never do; they're too toughened up by their work for fainting, even the women."

"Meddies?" She repeated the unfamiliar word.

"Medical personnel," he explained. "Like the ones who belong to Greenwoodweb. Healers."

"How do you know—? Why call *me* a meddie?"

"It must've been something you told Eleazar that

he told the others in council. No secrets in Carsonelic; we're good little webwalkers and all our paths are duty, cheerfully shared." The way he spoke, Becca could nigh taste the bitterness.

"You're part of their council?" She didn't care to add that Van hardly looked old enough to have a share in something so high-sounding. "Or were you spying there too?"

He took no offense at the barb. "Why go to the trouble? Auntie Salome tells me everything."

"I don't think I recall meeting your Auntie Salome."

"You'd remember if you did. You will, in time. Not that I could tell you *when*: She's a busy woman, scary how busy. Anyhow, she took the time to quiz Eleazar all about you. She told me you're supposed to be a pretty good healer, for someone with next to no training." He got a cunning look on.

"Gilber's another," Becca said, recovering herself. "When I lived on Wiserways, I wanted to be an herbwife, so I got what lessoning I could."

More calculation fed into his eyes. "I hear too you brought some supplies with you."

"Gilber's, really; I'm keeping his herb box safe in my room. Eleazar said he wouldn't be needing it at Greenwoodweb."

"No, not with all the meddies there! And if we want to see everything I've got planned, we'd better get moving."

"What's to see besides the way there?" Becca asked, but Van seemed to have her brother's gift for going

deaf when he didn't want to answer. He simply picked
up his pace, and she had to match his stride smartly
or count herself lost.

It wasn't that far to Greenwoodweb. Becca knew:
She'd asked Eleazar once, that time she'd tried to go
out on her own and failed. Her brother had taken
her onto the balcony and showed her where it lay, a
cluster of buildings white as bone. It wasn't supposed
to be far from Thirdweb to Greenwoodweb at all.

*There's leagues that lie between things as they are and
things as they're supposed to be, and you'd do well to
learn it!* As Becca trotted along with Van, she could
hear her mother's prim voice rattling off that bit of
rote wisdom. The city was all towers around her, some
tall, some low. What had seemed like a short, fairly
straight route when seen from on high had become
a long and twisty business. The array of streets and
byways was a thousand times more complex than the
sprawl of Verity Grange. Still, the longer she and Van
walked, the less overpowering it all became. There
were signs on some of the towers that must be clues,
and places where the cobbled-together walkways were
marked all of one color.

There's meaning to that, she realized, noting where
one color ended and a different one began. I could
learn it. *I can learn the customs, too. Give me a little
more time and I can find my own way around. And
wouldn't that be a comedown for Van! Call Gilber a
wildman, will he? Mary Mother only knows what he calls
me behind my back.* The thought made her seethe. In
that moment she became even more determined to
know the city on her own.

She forgot to gape indiscriminately at every new thing that caught her eye. Instead she focused her attention on memorizing distinguishing details of the places they passed. She repeated the more vital facts under her breath, to aid memory, the way she'd done on stead in Katy's schoolroom.

"You could study a city plan. It'd be easier, and you wouldn't make such a spectacle of yourself with that god-awful muttering." Van's sarcasm cut rudely through her concentration.

"I would, if I knew where to come by one," Becca muttered, striving against distraction.

Van snickered. "If you're trying to memorize the way we're walking, save yourself the trouble. This isn't the route to Greenwoodweb."

Becca stopped stark in her tracks. "You told me you were taking me there."

"I am; just not right away. There's somewhere you need to go first. Oh, and we've got to get you different clothes and a haircut before that. Where we're going, if you don't look like a man you'll wish you did." He continued walking as if he'd said nothing extraordinary.

Becca stayed right where she was. The crowd swirled around her, parting like stream water at a rock. The confidence she'd found so easy to claim vanished within minutes. While she'd kept walking with Van beside her, safe in his borrowed familiarity with the city, she came to ignore the press of people. Now, standing still and alone, the multiplicity of faces, colors, and smells conspired to dazzle and befuddle her.

There were just too many new things, too fast, too different. Her dreams had painted the city as a place of order, even down to a like-dressing populace, and her vision had populated it with angels, identical in their glory. The reality was a shock like a blow between the eyes. The variety was overwhelming. Apart from the elite security force Van called Highlandwebbers and some skinny, sad-faced, slow moving youngsters in yellow coveralls, there were no uniforms. She would have rejoiced to see more uniforms.

Stubbornly she refused to call after Van. A covert glance up the street showed that he had disappeared from sight anyway. Shaking inside, she decided to strike out on her own. She knew where she was going, didn't she? And she had the freedom of the city! What was the worst thing that could happen to her? Getting lost? But then she had her card, and she knew her brother's web and elic by name.

"Greenwoodweb," she murmured. "I want to get to Greenwoodweb." She'd go to Gilber first; she didn't need a guide. Yes, she would show Van.

The first person she stopped was a gray-haired older man who was coolly polite. "Greenwoodweb? Are you sick?"

"No, sir," she replied with the respect due age. "I just want to go there to see a friend. Is it far?"

"Not very, by the direct route, but you'll want to go the long way around. Now you take this street up five—"

"Please, I'm going there the quickest I can."

A frown. "You don't care?" A closer look at Becca's

plaited hair, her sunbrowned skin, and the way she carried herself. "Are you a new recruit?"

In too much of a hurry to be gone, the sooner to rub Van's nose in her triumph, Becca decided to let truth take the long way around too, and just nodded. The stranger was immediately mollified.

"Well, if you're a new one, that explains it. Fresh in from the fields, eh? Fine. In that case, you just go up this street one intersection, turn left, follow the way down past Hyacinth and Jasmine Webs—oh, and Peony; it's been a long time since I was down there— and after you pass the Hesperides Arch you'll see the hospital complex straight ahead." Then the old gentleman did a peculiar thing: Smiling softly, he pinched Becca's cheek and said, "If only you'd been here twenty years ago."

He might have been odd, but his directions were accurate. Becca followed them and found herself in a street whose traffic was a dramatic relief from the cheek-by-jowl conditions she'd endured with Van.

In this place the way was a lot narrower, with no possibility of anything but foot passage. The towers were not so tall, and they leaned in closer from either side of the street, overshadowing the passers-by. A sweet, musky scent cloyed the air, undercut by the more potent smell of stale frying grease. Here there were no raised walkways, no color-coded curbs. No windows showed their faces at street level, and all the doors were cheerless gray slabs of wood or metal. Above each one was a plaque with the feathery relief carving of a flower. Thin music trickled through the air.

There was color enough though, above street level. Boxes full of profusely blooming flowers—white and pink, red and gold—pressed up against the decorative black grillwork at the second-story windows. The sashless glass panels of the upper floors were overhung from the inside with jauntily patterned cloths of every hue. Becca was craning her neck to see how far up the building the pretty display went when she heard a door behind her open.

"Hey, you! What web?" The woman hailing her stood splay-foot in the doorway, arms akimbo. She was gargantuan—the first really fat person Becca had ever seen—so that her sheer plenitude of sallow flesh became the stuff of nightmare excess. All of her mounds and bulges were scantily covered with pastel robes, the tissues shot with silvery threads, an illusion of luxury. "Are you deaf? I asked what web?"

"Th—Thirdweb," Becca stammered.

"Sure you are." The fat woman's reply was ever so lightly washed with caustic bite. "You kids, what an imagination! You're not one of mine, so whose are you? Really, this time."

"I told you, Thirdweb. Carsonelic, Thirdweb." All of a sudden it became very, very important to Becca that the fat woman believe her. "I can show you my card—"

"Not another one!" The woman's obscene bulk doubled over as she slapped monumental thighs in laughter. "Come inside, dearie, and I'll show you my collection of otherweb cards I've pried off my own girls. It's the young sprats who give those as presents, 'specially if the girl's their first time fuck. And the

sorriest thing of all is, the poor little bitches buy into
the fantasy! But in's in; you're better off knowing it.
You're fresh yet, by the look of you, so I'll try it once
more and *then* I'm going to get Jude up. He's not one
of the best Highlandwebbers in this city, God knows,
but he's one of the biggest and he don't like having
to go on duty early. Kind of likes to make someone
pay for his lost sleep, and your credit's a lot less
overcharged than mine." She roared at the joke
Becca couldn't understand. "Now tell me your true
web and I'll just keep an eye on you 'til you go in
the proper door."

"Ma'am, if you'll only listen, I'll—"

"Oh, fuck." The fat woman sighed, then leaned
back to holler into the darkness: "Jude! Get up, Jude,
it's an early night!"

Becca didn't wait to see whether Jude was as big
as the fat woman claimed. She took off running,
heading up the narrow street without a glance
backward or sideways. The shrill blast of a whistle
cut the air. Other gray doors on the street opened
and other folk in the uniform of the Highlandweb
security force lumbered out. Their garb might have
once matched that of the Steadway Gate guards, but
now it was shabby and carelessly worn, the visored
helmets smeared and battered. There was nothing
wrong with their legs, though.

Becca ran, but they ran fast and faster, and some
of them popped out of doorways ahead of her, cutting
her off. They ringed her with a faceless circle that
cast back the warped reflection of her own panic-
stricken eyes from twenty pocked and dented visors.

The first gloved hand fell on her shoulder, fingers digging into the collarbone.

"There you are, Becca! I told you not to wander away." Van shoved his way through the circle with no more care than if the guards had been grain stalks. He spared a moment to wave at the fat woman. "Hello, Sabrina! Has she been giving you trouble?"

"She's with you, Van?" The fat woman was perplexed. "Your web and all, like she says?"

"Exactly as she says."

"Then what's she doing here? Looking for trouble? 'Cause she's come near enough to getting plenty." Sabrina scowled at Becca as if it were all her fault for telling the truth and not being believed.

"She's very, very sorry and she won't do it again. She just didn't know any better—right off the land, poor little seedgrub, she can't be faulted. It's not as if she'll be staying in the city."

Sabrina was unassuaged. "Well, you keep better watch on her until she's gone, hear me? We had enough of a dust-up with *your* doings last week, and don't tell me *you* didn't know any better!"

Van's wide, false smile froze into a rictus. "I know better now." The time for friendly sparring was dead. "And when my training's done and Webmaster Steven steps down, I'll know enough to remember *you* at the first inspection assizes."

Becca didn't entirely follow what was going on. She sensed enough to suspect that here was a battle challenge subtle as spider silk, but strong. The fat woman tried to brazen it out. "Huh! Mighty sure of yourself, aren't you? After what you did, Webmaster Steven's going to look elsewhere for his heir!"

"If that were true, why keep me alive at all?" It was softly said, and dead on, to gauge by how radically Sabrina changed her tune.

"Now, now, you know I was only joking. You know how I love a good laugh. We've had a few between us, haven't we? I'll tell you what, you come here tonight, after we open up and get going good. I'll fix you up with a new girl—fresh, pretty, plenty of spirit—and we'll let all this pass."

"Of course we will," Van said in a way that made the fat woman cringe. "Come, Becca." This time when he walked away, she followed close after.

He did not take her straight to Greenwoodweb, as she had hoped he would. At the next intersection he made a sharp right. The towers here followed the style of the ones on Sabrina's street, and when he turned left three streets further on there were more with the same heavy, gray doors, the same black bars on the second floor windows, the same bright cloths curtaining out the light. Becca darted glances down every cross-street they passed, hoping to see the crowds she'd formerly feared. Every path was deserted, or nearly so.

"It picks up at night," Van said, as if divining the reason for her hasty looks to left and right. "Oh, and for the harvest feast—What do your people call it—?"

"Harvest home."

"Yes, that. That's the busy season here, especially all the boys back from their first grange trip if they're trainee traders. That was the first time that I— Ah, here we are." He stopped before a door that looked no different from any other and knocked. It was answered by a black woman who could have been Virgie's grandma.

"Thank Mary Mother it's you," she said when she saw Van. Iron suspicion clamped down over her face when she saw Becca behind him. "Who's this?"

"Don't worry, Kethy, she doesn't know enough to tell anyone anything. I wanted to get her fixed up before we came here so she'd be inconspicuous, but she had other ideas. Maybe she'll listen to me next time."

He shouldered his way past the woman and Becca could only come after. Kethy shut the big door securely. A single light glowed overhead from one of those bizarrely cool globes the cityfolk used to capture the sun. It was a very poor sib of the array that made Carsonelic's quarters bright by night, and it could not be taken along to illuminate the hall up which Kethy now led them.

Becca was just thinking that these cityfolk were stupid not to use plain, common candles when the black woman struck a spark in the darkness and lit a fat yellow taper. Her eyes cast back oily reflections of the flame.

"I could get in a lot of trouble for this, Van," she said.

"You're in trouble already, Kethy." Van chuckled, a wintry sound. "That's why you're doing this. I'm in trouble too, for all that, and my new friend Becca will be in more trouble than she ever thought possible if her precious brother learns where she's been today."

"I didn't ask to come—"

"But here you are anyway." Van waved aside her objections. "And now I even have witnesses to prove that you entered this webquarter unescorted, of your own free will. I did offer you the chance to come here so that no one would recognize you, and you turned it down."

"To cut off my hair, change clothes, play the man?" Becca was livid. "You ever expected me to consent to such abomination?" Her voice rose to a shout, sending poor Kethy into fits of desperate shushing.

"Don't you understand anything? People think this web's *closed*," she said. "They hear voices, they'll get a couple of those damn guards to come see. Then where'll I be?"

"Where indeed," said Van. "At a new assizes, I expect, and completely disenfranchised after. I've been a good boy, Kethy, studying my lessons with Webmaster Steven as if nothing happened. The law is simple, but direct and to the point: Judgment must be swift and without appeal. The few innocent who fall do not detract from the great work of punishing the greater numbers of the guilty. And so on, and so forth."

He looked at Becca by candlelight and smiled. "We're not so haphazard here as where you come from. Certain jobs are the province of certain webs, though almost all webs do manage to keep a sufficiency of traders. Thirdweb's claim to fame just happens to be the administration of justice. Even our elic's Auntie Salome knows the twists of the law, even if she does prefer the trader's life."

"Then an elic's like—like family?" Becca hazarded. "Like a stead?"

"Yes, just like a stead, and just as full of all the warmth and love any child could ever hope to know," Van purred. "Now you see, that was Kethy's mistake, confusing work and family. You were stead once, weren't you, Kethy?"

The black woman looked away. "It's been a long time. I forget."

"Don't worry about it; I can look it up. Well, stead or city, Kethy took it upon herself to run her web as if there were some kinship between her and the girls and their—accidents. Did you know, Becca, whores have babies, too?"

"Whores..." It was a word that once had no meaning for her outside of Scripture. It was what good steadwives lessoned their daughters to call a female who gave herself to honest men for any reason other than thanks for feeding her and keeping her from harm.

It was what Gilber Livvy had called her, before.

"What a face!" Van's perfect teeth flashed. "Kethy, Keth' love, come bring that light nearer; you've got to see this! It's like losing your virginity all over again. Yes, *whores*, Becca! What did you think they made in these webs—flower garlands?"

To her surprise, and somewhat to her pride, Becca did not feel anything like a blush touch her cheeks at Van's crude words. Good: She would not give him any more satisfaction than she could help.

"You're an idiot," she replied levelly. "Seven kinds of fool beside if you think we steadfolk don't know what whoring is. Sodom was a city, too. There's just one thing I don't understand: Why call the babes anyone's accident? A taking woman nigh always turns fruitful, unless…" The thought of the ways—the blasphemous, demon-given ways—that folk might thwart the Lord's will for giving new life refused to be spoken aloud.

"Well, well." Van tilted his head, studying Becca as if she were an especially convoluted text of law. He shifted his glance to the black woman. "She knows more than she lets on. Shall we improve her education a little, Kethy?"

"I just want you to keep your word to me, that's all," Kethy muttered. "Then you can teach cows to sing, for all I care. Now you come along, get this visit done, go home. Then see about getting us the supplies we need. I can't feed her on my shares."

"You'd better feed her, or you'll find out how closely I do keep my word," Van said. "Very well, Becca; it looks as if I'll have to teach you the way—the absolutely sanctified way, never fear—that we manage these things in the city. You'll help me, won't you, Keth'? The woman's touch—?"

Kethy made a noncommittal sound and went on to the end of the hall, then up three flights of stairs. Becca saw several light globes along the walls, but all were dark. There were carpets underfoot, and what little she could see of them by the candle's light revealed poor quality and cheap showiness. Upstairs was another corridor, and halfway down it was the door that Kethy opened.

"Van!" The girl knelt naked on a towel beside a basin of water, washing herself. When she saw him, the joy in her eyes lit up that room brighter than a hundred candles. He was all that mattered to her, all that she could see, for she forgot her nakedness and raced into his arms just as she was.

Without the cheesy draperies to hide it, her pregnancy stood out like an unnatural growth, its swelling a terrifying contrast to the frailty of her limbs, the birdlike quality of her bones.

She was split, and a long time dying. That was the fear-tale the steadwives told of women captured by rogue bands, used in the begetting way even though they weren't taking. A man could do that to a woman; the woman usually died of it, broke and bleeding. But there were other ways a woman could die broke and bleeding too. Becca had heard the stories of births gone hard, women too small to release the babes they carried.

Too small... She looked at the girl in Van's embrace. *She was split, and a long time dying.* It was that wayward memory of the past, that ghastly intimation of the future, which ultimately made Becca sink to her knees, eyes covered, praying aloud for the mercy of a god in whom she no longer believed.

Chapter Five

Two men once stood facing each other before battle. They knew it would have to be to the death because that was the way it was, in those days.

The first man said, "I'm going to win this one."

"Oh, are you?" his rival asked, not really asking. "And why might that be?"

"Because I've got everything to lose," came the reply.

The second man shook his head. "I'm afraid I'm going to have to give you the lie there, son. I'm going to win this one."

"How do you figure?" the first man asked.

"Because I've got nothing to lose," the second man said. "Nothing at all."

The white stone steps that led up to the main building of Greenwoodweb shone like mirrors, polished sleek and slippery by the passing of uncounted feet. Becca stood at the bottom and told Van, "Thanks. I won't be long." They were the first words she'd spoken to him—that either of them had spoken—since leaving Kethy's place on the street of the gray doors.

She started forward, but hadn't gone more than eight steps up before she felt a hand on her arm, holding her back. Van turned her around so sharply that she nearly lost her footing on the slick stones.

"Where do you think you're going?" he demanded.

"In there as a case for the bone doctors, if you pull a fool caper like that again," she snapped, wrenching her arm free of his hold. "Unless it's my neck you want broke."

"You can't just walk into Greenwoodweb like it was one of your country barns. They'll throw you out so fast and so hard it won't be your neck that's broken." He gave her a swat on the rear for emphasis.

Becca rose up bristling. "Don't you *touch* me, you ill-mannered clod! How do you *dare*—?" She would have stamped her foot with rightful anger, but the steps' smoothness was a caution. Instead she gave Van a look fit to sour milk and marched to the top of the flight without a backward glance.

He was waiting for her when she got there. He could move fast, for a city boy. "Now look—" he began, leveling a finger at her face. She slapped it away, and in its place got a smile that was even more provoking. "Who's stepping out of line now? You're a strange girl, not what I've been trained to expect from stead blood at all. I don't know whether to be overjoyed or revolted. Webmaster Steven would, though; Webmaster Steven always knows best."

"Say what you're going to say," she muttered.

Van only shook his head. "I think the time for trying to teach you anything like common courtesy or common sense is long past. You'd better have this your own way. May I—?" He stepped up to the double doors at the head of the stairway and held one open for her with a little bow.

She stepped over the threshold, giving him a chary glance as she passed. She no longer trusted him, not after what he'd put her through to get here. He took her frown and gave her back a grin that guarded secrets. He continued to wear that same irritating curve of the lips as the pair of them walked through the halls. Simply looking at his face made Becca itch to strike him again, and more than just a slap on the hand this time.

The hall was long and narrow, cluttered with chairs, bedding, and wheeled tables that groaned under a load of boxes and bizarrely shaped glassware. Becca tried to keep her mind on what had brought her here (*I must find Gilber, we ought to see Virgie*), but it wasn't easy. At every turn was a new curiosity to distract her. When the hall ended in a larger space, high-ceiled and lit from above, she didn't focus on the lone desk there or the person behind it. Rather it was the stacks of paper piled atop the desk that held her eyes. She'd never seen so many of the precious, fluttery sheets all together in one place—

not outside of books, any road. When Eleazar had shown her the room holding Carsonelic's collection of books, it had been all she could do not to lock herself in and devour them all at a sitting, or die trying.

"May I help you?" The words jerked Becca from her daze. The voice was deep, though the face was a woman's. She sat with hands folded on the desktop, regarding Becca with honest eyes the color of well-baked bread.

"Yes, please." Becca took a step nearer the woman, a step to distance herself from Van, and said, "I've come looking for Gilber Livvy."

"Gilber Livvy…" The woman ran the name over her tongue as if it carried a questionable taste. "That one. What's your business with him?"

"I'm a friend."

"Ah." There was no change at all in her flat expression, her steady gaze. "And are you a friend with a name?"

Becca felt the first twitch of annoyance. "I'm called Becca of Carsonelic, Thirdweb." She still didn't feel entirely at home with the new name Eleazar had given her, even if it was supposedly hers only for the time being; her heart refused to close the door on Becca of Wiserways.

"Thirdweb…" Again that peculiar way of repeating the facts. The woman behind the desk lowered her eyelids as if their undersides carried special instructions only she could read.

All around the desk, the people of Greenwoodweb came and went on their unknown errands, emerging from one corridor and disappearing down another. Some wore yellow coveralls, some green with thin yellow bands at the sleeves, some wore only pale green tunics above the waist and whatever they fancied below. Their shoes clicked over the smooth flooring like tiny heartbeats marking time. Becca felt her skin crawl whenever one of them gave her an inquiring look in passing. *What are you doing here, girl? You don't belong,* their eyes told her plainly.

I know, she replied just as silently. *But I had to come. I have to see Gilber.* She couldn't blame the Greenwoodwebbers for staring. One look at her clothing was plenty to declare that she was a Ruth, an alien sojourner among them. She still wore the same garb that had seen her here from Wiserways, the long, cumbersome skirts and roughly woven blouse of a steadwoman. She had resisted all of Eleazar's attempts to make her exchange them for citywear. Her one concession to him was accepting a pair of decent shoes. She'd also allowed him to have her wayfaring garments laundered. No matter how sharply they made her stand out, even in the midst of the Coop streets' motley crowd, she couldn't give them up.

Not yet. Not until I've got somewhere to hide it. Secure in its underskirt hammock, Pa's gun weighed her down with secrets.

"Carsonelic, Thirdweb…" The woman's eyes shot wide open and she stated, "You don't belong here. You'd better go."

"What?"

"This is Admin, not Admitting. The only place

here that anyone from Thirdweb could possibly belong is Admitting. That's over in the Union building."

"Is that where I should go?" Becca asked.

The woman shrugged. "If you like. It won't make any difference; you don't look sick. They won't have you."

"I *know* I'm not sick," Becca said sharply.

"Then you shouldn't go to Admitting," the woman replied, always in the calm voice of reason. "They don't like having their time wasted any more than I do."

"*I* never said I was sick. *You're* the one who said that the only place I could go was Admitting. Fine, forget all that: Just tell me where I should go to find Gilber Livvy and we can both stop wasting time."

"I can't do that. I told you, this is Admin. Weren't you listening?"

"Well enough." Becca's words were starting to come out between clenched teeth. "I still don't see why you won't tell me where Gilber is."

"This is Admin," the woman repeated slowly, teaching a lesson to a backward two-year-old. "We do not have that information here. It's not our job. You should know better. How would you like it if someone came into Thirdweb asking for jam when the only thing Thirdweb's got to give is justice?"

Becca stared at the woman as if she'd sprouted horns. "I think I'd at least try to send them somewhere they *could* get jam," she replied, resting her palms on the desktop. She knew that if she didn't press her fingers down hard, they'd wind up around this creature's neck.

"Of course you would, child." The woman leaned forward and patted Becca's hand; Becca jerked away from the smarmy gesture. "Of course you would. And with no thought at all for the way things are supposed to be run, I'm sure."

"All I want is information."

"Which would be no trouble to me at all…*if* we had an Information department. In that case I could send you there and let you be their problem."

"Perhaps the information she wants could be found through Personnel?" Van suggested. Becca was so flustered by the woman behind the desk that she didn't bother telling him to mind his own business.

"She could apply there; it's all the same to me. That's in the basement of Tion Hall. Go back out the way you came in, make a sharp right, and it's two buildings over."

"I know where Tion Hall is," Van returned. He was no longer smiling. There was something about his stern, stony look that reminded Becca of her first encounter with Webmaster Steven. "What I *need* to know is whether they'll be able to help this girl."

"That will depend on her friend. If he's a patient here, it won't. New patient inquiries should be addressed to Admitting, long-term to Nursing."

"Gilber's not sick either," Becca said.

"She knows that, Becca," Van said. "Didn't you observe her reaction when you first gave his name? She knows who he is, she's just too stupid to know how to find him, so she's—"

"He came to Coop with me, from the outs." Becca spoke over Van's words, trying to take back control of the situation. *I can do this myself. I don't want his help; it costs too dear.* "He had questions to ask for his tribe's sake that could only be answered here at Greenwoodweb, so he's living here until the, um, the meddies can help him. Webmaster Steven arranged the whole thing."

"In that case, Webmaster Steven should have told you where to apply for proper information. You should go back and ask him. Now if you'll excuse me, I'm busy." The woman at the desk didn't move. The stacks of paper before her remained untouched.

Van stepped smoothly between Becca and the woman. Lips taut in what might have been a smile, he scooped up a pile of papers from the desk and dropped them on the floor. They made a splattering sound when they hit. The passers-by paused in their tracks to goggle as crisp sheets swooped and slid everywhere. The woman jumped to her feet.

"*What the hell do you think you're doing?*" Outrage deformed her face, dyed it with crimson blotches. The loiterers took one look and cleared out.

Van laid a finger to his lips. "Shhhh. There are sick people here." His eyes suddenly took on the look of fire stones, ready to shoot sparks. "And you're about to join them."

Becca never saw how the little knife appeared in his hand. Light from above winked over the blade. The woman's eyes were perfect circles now. "What do you mean?" Her words were scarcely more than whispers.

"My name is Van, Carsonelic, Thirdweb. You may have heard of me. If you haven't, permit me to educate you: Some days ago there was an uproar in the city over a pair of runaways. I was one of them. As you can see, they found me and brought me back."

The woman nodded her head stiffly, eyes never wavering from the knife. "Yes, sir."

"Now tell me what else you see…here?" He stretched out the hand that didn't hold the blade so that the woman could have a clear view of his sleeve, then swapped the knife to that hand and extended the other arm. "Or here?"

"Nothing." She swallowed and said again, "Nothing, sir."

"Not even the shadow of a yellow stripe, hm? And that's exactly as clean as they'll stay even if I stick this—" He made a feint with the blade "—right through your eyeball." A twist of the wrist, and the knife was gone as quickly as it had appeared. "Now do you know who I am?"

"Yes, sir."

"And will you help us?"

"Yes, sir," the woman repeated. Her voice had become a thin mewl of misery.

Shortly after that, Becca found herself trailing after Van and one of the Greenwoodwebbers. Their guide was a young man in yellow coveralls who looked as if he had only a few years advantage over Van. There was something about his expression that minded Becca of the third man in Galen's patrol, the one who hadn't spoken up once. Now that she came to think of him again, she thought she'd seen a yellow band marking his sleeve, though by night and firelight she might've been mistaken.

This man had the use of his voice, though he didn't overdo it. A grunt was the only way he acknowledged the assignment that the still-trembling woman gave him. In silence he led them from the desk, out of Admin, down the slick steps, and across a small space paved with crushed rock to the door of a different building.

If this is where Gilber lives, I'll have no trouble finding it on my own another day, Becca thought. *All the other Greenwoodweb places are white as salt, but here's a spot partway up the wall where they're rebuilt in brick. And look there!* She tilted her head back to gape at the wondrous thing that hung in a wooden frame atop the building's flat roof. *A bell! God's glory, a bell the size of a cauldron. After this day, I can come back to this place with no help at all.* She hurried inside.

"In here," said their guide, jerking his thumb at a closed door. They were the first and last words he bothered to address to them before lumbering away.

"Well, there's manners for you." Van smirked. "You could take a lesson from him, Becca."

She scowled. "I'm proper grateful to you for getting some help out of that lump behind the desk," she told him. "But if we're talking manners, what you did for me doesn't give you free rein to give me that sass."

"Weren't you paying attention back there?" Van asked. "I've got free rein to do whatever I like, short of murdering someone. Webmaster Steven's my pledge for that. But why do I need his sanction to speak to you as I please? I didn't think that steadwomen ever said boo to a man without their alph's blessing, let alone criticized the way any man spoke to them. And as for gratitude—" His lips twisted into a leer.

Becca could feel her face closing up over hot anger. shutting away every sign of unwomanly rage. *What did I expect? Not so different from stead here as all that.* The bitter thought was followed by a private curse. There was nothing she could do but comply.

"If that's what you want of me, I'll oblige. Here? Now? Must be city ways. On stead we're taught that a woman's fitting gratitude needn't compromise her modesty. Apart from harvest home, our men are *mannerly*." She hit that last word hard, on purpose, then hiked up her skirts just enough so that she could kneel without getting her heels tangled in the hem. Looking up into Van's face she asked, "You want the kiss or the sign?"

"*Jesus!*" Van flushed dark red and yanked her to her feet by one arm. "Are you crazy? Because you've picked the right place for that."

"I thought it was what you wanted." Becca rubbed her aching arm. Van's reaction had left it wrenched and tender. Her thigh stung too where the hidden gun had slammed against it. She didn't like to picture the bruise that would leave.

"Dear God, *no*." He spoke so emphatically and looked so repulsed by the very thought of what he'd just been offered that Becca came nigh to feeling insulted. "I was only joking."

"The way you were when you said I could learn manners from the man who brought us here?"

"No, then I was serious. If you knew what he is, you'd understand."

"Well, what is he?" Becca demanded.

Van only replied, "Do you want me to give you a lecture or do you want to find your friend? We haven't got all the time in the world. If I know Eleazar, he'll want you home by dinner. That's when I need to be back too, or overstep parole. So, your choice." .

Becca didn't need to think it over. "Find Gilber."

She expected that the door before them would open onto Gilber Livvy's room, but she was mistaken. It swung back to place them in another hallway, just as cluttered as those back at Admin. Becca made herself a promise to return another day soon, when she'd have the time to investigate all of these fascinating objects. She guessed that most of them must have something to do with healing—Wasn't healing Greenwoodweb's sole charge?—but she yearned to learn the exact function of each.

If only Miss Lynn could see all this. Wouldn't she be thrilled! For once the thought of the herbwife who'd been her friend and mentor didn't pain her heart.

The corridor ended in an open space almost twin to the one at Admin, only far smaller. There was an identical desk, garrisoned by another woman. When she saw her, Becca covered her eyes with one hand and couldn't help but groan, anticipating more trouble, another tooth-grinding duel of words. She was too weary to face it.

She didn't have to. Van stepped up to the desk and

told the guardian, "You've got a Ruth here called Gilber Livvy. We've come to see him."

Becca braced herself to have the woman recite a dozen reasons why she couldn't help them find Gilber and why they weren't supposed to be in this building to start with. What she did hear was: "Gilber Livvy? Of course. Such a nice young man, so helpful. It's as if he were born to us. It breaks my heart to think of the day he'll be leaving. Well, that's not your problem, is it? He's in room 140 right now, just down that hall, fourth door on the right."

Gilber was where the woman had said they'd find him. "Becca, love, what's wrong with you?" he asked urgently, rising from the table where he'd been busy reading. "You look like you've had another vision. Is that what's brought you?"

"*Another* vision?" Van echoed. He gave her a look part mockery, part speculation. "Do you make a habit of prophecy?"

Becca ignored him. She rushed into Gilber's arms and buried her face against his shoulder. A tiny knot of iron formed in her chest: He no longer held the sweet, clean scent of pineywood. There was a different odor to him now, something that made him smell *too* clean, like a boiled stone. Over her head she heard Gilber tell Van, "You speak scorn like that to every woman?"

She expected an explosion of temper from the boy, maybe even a second flash of the knife. The mildness with which he responded to Gilber was an astonishment. "I'm sorry; that was inexcusable and ill-timed. We were just discussing the importance of good manners."

"It's all right, Van," Becca said. Gilber settled his arm around her waist, took her close into the warm curve of his side. Secure, she was able to be generous, even if it stretched the truth of things. "You've been more than mannerly to me, seeing me here safe and sound. I won't trouble you any more."

"If you want to be left alone with him, just say so," Van told her. "My time's my own these days, damn the luck, and I've already taken care of the only business I've got." His cocky look dimmed; Becca could tell his thoughts were with his sweetheart. It made him look older. "I'd like to have a word with both of you, but it can wait. Tend to your own affairs first; I'll be down at the reception desk."

"I know where that is," Gilber said. "I'll fetch you."

"I'd be most obliged." With that, Van left them.

"That's queer," Gilber commented more to himself than to Becca.

"What is?"

"Do you think he didn't know me? Or could be that there's something ailing his sight? I know I got a close enough look at his face when we pulled him out of hiding. I got more than a look from him." He pulled back the loose-fitting sleeve of his green tunic to show Becca the yellow blotch of a healing bruise on his forearm. "Now here he is, and not a word about all that. Not one! And him boiling over with curses that'd peel paint when it happened. Mighty queer."

"He does know you, Gilber, only—" Becca hesitated over he next words. "Maybe he's come to realize it was all for the best." It was an answer she didn't believe herself. "His girl—her name's Isa—she's fruitful. They couldn't have got far with her that way; she'd never have survived." Becca didn't have the bone to add that Isa didn't look long for the world any road.

"I hope you're right," Gilber said. "I guess you must be. After all, you were there with me too, when we dug them out of the ruins. He'd have to hold you just as much to blame for their capture, but you say he's been mannerly." His hands cradled her face like a blossom and his kiss was water after thirst. "I couldn't bear it if he'd turn on you to get at me."

"Gilber…" Becca took Gilber's kiss greedily, gave him back a dozen more, trying to make each add its flame to the ones that had gone before. Her body burned for his, her hands lost to any hint of modesty or restraint.

If Van could see me now, he'd laugh out loud. Is this Eleazar's prim and proper stead-reared sister? A fresh sweep of fire in the blood whisked away her random thoughts. She pressed Gilber backward until he bumped into the table where his abandoned book lay.

"Becca, love, wait." He grabbed her questing hands and held them firm. "We can't do this here, not now."

"Why not? Don't tell me you've got Virgie hid somewhere in this room?" She made it sting.

He didn't try to defend against her biting words, only let her hands go and turned to face the table. With a care that was nigh reverence, he closed the book and set it aside, then stood there wordless, gazing down. His silence scared her. Tentative as any untried maiden, she touched the fine green cloth sheathing his arm.

"Gilber?"

"You think I don't love you anymore," he said. It hit her ears without mercy, a plunge into the abyss.

"I never said—" She paused, unsure of what to do. Deny it? That would be to cast aside the truth. *Why don't you deny it, Gilber? Why don't you tell me I'm wrong?*

Unless it's so.

"That's the way Virgie tells it." She peered over his shoulder to watch him run his fingertips over the book's worn clothbound cover. "I've been to see her every day. They've got her over in the creche ward with the other children, in Ergen Building. I didn't know she was so sick." He sighed. "Good thing we didn't force her to go back to Mark's stead when she joined us. Bringing her here was her salvation."

"I'm joyed to know that," Becca said, though how she said it gave her the lie.

"I'd rather you were happy to know how wrong she is," he said. In one unexpected movement he whirled from the table and held her in his arms once more. "I do love you, Becca. I could stop breathing sooner than stop loving you."

"Then why won't you—?" She couldn't say it. The fire in her was dead, and all the lessons that Wiserways taught her maidens had risen from the ashes. A proper woman wasn't forward with a man.

"It's not for lack of wanting, believe me," he told her. "It's just— All this is so strange to me, this place, these people and their ways. I'm feeling my path.

Inside these walls, I don't know what's right and what's forbidden. What if we were caught?"

"I'm not afraid to face punishment for that," Becca said. Her heart was singing, exalted. *He does love me! I can read the truth of his soul in his eyes. Oh Gilber!*

"Don't you see, love? It wouldn't be our punishment alone." He kissed her brow, his lips warm. "There are so many others relying on us: my tribe, your stead, the children Virgie left behind. If we break a law here, we take them down with us."

"But you don't even know if there is a law forbidding us to be—to be the way I want—I need—"

"I want too, love; I need too." Another kiss, this time on her lips, so sweet she thought she sipped honey from the comb. "That's just the sorrow: We don't know. Until we do, until we learn, we've got to walk over dead leaves without a crackle."

She sighed and let her head rest against him. He was right. Blinking back tears, she put on a brave face and said, "We won't need to bide long for the knowledge. Eleazar's from Thirdweb and Thirdweb deals justice. If there's any place to learn Coop law, it's with him. I'm a quick study."

"There's my angel!" Gilber's happiness lit up the room. "We'll be together before another moon changes her face."

"Another moon..." Becca clung to her lover. "Sweet Mary, that's half what's brought me here, Gilber. When the moon changes—"

Gilber's hand stopped her mouth gently, before she could say another word. "When the moon changes, it's a beautiful sight," he said, giving every word its weight.

She thought she caught his intent: *So much we don't know about this place! Like whether we can speak openly of all things without fear of being overheard. Tread softly, for now.* "Not everyone thinks that way, though Lord witness I do. You taught me to see it so."

"You think people in your brother's house might not share our views?" Gilber asked. She nodded. "Well, a good guest doesn't trespass on his host's prejudices. Listen, love, the Greenwood folk like me. I earn my keep by lending a hand to the hobays with the heavier chores."

"Hobays?" She thought she'd heard that word before.

"The ones in the yellow coveralls. It's their work to keep the whole web clean. I help them with the garbage. No reason why you wouldn't be welcome to visit here even when I'm working, especially if you work alongside me. It's not the most fragrant work under heaven—"

"It'll suit me." Her smile mirrored his, sealing their unspoken pact. In a place of healing, who'd go tracking the source of every scrap of blood-stained cloth? When the moon changed, she could hide the telltale rags, then come here to dispose of them daily.

"I didn't expect any less." This time his kiss was brotherly, a peck on the cheek. "So what else brought you here to see me?"

She reached under her skirts and undid the knot holding her sire's gun. "This." She laid the heavy weapon on the book.

His fingers closed on the sleek handle. "Are you sure you want this out of your keeping?"

"I need you to mind it for me. Eleazar's been wanting me to dress like the other women in his elic. He won't say it in so many words, but I can tell I'm an embarrassment to him garbed like this. I can't put him off forever, and these clothes of mine are about to fall to threads any road. If I do dress Coop, I'll have nowhere to hide it that's truly safe."

"I do." Gilber raised the bottom of his tunic and tucked the gun into the waistband of his trousers. "They don't meddle with my things here. I've been allowed to keep my rifle in my room. What a fine place they've given me, too!"

"This it?"

"Oh no, this is just the room they've set aside for my studies. Isn't it a wonder? Course if they had need of more space here in Bell Ward, I'd have to move in with someone else, share quarters. I'm thankful for the moment."

A sharp, impatient rapping sounded at the door. Before Becca or Gilber could speak, Van came in. He no longer looked like a man whose mind was on being mannerly.

"You've had long enough," he stated. "It'll be dark out soon, and my parole ends with dusk. I'm not going back with my business unsettled just so you two can indulge yourselves."

"What business do you have with us?" Gilber asked, on his guard.

"Plainspoken business: You have healing skills,

Gilber Livvy. That's what the Greenwoodweb records say. I need them."

"You mean she does," Gilber replied softly. "Your girl."

Van's eyes flickered in Becca's direction. "Chatty little thing, aren't you? Fine, it's no secret; I'll want your help too. Isa's going to have my child. Between the two of you, there's enough knowledge to see her through the birth."

"If that's your business with me, I'm sorry for you. The little healing lore I've got doesn't touch much on midwifery," Gilber said. "Wouldn't it be best for the girl to bring her here?"

"That's impossible."

"Why—?" Becca ventured.

"It's impossible because I *say* it is!" Van shouted at her. "Who made it your place to question me?"

"You'd better put a kinder rein on your tongue when you speak to the lady." Gilber's tone was no longer soft. "If you won't bring your girl here for help, Becca's your only hope; don't count on me. I can't uncover a stranger woman's nakedness like that, or touch her when she's in her impurity. I can't help you with her at all."

"Can't?" Van's eyes narrowed. "Can't or *won't?*"

"Both, I guess." Gilber would have said more—Becca could have told Van that much—but Van didn't give him space to speak.

"Damn your soul, you won't help us? But you were ready enough to help Webmaster Steven and his hounds track us down, drag us back into hell. All right, Gilber Livvy, I'll remember. And when the day comes that you beg for my help, I'll throw those same words back in your face like this!" He spat hard and straight into Gilber's eye and stormed from the room, slamming the door behind him.

Chapter Six

They tell me times are hard and that's no lie,
Tell me to be grateful 'til the day I die,
Say it's not so much that I can't have no more,
Say it's the salvation I've been looking for,
Tell me that it's something that I can control,
Give me a full belly and an empty soul.

"There you are, Becca." Eleazar was waiting for her by the stairway door. Eleazar was always waiting for her somewhere whenever she came back into Thirdweb's tower. He'd been waiting when she came home from Greenwoodweb without Van, that first time, and every time since. Sometimes she found him biding at the very door of her room, sometimes all the way downstairs at the entrance to the tower itself. Becca found it warming and uncanny at the same time. She couldn't tell whether she was being cherished or merely watched.

She'd grown up under a man's eye, but always her sire's, her alph's. Eleazar was kin, not alph. In fact he'd been the one to tell her that there were no such things as alphs in the city. He'd wanted to tell her more, but he'd been summoned away on web business and hadn't found the time to take up the subject since.

Becca thought how odd it was that a busy man like Eleazar was never too busy to meet her when she came home.

He held her at arm's length, beaming. "Now let me look at you. Let's see if Sandersweb is worthy of their hire." He took her borrowed jacket from her and gave her a once-over inspection, then nodded his satisfaction. "They do work magic with cloth and thread. You look just fine."

"Like I belong here?" Becca teased, turning around slowly to show off her new garb. There was a hard chill outdoors, and her cheeks flamed as much with the cold as with pleasure and a little shame. The dress only reached a handspan below her knees. Hattie would have been shocked to see her daughter turned out so brazen, but she'd have been outright scandalized to know how close Becca had flirted with the idea of wearing breeches. The tailors of Sandersweb had given her a choice of skirt, dress or pants as if it were no great matter. "Like I'm Coop, not stead?"

"Exactly like," Eleazar said, laughing, then added, "Until you open your mouth."

"Oh." Becca's elation subsided.

"I didn't know it was your ambition to be Coop." He led the way into Carsonelic's apartments. His adopted family took up three levels of Thirdweb's tower, their allotted floors connected by internal stairways. "You should have said something. There was a vacancy over in Greenwoodweb two days ago. They tried persuading your friend Gilber to take it, but he refused. It's filled now, of course. You've studied healing and you're young enough to learn more, it would have been the perfect place for you. Too bad."

"I don't want to be Coop," Becca said, all joy in her new clothing forgotten. "I just want to pass for Coop while I'm here. So I won't shame you, Eleazar."

"Not a chance of that." He patted her cheek. Though he didn't have more than nine years on Becca, he carried himself like her elder by twenty. "Why, you're frozen! Come and have something hot."

He shepherded her into the big room where the whole elic gathered for meals and motioned for her to take a seat at the long table. There was a miracle-pitcher on the sideboard, a wonder that stored strong tea good and hot for hours with no fire. Eleazar poured them out two cups of the brew. He treated the miracle-pitcher the same way he treated the host of other daily marvels surrounding him, never giving them a second thought or look unless they failed to serve him.

I wonder how long he lived here before he got that way? Becca thought. *Not too long, I guess. He'd have to pass that test Van mentioned before he could live here for good.*

The cityfolk mightn't take a boy who was always gawping at things that're commonplace as brooms and buckets to them. She sipped her tea. It was nice and sweet. Eleazar always remembered how much honey she liked.

"So!" He took the chair across from her. "And how was your visit? How's the little girl coming along?"

"Virgie's fine," Becca replied. "The nurse told me that she'll probably be fit enough to leave in another week. Eleazar…" She looked at him sideways, shy of begging favor. "Eleazar, do you think she could come live here then?"

"Hmmmmm." Eleazar leaned back, steepled his fingers. "That wouldn't be up to me."

"But you said you saw promise in her."

"No doubt. She's a most impressive young lady. But to have her move into this elic— I don't have that authority."

"But you took *me* in!"

"You're only here on a temporary basis, a visitor. We have enough flexibility to our supply allowance to cover that, and as your blood kin I can vouch for you. Besides, you stated under oath in the webmaster's presence that you'd return home as soon as your grievance against the new Wiserways alph was heard. The girl has no home to return to. She'd be needing a permanent berth, which makes it a different case entirely."

"That's another thing, Eleazar," Becca said, hands wrapped snug around her cup. "What about Virgie's old place?" Lately she'd come to feel uneasy in her mind calling Mark's domain *stead* or *home* when it was a thing so much darker. "Winter's coming in. As bad off as Virgie was when she got here, those poor babies she left behind have it worse. We've got to go to them, bring them out of that place, fetch them here, give them decent food, clothing, warmth—"

"Yes, yes, I read your deposition for Webmaster Steven myself."

"Well? What did he say? What's he going to do about it?"

"What the webmaster of Carsonelic always does: He's going to ponder the merits of the case and render justice."

Becca pushed her cup away. "When?" was all she asked.

Eleazar made a noncommittal gesture. "Add that to the list of things I can't decide for you, Becca. Of course if you're that edgy to know, we do have right of petition. Even for you Ruths, as long as you're living within the wall of the law."

Becca was bewildered. "What right's that? What good is it to me or Virgie's kin?"

"What it means is you can apply for a personal interview with Webmaster Steven and ask him for a progress report on your case. It's not something we do too frequently: Some people feel that hurrying the webmaster might anger him enough to give a decision they don't want to hear. It's only a belief, no proof to back it. You can risk it, if you like."

"Would you, if you were me?"

"I can't even begin to imagine being you, Becca," Eleazar told her. "Coming so far, calling out for judgment against your lawful alph—"

"Adonijah's *not* my lawful alph!" Becca's fist thumped the table, made her cup dance. "He didn't come to power in a fair fight, he *murdered* our sire, and I can prove it!"

"That's just what you'll have to do, when the case comes before us," her brother said dryly. "Charges like those demand a panel of judges, but Virgie's case concerns only Webmaster Steven. You won't harm your own chances for a good verdict by approaching him about this."

"I wouldn't care if I did."

"You know, I believe you." Eleazar finished his tea, then smacked his lips and said, "Why don't I take you to him right now? Not exactly the normal route for a petition, but I happen to know he's in the garden at this hour. You could speak to him off the record."

"Is that something that's...*done* here?" Every time Becca visited Gilber, he reminded her of the need to tread lightly among the city customs. It bothered her that of all the books in Carsonelic, not one laid out the laws or the usages of Coop. *Not one of the books they've let* me *near*, she realized on second thought.

"Well, it isn't standard procedure, but you won't be punished for it. If Webmaster Steven gets angry, tell him it was my idea."

"Oh no, I couldn't—!"

Eleazar squeezed her shoulder. "What's the use of being bound by blood if we don't use the tie now and then?"

Becca had never been to the garden. It was planted on the tower roof, and it boasted plants both useful and purely decorative. A glass enclosure kept the air inside warm and moist, charming heat from the miserly winter sun.

Eleazar stopped short of going in. "It'll look better if you approach him on your own."

Becca stared at her reflection in the misted glass. "You couldn't go in with me? Just until I spy him out?"

"I'm telling you, there's nothing to be afraid of. I thought you were brave?"

Becca nibbled her underlip. "I—I guess so." She made herself think of the children. "All right."

"Good girl. Go on. I'll be waiting for you just inside the stairwell. It's freezing out here." Clapping his arms around himself, every breath trailing a thin ghost, Eleazar took himself off and left Becca facing the garden's glass door.

He was right about how cold it was. Without a jacket, wearing only her new city garb, Becca felt the keen chill. She got herself inside the glass and gave a little shudder of pleasure as the captive warmth worked its magic on her bones.

It didn't take her long to find Webmaster Steven. In the green stillness surrounding her, she heard the faint snip of scissors. She followed the sound and saw the webmaster absorbed in trimming dead leaves from a little shrub. There was a spicy smell in the air.

If he knew she was there, staring at him, he gave no sign of it. Becca hesitated, unsure of how to make her presence known. Her fingers twisted together, a nervous habit she loathed. She would have hidden their contortions in her skirt, but her new clothing had so much less fabric than the old; it was impossible to do without hiking up the hem even shorter. She left off trying.

A deep breath filled her lungs with moist, fragrant air, drove back the fear enough for her to call, "Sir?"

Webmaster Steven looked up, his face expressionless. Then recognition warmed it and he smiled. "Well, here's a nice surprise! You're the stead girl, aren't you?"

"Yes, sir." Becca made a shy reverence. "Becca of Wiserways, Paul's get."

"That's a big mouthful for such a little girl. You won't mind if I just call you Becca?"

"No, sir." Even though she knew he was speaking to her as if she were younger than Virgie, Becca couldn't find the bone in her to be angry for it. He wasn't riled to see her; that was enough.

He returned his attention to the little shrub, but still he spoke to her. "Come here alone, have you? Exploring our home, or did you know this greenhouse was up here?"

"I knew where I was going." Becca clasped her hands behind her back to still their nervous motion. "In fact—" *Say it right out cold, Becca! Quick's always easiest.* "In fact I came here on purpose, to speak to you."

"Did you?" Another snip of the black scissors against the withered leaves. "What about?"

Becca told him. She spoke of the weather turning harsh, and the hard life that Virgie's kin and the rest suffered in the best of times, in that strange, half-buried place they'd claimed for shelter. She spoke of

Mark, the child who'd set himself up as alph of that place, and of how dead his eyes were to anything but survival.

She didn't speak of what she'd seen the children do in survival's name. She didn't want the shadow of their abomination to stand between them and the city's peaceable, plenteous haven.

When she was done, Webmaster Steven stood tall and tucked his scissors away in the small mesh bag that hung from his elbow. He produced a bottle and a leather cup from the same bag, had himself a drink, then poured a second and offered it to Becca as if she'd said nothing at all.

She shook her head and said a few polite words of refusal. He shrugged, drank the offering himself, put away bottle and cup, and only then chose to say, "It seems I recall hearing just such a case from your brother."

"Yes, sir." Becca wet her lips. "It's the same."

"I thought so. Did your brother happen to tell you how long it takes us to pass judgment on a case here in Thirdweb?"

"Uh...I didn't ask." *Dear Lord, what've I done? How could I have been so stupid? I've been forward, given offense, pushed myself in where I had no business being! What if my foolishness costs Virgie? What if it costs Gilber's whole tribe, because he came here in my company?* She could feel her every heartbeat right down to her knotted fingertips.

Webmaster Steven laughed in her face. "Oh child! You look ready to bolt, poor thing. Don't be so afraid of me. I'm not that ugly." Becca couldn't even find the breath to agree with him. He laughed at her again, then took her hand. "Come, let's find someplace where we can sit and talk like civilized people."

He led her through beds of low growth and between trees that grew and flourished in huge clay pots. She felt sweat seeping into her new clothes at the neck, the waistband, under the arms. At last he cried, "There we are!" as if he'd discovered a new world. What he had found was a white stone bench set between two bushes with shiny dark green leaves and waxy white flowers. Their fragrance closed over Becca like a giant's hand the instant she sat down.

"Now listen, my dear," Webmaster Steven said in a kindly way. "You're a stranger here. No one expects you to know all our customs straight off, by osmosis."

"By what?"

He chuckled. "Don't worry about that. While you're at it, don't worry about anything. I've seen how you carry yourself, how you behave to others in the elic and in the web, and I've got no complaints. You're a clean, quiet, well-mannered girl, no trouble to us at all. If you step on a few minor rules, that's to be expected. Nothing will happen to you for that."

Becca's breath left her in a great gust of relief. "That's a mercy," she said.

"Why, you can even have your gun back, if you like."

He might as well have pulled out that same gun and shot her with it where she sat. Her mouth fell open, wanting to speak, powerless to make a sound.

Webmaster Steven clicked his tongue. "I'm sorry,

dear, old knives grow blunt with age. You know your friend, the young man who was such a great help to me the day you arrived? We're all deeply indebted to him."

"Gilber Livvy." Becca had the sure and certain feeling that Webmaster Steven had forgotten the name long since, despite all his talk of gratitude.

"Yes, just what I was about to say, Gilber Livvy. Well, the first time you went over to Greenwoodweb to visit him, we had a call here from Highlandweb. A meddie noticed your friend Gilber was carrying something under his tunic and when he stopped the lad for questioning, it was like talking to a rock. He had no choice but to call a guard, the guard found the gun, and your friend found himself in a bit of trouble."

"He never said a word of it to me!" Becca protested. "I've been to see him more than once since then, and he didn't say a thing!"

"Why should he? Women worry so, and the case was already settled by the time you paid your next visit. The problem wasn't that he had a gun, or even that it was yours. The real trouble was that he was found carrying that gun in Bell Hall, of all places! That's a felony. He might have been imprisoned for it."

"I'm thankful he wasn't." Becca spoke her heart. "Was it your doing, sir? You've got all my blessing for it." She'd learned better than to offer Coop men her gratitude; they saw it as meaning just one thing, coming from a steadwoman's lips.

"I'm not the one who's earned it. I'll tell you

frankly, Becca, when Highlandweb contacted us my first reaction was to lock up your friend for a long time. A gun in Bell Hall! It might have been disastrous. I rushed over there intending to teach that young man a lesson he'd never forget."

Becca wanted to ask *Even after how much he helped you?* She could guess the answer she'd get, and thought she'd do better to keep still.

"Fortunately for him, my judgment was tempered. I suppose you could call it a divine sign—we don't seem to get those here in the cities so much as your people. Or you could call it a coincidence, but on my way, I ran into young Van. He was rushing to get home before dusk—the way he honors his parole is an example to us all. I gave him leave to stay out past the hour and to accompany me to judgment. He needs the practice. One day soon it will be Webmaster Van who rules Third."

"Oh!" Becca's eyes were bright with sympathy. "Has he challenged you already?"

"Challenged!" The webmaster's laughter went on so long that it turned hoarse before it was done. Wiping moisture from his eyes, he said, "Forgive me, my dear, but I couldn't help it. Ah, you're blushing! Don't be ashamed. Shame on me for assuming you knew: That's not how we do things here. To be a webmaster requires more of a man than mere brute strength and cunning. If we'd allow the office to go to the man capable of killing his predecessor barehanded, this city would be nothing but a pile of rubble by now."

"Then how do you manage—" She tried to recall

the word the Coopfolk had for it. "—your changeovers?"

Webmaster Steven was visibly pleased to hear her speak so. "You are a bright one. Not that I'm surprised: Your brother's one of the best we've ever chosen. Oh! I apologize again; I shouldn't have said *chosen.* I forgot that there's a particular meaning attached to that word where you come from."

"Don't bridle your speech on my account," Becca said. "You've been good enough to overlook my missteps. And Gilber's."

"Back to that, are we? My word, I do wander from the mark. We can't prep Van fast enough, if you ask me. Age, age…" Webmaster Steven shook his head, a self-mocking smile on his lips. To Becca he said, "It's Van who'll be my successor as webmaster of Third; not because he's strong enough to kill me but because I'm wise enough to pick him. From the day I was given the post by Webmaster Benjamin, I've had my eyes open for an heir. Since then I've searched among my own sons, and the sons of other men, and among the sons we've brought into the city full grown. There was a time I thought your brother would be ideal for the post, but then I began to notice young Van. He's the one, I have no more doubts."

"But he—" Becca bit her tongue. *But he has doubts,* she thought. *More than doubts, or why did he try to run away?* She became aware of the webmaster's knowing look and realized she might as well have spoken her thoughts out loud.

"*Young* Van, I said. He is very young; misguided,

as the young so often are. He's been swept up in the enthusiasm of the moment before this. It's natural; I wouldn't want him for my heir if he were some sort of emotionless monster. The law lies here—" He tapped two fingers against his temple. "—but justice dwells here." He laid a hand over his heart. "And because unlike law, justice can never change, there is no appeal once the verdict has been pronounced. That makes it all the more vital for the webmaster of Third to know both the law and the heart."

Suddenly Becca understood what had happened that day she left her gun in Gilber's keeping. "So the verdict you pronounced on Gilber was Van's doing, and he said he should go free."

Webmaster Steven nodded. "He argued that if anyone were to blame in the case it was the Greenwoodwebbers for not having warned your friend about the rule governing Bell Hall. *Now* he knows, and he even agreed with the wisdom of the law. He's pretty smart, considering. Both firearms are safely stored in Gilber Livvy's quarters for the present. So, *do* you want yours back?"

"No, sir, thank you. If Gilber's still got it and it's no harm to him, let it be. But sir—" She gulped air. "Sir, you still haven't given me the answer I came for. What about those poor children out there in the ruins? When will you send folk to save them?"

"I don't think we'll be doing that, child." Webmaster Steven plucked a single petal from the flowering bush beside him. "The verdict's not final nor formal, but I see no point in keeping it from you, since you went to the bother of seeking me out. We'll let them be as they are, and God will look after them."

"Sweet name of Mary, *why?*" It was meant to be a question; it came out a cry of pain. "Isn't there enough bread here? There's not so many of them. I'd give them the full half measure of my allotment, and so will Gilber! Let me go out into the city, find other folk who'd be willing to do the same, for mercy's sake. You *can't* leave them to die; they're only babes!"

As she spoke, her words built up a hill of little bones that only she could see, and a darksome slope where baskets and swaddlings and vessels baked of clay shook with the famished cries of their small nestlings. Red-eyed scurriers haunted the hillside, waiting their time until the cries grew weak, then ceased. The long shadow of the Lord King Herod bent low over the makeshift cradles, summoning his chosen children with the bright glory of His sword. When the Lord King departed, the scurriers came forth boldly to feast on the shells left behind. Sometimes the scurriers grew impatient, nibbled at the living along with the dead. Becca's infant sister Shifra had known their bite, venomed with uncleanness. It had cost her a foot and came nigh to costing her more.

Becca swayed, dizzy, unaware that she'd somehow risen to her feet before the webmaster. "You have to save them," she moaned. Her words blew through the piled bones of Prayerful Hill, sang through the empty sockets of uncounted skulls, each no bigger than a grown man's fist. "In the name of God—!" The bones plunged into the black womb of the earth, dragging her down in their wake.

She came to her senses in her own room with someone at her bedside watching her. Before she revived fully she thought it must be Eleazar. Then her vision cleared and she saw that it was Van.

"You gave Webmaster Steven a bad scare," he said by way of welcoming her back into the land of the waking. "I don't know whether to kiss you for it or not. I wouldn't want you getting the wrong idea."

"He can't do it," Becca muttered, ignoring the boy's jibe. Her thoughts were still fixed on the children. "He can't, not if he's human."

"He gave up his humanity a long time ago." Van waved it all away casually. "Even before he took over as webmaster."

"I think you're right." Her mouth was full of ashes. "Everything he said to me about justice, the heart, it was all words. Only words. If not, how could he decide to abandon those poor little souls out there?"

"Oh, that wasn't his decision," Van said. "It was mine."

Chapter Seven

What's the password?
Never ask the password.
Pass, friend.

The crowd outside the theater rocked and surged back and forth like cream in a churn. Becca was shoved and jostled on every side, yet she held her ground. She didn't want to be here—she had no idea what was in store once those doors up ahead opened, and the tumult was making her head ache—but she'd lose her hope of heaven before she'd show a lick of weakness in front of Van.

"Are you sure you don't want to take my arm?" he inquired. He offered it, elbow first.

Becca took advantage of a sudden shift in the mob

to use her own elbow to jab his away. "I'm fine," she said.

"Are you? You sound taut enough to plunk a tune. Well, suit yourself."

"If I could suit myself, I'd be home now," Becca rounded on him. "Or with Gilber."

"Home?" Van's brows rose in feigned innocence. "Is that how you think of Thirdweb these days? Webmaster Steven *will* be pleased. I think he likes you. You're a rarity. The old boy always did have a taste for freaks."

"No wonder he picked you, then."

Van took the barb out of Becca's words by the simple act of agreeing with them. "Naturally. You know the old saying: The fire goes to the flame."

"That's not one I heard."

"That's because I just made it up."

Becca snorted and turned from him, angry with herself for having tumbled to his jest. The clamor of the crowd was too loud for her to tell whether or not he was laughing at her behind her back.

At length the doors opened and the crowd streamed toward them, sucking Becca along. A hand closed on hers; she assumed rightly enough that it was Van's. *Does he think I'll try to escape?* By the time the inrushing tide slowed and thinned enough to give a body room to breathe, they were well inside the building.

Becca looked all around, wonderstruck. She'd read of theaters, just as she'd read of guns, in the old books on stead. She'd known what to expect—places to sit, a raised platform where the players could perform—

she wasn't stupid or ignorant. But the few words and the one tiny picture she'd seen weren't enough to prepare her for the stunning reality surrounding her.

The size of the place was enough to awe anyone. The interior of the theater was vast and dark, a manmade cavern generously lit by a multitude of cool glow globes bubbling from the walls. More clustered on multibranched perches overhead. Whatever wasn't covered with brown and green cloth, brown and green paint, was brightened with slick white or cautiously enhanced with gold.

Van stepped in front of her, still holding her hand. "We've got to move," he said in a hushed voice. "We're blocking the aisle." He led her down a sloping walkway to one of the rows of chairs, then edged past the people already seated. Becca stammered pardons and excuses for trodden toes as she stumbled after him. When they reached their places and he motioned for her to sit down, she could have hugged the chair.

"If you watch the play the same way you look at the theater, for once I'm going to enjoy the performance," Van said.

"And what's that mean?" Now that she was settled in, Becca's annoyance with her companion and her situation returned at double rate.

"Fresh eyes are a great advantage. I can't remember when I last had them. I used to love the theater when I was a little kid. Then Webmaster Steven took notice of me; next thing I knew, he was dragging me to every production in the city. He wanted to see how I'd react to some of the situations on stage. It wasn't

just a pastime for me any more, it was a moral lesson.
Can't have the heir to Thirdweb siding with the
villains, can we? He'd cross-examine me after the
performance too, until I stopped enjoying the plays
because I was too nervous about getting all the
answers right. I think I've seen every play they ever
do here at least three times over."

If he intended his story to draw her sympathy, he
was knocking at the locked door to an empty room.
*Fresh eyes! I could hand him his own reborn. Let him
come out with me to Mark's place if he wants to see
something new.* Becca couldn't scrape up the smallest
measure of pity for the child Van when her head
ached with lost children in the wilderness, little ones
who had problems more pressing than being forced
to watch a play.

She gave him a long, cold look and didn't bother
hiding her contempt when she said, "I'll do my best
to please you, then. It would be a shame if you
couldn't enjoy yourself tonight on my account. Will
it suit you if I gasp out loud? Oh! And will you also
be asking me questions about the play after?"

"No." His easygoing smile turned sour; his eyes
gave hers back cold for cold. "Nothing's demanded
of you here."

"Nothing except that I be here."

"I thought you might enjoy it. It's like nothing
you'll ever see in your life again, once you go back
to the other seedgrubs, where you belong."

"Then what's the use of my seeing it even once?
None of my kin would ever believe me if I told them
about it, any road. A place this big, this rich, given

over to pure vanity?" Her gesture took in the entire theater with all its splendors. "If they did believe me, you'd never see another peck of grain from Wiserways. Are we breaking our backs to feed *this*?" She said it solely to provoke him, not because she felt so.

"Is that what you thought when Eleazar showed you Thirdweb's library?" Van's voice was low as the hum in the air before a thunderstorm.

"If there's a library belongs to all Thirdweb, I never saw it; only the book room that's Carsonelic's."

"Then you've seen next to nothing at all," he said. "There's Wiserways grain in the bellies of the Essexweb people who restore the old books, recopy and recover the ones too far gone, sometimes create the new. Do you want to take back that bread too?"

Becca folded her hands in her lap and forced herself to keep a calm mask over her face even though the thought of a library proper to the whole web made her heart beat fast. *So many books! And maybe that's where they keep the ones that speak of city law and lore.* She couldn't let Van see her true feelings; he was the sort to bend all such knowledge to his own use. So she sat still and took Hattie's voice: "That's not my place to say." Then the lights dimmed and went out, and the curtain shielding the stage parted before Van could respond.

The play was a wonder that surpassed its setting. Becca had thought it would be like schooling back home, with Katie reading to her children from the book, prefacing each part with "Now *he* says—" and "Now *she* answers—". Sometimes she'd drop all that, when the story was especially exciting, and pitch her voice different ways to let the children know she was different people talking. Becca had liked that.

This was better. This was as far above Katie's readings as the stars were above the earth. Here there wasn't just one person pretending to be many, but as many people as the scene demanded, each so artfully persuasive that before long Becca forgot that these were only players saying words they'd memorized. For her, they became the very people they feigned to be, each speaking his own thoughts aloud just as they occurred to him.

Those same thoughts were odd ones, to say the least. Things that happened on the stage could never have happened anywhere else, yet for all that, Becca didn't mind. The story centered on two men, friends, though only one of them seemed to belong to a city elic. He was a trader who drove his own tram, his friend's job was to carry away nightsoil. The second character's bright yellow shirt kept every eye in the audience on him whenever he was on the stage, and his words never failed to make Becca laugh.

There were women in the play as well, members of the tram driver's elic, but they treated him shockingly. They scorned him for nearly the length of the play, making fun of his schemes to make his webmaster notice him and make him his heir. Their sass was so funny that no one in the audience seemed to mind that they went unpunished for it.

Only after all the tram driver's grand plans were brought to nothing did his favorite wife offer him any words of praise or comfort. Instead of striking her as he'd threatened to do several times, he took her into his arms to the applause of the audience. Becca was only a little surprised to find herself clapping as loudly as the rest of them.

She blinked and rubbed her eyes when the theater lights brightened. The crowd murmured with renewed conversations. Women carrying trays laden with bottles and small packages began to walk up and down the aisles.

Van nudged Becca and said, "If you're hungry or thirsty, take this." He passed her a thin square of pimpled red metal. "Give it to the vendor; she'll tell you what she's got for sale that you can afford."

Becca eyed the token askance. "I don't want anything." She lied; her mouth was dried out from all the laughter, but she was feared that this was another of Van's jests. *How do I know what that bitty slip of metal really is? I won't give him the chance to humble me with his tricks.* When he offered it to her a second time, she refused more curtly.

"Have it your way." He said no more to her until the lights dimmed again.

The next play didn't make Becca laugh. It was about two people who were in love, who desired each other with so much passion that Becca felt an answering desire rising from the pit of her belly. Her mouth ached for the feel of Gilber's lips, and when the man on the stage kissed the woman, she could swear she felt that too.

Desire was not enough. An older man came onto the stage, saw the lovers, ordered them apart. His words sounded strange to Becca's ears, but she didn't need to understand everything he said in order to follow his intent. By his command, the young man went away, leaving his beloved collapsed at the old man's feet, weeping and calling after him in vain. The curtain fell and the lights came on.

"A fragment," Van explained. "Not very satisfying, was it? It isn't one of my favorite pieces, but they keep presenting it for some reason. The language itself, Webmaster Steven would say. I don't see the point." He stood up and stretched his bones.

People all around them were also standing up, stretching, chatting, putting on coats and jackets, starting to make their way into the aisles and out of the theater. Becca glanced from side to side. "Is it over?" She couldn't help sounding disappointed.

"So you liked it."

She refused to give him the satisfaction. Getting her voice back under control she shrugged and said, "It was all right."

Van's finger touched her cheek lightly, hovered before her eyes so that she couldn't avoid seeing the teardrop he'd reaped trembling on its tip. "More than 'all right', if this is any gauge. They were only actors; they're probably backstage right now, putting on their real clothes, laughing, bickering over whose turn it is to cook. How can you weep for them and not for Isa and me? How can you believe their pain and not ours?"

"The same way you can't feel anything for anyone but yourself!" Becca snapped. "Why did you tell

Webmaster Steven to rule against Virgie's case? Because you think Gilber and I turned you down for no good—?"

A slap cracked against her cheek, shattered the words from her mouth. "We'll speak of this elsewhere," Van said in the soft voice Becca had come to hate and dread. The people nearby who witnessed the slap paid no notice. They'd given more attention to the nightsoil man in the play.

Becca followed Van out of the theater, her cheek stinging with renewed pain when the cold air hit it. "Now can I speak?" she gritted.

"No. *Now* you can come with me. It's early yet, and I don't want to waste my first night out by going home to bed at this hour." He reached for her hand, but she jerked it away. "If that's what you want…" He started up the street.

"Where are we going?" She easily matched his pace, stride for stride, though he was taller by almost a head and his legs were made to gobble up distance. "To see—to see Isa?"

Van kept his eyes aimed straight ahead. "Why, do you want to?" Becca didn't answer. "That's what I thought."

"Van, I'm trying to explain—"

"You couldn't get into the Flower Market at this time of night anyway. It's against the law. I've just gotten off parole and I'm not going to risk getting knocked back into it so soon on your account."

"Then where are we going?"

"I'm taking you someplace we can talk. You did say you wanted to talk with me?"

"And you said you wouldn't even listen if I didn't come to the theater with you," Becca said bitterly.

"I wanted company on my first night out."

"Forced company."

Van stopped in his tracks. He looked ready to slap her again, and not leave off at a single blow. "Tell the truth, Becca: If I'd given you a civil invitation, would you have accepted it?" Once more there was no need for her to give the answer he already knew. "No, not for the world. You'd have turned me down out of pure spite. You'd have thrown away the chance to experience something you're never likely to see again in your pitiful mudscrabble life. For what? Just to teach me a lesson, to win a petty little war that you're the only one fighting. Webmaster Steven says you're bright; so do a lot of others in our elic. How can someone who's supposed to be so smart be so stupid?"

Becca's palm connected with Van's face before she knew what she was doing.

An instant later, she wished she could bite off her hand. *You fool!* she wailed inwardly. *Oh, that's helped Virgie no end! Why don't you just go back to the child and tell her how well you've looked after her affairs. She won't be able to find the words to thank you.*

Fingertips to her mouth, she said, "I'm sorry, Van." It was almost a whimper.

Van cupped his cheek with one hand, drew out a pocket kerchief with the other. He dabbed it to the corner of his mouth and it came away red. He said nothing. The few people sharing the street with them glanced at him curiously as they passed but didn't stop or even linger. One young man noted Van's bloodied kerchief, then looked Becca right in the eye and *winked* at her! She loosed a shallow gasp and shut her eyes tight, wishing beyond hope that when she opened them again, all this would have vanished.

I want to go home, she thought urgently, and the image behind her eyes was her room in Thirdweb tower.

"Hey." Van gave her elbow a firm squeeze. "Anyone home? Open up in there." He didn't sound angry. His voice was soft, but not that skin-prickling softness she loathed. Becca opened her eyes; he was smiling.

"Bit the inside of my mouth," he explained, holding out the stained kerchief. "You don't *look* that strong, but oh boy! Where'd you get all that muscle? Swinging a scythe? Pulling a plow?"

"It's forbidden for women to come nigh any work that's got to do with the harvest," she rattled off. "And as for plowing—" Suddenly she caught his eye, saw the glint of mischief there, and knew she'd been well and truly taken in the snare he'd laid. To her surprise, she felt no resentment, only the urge to laugh at herself. It would feel good to laugh, but she couldn't give in to it just yet. *Two can play this game.* She folded her arms and tried to look severe. "Proud of yourself, aren't you, you rascal? Turn the other cheek, Van, and maybe I can smack some sense into you from that side." She tried to scowl, but it must have looked ridiculous. Van was staring at her, lips working hard to hold back the spate of merriment. The look on his face cracked her mask into shards of laughter for both of them to share.

When the mirth left them he said, "I think we ought to start fresh, Becca. I'll try if you will."

"Give you my sworn word I will," she replied. "Fair questions, fair answers between us, if that'll suit you."

"I couldn't ask for anything more." All of his anger seemed to have left him. His face was open, bright with sincerity. Without grudge or sneer to warp his looks, he was a passing comely young man. He took her hand the way her brother might, to lead her on down the street while they spoke. "Why don't you ask first?"

"I don't really need to *ask* anything," she said. "I think I know the answer. You told Webmaster Steven to rule against Virgie because you're mad at Gilber and me."

"You make me sound like a spoiled child, breaking things just because I can. How about *why* I'm angry with you? Do you know the answer to that too?"

"Because you love Isa." Every time she mentioned that poor girl's name, her image rose before Becca's eyes, then was quickly blurred away by tears of pity.

"It's more than that, Becca. You know what Isa is, what she does—*did*—before I dealt with Kethy and made her mine alone. It wasn't her choice, believe me. You said that you know about whores, that Sodom was a city too. Of course you know: You steadfolk are so—so damned *godly*."

"Van—!" Becca's protest was weak, her fear strong. There were other people on the street. What if one of them overheard his wicked tongue? Surely that would be cause strong enough to break through any Coopman's thick skin of indifference?

But no one paused, no one slowed, no one so much as looked in their direction. So damned godly! Van hadn't bothered to lower his voice when he linked the Lord's name to blasphemy, and still no one cared.

Sodom was a city too.

"That's why you won't help her," Van was saying. "Because of what she is, because you can't dirty your hands on a whore."

"If that's what you think, you're wrong." Becca said it plain and simple. The truth needed nothing but itself to stand at judgment. "Miss Lynn who was my teacher told me that our sole care's to cure those who need us; heal their bodies, leave their sins to their alph's verdict and the Lord's."

"Then why won't you help Isa?"

Becca sighed. This would be hard, harder because she'd told him the same thing so many times before this. Each time the verdict came more painful to pronounce, each time he refused to accept it as given. "*This* time will you believe me? We *would* help her— I swear we would!—but what would it all be for? You only see Isa with the eyes of love; I see her as any herbwife would. I wish I didn't. She's weak, Van, a stem of broomstraw. Her bones were never made for childbearing. She's too frail to live through travail even if she can carry the babe to birth."

"It would be for the baby's sake." The old soft voice was back. Van picked up the pace, heels clicking more and more rapidly against the city pave. "How many times have I heard you pleading for things for the sake of the children, Becca? Virgie's sibs, the others with them, your own murdered kin on

Wiserways… Do you only love them as an idea? Is the thought of saving just one small infant too unimportant to trouble you?"

Because he'd said it without malice and without scorn, she answered without anger: "Sometime you ask Gilber Livvy what we did to save one small infant. The Lord King's sword chooses His children in their thousands, and from the hungering times in their ten thousands, but the blessed Child that sweet Mary Mother birthed was only one."

"Then why won't you do it?" There was no more challenge to his question. It had become a prayer.

She stopped where she was and clasped both his hands. "Oh Van, we *will* help you and Isa and the baby, only—only not yet. Not yet. I spoke of it to Gilber, he was willing, but then I overheard something back home. It was Eleazar talking with Bai about a case they had to judge. Someone had been caught trespassing in the Flower Market. From what I could gather, those streets aren't for all the cityfolk to walk; it's a transgression to go there if it's not your right. Later on I made confession to Eleazar for being big-ears, as was right to do, and I asked him some about that place." She lowered her eyes as if ashamed.

"I can guess what he told you," Van said, vinegar on his tongue.

"He told me nigh nothing. He scolded me some for eavesdropping, but more for asking questions. He's got no idea that I already know it's where the—the whores live." For all her boldness, she still found it hard to mouth that word. She could feel her mother's disapproving eyes boring into the back of her skull even though Hattie was leagues away, on Wiserways Stead. Breeding died harder than life itself. "He made it clear enough that it's a place for me to keep clear of, word and deed. I don't like to think what would've happened if he'd found out you tried to take me there."

"He'd probably scamper off to tell Webmaster Steven and I'd be back on parole." Van didn't sound worried. "Unless you'd testify to the truth: that you ran off and stumbled into that webquarter on your own."

"But you wanted to bring me with you, dressed as a man!" Becca protested. No matter the differences between stead ways and city, there was an abyss between a woman wearing trousers and a woman caught in abomination.

"Also true, but my *intentions* aren't evidence. If an unauthorized woman wanders into the Flower Market by chance, it's a pardonable offense. Once."

"That's not how it is for a man," Becca said. "Eleazar told me that much. He said he hoped that the meddies had warned Gilber off. 'God help him if he's caught there,' he said. I asked him what if Gilber just happened to be there, not knowing it was wrong? He shook his head, all solemn, and said, 'The only difference that would make is how badly he'll be hurting when he's put outside the city walls.' Oh don't you *see*, Van? We can't risk it, Gilber nor I, we don't dare! We can't chance being thrown out of Coop, not until we've done all we came here to do. There's all the folk of Gilber's tribe to think of, all my kin left living on Wiserways, so many lives—!"

"I do see, Becca." Now the softness in his voice came from having all the bone in it broken to dust. "Responsibility. Do you know how often I've heard that word since Webmaster Steven named me his heir? Do you know how much I hate it? And now it's come to settle its full weight on your slim shoulders." He gently patted the same cheek he'd slapped so cruelly in the theater.

The unexpected touch of kindness filled Becca with relief. "You do understand."

"Finally. I might've seen it sooner, if I hadn't been behaving like an idiot. All the time that I thought you two were abandoning Isa out of selfishness, I was the selfish one. I should have looked deeper. Webmaster Steven says that a good judge knows how to do his work on many levels, from skin to marrow. I won't ask for your help again, I swear to it by holy Scripture." He made the sign of the cross over his lips. "And I also swear I'll do what's right for the sake of someone besides me."

Becca's soul felt so lightened of all burden she thought she could soar up to touch the stars. She pressed Van's hands to her lips and kissed them both, back and palm. "You've fed me peace. I can't come to Isa, but I can give you doses for her to ease pain and lend strength to the blood. It's not much, but—"

"Not another word." His forefinger sealed her lips with the cross as well. "Now come. Let's not ruin what's left of the evening. We've had our say, you and I, and can live peaceably together after this. Time to start making things right: Let's celebrate." His arm settled over her shoulders. It was warm, even through her jacket, a comfort against the cold. "Remember that place I said I was taking you? The place where we could talk? Well, there's more than privacy there: There's music and laughter and fine drink and—"

"Wine?" Hattie's breath was searing the back of Becca's neck. "I can't have wine, outside what's sacred."

"Then we'll *make* it sacred," Van said with a bark of laughter. "Just for you." He tightened his hold on her shoulders and hurried her along.

Chapter Eight

As long as I feed you, I'll tell you what's natural.

Where were they going? Becca didn't know. Everything looked different by night. Coop streets were lit only a little better than those of Verity Grange. Someone had decided which avenues were of enough importance to merit light, and the rest could wait for dawn. If the darkness held any dangers to reach out and seize an unlucky soul, it was a fool's own fault for sticking his nose where it had no business being.

She tried to catch sight of the signs as she and Van hurried along. Too many lay in shadow for her to get her bearings. She'd memorized the route to Greenwoodweb, but that was all. For her other excursions away from home she relied on asking directions in the street. There was a city grid tucked under the pillow back in her room, but she hadn't had the chance for committing it to memory yet.

I wish I'd done it, she thought, breathing hard. Van had a stride that would give Gilber a challenge. *I wish I'd learned the streets by heart, but there's so many, Coop's so big, and when've I had the time—? Always something eating up my days, here; less work to lay my hands to than on stead, but still the hours slip away. I wouldn't mind so much not knowing where we're going, if only I could tell where we are! What if he loses me again?* She didn't much fancy the possibility. She remembered too well what had nearly befallen her that time she'd stumbled into the Flower Market by daylight. Nightfall made it all worse by a thousandfold. Ignorance turned her helpless, helplessness turned her to a babe inside a woman's skin, and she hated that.

"Van, wait up!" she panted.

He didn't heed her plea at once, but gained the next corner before stopping. A lone glow globe on a yellow-striped pole shed a sorry light over his dark hair. "Sorry. When I'm moving I like to move."

"Are we nigh there?"

He laughed at her question. Even his teeth looked the sickly color of weak tea in that amber light. "You sound like me when I was a kid and Auntie Salome used to take me on trips with her. Yes, we're almost there."

"I hope this trip's worth the walk," Becca said as they resumed the pace. She sounded sulky as any

child, but she was a little winded and not happy with
the realization that Van was in full charge. He'd
borne her a grudge too recently for her to place all
her trust in him just yet, much as she'd like to.

It rankled her to walk with a man as if he were
suspect, maybe even enemy. Mistrust too easily
ripened into hate. Some folk—she thought of Gram
Phila's Martha, of Thalie, of Weegee's silent girl—
had hearts that relished hatred. They bloomed with
it, like good land with barley. For herself, even
mistrust left her sour-stomached. What she'd done
to Adonijah, how she'd killed Corp, those were acts
so far from her own nature that she'd become another
when she did them.

That's the comfortable thing to believe, any road,
something whispered inside her. *Or how could you live
with yourself?*

*Could I have let Adonijah go unpunished? Should I
have let Corp kill Gilber and me?* She argued against
herself and found an adversary without pity awaiting
her.

You were a very angel of divine justice. The voice
mocked her. *Everything you did, everything you do, you
do for the best of all possible reasons. The same as the
rest.*

She heard her voice; she knew it was true. In the
quiet place inside her, the place where once she'd
imagined she housed Satan's own worm of doubt and
rebellion, she now answered words that were all her
own: *We do what we must to live in this world.
Sometimes it's sin.*

For all sins but one there's forgiveness. Becca's inner

voice was fading now. It had lost its scorpion sting, and the dark place where it dwelled seemed to lighten.

What sin's that? she called into the dark. No reply. The answer remained unspoken, though she knew what it must be. It was built on the bones of all who had died in the hungering times and all that the great famines had brought forth from their cracked and wrinkled wombs. It was hiding among the bodies of infants left to live or die on a hundred hillsides. It was standing at the side of every alph who hugged Scripture to his heart so long as it gave him leave to do his own will. She knew the answer: all that she lacked were the words to frame it.

And then, from her own soul, a parting gift no louder than the breath of dawn: *To lay the mask of God over the face of evil, that is the only true sin.*

"Hey! Where do you think you're going?"

Becca startled. She'd been so rapt by her own thoughts that she'd fallen into a sleepwalker's tread beside Van. When he'd come to a halt at a door like so many others, she'd kept going until his call brought her up short. He sprinted after her and fetched her back. "What planet were you visiting?" he asked pleasantly. Now that there was no resentment or sarcasm tainting his words, he had a lot of charm. Becca could see why Webmaster Steven was so taken with the boy.

"I guess we must be there," she said, sheepish.

Van smiled at her. "Right through this door and then you can tell me for yourself whether it was worth the hike." His knuckles rapped against the portal in a particular rhythm; the metal panel rang like a badly battered bell.

Someone Becca couldn't see opened the door a shaving. "Friends of Rahab," Van said, and the shaving opened wide.

Van bowed Becca in ahead of him, into the care of the porter. The door slammed shut behind them, closing Becca into a world of shade. "Have you brought your own?" the porter asked. Becca still couldn't see that person's face, but the voice was feminine.

"I forgot mine and it's this young lady's first time," Van replied. "I think you can sell us some."

"First time?" the porter echoed. She sounded dubious. Though Becca couldn't see for herself, she had the feeling that a pair of eyes accustomed to the dark were giving her a thorough, critical examination. "It's a pretty busy night. I don't know if I'll have the time to teach her the rules."

"Don't bother. I can do that myself. She's a quick study," Van reassured her.

"Oh, is she." The porter didn't sound convinced.

"She won't be causing *you* any trouble, in any case." Now Becca heard Van take on that same imperious tone he used the instant someone placed themselves in his way without good reason. (*As if he'd call any reason good if it blocked his will!*) He reached out and flicked at something on the porter's chest, something that fluttered in the dark. "Care to sell them to us now?"

Grumbling, the porter turned away from them. Becca was utterly bewildered by what had passed between this woman and Van, but she was avid to learn. She tapped him on the shoulder.

"What rules?" she asked.

"I'll tell you once we're inside," he said, lightsome as a summer breeze.

"But if there's something I ought to know—"

"—then I'll tell you when you need to know it." He laughed friendly, not mocking, then added, "Look, Becca, if you follow my lead you know you'll be all right."

"Well…" There was sense in what he said, and memory of his recent promise to her, sealed with the sign of the holy cross, lent him credence. She decided to let it go. Her eyes were slowly growing used to the dark. Not so far up ahead she could see another doorway, this one curtained instead of paneled. A vertical thread of light showed itself between two impenetrable wings of cloth, and the muted sounds of talk and music filtered through.

"Here." The porter was back, thrusting a tray under Becca's nose. It rustled with a pile of shiny paper flowers, yellow and white. "Take your pick. And pay," she stressed, staring at Van.

For answer, Van produced the same pimply red metal wafer he'd offered Becca in the theater. He flicked it into the laden tray, among the heaps of flowers, and plucked out one of each color. He pinned one to Becca's blouse so that her jacket covered it, pinned the other to himself, and said, "You can bring me my change," before shouldering past the porter and through the curtain, Becca in tow.

It was another world beyond the dark. Candles

shone with a brighter, more familiar light than the cool glow globes out in the street. Along one wall was a bar, piled high with glasses, fortified with bottles, backed by a tower of wooden casks and tuns, spigots shining.

In one corner of the room five musicians played on wooden flutes, guitars, and tabor, filling the air with tunes Becca had never heard before. It didn't matter; even unknown music had the knack to call up a dancing spell in her feet. She hadn't danced since Harvest Home, a thousand years ago, a thousand leagues away, another life. The melody set her body rocking back and forth, heel and toe. There was a cleared floor space near the musicians where other folk were already dancing, a circle of women, many squares of men. She started forward to join them.

"Hold it a moment, Becca." Van's hand on her shoulder kept her back gently. "That's not how we do it here."

"Oh!" She felt the blood flood her cheeks. "I'm sorry, I only—"

"Don't worry about it. You haven't stepped on any toes yet. Just stick with me and pay attention, remember?" He slipped his arm around her waist and steered her away from the music.

They passed among many round wooden tables where men and women sat together, chatting and drinking in a manner that would have been cause for scandal and swift punishment on stead. Boys and girls in butter-colored aprons glided behind the chairs, setting down fresh bottles, clearing off dirty glasses.

Becca thought she recognized a familiar face or two in the crowd, people she'd caught sight of back at the theater. A few folk hailed Van by name, but he only waved to them and hurried Becca along to yet another doorway.

This portal had neither panel nor curtain. It stood wide open at the head of a steep flight of stairs leading down. Light from above met light from below, all that there was to illuminate the way. Becca heard Van purr in her ear, "It's too crowded up here. They serve the same drink downstairs, the music's better, *and* there's more privacy."

He guided her down the stairs with an elder brother's tender care. Ahead, she could hear more music, more voices. She stepped into a room that seemed much snugger than the one above until she saw that the area had been divided up into a series of little booths surrounding the main floor. The bar was twin to the one upstairs and took up another significant chunk of space. There were musicians here too, as promised, and a smaller place for dancing, and the same sort of tables as upstairs. The crowd was thinner, for a relief.

She took another step forward and felt her jacket leave her shoulders. "I'll just go find a place to hang this up for you," Van said, holding it to his chest. "Why don't you go ahead and get us one of those booths. Draw the curtain; that way no one will bother you until I get back."

"Couldn't we sit at a table near the music?" Becca pleaded. Her eyes were sparkling, brimming with joy in the lilting melody. The dance floor was deserted except for one square of men, none too graceful. If the women formed a ring, she longed to join it and show everyone how well they danced on Wiserways. Van had spoken truth: This place *was* worth the long hike here.

"Take the booth first," Van said. "You don't know how things are done here. If you sit out in the open, one of the servers comes up to take your order. You'd better be ready to pay on the spot or you'll be asked to leave. I brought you all this way to have a time you won't forget. It'd be a shame if it ended so soon, with you back out on the street. They *don't* let people back in once they've left the premises for the night. The porter's got a memory for faces, believe me."

"All right, Van." Dutiful, Becca headed for the closest booth and pulled the sunshine-striped curtains shut after her.

It was very pleasant in the booth. She could still hear the music. After a few moments the band struck up a tune she recognized from something she'd heard Eleazar humming over his papers. She sang along under her breath, fingertips drumming out the beat on the polished tabletop. A trio of candles burned merrily inside a clear glass bowl. Becca studied her reflection among the bobbing flames. The bowl nestled in the midst of a ring of folded paper flowers kin to the one pinned to Becca's blouse. Absently she ran her thumb over the slick paper, almost as yellow as her hair, and wondered what was taking Van so long.

The curtain rippled. A face popped through. "Excuse me, but is this place taken?"

"Yes, it—" Becca's automatic reply stopped cold. "I *know* you!" she exclaimed, glad to have her solitude broken by a familiar face.

"Ha! You're one of that little black girl's friends. Well, how about that!" Solomon's smile was twice as wide as her own. "So you made it inside after all. And just look where we meet! There's a joke on them, I'll say." The trader turned over one shoulder to call, "Matt! Hey, Matt, come see what I found!"

Matt was as joyed to meet up with Becca again as Solomon. They slipped into the side of the booth opposite her and soon the three were deep in conversation. Becca told the traders how she and Gilber and Virgie had fared since parting ways with them. Matt leaned forward into the candlelight, laughing readily. Solomon held back some of his mirth, but there was no hiding how glad he was to see Becca safe within city walls.

"So it wasn't Sela got you in," he remarked. "You're better off. If she'd done you a favor, she'd never let you forget it. I never knew a trader to keep such close account of what's owed her as that one."

"She here tonight?" Matt asked.

"I haven't seen her. That's another thing: Of all the traders ever born, I never knew one so much in love with the road as Sela! Out there on any excuse, taking the tram when she can and going afoot when it's denied her, off traveling right up to the minute they close the gates for winter. Even then she's first to volunteer for emergency trips, can you beat that?"

"Well, it makes sense if you think about it." Matt folded his arms across his chest. The gesture knocked loose the yellow flower pinned to his shirt. He picked it up by the twine stem and tucked it behind one ear. There it wobbled, ready to fall off any instant. "It's not what's out there that Sela loves, it's what's in here that she's not too fond of, if you follow me."

Solomon snorted. "Like she's the only one!"

"Well, it's harder for a woman."

"Your pardon," Becca said, tapping Matt's hand lightly. "I'm not sure I do follow you."

Matt stood up and stretched, though the low ceiling didn't give him room to make a proper job of it. "I'll tell you what," he said. "Solomon can explain to you; he just *loooooves* to hear himself talk." Solomon put his tongue out and Matt laughed. "Me, I'm going to go get us all something to drink. In here like this, having a nice talk, I forgot those servers'd sooner die than intrude when the curtains are drawn."

"While you're out there, give Oli a punch in the nose," Solomon suggested.

"Any good reason or have you just taken up a new hobby?"

"Hey, he saw us come in here with Becca, you know he's going to say something stupid. Maybe if you punch him first, you can avoid the trouble of punching him after he says it."

"I see." Matt nodded as if he'd just received the wisdom of the ages. "You're an idiot. That explains so much."

"Ah, just go make yourself useful." Solomon looked at Becca. "Beer all right for you?"

She nodded nervously. *Beer? I shouldn't*, she

thought. *Strong drink for a woman— But that's only stead ways. Things are different here. I thought I saw some of the women upstairs drinking brew and wine. Still...I've never taken such drink. What would it do to me? I might turn Noah, shame Van, Eleazar, anger Webmaster Steven if word gets back. Best to be safe. I should speak up, ask if they serve something else.* But by the time she opened her mouth, Matt had vanished.

Solomon was unaware of her misgivings. He was enjoying himself and the evening ahead. "We'll show you a good time, Becca. We'll share a pitcher and then maybe we can introduce you around. You don't look as if you know anyone here. That can't be much fun."

Becca nibbled her lower lip. "I do know someone here but—" She wondered what had become of Van. "He went to hang up my jacket. He's the one who can pay. I think I'd better go see—" She started to rise from her place.

Solomon's hand closed on hers. "'He'?"

The crash came first, and then the screams. Becca jumped, gasped out, "What was that?" Solomon said nothing, turned to stone. The sounds beyond the curtain got louder: running feet, shouts of "Halt! Stop where you are!", dull thuds, breaking glass, wordless cries of fear.

"Matt..." The name shook and broke on Solomon's lips, but it brought him back to life. He stood up and made for the fluttering curtains. Becca hurried after him, afraid of what was out there, more frightened still to be left behind alone. Solomon yanked the curtains aside so hard that he tore them from their rings. "*Matt!*" he hollered.

Three tall men wearing the sign of Highlandweb stood waiting for him outside the booth, blocking his path. Two of them seized him fast, before he'd taken three steps. The third grabbed Becca.

She acted without thought, bringing her linked and fisted hands up under the man's chin, knocking him backward. One of Solomon's captors saw and exclaimed, "Dear God, is that a *woman?*"

"Down here, who the hell knows?" his partner snarled. A pair of chained bracelets flashed silver in the candlelight. He manacled the trader's hands securely behind his back, then ordered, "Don't just stand there goggling, you lump; get her!"

The guard obeyed. Becca saw him coming and prepared to meet him. His attack was clumsy, random, a simple lunge with arms outstretched. She sidestepped, ducking under to one side, and gave him a kick from behind to encourage him on his way. He flew forward, ramming his gut into a heavy tabletop. Bottles and glasses sailed off to smash into showers of twinkling shards. He groaned, doubled over, holding himself, gasping. Becca didn't waste time gloating over small victories: She ran.

She was one of many running. The downstairs area had changed from pleasant retreat to pure chaos. Yellow-aproned servers shrieked and cowered under the tables, holding their trays in front of their faces. Customers jammed the stairway portal to the upper floor. Some stood where they were, shouting that it was no good trying to get out that way, that there were more Highlandweb troops waiting for them at the head of the stairs, that it was like netting fish in a pond. Others hugged the walls, edging slowly along to the place behind the bar where another doorway stood, modestly veiled by shadows. By ones and twos the fugitives slipped away by that route. If there were guards waiting to capture them beyond, no one came back to give warning.

Becca ran for the bar, dodging panic-stricken men and women rushing the other way, sidestepping the Highlandwebbers when she could. They had prey enough to keep them busy. They gave most of their attention to capturing the men. For a string of heartbeats Becca dreamed she had a chance of freedom. She reached the bar, slipped around it, dove for the little doorway.

Then she heard a voice cry, "That's the one! Don't let her get away!" and suddenly eight hands clamped her arms to her sides. She lashed out with her feet, but only struck thick boot leather. Someone spun her around. A soot-haired guard was grinning at her. She brought her knee up hard and sharp between his legs. The grin stayed, but her knee throbbed.

"See, Bill?" the man said to one of his fellows. "I told you it pays to dress right, take the extra few minutes to shield yourself."

"All right, all right, you made your point," Bill grumbled. He wore the pained expression of a man who'd just learned a lesson the hard way. "It's not my fault the raid call came in so fast." He produced another set of manacles and snapped them over Becca's wrists.

"Fast or slow, a few minutes more is all it takes," the black-haired man lectured as they hustled Becca to the stairway. "Now when we go to collect our reward, who's going to enjoy it more, you or me?"

"Oh, shut up," said Bill. His gloved hands dug into Becca's arm painfully, taking out his anger on her. By now the downstairs room was almost clear. The servers remained where they were, under the tables, but their patrons were all either vanished or in custody. Bill shoved Becca into the stairwell, up the stairs, and into the light of the upper room.

When she saw how things were there, she stood dead still. She couldn't have been more dumbstruck if she'd come across a new winnowing, with every one of that place's patrons lying slaughtered in their own blood.

There was no blood. There had been no winnowing. Nothing had changed. The people still sat at their tables, laughing and chattering, enjoying their drinks. The musicians still played, the dancers still danced. All the time that the guards had turned the lower room into a pandemonium of terror, in the upstairs room nothing had happened at all.

As the Highlandwebbers took her to the street door, Becca glanced back over one shoulder. "Van?" She thought she must be dreaming. *"Van!"*

He sat at a table with two other men and a pair of women. When she called out his name in desperation, he merely looked up and raised his glass in her direction. It was garnished with a white paper flower. He drank her health as she was dragged away into the night.

Chapter Nine

And now, if you will turn to the images of common incarnations for abstract concepts, may I draw your attention to the accepted representation of Justice? Here we see a woman, her eyes blindfolded, a balance in one hand and a sword in the other. There is perhaps no other image which has survived to our day that so clearly shows the ignorance of our forebears. The balance was intended to indicate that Justice weighs all cases evenly. Why did no one point out that from antiquity onward, the balance has always been the first tool suborned to their own purposes by dishonest merchants? If anything it speaks of how readily Justice became a marketable commodity in those days. The blindfold was meant to convey the message that all are *equal in the eyes of Justice. Why did no one ever remark that the blindfold merely guarantees ignorance, not fairness? And as for the very idea of incarnating a concept of such moment and intellectual import in female form—!*

At least they got the sword right.

She was kept well fed and warm. She was the only prisoner in her cell, though there were four women crowded together in the cell directly across from hers. She didn't need anyone to tell her why she was kept alone, why the warders of Wallweb didn't apportion their lodgings more equitably. She learned that from the prisoners themselves, the moment they saw the crumpled yellow flower still attached to her blouse. She didn't know the words they called her, but it didn't take long for her to gather their meaning: *Abomination.*

The cell had no windows. There was a mattress on the floor in the corner farthest from the drain-grate that served the place of chamber pot. Fresh water was offered at set intervals, and with meals. Becca had a small metal basin to bring up to the slot in the bars so that the warder could fill it with the hosepipe from her carboy-laden cart. What Becca did with the water after she got it was her own business.

There was no way to keep track of the time except by the passage of the water cart and the arrival of food. It was plain fare, enough to stay the stomach, no worse than what Becca had eaten on stead. The first meal she was given was porridge, bland but plentiful. The second was a thick slice of that same porridge, fried up to a tasty brown and covered with a syrup of burnt beet sugar. Anywhere but this, Becca would have taken it for a special treat. Evening brought a meal of stew and bread. The stew lacked savor, but the vegetables were fresh and the meat was easy to chew. The bread was soft and there was butter. After the evening meal the warders came around to take away the metal dishes and to distribute blankets for the night.

She knew it was morning when the warders made a new circuit of the cells, collecting the blankets and providing more water. She thought she would wash herself well with this allotment, but instead she only took one drink in cupped hands and then sat there, the basin between her feet, staring at the ripples on the surface.

Why does no one come? she thought. *I don't care how busy Eleazar is, he must've missed me by now.*

When the warder returned with breakfast, Becca asked, "How much longer do I have to stay here?"

The woman shrugged. She wore dark blue coveralls with a thin yellow stripe on both arms. "Can't," was all she said. Becca didn't know whether she meant that she couldn't answer the question or wasn't even supposed to be talking to the prisoners.

It was shortly after her morning meal that Becca finally had a visitor. She heard a familiar voice echo down the hall; she ran to the grilled cell door to peer out and determine whether she'd heard right. She had: It was Van.

He came sauntering after the cart, in no particular rush, waiting patiently each time the warder on duty stopped to pick up dirty trays and dishes from occupied cells. He wore a black shirt like the one Webmaster Steven had worn the first time Becca saw him, except Van's bore only four silver flowers over the heart instead of the webmaster's five. He seemed to be having a good time, looking into the cells on either side as he passed, sometimes pausing to have a friendly word with the inmates. Another warder accompanied him, an older woman wearing a plain blue dress unrelieved by any touch of yellow. They chatted like old acquaintances, though Becca thought the warder fawned over him too much for there to be an equal footing between them.

"Good morning, Becca." At least he had the good sense to keep from smiling when he greeted her, though she saw triumph dancing in his eyes.

She threaded her fingers through the spaces in the crisscross grill and pressed her face to the metal. "What did you do to me?" she asked.

"I don't know what you're talking about."

"Where you took me, where you left me—" She tore the yellow flower from her blouse and crushed it to the bars. "There was a reason yours was white."

His lip twitched up at the corner for just an instant, the thought of a smile and then gone. "So you are as smart as they say." He made a sign to the warder. A key turned in the heavy lockplate on Becca's cell door; the grill slid aside. Van offered her his hand into the free world. She glowered at it as if it were some vile thing and walked out on her own.

His hand closed on her elbow. "I'm afraid I'll have to insist," he said. "No prisoner leaves her cell unless in the physical custody of a warder, security personnel, or an officer of justice. The strict interpretation of that law calls for manacles, but no matter how thin we stretch things, this is really the least that's required."

Becca started to answer that she'd prefer the manacles, but stopped herself. She wouldn't give him the satisfaction of her spite. Instead she shrugged and tolerated his touch as if it were nothing to her. It was a pleasure to see how much this rankled him. There was nothing close to a smile on his face as he steered her out of the hall of holding cells, through a barred door, down a short hall, and into a little private room beyond. The warder walked after them.

There were two chairs and a table in the windowless room, all bolted to the floor. As soon as the warder locked them in, Van let go of Becca's arm, motioned for her to sit down, and took the other seat himself. She obeyed without true obedience. She worked hard to make her every action tell him, *You're not worth my while to fight with over trifles.*

"Now we can talk," he said.

"That's what you told me that night."

He stood up. "If you're going to snipe at me, I can come back another time. You aren't missed. In Carsonelic, they think you're visiting Gilber Livvy. It should take another day before they find out the truth. Gilber's helped by locking himself away from everyone for a good twenty-four hours."

"Shabbit," Becca murmured. But when Van asked

what she'd said she shook her head. "Nothing. I'll
speak civil, if that's what's wanted to get me free of
this place."

"You're not in here for rudeness. If your case comes
to judgment—"

"If it comes to judgment, I'll be found clean!"
Becca pushed the heels of her hands against the
table's edge, fighting for control. "To be guilty of
abomination, that's cause for the hard death. There's
not an alph alive will waste a working life just on
say-so. He'll want evidence, more than where I was
or who I was with. He—" Her words choked her. She
knew too well what was cause for condemnation in
this case.

Oh Jamie! Sweet Jamie, dearest Jamie, Jamie her
lost love. Sometimes when she was with Gilber, she
thought she could feel Jamie's eyes on her, poor
hungry ghost! *It wasn't your fault, Jamie, but it was
law.* He'd been taken by guile, forced into
uncleanness by his field boss, coerced by that first
sin into more. They'd been caught together. Paul
knew Jamie's heart was stainless, but that didn't
count for dust. It was what you'd done that killed you,
nothing less, and if you'd done it, there was no excuse
could save you.

"You keep talking about alphs," Van replied. "Have
you forgotten where you are?"

"I misspoke," Becca admitted. "Call them
webmasters or what you will, I'll still wager my life
that they won't condemn me without solid proof."

"That's exactly what you will be doing," Van said.
"Wagering your life."

Becca gave him a hard stare. "If that's what you came to tell me, you've said your say. I'll say mine when they bring me to trial. I'll tell them why you did it. I'll say what I know about Isa and Kethy and—"

His hand shot across the table to clamp across her mouth. "You'll say *nothing*," he hissed. "You do, and before tonight's out I'll serve your friend Gilber the way I served you, only better!" He released her and dropped back into his chair. "You're sharp, girl, but I'm wise. Why else would Webmaster Steven pick me for his heir over grown men like your brother? *He* knows me. And the first lesson he taught me was that knowing is everything. I know what makes people act as they do—*motive*, he calls it. He didn't need to teach me that it's a priceless tool, in hands with the skill to use it."

"What will you do to Gilber?" Becca said slowly.

At first he pretended not to have heard the question. "Do you know what sort of a place I took you to, night before last? It's a place that shouldn't exist at all, by law, downstairs *or* up. There are a lot of people inside these city walls who are still just as narrow-sighted as the lowest seedgrub from the outs. They don't approve of places where men and women can go to enjoy each other's company for its own sake, or find friends outside their elics and their webs. Too uncontrolled for their liking. But a place like that turns a big profit, and as long as it keeps a low profile—after hours only, tucked away in the hobay quarter—there's enough of that profit to share out so it keeps going along discreetly."

"Even for—even for the downstairs kind?"

"'The downstairs kind'?" Van lifted one brow. "That's the coyest thing I've ever heard them called. The masters of that place positively cherish them. They pay more, they never complain, and they make sure to keep things quiet."

"What about the raid?" Becca asked. "Not *too* quiet, I'd say. If it's all against the law, why didn't they roust out you and your friends upstairs?"

"Because they were only paid to raid the downstairs, Becca." He said it so that she didn't need to ask who'd done the paying. "And there's a constant bounty set on every arrest for *those* charges, if it leads to a conviction. I hear that the Highlandwebbers go to bed nights praying to find a pair caught in abomination the way other people pray to find love. The men I called in may very well get to collect twice. The raid was a great success; they're looking at so many guaranteed convictions that they might even forgive me if I whisk you out from under their noses. Anyhow, I already paid extra to the man who captured you."

Becca breathed deep, forcing the fury down. Van was right, even if he was the devil himself: *Knowing is everything.* Though it turned her innards to burning knots, she wanted to strike him and knew she couldn't. *Not yet. Not until he's told me more.* Holding herself together by a thousand fraying threads she asked, "What's all that got to do with Gilber Livvy?"

"Do you think they're true, Becca?" Van mused. "The old stories about how Jews don't know any loyalty? I'm going to find out. I'll go to him today and tell him how you've vanished. I'm going to be very worried about you. I'll offer to take him to the place you were last seen. Do you think he'll come with me? I hope so. I'd hate to have paid off that many men for nothing."

"Paid…"

"Your friend is strong," Van went on. "He's not almighty. How many men do you think it would cost me to drag him into one of those booths and—?" His hand sprang up to intercept her own before it could reach his eyes. "Tsk. You're the one who asked." His other hand slid under the table. A buzzer sounded and the door opened. "Thank you very much." Van gave the warder a winning smile. "I have to go now, but I'll be back to see this young woman after evening meal. Please see to the arrangements."

The warder took Becca back to her cell. She felt as if she were walking through a fog. Though Van had never used her as rawly, as harshly as Adonijah or Corp, his words alone left her feeling stripped of all worth, violated to the very core of her soul. He had reduced her choices to a single one: *Do as I desire or lose all.*

She sat on her mattress, staring at the blank wall. For a liar, he was clever about keeping the letter of his word. He'd sworn on holy Scripture not to ask for her help again, yet he'd still contrived things so that Becca would have to go to Isa as often as he demanded. It didn't matter how much she risked to do it, or how hopeless all her efforts would be: He only knew that this was what he wanted, and this was what he was going to have.

She couldn't escape. He'd shown her what he was.

That boy could lesson Adonijah in plain ruthlessness, she thought. *If I give him my word to help Isa and then break it once I'm free, he won't wait for my soul to burn for the lie: He'll find a way to destroy it while I live.*

She gathered her knees close to her chest and covered her face. *We can't let him win. We can't give him everything. I'll go where he says, do what I can for Isa—poor girl, it's what I'd do any road, if it was just me!—but I'll ask him to keep Gilber free of this. No cause for both of us to risk losing all we came here to gain. He can own me, body and soul, but Gilber's got to go free.*

With that thought in mind, she curled herself up on the mattress, turned her face to the wall, and fell into a restless doze. She was woken from a half-dream by the duty-warder, bringing the evening meal. Even though she'd slept through the noon feeding, she ate what there was on her plate more from training than from appetite; she tasted nothing.

As promised, Van came back when the pickup cart made the rounds, in company with the same warder as before. To Becca's surprise he wore a long face and wasted no pleasantries on any of the other inmates. The older woman carried herself as if she were treading barefoot over serpents. When she unlocked Becca's cell door, Van shouldered past her, grabbed Becca's wrist, and hauled her out as if she were a wooden doll and he an impatient child. He never bothered to acknowledge her with a single word.

Here's a change, Becca thought, bemused.

The way they went once she left the cell was different too. Instead of taking the lead and escorting

Becca back to the small interview room, Van fell into step behind the warder. The older woman walked briskly, like a fugitive trying to run away without drawing the unwanted attention of a flat-out run for it. She led them to a barred door, but this one opened onto another hall of cells. Here she stopped. A man wearing the same midnight blue as the other warder was waiting for them on the other side. All he said to Becca was, "Eyes front, miss," before he led them down the length of hall.

Becca saw no cause to disobey. She kept her gaze set on the back of the male warder's balding head. There were voices all around her coming from the cells, men's voices. Some were saying terrible things. Others only moaned or wept.

Then one called her name. It broke through the sounds of tears and groans and blasphemies. It startled her so deeply that she forgot obedience and turned her head.

Hands hooked to the bars of his cell door, Solomon's lean body looked as if it only wanted a breath more effort to burst free. "I didn't tell, Becca!" he shouted. "I didn't tell!" His eyes pleaded with her, a prayer she strove to understand and failed. Yet all the way to the end of that eternal corridor she heard his crying after her, "I didn't tell! I didn't tell!" as if those were the secret words to open the gates of heaven.

There was a pale sun shining low in the sky when Becca and Van stepped out into the street. The ironbound doors of Wallweb closed with an almost inaudible click that belied their weight. Becca thought there wasn't a sweeter sound on earth.

Almost at once her relief changed to shivering; she had no jacket. The cold got under her skin, making her teeth chatter.

"Here." Van took off his coat and tried to put it around her shoulders.

She stepped out of it. "I've g-g-got my own j-j-jacket," she managed to say.

"So you do, back home," he pointed out.

"Oh, you b-b-brought it th-there? I th-th-thought you'd maybe abandoned it the s-same way you abandoned m-me."

"For God's sake, I don't have time for this," Van muttered. He seized her arm and proceeded to stuff it into one of the coatsleeves by pure force. She fought him at first, then gave in and let him dress her. "There! Some of the alph in me after all," he told her, pleased with himself. "Surprised?"

"That I'd rather have you freeze than me? No," she replied. She dug her hands deep into the pockets of his coat, reveling in the warmth. When she'd banished the last of the shivers, she asked, "Where are you taking me now?"

"Nowhere," he answered, sulky. "Home, if you like. To hell, if I had my way. You've got the freedom of the city; you choose."

"I'm free?" She wanted to believe it; she didn't quite dare. She'd sooner trust the word of Ananias himself than anything Van told her.

"There are no charges against you."

"Did you do that? Tell them how I didn't belong down there with Solomon and—" She was about to say *and Matt*, but Solomon's desperate words dinned in her ears: *I didn't tell!* Neither would she. "—and the rest?"

His answer was a noncommittal grunt. Hands tucked snugly into his armpits, he began walking. It was clear that he didn't give a damn whether Becca came along. She let him get almost to the end of the block before she made her decision and hurried after him. By that time, he had already turned the corner at the cross street and was out of sight. She wasn't worried; if he'd taken off, she'd be able to find someone to ask directions from eventually. Even after dark, there were plenty of people about, just not everywhere. Some sections of the city were deserted while others throbbed with more life by night than by day. It was all a matter of finding them. Though she didn't know the area surrounding Wallweb, she was growing used to the city and its ways. She was no longer so afraid.

Her breath rose in little puffs of steam as she trotted to the corner. She half expected to find an empty street—Wallweb was no public attraction— and Van long gone. Instead she almost ran right into him. He was standing in the nearly deserted street, speaking with a woman. In the fading light, Becca couldn't avoid jogging his out-thrust elbow as she came to a halt at his side.

"Watch where you're going!" he snapped at her.

"Now Van," the woman chided. "Don't talk to her that way. You were raised better than that."

"Shut up," he responded, but kept it so low that Becca could barely make out the words.

"Hello, Becca. Long time no see." A strand of moonlight blond hair came loose from under the woman's green knit hat, dangled near her silver-shot eyes. She tucked it back with a gesture at once graceful and vaguely familiar. The voice, too, was one Becca somehow knew. "So you made it inside after all."

"Sela!" Becca exclaimed.

"Sela?" Van turned an inquiring look from the woman to Becca and back. "What the hell—?"

"Don't tell me you'd have continued to call yourselves Van and Isa on the road," the woman said. "Passing outside the walls changes so many things. What's a different name compared to a different life?"

"We didn't make it that far." Van's face closed itself off. "I wouldn't know."

"And whose fault was that? You should've listened to me. You should've waited for spring."

"Oh yes, that's right, how could I forget?" Van sneered. "Auntie Salome always knows best. Auntie Salome said <i>Wait until spring</i>, and we didn't listen. I wonder why. Maybe because Auntie Salome can't count up to nine!"

"Was that the way of it?" The woman Becca knew as the trader Sela didn't seem especially upset by Van's bile. "I was on the road, how was I to know the little darling was pregnant? If I had known, my advice would have been quite different: I'd have told you to sit tight and not waste yourself on lost causes."

She smiled at Becca. "I guess we both know how effective it is to tell him that, don't we, dear?"

"How do you know what I told—?" Becca began.

"Because she's a dirty spy," Van spat.

Sela/Salome laughed. "Listen to him! Now I'm a dirty spy. When I brought him the information he wanted for planning their escape, all I heard was 'You're a life-saver, Auntie Salome! We'll never forget you for this, Auntie Salome! We love you so much, Auntie Salome!' Oh, Van—" She sighed and tried to pat his cheek. He slapped her hand away, a pettish gesture that only made her laugh harder.

Becca felt herself go on guard. She was at a full loss to know just what this strange trader woman was, or even who she was, how it was proper to call her. Van named her Auntie Salome—he'd spoken of her many times before this. They shared a web, an elic, maybe even a blood tie. There was something more between them too. The scent of many secrets, deeply buried, fair and foul, made Becca edgy. *Knowing is everything*, Van said. He'd done his part to teach her that ignorance was danger; she lessoned fast, she'd remember that, she wouldn't need a second teaching.

She had the odd, insistent feeling that if she bought her lessons from Sela, they'd cost dear. What was it Solomon had said of her? *I never knew a trader to keep such close account of what's owed her as that one.*

A knot in the pit of Becca's stomach undid itself. At first she thought it was only her body letting go of the tension that had nested in her guts since her arrest. Then she felt an ache low down, and gasped as she recognized what was happening to her. She grabbed Van's arm. "Are we far from Thirdweb tower?" she demanded. "Can we go home now? Please?"

Van jerked away from her. "Find your own way."

"Van, please. I just want to go home." She pressed her knees together and prayed it wasn't far.

"What's your hurry?" He saw the urgency written large on her face and took cold pleasure in taunting her.

"Van, you're a clod." Sela wasn't laughing now. She linked arms with Becca and marched her off up the street. Swept up at the trader woman's pace, Becca tried to take tiny, rapid steps, tried to hold on, tried—

"In here." Sela made a sharp left at an unmarked doorway. A brief knock and it was opened. "Thirdweb," was all she said to the mousy woman who asked them for identification. The timid soul fairly jumped out of Sela's way. They sailed through a large room lined with gaily painted shelves. Becca glimpsed a few books and many toys, dolls made of cloth and clay and wood, little wagons, a Noah's ark on wheels, leather balls, a pile of small sleeping mats in the corner. Then Sela pulled her through another door and she saw a deep sink with a pump and a row of low, wide-mouthed clay pipes sticking out of the floor.

"Just in time, hm?" Sela smiled at Becca, then looked at the girl's feet. Her smile went out. "Oh. Well, almost."

Becca lifted her skirt slightly and followed Sela's glance. The thin line of bright blood inched its way inexorably down.

Chapter Ten

And when the Commandments were
given to Moses,
There was one that he chose to ignore,
For he thought that his people would have
enough trouble
With the ten that had all gone before.
But he learned the Lord's will is beyond
comprehension,
And past all our wish to evade.
It will find us at last, though we cower
in darkness,
A refuge our own fears have made.
The final Commandment is written in
heart's-blood,
Its sisters writ only in stone.
It will find us at last, be we waking or
dreaming,

In sin or about to atone.
The wicked, the pious, the fallen, the
angel—
In this, all their acts are as one,
For the words of the final Commandment
eternal
Are these: Look at what you have done.

"You don't say so!" Gilber finished winding another bandage and put it neatly in its place atop the pile of others he'd already wound. "And she's called *what?*"

"Salome," Becca answered, her own hands busy with the lengths of clean, white cloth. They were sitting across a small table from one another in the sunroom of Creche, over at Greenwoodweb. Whenever Becca came by to see Gilber, she knew that she'd find him there, nine times out of ten. Creche was where they brought the Coopwomen whose pregnancies wanted special care, skills, and supplies beyond what the meddie midwives could truck along with them on their normal rounds.

"Salome?" Gilber clicked his tongue. "Is that what she told you to call her now?" A young woman, newly delivered, walked slowly past them. Gilber smiled at her and called out, "How's your son, Lainie?"

The woman's smile answered his. "Beautiful! But you know that already, Gilber."

"Can't deny I do." He winked at her, she giggled and walked on. He sat farther back in his chair and sighed, content.

"She doesn't care," Becca said.

"Huh?" Gilber blinked himself back into the world.

"You asked me what I'm supposed to call her now—Sela or Salome. Well, I asked *her* that and she said she doesn't care." Becca's mouth went prim. "Appears she's not the only one."

"Ah now, Becca…" Gilber wheedled. "I'm sorry I wandered off there, angel, but Lainie's boy— Well, I was there to help at his birth. They'd brought her here from Heskethweb in a bad way. Their Webmaster Thomas died three months ago; she was carrying his last child and the midwife warned 'em it could turn touch-and-go. The new webmaster—Orion?—said it would be a shame to lose the child, so he sent Lainie here."

"The new webmaster *saved* the old one's get?" Gilber could have told her he really did have horns and a tail and she'd have been less shocked.

"Not the way your people do things, is it?" he asked, knowing the answer. She looked away. He leaned across the table to pat her hand and say, "When you go back, you can tell 'em how they do things here. They're human: They can change."

"They're stead," Becca said. For her, that told all.

"Stead *and* human," Gilber insisted. "I can't believe stead ways sprang up full grown overnight, or that they can't know change. City ways neither."

"Maybe once," Becca said. "Not now. Now they're set in stone." She shook off the little ghosts. "So you helped birth that woman's boy?"

"Uh…" Gilber's face colored up. "That's not what I said; I said I was there to *help*. Some. If that wasn't a time we had with the pair of them—! She birthed him weeks early *and* hindside first. She was on her way to noon meal when it came over her. I was just coming back from a meeting and saw her go down against the wall. People ran for help, but it was happening fast. I took a look at her and saw how things were. Back home, one time I saw a midwife turn a baby, so I tried."

Tried? And the woman steeped in her 'impurity', or I don't know birthings. Probably tried to turn the babe from the outside, through all the mother's clothing. Becca could nigh picture it. The thought made her smile.

"Oh, I know what you're thinking," Gilber said. "You're figuring I'm no more fit to handle such a thing than fly to the moon." A fresh blush touched his face. "And you're right. Thank *H'shem* someone came quick; I didn't know *what*-all I was doing. But later on, after she'd been safe brought to birth, she told me I'd been a comfort. She said sometimes that's just as important as being a help."

"So she's naming the boy after you?"

"No, after Amos, the meddie who *did* know what to do for her and could do it, besides. He's a good man. He's been a help to me too. He came from the outs, did you know that? From Hallow Stead! He knows Weegee."

"Hard not to," Becca remarked. Weegee was one of a kind, a dwarfish creature given to spells of "seeing." It was a miracle that someone with his stunted body had been permitted to survive past birth, but it was no mystery why he now lived out his days in comfort. Weegee spoke true prophecy, that was his salvation. It bought him some respect and a lot of fear, on stead and grange-wide. Some long-dead alph of Hallow even gave the little man his own house, far from the rest of the stead.

"But Becca, there's more than that: *Amos knows Shifra.*"

Becca dropped the bandage in her hands. It bounced away, unrolling itself across the sunroom floor. "How could he?" It was a whisper holding hope and dread.

"I told you, he's from Hallow. He left when he was small, but he still sends word back and gets news. We were talking about babies, him and me, and he mentioned how everyone back home was that surprised to hear that Weegee'd been blessed with a daughter. No one's seen her, mind, but they've heard her cry and Weegee's done his share of bragging."

"Shifra..." It had been too long since Becca had given her baby sister into Weegee's care. *His girl's care, not his,* she thought, and tried not to shudder.

Along with his house, Weegee had been given one of Hallow's unwanted children, a girl who'd lost her hearing young—a calamity normally cause enough to end the child's life along with her full usefulness to the stead. Most folk believed she'd lost her speech as well. Only Becca knew the truth of things: that the girl could speak when she'd a mind to, after a fashion; that though she couldn't hear a person's voice she could steal the shape of words from their lips; that while they'd never let her choose if she wanted to serve Weegee's house and warm Weegee's bed, she'd taken her own choices where she could. The child Weegee got in her belly hadn't drawn two breaths before she killed it, and no one the wiser.

She said she wouldn't harm Shifra, though, Becca thought. *Shifra's not Weegee's get. She said...* Sick at heart, she wondered how far to trust any soul's say-so these days.

She didn't want to think about Shifra, not when she was so far from being able to help her baby sister. *I'll be back for you some day, little one. I swear it in God's name.* To distract herself she asked Gilber, "Why does that Amos keep up with what's happening on Hallow Stead? His life's here now. Eleazar never sent back word to Wiserways." *No matter how much Ma ached for it,* she thought. Whatever her feelings toward Hattie now, she still couldn't help pitying the woman who gave up a son to the city and got nothing in return, not even a word of love.

"Amos isn't Eleazar. He told me he came here when he was barely ten years old, but he still remembers his mother and his sibs. I guess he never heard the saying 'Out of sight, out of mind.' But Virgie knows it by heart."

Becca stood up. "That was a mean thing to say, Gilber Livvy."

"Mean or true?" He continued winding bandages, unruffled by the burning stare on him. "How long has it been since we've come here, Becca? How long since we've been within the city walls? You come to look in on her even once, all that time? She's stopped asking for you. Time before last shabbit when I went to see her, she asked if you were dead. Time after that she said she hoped you were. Last few times, she said nothing about you at all."

"I told you what happened to me!" Becca protested. "How could I come see her if I was in prison?"

"It's a week and more since you're out, and what about all the days before that? Virgie isn't stupid."

Becca sat down again, clasped her hands in her lap and bowed her head over them as if praying for Gilber to believe her words. "I'm shamed to see her, Gilber. I haven't been able to do a thing to help her kin. First Van interfered one way, then another. He won't let go. Salome was the one stepped in to get me out of prison, but there's nothing she can do to sway Webmaster Steven's mind the way Van can. And Van won't."

"Maybe we ought to do what he wants, then," Gilber said quietly, his eyes on the bandage in his hands. "It'd be better if it was just me who went to tend that girl."

"Didn't they tell you what could happen to you if you got caught in the Flower Market?"

"Oh, I got told. But there's always a way. Whatever else he is, Van's no fool. If I come out to help him, he'll be just as eager as me to protect my skin. From what you say, he's got his ways around the law. Don't tell me he couldn't set things up so that I'd look like an approved Flower Market patron! I'll be safe."

"Until the birth," Becca said, pitching her voice so only Gilber could hear. "Did you ever see that girl? It won't be easy getting a baby out of her even if the child's turned right. And what if it's not? You just now admitted you can't handle such. Isa's going to die any road, barring a miracle—I think even Van knows it, though he'll never allow it's so—but what about the child? A bad birthing could kill it too, and then see how long Van lets you live! Then what becomes of your tribe?"

"And what becomes of Virgie's kin if I don't give Van his way? Poor babies! There's not a mouthful of food passes my lips but I think of them in their hunger out there. It's a wonder I sleep nights."

"You know there's blood at a birth. What about that? Won't it stop you?" Becca insisted, desperate to turn him from this path. "Or is it only impurity when it's mine?"

"There was blood at Lainie's birth." Gilber acknowledged her words in a voice smooth with reason. "We're taught that there's no uncleanness worse than turning aside from those who need our aid. So I was touched by her impurity, but I followed the proper rites to cleanse myself of it after."

"And what if Isa's brought to bed on shabbit?"

A frown creased his brow slightly. He hesitated before saying, "I think…I think there's commentary on the law that gives me leave to work if it's in the cause of life."

"But it *won't* be life," Becca maintained. "If you'd been the only one there to tend Lainie, she'd be dead now, and the babe with her; admit it."

"It won't be just me." Gilber had turned stubborn in the face of Becca's arguments. "You told me there's another woman with Isa."

"Kethy?" Becca snorted. "If she knew anything

about birth, would Van want us nosing in? She ran Isa's old web, that's all."

"A *woman* running a whole web?"

"The Flower Market's a different world, Gilber." Her fingers tightened on each other. "I've decided."

Gilber's frown returned, deeper. "What did you have to decide?"

"I've decided you're right, for one: We'd best give Van free way or he'll throw a hundred stumbling blocks in ours. Fact is, I decided that much while I was still in prison. And I've decided that since I'm the one with fewer lives riding with me and the most healing lore when it comes to births, I'm the one to go aid Isa, not you."

"Becca, no!"

"Lower your voice, Gilber, this isn't anyone's business but ours." Now that she'd spoken her mind, Becca felt a queer serenity settle over her. She picked out another length of cloth and wound it up with steady hands. "Don't fret for my safety; you're the one said Van's sharp enough to shield you. It'll be that much easier for him to protect me. Dress me up like one of the Flower Market girls, maybe. If he takes me to look after Isa by night, no one will question us."

"And what if she needs you by day?" Gilber countered. "I may not have your *long* experience with midwifing, but I do know that babies aren't particular about when they get themselves born. By the way—" He eyed her narrowly. "—just *how* many births have you handled all by yourself?"

"At least I've laid a hand to more than you ever

did," Becca shot back. It was as close to the truth as she was going to get with him. "Be sensible, Gilber: If you're caught helping Isa, your people lose every hope. If I'm caught, Wiserways will survive."

"For how long, Becca?" Gilber asked. He was no longer winding bandages. He set aside the one he held and rose from the table. Becca didn't move, didn't even follow him with her eyes. She heard his footsteps and at last felt his hands settle onto her shoulders before he asked again, "For how long? You left Adonijah blind. Anyone could defeat him now, take over your stead. You told me what happens after a new alph comes in."

Becca's eyes swam with the memory of Wiserways awash in blood. Children too small to save themselves, children not swift enough or smart enough to find hidey-holes in time, children who were only babies at the breast, all swept away by the new alph and the men hot to prove their loyalty to him. Take a woman's babe from her and she came back into her times all the sooner, ready to serve her new lord. If the old alph didn't have the power to protect his gets, why give hard-earned sustenance to the seed of a weak stock? Better to let the new alph sow a fresh crop, a stronger harvest after the winnowing.

"Six months," she said. "He's got six months' grace before another man can come to challenge him."

"Six months," Gilber repeated.

"That's how it's always been. That's the law. A little stretch of peace for the old alph, if he wins, a little healing time for the stead if he loses. It's the only reason I didn't kill Adonijah then and there, when I had him under my hand. Whoever would've taken his place would call for a fresh winnowing, maybe lay hands on some of the children who escaped Adonijah. That's why I let him live, for the six months' grace. Else there'd be no respite for my family, no chance to bring Coop justice home."

Gilber's fingers massaged the tautness from her neck. "If you're caught breaking their law for Isa's sake, what makes you think they'll give your stead their justice?"

"I've given my testimony to Eleazar. He can tell my story and speak for me if I'm gone."

"Will that be as good as you speaking for yourself?"

"I spoke under oath. It'll do." She found the lies coming more readily these days. She wondered whether it was the city working a change on her or if it was a change she'd learned to work on herself.

"I don't like what you're planning, Becca."

"You don't need to like it." She got up, shrugging off his hands. She made sure to be wearing a brave smile when she turned to him and said, "I think it'd please me to go see Virgie now."

⊱⊰

She went home with the early dusk, a small measure of comfort in her heart. Virgie had been so happy to see her! The girl looked well, better and better. She'd accepted Becca's apology at once, brushed aside the flimsy explanations Becca tried to make for her long absence. How her face lit up when

Becca told her that it was only a matter of days before city help was sent after her kin!

They'll act wise as well as swift when they take the place. That's how they'll be ordered to act, that's what they'll do. Highlandwebbers are born to follow orders.

Your orders? Virgie asked, worship shining in her eyes.

Becca had laughed and hugged the girl. *I can't give orders to Highlandweb, but I can get them issued by someone who can. There's one here who owes me that much.* She promised this to Virgie in the unspoken hope that Van's gratitude would prove it true.

Now all she had to do was find Van, make her surrender to him, urge him to fulfill his part of the bargain. She redoubled her pace back to Thirdweb tower, flew up the stairs so fast she didn't even see her brother waiting for her on the landing.

"Becca, what's your rush?" Eleazar trotted after her, a sheaf of papers in his hand.

"I have to find Van!" she called back, dashing into the Carsonelic apartments. She had searched all the common areas just three steps ahead of him before Eleazar managed to lay hold of her and bring her to a reluctant halt.

"Save your energy," he told her. "Van's not here."

"Where is he, then?"

"With Webmaster Steven, where else?" There was only a hint of envy in Eleazar's voice. "They've been closeted together in the office for three hours, and the last anyone heard was not to expect either one of them for dinner."

"Is something wrong?"

"When it's Van, something always manages to *turn* wrong," Eleazar replied.

The word that had come down from Webmaster Steven's office proved true: Neither he nor Van was present at the table that night. The webmaster's absence alone wouldn't have been noteworthy— Webmaster Steven shared out the honor of his mealtime presence among all the elics of Thirdweb— but Van belonged to Carsonelic until the day he stepped up to take the webmaster's place.

Something's going on, Becca thought as she sat sipping her soup. *Something big; the air's itching with it.*

Keeping her head bowed over her dish, she still managed to steal glances to left and right and all around the table. No one was talking. Not one soul there asked another how a specific case was coming round, or made inquiry about some obscure point of law. No one even asked Varda how her belly thrived, or begged to lay a hand on it and feel the baby move. Instead of the lively conversation that was a hallmark of all meals in Carsonelic, there was only silence. The clinking of spoons against bowls sounded unnaturally loud; everyone seemed ready to leap out of their skins.

When Eleazar cleared his throat, Bai almost shot straight to the ceiling. All eyes turned on her; she giggled and shrugged, then needlessly shifted her long braid of blue-black hair from one shoulder to the other. Salome looked at her and made a face. The meal ended without further disturbance.

If Van returned before Becca went to bed, she didn't see him. Under ordinary circumstances, the members of Carsonelic gathered in the large common room with the glorious view of the city from its balcony. Scattered in small groups of two or three or four, they would chat idly or play games. Eleazar had tried without success to interest Becca in learning chess, and she flatly refused to come near any game involving cards. She had read somewhere that it was wickedness.

Sometimes there was music. Bai had a sweet voice and could play the guitar. Becca enjoyed her performances and dearly wished Eleazar would arrange for her to learn that skill, but never found the bone to do it. Stead lore taught that though women might raise their voices to praise God, instruments were forbidden them.

Why are the small things that hardest to change? she asked herself, yearning after the music.

This night was different. There was no music, there were no games, no talk, certainly no laughter. Varda took advantage of her belly and was the first to steal away, Felix and Myra following almost immediately. Glendon and Hadar never even bothered to come to the common room. When Eleazar remarked on their absence, Salome announced that they'd decided to go straight to bed after they finished supervising the elic helpers clean up after dinner.

"They said they're tired," she added in a tone meant to tell just how far she believed *that* story.

"Maybe they are," Bai ventured. "I know I am." And she was gone.

Becca took herself off to bed soon after. Whatever unseen presence was haunting the folk of Carsonelic this night, it was none of her affair. So long as their secrets didn't touch her or Gilber or Virgie, they could keep them. That was what she told herself. She had to repeat it many times before she could force her way into the haven of sleep.

She was awakened by cool fingers gliding over her cheek. "Wake up, Becca," Salome said. There was a candle in her hand, casting shadows into the hollows underneath her eyes. "Get dressed and come with me. It's nearly dawn."

"Uh?" To wake before first light was no hardship for Becca; she'd grown up with the memory of five thousand dawns and more on Wiserways. But when she'd lived back on stead she'd always known the reason for early rising. Coop ran by another clock; this early hour didn't belong to the city at all. She sat up, the bedclothes held tight to her bosom, her heart whipping up its beat. "What for? What's happening?"

"What has to happen," Salome answered, grim. "The law's being kept and for once there's some justice to it. It's an honor to be invited to stand witness, or that's what your brother said. He's declined the honor himself—a sudden illness. I wonder if the meddies can diagnose a case of vanished backbone?" She didn't so much as smile when she said that. "Will you come? You don't have to. Eleazar's illness may run in your blood."

Becca swung her legs out of bed. "Are you going?"

"I don't have a choice. Van named me his second and Webmaster Steven approved it. There's a difference between a command appearance and an invitation."

"Was that who invited me? Van?"

"To witness this? To see how he'll stand up to it?" At last a smile no bigger than a fruit paring curled over Salome's lips. "He'd sooner die. That's why *I'm* inviting you. If you do come, you don't need to look at anything but him. That's if you come at all. Don't say yes or no on my account. When I had Van release you from Wallweb, I did it free of charge."

"Does Van know you invited me?"

"He'll figure it out when he sees you there."

"If I come, will it—will you get in trouble with him for bringing me?"

Salome's smile warmed itself by candlelight. "You're sweet, Becca." She didn't answer the question, instead only said, "Well?"

Becca thought it over. "I'll come," she said.

She dressed as quickly as she could, under Salome's eye. She didn't find the other woman's presence an invasion—on Wiserways she and her sibs had shared a dormitory. Privacy was for wives still young enough to hold their alph's interest. Her preparations were only a little delayed by the need to see to herself in the elic washroom.

There was a special place in that room, a curtained-off corner kept separate for the women's needs. Here Becca had soaked and washed and dried the bandages she'd used when in her times. Salome had provided her with all the supplies she needed and more, though she'd laughed at her when Becca insisted on laundering the stained ones herself. *You've been here*

how long and you still don't know what a hobay's for?
And Becca, too embarrassed to admit that she didn't
know what the other woman was talking about,
claimed that it was the custom of her stead for women
to look after themselves entirely when in their times.
So that we remember Eve, she'd said, the image of
womanly piety. That made Salome laugh even more.

Salome was waiting for her right outside the
washroom door when she was done, Becca's jacket
in her hand. She watched while Becca put it on and
even set down her candle to help lift the stead girl's
braids free of the collar. "What beautiful hair," she
said, letting the end of one plait slip through her
fingers.

The stairs to the street were lit by globes whose
brightness burned lower the closer it got to sunrise.
"You know, it's funny," the trader woman remarked
as they stepped outside into a gray world.

"What is?"

"How you came into your times, and no one the
wiser."

Becca's breath almost stopped. "What do you
mean?"

"I mean that no one in our elic noticed anything
different about you before, when you were taking.
You know what they always tell us about a taking
woman: Better get her locked away somewhere safe,
under a strong man's protection, or every other man
for miles will be on her!" Salome snickered, though
Becca saw nothing funny in her words at all. The
trader woman put her arm around Becca's waist. "Oh,
take that scandalized look off your face, I was only

joking. That's just what they say out where you come from, isn't it? I doubt any man in this entire web could tell a taking woman by smell alone even if you rubbed his nose in—" She clapped her other hand to her mouth, feigning that she'd shamed herself, but her eyes danced, proud of all she'd said.

In the hour before dawn, Coop streets near Thirdweb were quiet. Becca was accustomed to that by now, though it used to give her pause. The first night she'd spent under her brother's roof, she hadn't slept well and had gone out onto the balcony to watch the sunrise. She remembered how still the streets looked, how deserted, as though her arrival had scared off all the other inhabitants of the city. There was some bustle off to the west, where Steadway Gate lay, but nothing at all astir in the streets directly below.

A rumpled and grumpy Eleazar had found her on the balcony about an hour later. If he overheard her prayers for God to lift the all-surrounding spell of silence, he didn't let on. As he wiped the sleep from his eyes, he explained to her that Thirdweb tower stood in a quarter given over to residences and to those groups whose trades could be conducted from home.

Nothing heavier than books and paper to be trucked in and out, Becca, no motor vehicles, not even a horse. No reason to be up at this godforsaken hour either, unless it's your turn to supervise breakfast. It happens to be mine, worse luck. Now go back to bed and rest easy: You've got it more peaceful here than you ever knew it on Wiserways.

Knowing all this, when Becca turned the corner and saw the great tram chugging softly at the curbside, she was sure she must still be back in her bed asleep. Everything she'd witnessed so far today—from Salome waking her up so early to the advent of this monstrous, huffing apparition—were all part of the same mad dream.

"What are you staring at? The door's open, they're waiting for us. Get in." The dream Salome was as strong-willed as the real one. She dropped her arm from Becca's waist and gave her a hearty shove toward the machine. There was a panel gaping open in its flank and a man in black waiting to give Becca a hand up and inside. Salome scrambled after on her own and took a seat on one of the padded benches. Becca did the same just as the panel closed.

The tram started forward at a glide. The ride was remarkably smooth. Becca wondered how fast they were going. There was no way to gauge speed from where she sat; there were no windows, the interior compartment lit by a continuous strand of tubing that shone with the same cool, pale light as the glow globes.

All that Becca had to occupy her eyes were the faces of her fellow passengers. Besides Salome and the man who'd helped her in, there were ten others seated on the benches against the compartment walls. Only one was a woman, and she wore the same black shirt touched with silver flowers that Becca had first seen on Webmaster Steven. Hers only boasted two.

Now that Becca came to notice it, Salome and the rest were likewise clad in black. Salome's blouse was the only one unrelieved by silver flowers. Instead, a pin the size and color of a ripe ear of grain clung discreetly to one point of her collar. In her common city garb, Becca felt as out of place as if she were still wearing stead clothes.

The smooth ride ended and a bumpier stretch began. The tram lurched and jounced, swaying on its treads. Becca hooked her hands under her seat and held on. Her empty stomach protested this rough treatment and threatened to rebel. Luckily the tram came to full stop before that could happen.

A gust of cool air, heavy with salt, rushed into the compartment the instant the side panel opened. Becca didn't need help or encouragement to leap out and meet it halfway. She gulped down the fresh air gratefully and reveled in the soothing wash of a sea breeze over her face. Lighthearted, she turned to see if Salome was enjoying the return to air and daylight as much as she.

Salome was nowhere to be seen. No one but Becca had emerged from the tram. The opening in its side was dark and still. Up top, the driver sat staring straight ahead, the nose of his vehicle pointed back at the city.

"Hello?" Becca called up to him once, then again, louder: "Sir? Sir, are you supposed to tell them they can come out now?" The driver didn't answer, only pulled his head further down into the hood of his yellow jacket. His gloved hands stayed on the control levers, his eyes remained fixed on the city walls in the distance.

Becca rested one hand on the tram tread and

looked around. The driver had brought them north and east of the city to a steep headland. A giant hand had sliced its sides like a wedge of cheese. She heard a hiss and a roar from beyond the land's edge, a wild, alluring sound that stirred the small hairs at the nape of her neck and all along her arms. She turned her face to the wind and her eyes were stung with a sudden, silver-blue brightness. Dazzled, she walked toward it, sure that she was once more the vessel and the victim of a great seeing.

But it was no seeing, no vision of prophecy and dream. She drew nigh to the verge of the headland and her whole body went slack with wonder at her first sight of the sea. Nothing she had read of waves or waters prepared her for it. It spread away past any boundaries Becca's fancy might have set it, rippling like air-dances over the fields of paradise.

Becca gasped for breath and drew the freshness of salt spray deep into her lungs. All around the headland where she stood, strange birds rode the swirls of wind, swooping from the salt-shorn grasses at its peak to the rocky shore far below. Their sobbing cries echoed out over the unknowable vastness of the waters.

Feeling forlorn and small, Becca moved back toward the opening in the vehicle's side. "Salome?" she called, her voice faltering.

"*Ssshh!*" The admonishing whisper was curt, peremptory. It echoed from the tram's body like a spook voice from a wellshaft. Becca closed her mouth and was silent.

Now one by one the other passengers emerged.

When their feet touched the earth, they formed up into pairs and marched up the headland. Salome strode beside the other woman, last couple but one from the end. Confused, Becca wanted to run up to her and ask what was happening, where were they going, why? One look from the trader woman changed her mind. Becca had seen that hard look on her pa's face before, when he'd had to act as alph and not as man.

She found her answers soon enough, without Salome's aid. The twin column and its lone straggler climbed the gentle slope, keeping to the verge where the land plummeted away into swirling water and leaping foam. Where the headland thrust its narrowest point into the sea, someone was waiting for them. The sun was just beginning to show itself over the ocean at his back, casting his face into shadow, limning his body in flame, but even at a distance Becca knew that it was Van.

There were others with him, elite members of Highlandweb standing to his right. Drawn up three deep in their ranks, the new day's light reflected in blinding flashes from their visored helms. Salome's group marched smartly past the guards to take their place to Van's left. There was also another group present, people who didn't appear to belong to either Thirdweb or Highland. Becca felt eased of a burden as soon as she saw them. She let Salome's group go where it would and took her place in the midst of this one.

"About time!" someone said. Becca looked to her left. The black man beside her ran a hand over his shaven skull and added, "Thank God those Thirdies finally showed up. All we need's to miss the tide. I'm not dragging out here all over again tomorrow just because *they* couldn't wake up early enough."

"C'mon, Jon, you bark but you don't bite." The next man over gave the first speaker a friendly nudge in the ribs. "I was kind of hoping it would get put off. I wanted to lay bets on which team'd get their pole clear first, without drowning themselves."

"You would." The black man returned the nudge a little harder, a little less friendly. "Shoosh. They're starting. See? There goes the Face to the edge now."

"Pretty young to be the Face." Jon's companion stroked his chin. "Want to bet anything on whether he falls off?"

"Adam, I swear I'm gonna bet whether I push *you* off, and then I'm gonna turn it into a sure thing. Now shut up!"

Becca wished Jon didn't sound quite so testy. She wanted to ask someone what was going on, and approaching Salome was out of the question. The crowd around her was all male, except for herself and two women as far from her as possible. They had their heads together, whispering. There was too thick a press of people between them and Becca for her to sidle through, and here where the headland narrowed there was no other way to reach them. The crowd itself massed too near the precipice for her to go around. She shifted from foot to foot, a tangle of curiosity and anxiety, inwardly debating what to do.

"Young woman, *what* is your trouble? Someone stick a burr down your back?" The man Jon did sound ready to bite, no matter what his friend Adam claimed.

"I'm sorry. I didn't want to bother anyone. I—"

"Sshh. Don't talk, it's started." Jon cupped one ear. "I *think* it's started. Damn stupid place for it—the wind carries off everything the Face says, and besides, he mumbles. Youngsters always mumble. What good's being a witness if you can't hear a blessed word that's said? Whose idea was it to tap that infant to play the Face anyhow?"

"Why don't you just admit you're getting old and your hearing's going on you?" Adam suggested cheerfully. Jon gave him another poke in the side.

"Please, why do you call him the Face?" Becca asked.

"*This* is how they teach our kids!" Jon exclaimed dramatically.

The whole crowd turned on him as one and said, "*Sssshhhh!*" One of the nearby Highlandwebbers only half managed to suppress a chuckle. Jon glowered at everyone, in uniform and out, then lowered his voice and said to Becca, "The Face of *Justice*, do you remember your schooling *now*? The one the Thirdies send to be their official witness whenever one of their death sentences gets carried out. There's other Thirdies sent to bear witness too, but as long as they haul their bodies up here, their job's done. They don't *have* to look."

"The Face does?" Becca asked.

"No choice but," Jon confirmed. "And then to top it off, they haul a bunch of honest citizens into their silly little game. 'If we witness the deaths we decree, we will never call for death too readily,' that's what *they* say. And then it's 'If the people come to witness the full payment for transgression, they will not so readily transgress.' *Ha!* Shows what they know, those sanctimonious Thirdies. Let 'em spend a little more time studying human nature, a little less studying books and *maybe* there'd be a hope for 'em."

Someone in the crowd tried shushing him again.

"Shoosh yourself!" he shot back. He folded his arms and shook his head. "I could pity the lumpskulls, if they didn't make me so mad. Drag us up here, when we'd be better off asleep in our own beds. I don't see the point. We're supposed to be witnesses too, but we can't hear the Face rattle through all the legal gobbledegook to justify why they're killing those poor bastards down there, and we can't *see* the execution itself because the Thirdies keep the best observation spots for themsel—"

"Sir?" The Highlandwebber's visor twinkled with a new-made galaxy of stars. He held up one gloved hand before Jon's face and said, "Sir, I'll have to ask you to stop talking. The Face can't complete the ceremony unless there's silence and we don't have all the time in the world."

"I was just trying to explain things to this girl," Jon replied, drawing himself up in a huff. "She's bone ignorant, *no* idea at all what's going on, a *fine* witness and another *glorious* product of a city that always manages to buy *some* people bright, shiny new helmets while our children grow up dumber than a mud sandwich!"

The Highlandwebber sighed. "Yes sir. Sorry, sir.

Why don't I just take the young lady up forward where she can have a good view? You know what they say about one picture, sir." He didn't wait for an answer, but escorted Becca away.

Behind her she heard Jon grumbling to Adam about how the trouble with the world was how everything was catered to ease things for the young. She half-smiled, wondering what he'd say if he knew the truth of her life and how precious *easy* it'd been. Then the guardsman brought her to the edge of the headland, a little beyond the double row of Thirdwebbers in their black shirts, a little behind the spot where Van stood, arms held out to the inrushing sea, the rising sun. His hands reached up, but his eyes looked down. Becca looked down too.

She saw hell.

Chapter Eleven

Now let us be merry and put by our sorrow,
A star shines in Heaven with hope for the morrow,
The Son of the Father has come from above,
To feed us and keep us in plenty and love.

"There you are, Becca," said Eleazar just as she
walked into the tower. "Where have you been?" As
always, whenever she left Thirdweb on her own
business, he was waiting for her somewhere between
the street door and her room when she returned. He
was always ready to intercept her with a warm
greeting and a brotherly inquiry, but these days she'd
taken to putting him off with vague answers,
shrugging aside his attempts to hug her when they
met.

"Just out," she mumbled. "Walking."

"Anywhere in particular?" Eleazar could be persistent. "It gets dark earlier now and it's awfully cold. You were gone for hours. Couldn't they have loaned you a heavier coat at Greenwoodweb?"

"Maybe…if that's where I'd gone." She said no more, and when he tried to help her out of her jacket she gathered the collar more closely around her face, as if she were still outside facing the winter wind.

He placed himself between her and the stairs, seizing her arms so that she couldn't evade him or escape without a struggle. She made a half-hearted attempt to squirm away, but then relaxed, resigned to wait him out. She could be twice as obstinate as he, when she liked. Lately she had come to the conclusion that she didn't care for living under scrutiny.

At least on Wiserways I knew who the noseybodies were, man, wife or sib. They didn't bother hiding what they were—said it was their God-given duty to keep watch over would-be sinners. Wish he'd be half that honest. I know he's spying on me; he might as well admit it. But that wouldn't be city ways. Becca held her brother's gaze for some time, then looked away. He was regarding her closely, with a look of concern, the way she'd seen Miss Lynn examine an ailing woman. *Now what's he up to?* She wanted to get shut of him, but she was too wrung out to do more than stand there and wait on his pleasure.

"You look terrible," he said straight out. The real worry she heard in his voice surprised her. "What's wrong? If your eyes sink any deeper into your head, we couldn't haul them out with a rope."

At the mention of *rope*, Becca trembled and made another weak try to get away from her brother. "I'm fine."

"No, you're not." A little muscle set along his jawline twitched with suppressed rage. "Apparently the Lord thinks I need another reason to want to kill Van."

"Van?" Becca stared, startled by what she'd heard.

"You're not going to lecture me about the evils of envy, are you? Mother used to do that. How that woman did love to lecture!" It was the first Becca had heard Eleazar speak of Hattie in a long while. "I could live with envying that little snot. It's nigh—nearly Christmas. I'm surprised Webmaster Steven hasn't handed down orders that we're to build the creche around his darling heir. All hail the newborn king of Thirdweb! No wonder I can hardly get my mouth around the carols without feeling sick. I keep seeing Van's ugly face in the manger, haloed 'round with light."

Becca was about to say *He's not ugly.* If she didn't, it was because she knew her brother would take that simple truth and twist it into a woman's fancy for one particular man.

"Eleazar, if you envy Van, that's your quarrel, not mine," she said. "I don't have any complaint to lay at his door. I haven't even seen him for over a week." *Lord witness, for once I want to find him,* she thought. *How can I tell that boy he's won if he's vanished?*

Eleazar got a peculiar smile on his face, one that sprang from secrets. "That's because he and Salome are off together again, in the bower. You'd think

Webmaster Steven would learn. Nothing came of it
the last time, nor the time before. It's a waste of a
fine, taking woman, but the old man's got his heart
set on having one of Van's brats underfoot. He's gone
so far as to say we'll raise it here! Well, you can raise
a pipe dream anywhere."

"Oh." Becca blushed. "I expect that was his reward
for being—being the Face."

"Some reward." Eleazar's sarcasm could peel the
living hide from an ox and tan it up for leather. "Just
following orders, that's all. There'll be no more
rewards for our Van! Not in the usual way.
Webmaster Steven made *that* mistake two years ago,
and see where it got him! A boy's first trip to the
Flower Market isn't supposed to end with him
running away with the girl."

"But if Salome's taking, and Webmaster Steven
doesn't choose to bless her himself, isn't it a reward
for him to give her to some other man?"

Eleazar cupped her chin with thumb and forefinger.
"Little sister, you're a prize—and I don't just mean
that in the times you're taking! It's been decades
since Webmaster Steven laid with every woman that
came into Third. Oh, he'll do it as a one-time
courtesy, to welcome the new ones in, but after that
he sees to breeding the next generation from good,
solid genetic matches. That's his job. That's what he
claims he's doing, coupling Van to Salome, but he's
beating empty husks and wonders why he doesn't get
grain."

"Maybe Van doesn't…like Salome." Becca recalled
how he'd called her *Auntie*, but then she figured that

if there was a forbidden degree of blood-bond between them, Webmaster Steven would know of it. Lots of people here set a high value on knowing things.

Eleazar made a scornful sound. "Like her? Van's a sulky little bastard who *likes* things just one way: his. Even had the nerve to try persuading Webmaster Steven to let that Flower Market trash join our elic, can you picture it? What skill could she bring us for a dowry, besides being able to fuck a boy brainless? Not that he had much brains to start with."

"Poor Salome," Becca said half to herself.

"Don't waste your sympathy on her; she'll survive on pride alone. Salome's one of the finest traders in the city and she knows it. We're lucky to have her working for Carsonelic. How do you think she feels about being shut up in the bower time after time with a boy that doesn't want her? You'll sooner get a baby from a beet field than from those two." Eleazar grinned. "There's just so much of this nonsense she'll take. It's only a matter of time before she makes a public petition for dispensation."

"What's that?"

"*That*, Becca, is when a woman like Salome finally gets fed up and hustles herself over to Greenwoodweb. She tells them just what's been going on—what *hasn't*, I mean—and the meddies check out her story, and *then* the wind shifts so Van's precious piss blows right back in his face. Not even Webmaster Steven could save him then."

"Save him?" Becca wished she could understand

her brother's words as well as she understood that nasty gloating look on his face. "From what?"

"From judgment on a choice of charges: Onan's sin, for the mildest, and for the worst, abomination."

"Abomina—" The word came stillborn. She couldn't get it out without having everything from that awful dawn come rushing back into her mind. Her breath shuddered out in a whimper between clenched teeth and she dug her fingers into her arms so the pain would force her to stay on her feet.

"Dear God! Becca!"

She heard Eleazar's worried voice come from far away. She wanted to tell him to be calm, there was nothing he could do for her. She had walked with ghosts before this. It would take her time, but she would find the way to cast them out eventually. *If only they'd let me sleep!* Eleazar meant well, even if he was spying on her. They were still blood kin; he mustn't suffer on her account.

Then she felt his arms around her, and a sudden chill that sucked her down into dreams.

They were the same dreams that had besieged her ever since that day she'd accompanied Salome to the headland. She tried to make them stop, but they refused to go away. She tried to cheat them by staying wakeful, but her own body betrayed her to sleep. Night or day, it didn't matter. Whenever Becca closed her eyes, the dreams were waiting.

It began with darkness, then a sliver of light like the opening of heaven's own eye. The sliver widened, a mouth of fire. She stood with her back pressed hard to something round and smooth, her arms pinned behind her, and watched the light come on. She knew with the fearsomely irrational logic of dreams that when that burning mouth opened wide enough, it would engulf her in its flames.

Somewhere above her head she heard the sounds of sobs and wailing voices. If she tilted her head back, it banged against the wooden post to which she was bound by wrists and ankles. A shadow lay over her, a presence she could not see, and there was a dreadful pooling of cold around her feet.

She looked down and saw that her feet were ankle deep in icy water that swirled with limp green strands of rootless plants and a white scum of bubbles. Wavelets splashed playfully against her legs, soaking the long gown she wore. The water seeped through the coarsely woven sackcloth, prickling her skin with gooseflesh. A random wave struck a little higher, sending the sting of salt into her eyes.

That was when she knew that the dream had come back for her again. That was when the voices returned, pouring words down upon her head from above, whipping their barbs around her ears.

Confess! they cried. *Name your partner in abomination and you will know mercy!*

Give him up, they whispered. *Why should you suffer the hard death alone? Why should he go free to walk in the sun when your bloated body will lie slowly turning beneath the water, a thing of horror? Why should he laugh when you must rot? Why should he see another dawn when fish have devoured your eyes?*

Let him share the price you pay, they wheedled. *Why*

not, if he shared the pleasure? Give him to us, and we will give you the easy death in trade.

Look! they coaxed. Look! It is not such a hard thing we ask of you. The others have done it and see! See how much less they will have to suffer now!

And Becca did look. She turned her head slowly to the right and saw another pillar with its roots sunk deep in the surf. It was not straight like the one at her back, but split like the forked sticks the boys on stead used to hold down the heads of serpents, and it was made of iron instead of wood. Two men were bound to it. They were chained so that they faced each other through the cleft, rusted iron between their bodies but nothing keeping eyes from eyes. One man wore a slim noose around his neck—Becca couldn't see whether it was made of silk or rope or wire—and the cord trailed off to end in a small black box set into the pole within reach of the other man's hand. That was how it was for the other man too, neck in a noose linked to a black box. The chains that bound their right arms were slack enough to let them reach each box's toggle switch or to let their arms drop to their sides. Becca turned away.

It was as if she had never moved her head at all. To her left was another forked pillar, another pair of noosed men, and beyond them two women bound in the same manner. The whole cove was a forest of dead trees, the iron ones cleft, the wooden not, all heavy with a harvest for the sea.

The water was higher now. It lapped against her thighs, then shyly stole a hundred secret kisses. The fiery eye on the horizon rose with the waves but gave no heat with its light. Becca shivered as the tide crept past her hips to slip a lover's arm around her waist.

She pressed her cheek against the pole. The wooden surface was slick with brown slime, reeking of dead things. Her breath rushed into her lungs tainted with rust and salt. The sea caressed her breasts, hardened their tips to stone.

Still the voices reached her from above, begging, wooing, exhorting her to give up the name her heart guarded.

Tell us while you can! they cried. *Tell us while you have the breath, the time! When your chin feels the cold, when your tongue tastes the salt, it will be too late. The water will overwhelm you. Your mouth will open for air and draw down brine, your nostrils will flood with bitterness. Do you know how long it takes to drown? Do you want to learn whether the helplessness is worse than the pain, the pain worse than the panic as the dark comes on?*

And then: *Look there and see our mercy.*

Now when Becca looked to her right, she saw the two men begin to move their hands. Carefully, deliberately, with love, each pulled the little switch. A low hum rose as the cords began to creep back into the twinned black boxes. The nooses closed. Tighter now, and tighter still they drew. What was it Becca saw in the men's eyes as their faces darkened for lack of breath? Was it gratitude? But then the waters came and hid them.

You see, said the voices, complacent, serene. *You see how it can be. Death too can be the gift of love.*

She wanted to believe them. In her terror she

wanted to believe anything that might blunt the edge of the sword. She opened her mouth, ready to give them the name she had kept close-locked in her heart so long, through so much.

Then she heard the shrieking. She jerked her head in the other direction and saw one man slumped black-faced and lifeless against the forked pole, the other still alive.

"You *bastard!*" he shouted. "You fucking bastard, you didn't pull it! You didn't pull the switch for mine! You swore you'd do it the instant you felt the cord move, but you dropped your hand. You did it on purpose, left me alive to suffer before I die! God damn you, *why?* Because I gave your name when they caught me? You were as guilty as me! You ran away, you ugly coward! Why should I pay the price alone? I hate you! I hate you! I hope you burn in hell!"

His howls were not the only ones to ride above the incoming tide. All through that drowned iron forest, the same scene was being acted out with a dozen minor variations. Here was a forked pillar where both captives had dropped their hands from the switches and stood bawling obscene accusations in each other's faces while the tide came on. There was a couple where neither one would be the first to pull the switch, mistrusting the other to act in kind, all love destroyed by doubt. For every pair that used the instrument of mercy in their hands to set each other free, there were three others that saw old love crumble to hate before they died. Bound together in flesh, each soul entered the dark house alone.

I didn't tell! I didn't tell!

Becca heard Solomon's pathetic cry, and suddenly she was no longer chained for the tide, but standing free, high on the precipice over the cove where the city meted out the punishment for abomination. She was standing near Van, whose lips were moving in silent prayer, whose face was the sickly white of the bird droppings on the rocks below. Down in the tide's churn she saw the trader Solomon's golden hair vanish under the water and for the last time heard him shout those words: *I didn't tell!* It had become a shout of victory.

Solomon! I'll save you! she called. Though a gulf of space separated them, she knew herself resolved to rescue him. She didn't doubt for a moment that she could do it. It was a dream: Common sense didn't govern the realm of its possibilities. She called out to the drowning man and stretched her hand into the wind. Bones closed around it, a seaweed-draped skeleton's fingers that clamped themselves to her wrist more tightly than any iron cuff. It pulled her from the cliff, down into the water. Just as the sea filled her mouth and nostrils she managed to cry out a name, a condemnation: Van! *Van!* Then there was only the water and the dark.

Still she shouted "Van!" The sound of her own voice woke her, set her bolt upright in bed, clutching the mattress.

In the doorway of her room, Eleazar turned sharply, a look of surprise and consternation on his face. From behind him Becca heard a smug voice crow, "You see? She does want to see me. Now step aside."

Eleazar half complied, giving Van barely enough

room to squeeze through the doorway. He glowered at the boy. "You're the reason she's gone sleepless. Why did you have to bring her there, to witness that? Did she need to see your great *honor?*"

"I told you already: I didn't send for her," Van explained patiently. "I don't know how she got there. She never would have known about it at all, if it had been up to me."

"Why not, Van?" Becca said softly. "I've seen worse things and lived. I'll survive this too."

Van fairly beamed when he heard her speak, though it was a grin brittle fit to crack. He hurried to her bedside and took her hand without invitation or leave. "Then let me give you something good to see, a sight you'll welcome. I've just come from Webmaster Steven's office; he's sent out the word to Greenwoodweb and Highland: We leave within the hour. We're going to the rescue of those children."

꙳ ꙳

The coat was heavy leather lined with fleece. The collar felt soft as a cloud against Becca's cheeks, and the hat and gloves mated to it kept her body warm as if she were still snug inside Thirdweb tower. The chill lay over her spirit, not her flesh, as she stood beside Van and watched the Highlandwebbers enter Mark's stead.

Gilber was with them, leading the way into the dark labyrinth, showing them the mysteries of trailwire, seeing to it that every child was found. She had wanted to go with him, but Van had said a word to the leader of the Highlandweb guards and she found her way barred.

"The children know you," Van had said, trying to smooth it over. "It's going to be chaos in there, terrifying. It'll be good for them if you're here, a familiar face to greet them when they're brought out."

His theory was sound; but many theories worked perfectly well until they tripped over reality. She didn't know why Van's assumption turned out to be so very wrong—maybe the little ones were too crazed with panic to react rationally, maybe Mark had poisoned their minds with Lord-knew-what tales about her after she'd gone—but she did know this: When she went forward to welcome the first children to be led into the light, they shrieked like lost souls and clung to one another so tightly that the meddies had to wrap them both in a single blanket. When they tried prying away the small fingers, they saw blood. It was the same with the next children out, and the next. They saw Becca, they recognized her well enough, and the sight of her sent them into fits of terror.

She gave up, leaving them to the meddies, retreating back to Van's side. She pulled her collar up high to hide her face and tweaked the brim of her hat down low. Hat, coat, and gloves were all Van's gifts. She had tried refusing them, but he'd made her acceptance a condition for coming out so far into the maw of winter.

"So many," he mused as six guards emerged from the ruins, flanking a party of four older children.

They shepherded them into the belly of a waiting tram with the meddie crest of a healthy tree in full leaf. "How many of them did you see while you were there, Becca?"

"I don't know if I ever saw them all," she answered. "I tended to their hurts some, and I think I might've met everyone that way or at meals, but I truly don't know. That Mark was made out of secrets. I think he figured that knowing something I could never know made him richer than me, somehow."

"Then he'll fit right in when we get back home," Van said with a smile. "A wise child. I'd better keep him away from Webmaster Steven or he'll find a soulmate and the webmaster'll find a new heir."

Becca's brow creased. "I don't think they've brought him out yet. No one knows that maze better than him. What if he hides so well they can't find him?" A sudden thought frighted her: "We won't just leave him here alone, will we?" She squeezed Van's arm as if trying to wring out a promise.

"Your friend Gilber's a born finder, remember?" Van responded. His smile curled itself away. "I do."

"Van…" The cold had dried her lips; she wet them before going on. "Did anyone tell you I'd been looking for you? For days. I didn't know you were in— away with Salome."

"You mean in the bower? You should've come after me there. It would've given Salome and me something to do. We were desperate for a little decent conversation."

She let his words pass without comment. What passed or didn't pass between him and Salome was none of her concern. "I wanted to tell you that I'd changed my mind. I'll help—" She cast a covert glance around, but all the meddies and guards were too preoccupied with the children to eavesdrop. "I'll help your friend."

"Oh." He didn't sound like a man who'd just won his game. "Too bad you didn't find me earlier, then. Now that I've given you what you wanted, I suppose you've changed your mind back."

Becca's gloved hands burrowed beneath her collar and held tight. "Good to know what you think of me. I was raised to keep my word, even if I only gave it to myself."

"The noble savage," Van murmured.

"What did you call me?"

"Nothing. Something I read in an old text. Nonsense about how the closer you live to nature, the purer your soul. I suppose that makes you seedgrubs half a step below the angels…if the angels slaughter infants and call it holy."

Becca's hands clenched tighter under her collar. She would not let him rile her, she *would not*. She would tell him what she had decided to do and she wouldn't listen to any foolishness he cared to spout. She knew that if she did pay him any mind at all, she'd kill him.

Could be that's just what he's seeking, came the whisper in her head. *Someone to do for him what he can't do for himself.*

If he's wooing death, let him find it somewhere else, she thought back fiercely. *Not from me.*

Just see to it he doesn't take you along with him when

he does go a-courting, the cautionary whisper replied.

"I made up my mind to help you and I'll do it," she told him. "Unless *you've* changed your mind?"

"No." Van's throat was tense with misery. "She— we still need you and Gilber to—"

"Only me," Becca said quickly. "Not Gilber. If we're discovered, I don't want him or his tribe suffering for it."

"You won't be discovered." He spoke as if he could will all his desires into reality.

"I'm joyed you think that. All I ask is you take whatever steps seem needful to protect me. I won't cut my hair or dress as a man, though. I've seen how your folk deal with abomination. Pity us poor seedgrubs, we can't do it up so fancy; all we know to do is stone the unlucky souls to death." She'd never intended to sound so caustic, but it was past her control.

Van dug his chin into his coat collar. "I didn't want you to see that. When I knew you were there, standing witness, seeing what could've happened to you because of what I—" He gritted his teeth. "I could kill that bitch Salome."

"Forget Salome. Keep your mind on our business. I'll want to visit once a week. In the last month, more often; I'll tell you exactly how much more after I've looked her over close. She's my job. Your job's going to be to get me there and back safe. Gilber doesn't come into this at all. Is that clear?"

He nodded, but also said, "I thought he could help. He's at Greenwoodweb, he could get you supplies and—"

"Gilber stays free of this business." Becca stressed each word so there could be no mistaking her will. "Anything I need, you can fetch for me."

"When do you want to make your first—?"

A clamor from the mouth of the ruins cut off Van's question. A guard dashed out into the fading sunlight, disarmed, helmet gone, blood flowing from a gash across his cheek. He yelled for help from Highland and Greenwoodweb alike, his cries sending a stream of personnel rushing down into the gaping entryway. More noise echoed up from within, the sounds of shouts and blows, grunts and screams, and then a single gunshot.

There was quiet.

The first to emerge were two guards carrying the body of a third. A meddie walked briskly beside them, doing what she could to stanch the victim's wound. A wedge of flesh and bone had been hacked clean out of his upper chest, just below the collarbone. He still wore his helmet, and it made the gurgle and wheeze of every breath echo eerily. The ghastly, tearing sounds stopped soon after he was hustled into one of the troop trams. Becca told herself it must be because the meddies had done something to help him.

There were more guards coming out of the ruins now. Some bled from superficial wounds, though most were untouched. They walked slowly, muttering to one another, shaking their heads, and sometimes casting uneasy backward glances into the darkness from which they had just come. The meddies followed, some taking charge of the

Highlandwebbers' light wounds, others getting back to tending the rescued children.

The last to emerge was Gilber Livvy. Becca saw the blood and dirt streaking his face and ran to him, crying out as if the hurt were all her own. He hugged her to him hard. "That child..." It was all he could say.

She led him back to the Greenwoodweb tram and helped herself to supplies to clean his wounds. "So many!" she exclaimed. "You're lucky they're mostly scratches."

"Lucky," he repeated.

A loud, metallic click made him jump. Six guards were massing around a meddie who carried a strange looking gun. "Take it easy, Gilber," the fellow said. "We don't mean to kill him."

Van joined them. Becca had forgotten all about him the instant she saw Gilber's hurt. "If that's the boy who almost killed that guard, don't bother with the niceties. You've got my permission to take him down any way you can."

The guards murmured their approval, but the meddie said, "I'm afraid your permission isn't worth dust. The orders for this mission came from Webmaster Steven, and he said the children were to be brought back with as little trauma as possible. *If* we can find that boy in there again, we'll make our best effort to take him alive. All I need is one clear shot and a lullaby." He patted the butt of the gun.

"Suit yourself." Van shrugged. "I still think you're making a mistake. That's no child down there, that's an animal."

The meddie looked Van in the eye. "That's a child," he replied, and went back into the ruins. Gilber gave Becca another hug and followed. The guards tagged after reluctantly.

Last to go in, they were the first ones to emerge less than an hour later. Gilber came staggering out behind them, the strange gun slung on his back, Mark's limp body in his arms. The folk from Greenwoodweb swarmed forward to take the boy from him and get him secured inside the tram.

The Highlandwebbers remounted their vehicles and turned them back toward the city. The meddies lingered, trading puzzled looks, staring at the now silent entrance to Mark's old stead. Gilber leaned against the side of the Greenwoodweb tram, head back, eyes closed.

"Gilber?" Becca wanted to take him in her arms again, but she hesitated. There was a heavy air about him that warned off all contact. Locked out, she waited for him to notice she was there. "Gilber?"

He opened his eyes. "I guess I should go back," he said. And then, "I guess I should tell them Kaith's dead." He unslung the tranquilizer gun from his shoulders and handed it to the nearest meddie. "You can come back in there with me to fetch the body, if you want. And see to this rifle. It misfires. The boy dropped a rock the size of a water bucket down on Kaith's head while he was trying to fix it. Lucky it worked for me, before Mark could find another chunk of stone. Lucky it was too dark for those guards to start some real shooting. Lucky..." He sighed. "He never had a chance."

Chapter Twelve

Blessed be,
Root, limb and tree,
And joy be ours this day.
Mary's child,
So sweet and mild,
Is born to show the way.
Sinners all,
Our faults appall
The heart of God on high,
Redeemed we
Must surely be,
Lest in our sins we die.

The sky was a peculiar shade of gray all the way from Thirdweb tower to Greenwoodweb. Becca could never remember it being so cold on stead at this time of year. She wondered if this too were part of what it meant to live in Coop, the unusual weather, or if back home the women were even now gathered together to discuss the intense, unseasonable chill. Hattie would say it was God's will, of course, and scowl at anyone who tried to take the talk further than that. Gram Phila would be there too, holding forth on all the winters she'd witnessed over the years and how this one compared to them.

Back home... She hadn't thought of Wiserways like that for a good long time. *The only thing more peculiar than the weather around here is you, Becca,* she told herself severely. *Now stop your woolgathering and get along!*

She adjusted the straps of her knapsack and slung the canvas bag she also carried over one shoulder. Together they made for an awkward load, but she'd see herself skinned raw before she'd give up either one. She took up a brisker pace and before long she saw the familiar shapes of the Greenwoodweb buildings. "About time," she grumbled. Her spine and shoulders were sore from the burden on her back and her arms ached from keeping the canvas bag from sliding off every few steps.

Greenwoodweb was known territory to her now. These days she didn't waste time with the desk folk asking for whereabouts of anyone she sought. She knew the few places where Gilber might be found, she knew where Virgie stayed. Nigh all of the others lodged with Virgie, except for Mark. Becca didn't know where he was kept, and somehow she never got around to asking Gilber if he did. She couldn't think of the boy without sickness laying hold of her innards, though her mind told her and told her that Mark wasn't wholly to blame for what he'd become. There were some feelings that not even solid common sense could shake.

"Doesn't matter," she muttered to herself as she walked up the steps. "He probably doesn't want to see me, either."

They had made the ward bright for Christmas. Shiny garlands of metallic paper, red, green, and gold, festooned the walls of the common room. Becca's eyes went wide to see a lush evergreen tree set up on a stand in the middle of the sunroom. Bits of colored paper, lacquered slick and cut into the shapes of shepherds and sheep, angels and oxen, hung from its branches. The children clustered at its feet, gazing up into a heaven of green boughs and twinkling candles like captive stars.

In their midst sat Virgie, a queen in glory. Her arms were around two of the little ones, her sibs. Other times when Becca had come here to look after how the children were getting on, she'd never seen Virgie go more than five paces away from those girls. It was all Gilber could do to persuade her to let them sleep in their own beds. Virgie had compromised only when the meddies moved Rina and Drusa's beds right up next to hers.

"Becca!" Virgie's face held all the joy of a spring day. She came forward to greet her, the little girls trailing along at her skirt. Becca noted with approval that these two, like the rest, were now scrupulously clean. Their hair was washed and brushed, the worst of the tangles shorn away, and there were even signs that they were starting to put on weight.

Becca dropped her sack and slid her knapsack to the floor before giving Virgie a hug. "When did all this happen?" she asked, sweeping her hand to take in the tree and all the rest of the decorations.

"Don't they do like this where you stay?" Virgie asked. Becca knew that look. Some of it was doubt, some disbelief, and the rest suspicion. Virgie was a smart girl; it hadn't taken her long to learn that the most valued coin in Coop was knowledge, and Lord help the soul she thought was trying to keep something from her.

"We've got some pretties on the walls, but nothing like this." Becca indicated the tree.

"You don't say so." There was that look again. What Becca said was at odds with what Virgie believed of the world outside Greenwoodweb. If here she had enough good, plain food to eat, then beyond these walls the cityfolk must be choking on delicacies past dreaming. If here she had a sparkling tree, then out there they must have called down the very stars of heaven to adorn their homes for Christmas.

Becca made the cross sign at the base of her throat. "Gospel true. Why don't you come with me and see for yourself? Gilber says you're well enough to leave."

"I don't think so." Virgie didn't move, but still she seemed to shrink back into herself. "I can't. Not until we're all well enough." She put her arms around Rina and Drusa, an angel mantling its wings over the holy Child.

"They look fine," Becca said. She squatted down

to get her eyes on a level with Rina's and held out her hands. "Come here, honey, let me look at you." The child stared at her, mouth full of thumb, and pressed her cheek against Virgie's leg hard enough to leave a mark.

Virgie grinned. "Rina says you can look at her just fine from where you stay."

"Oh, I think I can make her see things my way," Becca replied. She loosened the drawstring of her sack and pulled out a raggy doll with a knot of blue yarn for hair and a stitched-on smile. "Here's something for you, baby," Becca coaxed. "Yours to keep."

Virgie tilted her head, trying to steal a peep inside the bag. "That the only one?"

"I've brought dolls for them all, some like this one, some little lambs, only one cow—it took me too long to stitch up the horns." She waggled the doll like a hunter's lure, tempting Rina. Before the child could make up her mind, her smaller sib Drusa made a decision and leaped forward, snapping the doll out of Becca's hand and hugging it fiercely to her chest. Rina's jaw dropped, her thumb fell from her mouth. She took in a deep breath and let it out in an ear-shattering wail of affront and rage.

Becca hastily dug out another doll and pressed it into Rina's arms. The little girl's shrieking stopped the instant she laid hands on the stuffed cow. Becca watched as the horns she had taken so much pain to sew went right into Rina's mouth.

By now the other children were gathering around, eyes full of longing. Not one of them said a word, but Becca could feel the yearning in their hearts. She handed out raggy dolls as fast as her hands could move. When every child there cradled a new toy, Becca sat back flat on the floor and sighed with relief.

"Only these few left," she told Virgie, checking out the remnants in her knapsack.

"Not all the children are strong enough to leave their beds. Gilber can take you to them." The girl gazed fondly down at her sibs with their new playthings. "Been so long since they had such. It was real nice of you and Gilber to do this for 'em."

"It wasn't—" Becca was about to say *It wasn't Gilber, it was Van.* If she didn't, it was because she could hardly believe it herself. He'd been the one to suggest bringing the children gifts to celebrate the season and their rescue. He'd been the one to send Salome to strike a bargain with the folk of Sandersweb for the cloth and yarn, the thread and needles, even for some of the apprentices to lend a hand in making the toys. And he hadn't asked for any favors in return, not a one.

Becca no longer knew what to think of him. Ever since that horrible dawn when he'd been forced to play the Face of Justice, a change had come over Van. Webmaster Steven's high-handed, spoiled favorite was gone, at least as far as his dealings with Becca went. He made requests, not demands. If she voiced an objection, he no longer countered with a threat. When she had made her first trip to examine Isa, he had let her name the hour and every other particular of the visit. Becca knew that she wasn't imagining the new Van—she could tell by the way Kethy looked at him that this was not the same boy. She was glad of the change, but she still wasn't sure she could trust it.

"It wasn't such a much," was what Becca chose to say. No sense confusing the child. Virgie didn't know who Van was, didn't need to know. Becca got to her feet, knapsack and bag both dangling from one arm. "I'll go hand out the last of them."

"I'll come help you," Virgie offered.

"No need." Becca felt a pang to see how her refusal put out the eager light in Virgie's eyes, but she had no choice. The dolls were Van's idea; but they weren't the only thing that had brought her to Greenwoodweb. "I'll be back soon," she lied.

She hurried from the common room, heart aching for how she'd treated Virgie. *She deserves better than that. I'll make it up to her some day. Now—*

Now there was much to do. Becca got as far from the children's ward as possible before hailing a meddie and giving him the last few raggy dolls in her pack. "They're for those children brought here from the outs," she told him. "The ones still too sick to leave their beds. I'd give them their gifts myself, but I don't know where their rooms are and my webmaster said I'm wanted home early today."

"I'll see to it," the man assured her. "If your webmaster's anything like mine—" He rolled his eyes and made a face.

Becca thanked him and dashed away exactly like a girl with a crotchety webmaster to placate. As soon as she was out of sight, she slowed down and looked around. What was it Gilber had told her about the way Greenwoodweb was organized? "Find the stairs," she told herself. "Sicker patients stay on the lower floors, patients on the mend up above—they can take the steps—and top floors are for storing supplies." It made sense: Meddies and their yellow-suited aides could hustle up and down any number of stairs, freeing rooms on the lower floors for the sick, who couldn't.

She didn't go all the way to the top of the building. Though the storeplace there would contain everything she needed, how could she hope to get in? It would be locked, or she didn't know Coop ways. Within the city walls a person prospered by holding tight to what was his. Becca could understand if that rule only applied to food and drink and shelter—any sane person would—but in Coop it included things you couldn't eat or wear or sometimes even touch.

She didn't have the time to puzzle over the whys behind Coop ways. She had a task that wanted doing quick, that was her sole concern. When she found the stairs, she went up a couple of flights and came out on a floor that was pretty quiet. She'd be willing to bet her fine new fleecy coat that there was hardly anyone up here at all.

The stairwell was at one end of the building, its door opening on a long hall with a row of windows lining one side and a row of rooms the other. Becca craned her neck and saw that most of the rooms were closed. Only three had their doors left open, and two of those were just halfway ajar.

I wonder if it's a closed door or an open one that means a patient inside? It was more than an idle question. If someone saw her up here, she might be challenged. She had no business being on this floor. There'd be no great penalty to pay for her trespass, but being caught would still mean an unsuccessful end to her mission.

Her eyes lit up when she saw the supply cart. It stood in the hall opposite one of the open doors. Even from the stairwell, Becca could see that it was well laden. She was too far off to tell exactly what sort of treasure all those small brown boxes might hold, but finding out would be the work of a moment.

Of course there was the matter of that open door. Was there someone inside? Someone who might see her?

So what if I'm seen? I can brazen it out, claim I'm supposed to be here. Becca was determined. *How would a patient know who's a Greenwood worker and who's not? Besides, it might not even come to that. These upper floors are for patients who want rest for their best care. Anyone is in there, he's sleeping, most like.* Whether that was true or not, it was heartening to think so. She was resolved to be bold about this. Boldness struck quickly and was gone; she wanted speed more than courage.

She took off her coat, folded it neatly, and set it in one corner of the stairwell. The canvas bag and knapsack were piled on top of it. She fished in her skirt pocket, pulled out a length of yellow cloth, and tied it around her right arm. She didn't need a mirror to know that she looked close enough like one of the many Greenwoodweb workers who weren't true meddies.

If Van could see me now, he'd pitch a fit. Her lips tweaked into something not quite a smile. When she'd gone with Van to Sandersweb to see about making the raggy dolls, they'd been ushered into a room packed solid with bins and drawers full of cloth scraps. These were sorted out by color and material, waiting on some project that wanted them. Becca had been attracted to a bin holding silky remnants the color of summer sunshine. She'd rummaged through it while Van spoke with the needlemen, pulling out a square piece large enough to make a decent kerchief. She draped it over her head and called to Van to tell her how she looked.

Would she ever forget the expression in his eyes? Shock first, then a ferocious anger that colored up his face. The needlemen shrank back, whispering, goggling at her for the few moments before Van strode over, tore the scrap from her head, and ripped it in two.

You idiot girl! he bawled in her face, then whirled and stomped off with no more explanation. Later on, when she'd tried to make him explain, he turned sullen and said, *I thought you knew how to use your eyes. That color's what marks out…workers.*

She didn't understand. Who *didn't* work? On stead even children did their part as soon as they were past being milkfed, and sometimes sooner. She told him so.

You're not on stead now, he said, and would say no more.

They hadn't taken any of the yellow scraps to make the raggy dolls, though there were plenty to be had.

While Van and the needlemen looked elsewhere, though, Becca had pocketed this length of cloth and now she used it for her own purposes.

Who would ever think to stop a common worker from walking down the hall and laying hold of the supply cart? People had their own business to tend to. And if she wheeled that cart into the stairwell, that was still nothing extraordinary. It was all very simple. Once out of sight, she would plunder the cart for all the things she needed—clean cloths, clean bandages, clean pads and sponges made of gauze, and the strong-smelling bottled spirits that made water clean.

She walked primly down the hall, past the closed doors, past one that stood halfway open. She kept her eyes on the cart, not sparing so much as a glance inside the open room. Her hands closed around the steering bar. She turned the cart and started pushing it toward the stairwell.

"Where do you think you're going with that?" A dark woman in a pale green dress with the flourishing tree of Greenwoodweb embroidered over her heart stood in the doorway of the open room. If ever Becca had seen a woman out of patience, she was seeing one now. "Stupid hobays, can't work where you're wanted and can't leave off meddling where you're not. I thought I made it clear downstairs: No one takes off with my supplies until I call for you to clear them away."

"S-sorry. No one told me," Becca said.

"What, you missed the morning meeting too? I swear, you people aren't worth the bread to—" She paused, a frown plowing twin furrows between her brows. "You know, I don't remember seeing you at yesterday's meeting either. I don't remember you at all."

"I'm from another building," Becca said quickly. *If she swallows that, the worst'll happen is she sends me back. Better name one where I'm bound to find what I need.* She flicked through all the names of the Greenwoodweb buildings she knew and seized on one: "I'm from Bell."

"Are you, now?" The woman didn't look ready to swallow anything. "Then why aren't you there?"

"They sent me here." Becca shrugged away all responsibility for it. "Guess we had enough hands to help over there today."

"Since when does anyone flock to Bell? My guess is you belong over in Bell but you don't want to be there. You're not stupid after all, you're just a liar. I don't blame you. It's been hell over there lately. Why they don't just slap a chain on that beast and drop him into the sea—Ach!" She crossed her arms. "Well, that's none of my worries. You get back over there, where you belong, and we won't say any more about it."

"Yes'm." A load lifted from Becca's mind. She started back for the stairwell.

"Just a minute! *Now* where do you think you're going?" The woman caught up to her, seized her arm. "Fastest route to Bell is *that* way." She pointed down the other end of the hall to a second stairwell. "A liar *and* a slacker. I think maybe I'd better take you over myself, or I'll be tripping over you here all day."

There was nothing Becca could do but allow herself to be led. The woman took her down the stairs, out into the cold, and over to the distinctive building that was Bell.

Becca walked fast, trying to throw off the chill. She missed her heavy coat badly. *Looks like I'm turning Coop,* she thought. *I never did have anything so warm to wear back home—I didn't need it—but now I've gone soft enough to want it. I hope it's still in the stairwell when I get back.* She cast a glance back across the grounds and sighed. *No use longing over what's as good as lost. Leastways some good's come out of it: Bell's where Gilber spends most of his time, it's a place I know top to bottom. I've seen more than one of those supply carts untended in the halls, and sacks for the bed linens. If I can't lay hands on a bag, stuff it brimful, and be gone before you can say wink, I might as well give up.*

The warmth that swept over her when they stepped through the main door of Bell was a blessing. She thought that now the meddie woman would leave her and go back to her own territory. She was wrong. The woman didn't let go of Becca's arm, didn't even slow, but kept right on marching down one hall, through the reception area, down a second corridor, and up an open stairway.

"Ma'am, I can find my way from here, truly I can," Becca said, or tried to say. The meddie wasn't in the mood to listen.

"I'm going to see to it that you wind up where you belong and *stay* there." She was a young woman, healthy, and her feet raced up the stairs, Becca scrambling behind her. After several flights, the stairs ended at a heavy door banded with iron. There was a small slit cut through the reinforced wood at eye level. As well as Becca had thought she knew Bell, this was one part of the building she'd never seen until now.

A weary voice answered the meddie's insistent pounding on the door. "Now what?" Brown eyes appeared at the slit.

"I brought you a Christmas present. Open up."

The door opened a crack, the space blocked off by the most powerfully built man Becca had ever seen. He looked her over head to toe, eyes lingering on the yellow band around her arm, then said, "Thanks," and yanked her in without another word to the meddie, slamming the door in her face. As Becca followed her new guide away, she could hear the woman retreating down the stairs, holding forth on how some folk were no better bred than seedgrubs.

The man took her into a tiny room not far from the banded door. It was scarcely bigger than a cubbyhole. A glow globe shielded in a metal cage shone over rows of clipboards hanging from nails in the walls and a lone chair bolted to the floor. The man sat down and stared at Becca until she wanted to squirm. Finally he said, "You're not one of ours. What in the hell was that fool woman thinking?"

"I—" For an instant Becca flirted with the notion of confessing her deception and going back to Thirdweb in defeat. There would be other days. She could return to Greenwoodweb and try again to get the things she needed.

But I need them now. Isa needs them now. I could

ask Gilber, but I don't want him involved, and Van— Van doesn't want to know.

She remembered how Van had reacted when she'd shown him the blood-stained cloths, after she first examined Isa. They came to light when the girl disrobed. *What did you do to her?* he demanded. Then he crumpled up into tears, and Isa had to hold him, to assure him that the bright red stains were old, to insist that the fault lay with Kethy's indifferent hand for laundry. Later she'd pleaded with Becca to say no more about it.

I feel fine, and there are just a few spots, she told Becca. *It only looks like a lot because Kethy can't get all the old stains out of the cloth. Don't trouble Van over nothing. There are some things he can't accept; he isn't strong. Let him be.* The irony of fragile little Isa trying to protect her beloved seared Becca's heart.

That didn't change the fact that Isa needed clean bandages for the blood.

"I tried to explain to that woman," Becca said. "She wouldn't listen. I'm new here, I got lost, went into the wrong building and when I told her I belonged in Bell, she thought I was running away from my proper place."

"That's sensible." The man chuckled. "I'd run away myself if I could. You know, you're mighty chatty for a hobay. What's your name?"

"Rebecca." It was a common enough name to betray nothing.

"Tell you what, Rebecca, I've got break coming up soon. You stay here with my relief and I'll check out your story. Don't worry, it won't take long." He stood up and stretched his limbs. His hands touched the ceiling with ease. "Might as well get started on it now. Two minutes one way or the other won't make much difference. It's been a quiet day. Have a seat." He motioned her into the empty chair and left. She heard a series of soft clicks, then a loud one following the sound of a door swinging shut.

She wasn't about to wait for his relief or his return; she had things to do. There was still time to scare up supplies for Isa. She only waited long enough to be sure that the stairs would be clear, then she made for the door.

It was locked. The knob refused to turn under her hand and there was a palm-sized metal panel with nine numbered buttons set into the door just above it. She pushed one by way of experiment and heard the same soft click from when the man had left. She tried the knob again; no good. She tried to recall how many of those soft clicks she'd heard before, but gave it up. Every button she pushed made the same sound; she had no way to know which combination of the nine would let her escape.

"You have to know the magic."

Becca whirled around. The woman facing her looked about Kethy's age, but her face held the happy innocence of a child. She shoved past Becca to run a fingertip over the panel buttons, then she giggled. "If I could know the magic, I'd be free. They promised me castles and a handsome prince to be my alph and all the food I could ever hope to want. All I had to do was learn the magic. But I couldn't." She held out her arms. The wide sleeves of her loose white gown looked like wings. "I couldn't," she repeated, tears trickling from her eyes. "And it didn't even matter to them that I could read or that I actually know what a prince is. Was. I couldn't learn the magic, so they took me here."

"Are you...sick?" Becca asked. Suddenly she knew why the door to this floor was so heavy and locked so well. There had been a time when she'd doubted her own sanity, when the gnawing voice of doubt inside her left her terrified that she was losing her mind. On stead, the mad were turned off to fend for themselves, given over to God's mercy the same way unwanted infants were left out on the hillside. The difference was that sometimes one stead took in the castoff births of another, but no one ever came for the mad. They wandered the earth until they found their own deaths.

"I'm not sick now," the madwoman said. The tears were gone as abruptly as they'd come. "But I was after what they did to me. My whole body burned, especially there, where there's shame. They came and told me the cut didn't heal right, but I knew the truth: The stories we used to tell back home about the city were right. How do you make a meal of meat? Cut it, then throw it to the fire. Now it's just a matter of time." She pressed her palms together in an attitude of prayer. "I'm ready for the martyr's crown. I've paid the price for the pride that brought me here, out of my proper place. The Lord doesn't care if I can't learn the magic."

All at once her eyes narrowed. She gave Becca a

close look. "Is that why you're here? Did they send you to fetch me? Are they ready to eat me now?"

"No." Becca shook her head emphatically. "No, that's not it at all. I work here."

"You liar. You don't work here. Women don't work here. You're the first girl I've seen for years and years. It's always the men. Oh God!" Her hands clenched and fell as she went to her knees. "Oh God, make them stop hurting me! I'm ready to come to you, my sweet Lord! No more time of trial and sorrow, no more! Let me sleep without their breath to wake me, let me die decent or eaten up or anyhow, but let me be free!"

Becca tried to calm her. "No one's going to eat you," she said, patting the woman's back. "Let me take you back to your room and you can sleep peaceful."

The woman's eyes flashed. "Why *are* you here? Another one they lured inside to learn the magic too? Go home, girl. There's nothing here for you but blood and fire if you can't learn the magic. Did you learn it? No…no, if you did, you wouldn't be here. You'd be living in my castle, bedding my alph, breeding more princes, happily, happily, happily… No." Her hands snapped closed around Becca's wrists. "That must mean you failed too, and now they're going to— Oh no! No, they mustn't! We can't let them! Come with me, come, I'll save you!" She sprang up and dragged Becca down the hall so swiftly that the girl didn't have the chance to protest or struggle.

They ran past several other men in green, all of them built to the same muscular model as the one who'd let Becca in. "Who's that you got, Josie?" one called, grinning.

Another gave him a poke in the ribs and growled, "Who cares where she got her, that's not one of our cases. We better save her. Hey you! Josie! Let her go!" He started after them.

A third man stopped him. "Aw, let old Josie have her fun. We can pick the girl up later. Didn't you see her arm? She's just a hobay."

"A *female* hobay!" the second man spat back. "And it doesn't stop them from being human beings." He pushed the third man out of his way and ran after the two women, always shouting for Josie to let Becca go.

The madwoman's face flooded with panic. "They want you! They want to cut you up and throw you in the fire! Oh my Lord, save us Thy children in this our hour of need." She was breathing hard, panting as she ran. They were almost to the end of the hall. Josie's gaze lit on one particular door. The knob refused to turn under her hand, but this was no thick, iron-bound panel. Becca gasped as the madwoman kicked it wide open and jerked her inside.

"Get out!" Josie shouted, her back to the room, her body blocking the now open doorway. "I'll keep them off, you get out!"

"Mary Mother, don't I want to," Becca mumbled, stumbling away from the madwoman. "Just show me the way." The room was dark, the light spilling from the hall enough to show her that there were no windows and only a dead glow globe on the ceiling. This one too was boxed into a metal cage.

She was looking up at the useless light when she took another step and fell across the bed. It was no more than a mattress laid out on the floor, but there was someone on it. Becca felt a warm, breathing body under wide bands of canvas. "I'm sorry, I didn't see you," she said.

There was a sudden movement in the dark and pain fountained from her hand. She jerked it back and felt blood seep from the bitten palm. The body on the mattress snickered. "Too bad it's not the last thing you'll ever see," said Mark.

Then the man burst in past Josie. He had a light in his hand, a slim wand tipped with a miniature glow globe. He shone it full in Becca's face, then focused it on her hand. "Jesus," he said.

"Don't touch her! Don't hurt her!" Josie threw herself at the man's back. He reached behind him almost casually, grabbed her by the hair, and flung her against the doorjamb. She moaned and crawled off into the waiting arms of the other two meddies.

The man lowered the light-wand and held out his free hand to Becca. "You'd better get that treated downstairs. Mason's on door duty right now; he'll let you out. Tell him Les said so."

"Yes, sir." Becca cradled her bleeding hand. The initial shock had worn off, letting in the pain. She found it hard to keep the tears out of her voice. "Thank you, sir."

"Serve you right, bitch!" Mark shrilled at her from his pallet. "I wish it was your throat! I wish I'd killed you when I could! I wish—"

"Shut up," said Les, and with the same bland

disinterest as when he'd pitched Josie into the doorjamb, he drew back his heavily shod foot and kicked Mark in the head once, then again. The boy lay still. Les looked at Becca and smiled as if he'd done nothing more than knock a clod of earth from his boot sole. "You be on your way now," he said to her. "God be with you."

Chapter Thirteen

Brag all you like about how much lost technology we have managed to recover in these more settled times. I tell you, it will all come to nothing more than slag and fireworks. Our future lies not in what we can retrieve, but in what we have yet to explore. There are many unknown realms awaiting our studies, and the greatest of these is the study of the human mind. Without this knowledge, without knowing what causes another man to act as he does, without the thousand subtle forms of control this knowledge gives us, we would not have the leisure nor the security which we now accept so casually as our due.

We have the cities, you say. Yes, but can we hold them? Only so long as we can hold our brothers' minds. It is a calling that

demands our constant vigilance. And to
those of you who think me an alarmist, who
deem yourselves a breed apart from those
who live outside our walls, I say remember
this: Esau too was smug in his power just
before he lost his birthright for a mouthful
of food.

Gilber laid Becca's hand tenderly on the table and
unwrapped the bandages. The flesh around the
stitches was red and puckery as a newborn's face, and
there was a lot of purplish discoloration besides. He
let out a long, low whistle between his teeth. "He
did do you proud. This will be healing a long while
yet." He'd brought some medical supplies into his
little study room and now he used them to clean the
jagged damage Mark's teeth had done more than a
week ago.

"Did you find out?" Becca asked, keeping her eyes
on Gilber's nimble fingers as he rebandaged her hand.
It was pure pleasure to watch him tend to hurts the
way it was a pleasure to hear a gifted singer make
melody. He had a talent for it the way Miss Lynn did.
The good that the two of us could do together—! Becca's
heart beat a little faster at the thought. Then:
*Someday. Not now. Precious lot of good I can do now.
Not with my hand like this.* She forced herself to focus
on present matters. "Did you ask after him?"

"Only because you sent me," Gilber told her. "After
what he did to you, I couldn't begin to care what

becomes of Mark. And your hurt's less than nothing next to what he did to Kaith."

"Kaith…" Becca remembered the meddie Mark had killed, the one whose tranquilizer gun had jammed. There was that Highlandweb guard too, the one who'd been taken bleeding from the siege of Mark's stead. Despite all that the meddies had done for him, he had died in the tram on the way back to Coop. His death was the wild boy's work as well. "What did you find out?"

Gilber made an obstinate face. "I don't see why you should care. You didn't ask after Virgie this much."

"And I don't see why you won't answer my question," Becca responded. "Gilber, if you knew our Scripture you'd understand. The Lord taught us we're to forgive those who trespass against us."

"The way you forgave Adonijah?" His challenge was uncommonly sharp.

"That's different," she said, whether that was what her heart believed or not. "If it was just his offense against me, I might've come to forgive him that, given time. But all else he's done…" The tally of Adonijah's evil deeds passed before her mind's eye: Her sire's death by trickery, the winnowing in its wake, how he'd used little Rusha for his rough pleasure, the calmly ruthless way he'd tried to hunt out Becca's infant sister for slaughter, all these added to how he'd raped her in the very room where her sire's corpse lay waiting on burial. "It's gone past my portion to forgive," she finished.

"You'll have to excuse me from swallowing that whole," Gilber said bitterly. "It's just that I can't seem to remember your folk forgiving my people for being alive. Now here's this boy who's more wild beast than human, he's killed more than one grown man, he's bound hand and foot to keep him from doing more, he still manages to tear open your hand with his teeth, and all you can think of is taking him to your bosom and *forgiving* him. Why not try teaching a serpent to grow legs and—?"

"He's dead, isn't he?"

Gilber's mouth set to a razor's slice. At first he refused to say anything, then he looked away from her and said, "Yes."

"How did it happen?"

"Is knowing that going to make things any different?"

She could be just as obstinate as he; more so. "I want to know."

"I didn't even want you to know he was dead. He never had an easy life, heaven witness, and that made his mind all twisty, but he was still just a boy."

"That's a new tune," she said, looking at him askance. "One breath you say that, the one before you're talking about him like he was a wild animal. And you fault me and my folk for having two tongues!"

"Two tongues, one for each truth." Gilber leaned his elbows on the table and rubbed tired eyes. "Before I came here, I never would have thought I could see things like that. Half my heart's torn with pity for that child, and the other half—well, I could never rejoice over any death, but there's some I don't mind too much. Two truths…" His hands dropped heavily.

"When I was home, I could tell true from false without troubling my soul this way, but here—! This place changes people, Becca. I can hardly wait until our business here's done and we can get gone. Things are almost settled for me—the meddies showed me what ails my tribe and they're giving me the answer for it. What about you?"

Becca moved her hand experimentally. Despite how often she'd had the wound rebandaged, how carefully she'd looked after keeping it clean, it still hurt powerful bad, and there were times it felt like someone had shut it in an oven. "I asked Eleazar about my case today," she said, trying to get her mind off the pain. "He could only tell me what news trickled down to him from the webmaster's office."

"Don't they trust each other in that web? Or is it because he was only adopted in?"

"It's not that." She was a little annoyed with Gilber for drawing Eleazar's status within Thirdweb into question. "They don't make those distinctions. But he *was* born on Wiserways, even if he's cut off all contact years since, and Paul *was* his sire. It's because of what people *might* say about such things that he's kept out of the case. A justice can't take a personal interest. The law stays pure."

"What could he tell you, then?"

"Not much. No one who'll speak with him about it seems to be connected with the case. One says they've sent Highlandwebbers out to fetch Adonijah here for trial, another claims he's heard that an off-season trading party's gone to Wiserways to weigh evidence first." She held her hands out, palms up, to show how empty they were of solid answers.

Gilber took a deep breath. "I guess it doesn't matter all that much. We couldn't leave here until the spring anyhow. If there wasn't that much to live off coming here, there's just a hard rind and nothing under it out there now. And there's going to be a lot more of us to—"

"If it doesn't matter, then why'd you bother asking? I've got better ways to waste my time!" Becca's hand throbbed with pain and heat. It was making her testier than she cared to admit. "When I ask something, it's because the answer does matter to me. You never did tell me how Mark died."

"They killed him." Gilber was taut as stretched rawhide. He looked closely at Becca. "You're not surprised."

"I told you what I saw that man do to him," she said. "He'd've finished the work then, if I hadn't been there."

"Oh, you wouldn't have stopped him, not if he'd made up his mind. There's a certain kind of meddie works the upstairs ward in Bell. They turn it into their own private world. Other Greens don't try to interfere for fear they'd be sent up there and told *See if you can do better.* When you've got a job no one else wants to do, no one meddles with how you choose to do it."

"Why do they keep them alive at all?" Becca asked. "The crazy ones? They're no use to anyone, not even themselves."

Gilber's expression went from startlement to cool distaste at her words. "Heaven be praised for holding my tongue. I was going to call you heartless, but you can't be blamed for what they raised you to be." Blame or no blame, his voice let her know how loathsome she'd made herself in his eyes. Though there was a table between them, he still edged his chair back a bit farther from her, arms wrapped tight around his own body.

Her wounded hand ached unmercifully. She was tired of Gilber and his judgments, his piety, his thousand laws against pollutions she didn't believe existed. She rose from the table and said, "When I ask why do *they* keep the mad alive, that's what I mean: *They*. Coopfolk. You include me with them without my leave if you like, Gilber Livvy. Every man's entitled to his own stupidity."

She saw his body slacken even as the shame came into his eyes. "Becca, I'm sorry, I thought—" Her own pain dwindled to an ember beside the agony she saw searing through his soul. His eyes blinked rapidly, fluttering out a sudden gush of tears. He threw himself forward, hands pressed to his face with such force she was sure the nails must draw blood. His voice clawed its way free of his chest in a tortured prayer.

"Lord, what's happening to me? Be my witness, I never would speak so to this sweet woman outside these walls. Night and day I dwell among an alien race, a people whose ways aren't mine. But where's my choice in it? My tribe needs their knowledge. They're the ones who told me how we've lived in solitude too long, bred back into our own blood until the children come forth born lessened in mind and body. There are too few of us now, and if our breedings continue this way—" He shuddered with a dry sob. "What am I to do? What can I do but let the city have my soul, if it means the saving of our children?"

Becca's chair scraped back sharply. She was on her feet, reaching for him across the table with her good hand. She grasped his shoulder firmly and shook him like a washrag. "Gilber Livvy, you stop that! Don't you dare crumble away on me! If your Lord's the same one as spoke to Moses and to John, you're shaming Him. His help's for those who can take it. I've witnessed your strength, so no use trying to hide it from me now. What's ailing you, that you let a woman's crotchets tear you up this way? I can't help it if I've got a barbed tongue: I'm hurting, and it makes me meaner than winter." She got her hand under his chin and made him look her in the eye. "Coop can't change you more than you let it." She spoke with all the courage of one who needed to borrow belief in her own words.

Gilber looked at her, his breath shaky. "My Judith," he said at last. "A woman of virtue, sure enough, and me just a sorry excuse for a man."

"No more of that, I said!" Becca held up a warning finger.

"No more," he agreed. "You're hurting and I'm weary: It doesn't take much more than that to bring down the strongest folk. And we're both of us still finding our way in the dark, as far as city ways go."

"That's not so and you know it," she told him. "Why, you've fit in so well here, it's like you were born to the Greens."

He shook his head. "I've laid hold of a pebble, but the mountain's still a mystery. For every rule I know, there's a dozen I haven't heard of; maybe a score! And those are just the laws. As for ever hoping to learn all the unwritten rules, the customs, the usages—" He sighed, then clasped her hand and brought it to his lips for a lingering kiss. "You be my strength and I'll be yours. We'll fight free of this place."

Becca settled back down into her place. "It is a puzzlement, the city," she admitted. "So many ways they're like stead, but the differences—! There are times I think I'll never fathom it, then there's others when I'm sure that if I could only figure out the why of one thing—just one!—all the rest would come clear."

"Like the way they treat the mad?" Gilber provided. "I don't know if that'll be your key, love, but I can give it to you. There aren't all that many cases in the upstairs ward at Bell. A person's got to be far gone before they'll admit him, a danger to himself and his web. It's because those cases are so rare that they're kept on. Madness like that isn't something you see every day."

"So they keep them alive for study?"

"That'd be my guess."

Becca lowered her eyes. "The way they kept Mark."

"They were done with him. He wouldn't give himself over quietly to the visitors, tried to kill anyone got near him. In the end, they gave up on him. Maybe they didn't tell the keepers to kill him, but they let it be known how little it mattered what became of him. I wish I'd known before. Maybe I could've taken him away from—"

"Visitors?" Becca broke in.

"The ones who came to study him, the ones who come to examine any case here that's out of the ordinary. It's not just the meddies and the sick who come to Greenwoodweb," Gilber said. "I've seen whole groups of other Coopfolk walking through, all wearing a badge I didn't know. I asked one of my friends here who they were and he told me they hailed from Ravenweb, but when I asked what that meant he shut up tight. I had to gather crumbs. Whatever else Ravenwebbers do, they come here to study the mad and—" He hesitated.

"And?" Becca prompted.

"When I first got here, three of them came to talk to me. They asked me a lot of questions about my tribe and our ways."

"You didn't tell them anything, did you? Oh, Gilber!" Once more Becca felt the anguish she'd first tasted when Gilber Livvy had told her how steadfolk had come hunting Jews in years past. They'd called it *going to Moriah* and they made it into a fine game for young men to play until the quarry started fighting back.

"Stay easy in your mind, love, I told them everything but where we dwell."

Becca felt her mind blossom with the darkness of

cold suspicion. "That's the easiest of all for them to find out. When you leave Coop come spring, all they'll need to do is follow you home."

To her surprise, Gilber grinned. "I pity them if they try. My people will leave them to seed the wasteland if they do."

"But your people don't even know they're coming!"

"Not my people back in the mountains; my new folk." Suddenly he was all happiness. He sprang to his feet and caught her lips with one quick kiss. "*Our* new folk, angel!" He stretched his arms to heaven. "Praise be to *H'shem*, I went forth a solitary man and I return a great nation!" He danced around the table, taking her by the hand. "It's time you met them, Becca. It's time you saw our people, and it's past time they saw you."

She had a hundred questions on her lips. They all blew away in the wake of Gilber's high spirits. He ran with the urgency of a man trying to outdistance a ghost. She too felt the phantom Mark's hot eyes and cold breath beating down on the back of her neck and matched Gilber's speed with her own.

He raced her through the halls and down a stairway that took them into the underground reaches of Greenwoodweb. Becca hardly had the chance to note which way he led her through dimly lit passageways where huge tubes hissed above her head and others gurgled with the sound of rushing water. Openings dark and light gaped off to either side in a random pattern. Gilber always seemed to know which turning to take without a moment's uncertainty, as though this were a route he'd taken scores of times before.

They reached more stairs, and Gilber urged her to climb three flights of these. They came up into a space no bigger than a six-bedded ward room. It was bare of all furnishing, all signs of life, though when Becca took a breath she could swear she smelled something cooking.

"Here we are," Gilber said, squeezing her good hand gently. He took her across the room to where a sturdy ladder stood propped against a square opening in the ceiling. At the foot of the ladder he cupped one hand to his mouth and hollered up, *"D'va hasehr v'gan hadon!"*

And from above a timid voice replied, *"V—v'atz eelet b—b—* Oh Lord, I forget!" This confession was followed by the sound of slaps, smacks, and a general scuffle overhead, blended with other voices generously showering the first speaker with every low name Becca had ever heard and a few that were new to her.

Funny, she thought. *They're calling him all sorts of vileness, but they don't sound angry; they sound…joyful?* She listened more closely. Yes, there was only gladness under all that raillery, the way loving sibs might bandy harsh words with one another and never mean a breath of it.

For his part, Gilber was chuckling and shaking his head. "Poor Melky. He does have a mind like a fishnet, but he's a good worker. Come on, they know we're friends." He started up the ladder.

Becca had a hard time following him. Her hurt hand protested when she tried to use it on the ladder. She gave thanks that city-made skirts were shorter than stead garb. If she'd had to deal with that hand and the cumbersome clothes she'd worn back home, climbing the ladder would have been an impossibility instead of a trial. At last she reached the top and stuck her head through the opening.

"There she is, my friends." Gilber sat on the floor among a group of young people, male and female, and waved at Becca. "I promised you'd see her and I kept my word."

The group stared at Becca as if they shared one set of eyes among them. Becca felt the weight of their gaze pushing her back down the ladder. Her first impulse was to flee, but she knew she'd never be able to find her way back by the route Gilber had brought her, and she'd seen neither door nor window in the chamber below. Here there were windows, though the press of people blocked them from her.

Gilber wouldn't bring me into peril, she decided, and clambered the rest of the way into the upper room.

Almost immediately two of the youngsters scurried forward to help her clear of the trapdoor opening. "You're welcome, lady," said the girl. She had a plain face, fragile as a blown eggshell, and black hair cut to a prickly skull-hugging fuzz. Like all the rest of them, her clothing was yellow as the paper flower Van had once given Becca to wear.

"More than welcome," the boy said. He tried to press her hand to his brow, but he took hold of the bandaged one. Becca cried out with pain. The boy jumped back as though he'd uncovered his mother's nakedness, then cowered in a shivering knot at her feet. "Oh Lord, forgive me! What'd I do?"

"Sher, you fool!" The girl slapped his back. "Couldn't you see the binding, or did you just grab her all anyhow?"

Sher looked up, a beast afraid of a beating. "Thought it was maybe a glove," he said, nodding toward Becca's bandaged hand. "Where I work, we don't see too many wounds bound up. If a tunnel wall takes a dislike to you, it does the job thoroughly. No one's saved."

"No one's worth saving, you mean," another boy piped up from the crowd surrounding Gilber. Becca had left sibs his size behind who still hung close to their mothers. " 'Specially for the tunnels. They don't got to train us much to dig; it's cheaper to bring in new lives than to save the old. Bandages don't come cheaper than hobays."

"*Helem.*" Gilber's voice fell like a clap of thunder. "Helem, what did I teach you?"

The boy hung his head. "Not to use that word," he said. "Not to call ourselves by it because it's shameful."

"Not that," Gilber said more kindly. "Not shameful to you, but shameful to them. You're my people now, and there's no shame can touch you."

A sharp laugh, acid on the tongue, rang out in the little room. A girl wearing yellow draperies so very like Isa's stood up and pulled back the veil covering her flame-red hair. "We'll be your people once we've left these walls, not before. That's when we'll be free of shame." A chorus of assenting murmurs rose up from the crowd.

"You're wrong, Yemina," Gilber said in that soft

voice of his, a fire's warmth after bitter winds. "You became my people from the moment the Greens brought you to me and you gave your consent to be taught, trained, and taken back to my tribe. From that moment, child. Not after you learned reading or prayer or the law, but the instant you agreed to leave your old lives behind, that was when you became my people."

Yemina laughed again. "What do you know of our old lives, Abba? What do you know of our shame?" She shot a hard look at Becca. "What do *you* know of it, lady? Not much, or you wouldn't be looking at me so kindly. Unless he's kept you sheltered? He could, if that's his will. Abba holds the promise of our lives, our joy, our freedom in his hands; there's no questioning his power."

"Just his knowledge?" Becca said. She shook her head. "I know what you are. I've been here long enough to know what it means for a soul to wear yellow. You're hobays, *workers*."

"A soul... They try to make it seep into our souls, but some of us won't let them. Workers, are we?" Yemina's expression could chill bones to ice. "Whoever told you that—" She clenched her fists, then seized the front of her dainty robes and tore them wide apart. The flimsy material ripped away to show heavily bruised skin, small breasts scarred with many burnings, the traces of nails and teeth and blades branded deep into flesh too pale ever to have seen the sun.

"*This* is what we are!" she shouted, cupping one breast as if to give an infant suck. "We're what they cast aside. We're what they throw away. We're what they feed just enough so they can use us any way they will. *Any* way! We're the births not good enough for the elics and the webs. Some of us are the gleanings of the stead hills where they set out infants for their demon King. And because they don't actually set the knife to our throats, they can pretend they walk in godliness, in mercy. In *mercy*." The word curled like a snake. "If we die, we die; there are always plenty of others to take our place. They name us *hobays* not because it's close enough to what they first called us, the honest name for what we are. Do you know what that is, lady? Does even Abba know?"

Gilber crept near to put his arms around the girl, to try to settle her shredded draperies so that they would cover her nakedness. "Hush, Yemina. Hush, child. That's all done with now."

She flung away from him, weeping without tears. "*Whorebabies!*" she shrieked. The word reverberated through the doorless room. "*Whorebabies!*" She staggered back a step and collapsed in a swirl of yellow cloth at Becca's feet.

Chapter Fourteen

Sleep, my little one,
Sleep, my pretty one,
Here in your mother's arms.
Peace, my little one,
Peace, my pretty one,
Father will keep you from harm.

Becca dreamed of Yemina and the tower where the whorebabies dwelled for days after. They weren't pleasant dreams, but they never rose to spread black nightmare wings over her spirit the way her dreams of Solomon's death had done. She never awoke screaming, though many times she found her pillow wet with tears. Her sleep was restless, leaving her worn instead of refreshed.

Eleazar remarked on this new change in her. Eleazar

remarked on everything. "You'd better go over to Greenwoodweb today," he told her at the breakfast table. They had it all to themselves. Greenwoodweb didn't admit visitors until midmorning, and she never went to see Isa before noon. The other members of Carsonelic usually bolted down their food irreverently and took off about their business at an early hour, but never Eleazar. She wondered why he was different, with no pressing business to demand his attention.

When will you see that you're all his business now? came the knowing whisper.

"Not today," she told him. "Yesterday, when I saw Gilber, he told me he'd be busy."

"I didn't mean you should go there to see him. I meant you should go there to be *seen*." Eleazar sipped his juice. "You look ill, Becca. How's your hand doing?"

"All right," she lied. She tucked it under the napkin in her lap. The searing pain had settled into a dull, intense throbbing that refused to be stilled, day or night. The wound itself had closed, but there was an ugly yellow swelling around the stitches. The last time Gilber had rewrapped it, he'd used an ointment compounded from the last of the dried herbs in his traveling kit. *I don't know if these are still potent,* he'd said. Judging from the pain that assailed her, Becca would say no, they were done. Still, when he asked if they'd worked, she smiled and lied through her teeth, saying she felt fine. When he offered to fetch some of Greenwoodweb's supplies to treat the wound, she startled him so with the fierceness of her objection that he said no more about it.

"I'm not busy today, even if your friend Gilber Livvy is." Eleazar wiped his mouth with a fine cloth napkin and stood up. "I could take you over there."

"If you need something to be busy with, I wish you'd try finding out what's become of my case," Becca snapped.

"Now Becca, you know I can't touch that."

"No, but you could put your ear to the ground some. I know you do that when it suits you. It's been *months*, Eleazar! By the time they bring Adonijah to judgment, his half year's grace will be done and a new man will come to challenge him for Wiserways. He's blind; he'll die and there'll be another winnowing when there shouldn't even have been the first!"

"I thought you wanted him dead."

"I want him to go into the earth alone. Prayerful Hill doesn't need any fresh little bones to feed on." She thought of her sib Rusha, so young, dragged unwilling to Adonijah's bed. A taking woman seldom left a man without his seed rooted firm in her belly. Rusha had a fond, soft heart for babes, so tender that maybe she could gather some comfort from a child, even if it came of Adonijah's forced begetting. But a new alph meant she'd bear the babe only to see it taken from her and given up to the Lord King. *She'd run mad*, Becca thought.

"Prayerful Hill," Eleazar repeated with a fastidious shudder. "Of all the things I left behind me, that's one I miss least. What a monument to horror."

"Other Coopfolk feel the same?" Becca asked cannily.

"What a question! Of course we do."

"Then why not send out word to Grange, tell all your allied steads to leave off such doings?"

"And stand opposed to the Lord King Herod Himself?" Eleazar chuckled. "You go home and try it. Tell them that all their holy worship's been murder. See how they reward you for it."

"I'm just one girl. If Coop made a stand—"

"Coop has better things to do than stir up trouble we don't need." He stalled toward the doorway, saying, "Look after yourself, then, if you don't want my help. But don't be a fool about it." And he was gone.

A fool... Becca brought her injured hand out from under her napkin and laid it on the table. The pain mocked her, ebbing just enough to give her false hope before surging back with renewed force. *I ought to let the meddies see this. They dressed it first, then I had Gilber tend it after. It hurts so much, maybe I should— but what if there's something truly wrong with it? What if it's something beyond their lore to mend?* She shivered.

She remembered what had happened to her infant sister Shifra, when the babe's scurrier-bit foot was too far gone to save. What if the meddies took one look at her hurt now and decreed that it couldn't be saved either? They'd cut it off and be done. Becca couldn't face that possibility. She'd put it off, if she could, live with the pain. She wouldn't even let Gilber treat it with anything save the healer's kit he'd brought with him from the outs, afraid that if he went seeking Greenwoodweb supplies for the job, the meddies would take notice, ask him what was going on, and come to see for themselves. And once they say her hand… Becca's heart chilled with dread. She knew she wasn't thinking rationally about it, but try as she might, she couldn't force herself to see sense; not with the specter of Shifra's fate before her.

Someone better mend it, came the voice that was never far from her. *Someone soon, for Isa's sake. It's that useless now, it might as well be cut off. I never did hear tell of any midwife using just one hand to bring a babe to birth.*

"Isa…" Becca closed her eyes against the pain and saw Van's sweetheart, so fragile, so brave. The girl had been in good spirits the last time she'd seen her. *Look what Van brought us,* she'd said, and showed Becca a box full of clean cloth bandages and other medical supplies, proud as if it were the Wise Men's gifts of gold, frankincense, and bread.

He's a smart boy, Becca thought. *He knew that we'd need to help look after her without anyone saying a word. We sheltered him for nothing, and I got my hand tore open for nothing too.*

A fresh spasm of pain made her drive her teeth into her lower lip. She refused to cry out. Eleazar had left the room, but she'd wager he hadn't gone too far. Likely he'd taken up a watch post where he could know at once if she left Thirdweb tower. As far as she could tell, his spying kept itself to her comings and goings but not her destinations. She was grateful for that.

Even if he did keep closer vigil on me, Van would find a way to throw him off when we visit Isa. Yes, he's a wise one, Van.

It was then that she knew what she must do.

❦ ❦

Gilber Livvy took Becca into his arms and held her close. "Don't blame yourself, love. You did what's right, bringing me here."

She breathed in his scent. There was no doubt about it any more: The last trace of pineywood had seeped away, along with the strong, pleasing odor of his travel leathers. Now he smelled the same as every other man who lived within Coop walls, except for the tang of medicines and soap that hung about him and the meddies. "I'm sorry," she repeated for what felt like the fiftieth time. "I didn't want to involve you with this."

"What else could you do? You'll be no help to Isa when her time comes, only one hand."

"I should've asked Kethy, seen what she could do to help." Becca pressed her lips to Gilber's neck, clung to him like a last hope. "If you're caught here, what's to become of those ho—whorebabies?" It was hard for her to remember not to call Gilber's new tribe by the name the Coopfolk used, the name the whorebabies themselves scorned and despised.

"We've been over that. Van's covered our tracks along with his. Look here at what he just gave me." He distanced himself from her just enough to draw a gleaming yellow card from the breast pocket of his shirt. "Like you said, he's a smart boy. Besides, I owe him. I confess, I was worried with how poorly your wound was coming along, but he healed you."

"Him?"

"Not hands-on, I don't mean that, but he set things so that you got what you needed to cure your hurt. The healing dose they gave him, no questions asked, why, it works like nothing I've ever seen!"

"It does work a blessing," Becca admitted, holding up her bandaged hand between them. It no longer ached or pounded with pain, and her nights had won free of evil dreams. She gave Gilber a sheepish look. "I'm sorry I was such a coward about it, but I was feared they'd take one look at my hand and say it had to be—"

"Hush." Gilber laid his finger to her lips. "No need to speak of it any more. You're my brave girl and no coward. Anyhow, it all worked out for the best: That stuff they gave Van, it's nothing I could've got you. I didn't have a clue such a thing even existed, never mind all the work I've done at Greenwoodweb."

"I don't see why it's not common knowledge, there for anyone who needs it."

"Well, I did wonder that myself," Gilber said. "I even asked Van about it and he said, 'Rank has its privileges.' Good enough words as any to explain why Greenwoodweb holds back some of its lore for webmasters only."

"Webmasters and their heirs," Becca added. She grew thoughtful. "Now that my hand's healing, I can tend to Isa without you. You needn't—"

"Or I could tend her alone." Gilber waved the

yellow card under her nose. "With this, I can come and go around here easier than you."

"I wish you'd—"

"No. It's settled."

He sounded less like the Gilber who'd brought her through the wilderness and more like all the other men she'd known. *All save Jamie,* she thought. *And who knows how he might've changed toward me if he'd lived?*

She broke from him reluctantly and went to the window. Pulling the green and orange curtain aside, she looked down at the streets of the Flower Market. Evening was coming on, sauntering lazily along byways where the true dark lay hid behind dead gray doors. The first clients were already strolling the sidewalks, laughing and chatting, trading jokes.

She saw a boy barely out of childhood walk by in the company of three older men. He tossed his bright yellow pass of favor or reward from hand to hand, strutting out as if he were a familiar face on these streets. He paused beneath Becca's window and looked up. His cocky smile wavered the instant he realized that a woman was looking back at him. In the instant their eyes met, Becca saw desire war with fear in his eyes. He opened his mouth as if to say something to her, but before he could speak, his companions surrounded him. One pointed to the closed door, whispering in his ear. The shame that had closed Peony Web was common knowledge. The boy's face paled; he let himself be hustled away.

"What are you doing? You get away from there!" Kethy jerked Becca back into the room. The striped curtain fluttered down to veil the window. "What, you think we need more trouble than we got now?"

"Let her be, Kethy," Gilber said, touching the woman's arm. "She didn't mean any harm."

She snorted. "Huh! Your kind never do. Same way Van never meant any harm. Lord mark me, if I'd had the sight to see the future, I never would've let that boy into Peony Web that first night!" Abruptly she realized that anger had made her raise her voice. She cast a furtive glance toward the closed door leading to Isa's room.

Gilber never could bear to see another soul so frozen with fear. "I don't think he heard you."

"No, likely not," the woman murmured. "When he's with her, she's all he hears and all he sees." She folded her hands and pressed them to her bosom where they clutched soiled draperies that had once been fine to see. "What's to become of me when she dies?"

"We don't know that's what will happen, Kethy." Gilber tried to give her a comforting hug. She stiff-armed him away.

"Don't lie to me, Jew-boy. My mama always lessoned us that it was Jew lies killed our Lord Jesus, but she was wrong about near everything else. Don't make me start believing she got *that* right. You came, you saw her, and now you want to try telling me she's going to live through birthing that child?"

Gilber's face colored up. "You want the truth? It'll be a miracle if she survives the birth. It'll be a bigger one if she carries to term at all." He sank into the rump-sprung chair in the corner. "Those bones...those miserable little bones."

Becca rounded fiercely on the woman. "If you're so keen for truth, why don't you tell Van what we all know? That Isa's sure to die, and the babe more than likely with her."

"That's one truth he'll know soon enough," Kethy replied calmly. "Like I said, we don't need to go borrowing trouble ahead of time. Besides, long as we're speaking plain, why do you even bother coming 'round here if you're so sure she's doomed? Unless you're as feared of Van as I am."

"I'm not afraid of him," Becca said.

"More lies. He's Third, Third's law, and law's more feared than the Lord King's sword inside these walls." Her fingers worked the edge of her veil. "There've been nights I lie awake thinking how maybe I should just kill him and be done, fix it so I don't have him at my back, threatening what he'll do to me if Isa dies. If! There's a laugh. I could do it. I could slip a little blade right in under his skull when he's in there with her and he'd never notice he was dead 'til the worms bit his eyes. Maybe I could get away with it— hide the body, get it elsewhere, or maybe just leave it here in these rooms and get away myself, out of the city, back to the steadlands. But then I remember that there's nothing for me out there anymore. Even could I find a stead would take me, they'd cast me out as soon as they learned I'm no use as a bearing woman. If the wives didn't kill me first."

Becca too tried to put a comforting arm around the

woman, and again Kethy pulled away. The girl sighed.
"You're feared for nothing," she said. "Van's changed.
See Gilber there? He was the one ran him and Isa to
ground when they tried escaping the city. By rights
Van should hate him worse than poison, and he did,
but now—now there's truce between them. Van is
Third and Third is law, but Van's seen how far the
law can go and it's marked his soul."

"Since when do webmasters have souls?" Kethy
asked, a jest without mirth behind it.

"If he didn't have a soul, would he have come to
love Isa?" Becca countered. "Even if she was his first,
she was just flesh for his use. He could've had her
and forgotten her, gone on to a dozen others like her."

"Wish he had," Kethy mumbled. "I'd still be
running a working web if he had, not living on his
charity, and my girls—" For the first time since Becca
had known her, there were tears on Kethy's cheeks.
"Dear lady Mary, what've they done with my poor
motherless girls? Who's working them and how hard
and are they ever shown any mercy? When they
worked here, I saw to it that no man went in to them
who ever used a woman for pain. It wasn't Coop law,
but it was my rule and I had my ways to enforce it. I
had to. I was all the shield those babies had and they
were all the daughters I'll ever know."

She knuckled away the teardrops and glared at
Becca as if she bore all the world's blame. "He
promised me he'd find them, use his influence to
gather them all back, open up Peony Web again once
his baby's born. I'm to keep the child here, hidden
safe, until he's webmaster and can adopt it into Third.

But what's going to happen to my girls if the baby's never born, what happens when Isa dies? God knows she's ready for death. These past weeks it's been Van's will alone that's kept her living. All that blood—"

Gilber hauled himself out of the battered chair. "Kethy, don't fear anymore. Not for yourself, not for your girls. Becca's told you true: Van's changed. He's had a taste of vengeance and it almost burned the tongue from his mouth. He's had to face what law can do to lives. My folk live by law, so I know how it can be a better, a worse weapon than any gun. That's one lesson Van's finally learned. If Isa and the baby don't live through what's to come, he won't hold it to your account."

"Small mercies." Kethy bit off the words. "So he'll let me live, so what? How will I live? He'll turn his back on me, on my girls, on all the old promises. Cityfolk can turn you to glass with their eyes and never see you again."

"If that happens, you'll come with me." Gilber was set in his mind. "I'll tell the folk at Greenwoodweb I want you and your girls—you'll have to name 'em, though, so we can gather them in. You'll have to study with the rest, learn our faith, take up a skill my tribe can use, but as long as you're willing to travel all the way to the mountains—"

"What?" The woman's face tightened with suspicion.

"Gilber's tribe needs to be renewed," Becca provided. "Too few of them left, too few breeding. Then too many of their children are born different, never do come into their full strength or wits."

"The Lord King must rejoice in you, to choose so many," Kethy said to Gilber, each word twisted around a bitter core.

"We don't serve your Lord King," he answered her quietly. "Every birth *H'shem* gives to us we raise up in the light of the law. But that doesn't change the fact we need healthier births. If you and your girls can come with us, you'll find a true welcome and you'll end your days among us as honored wives and mothers of children, happy in your homes."

"Mothers of children..." Kethy's body began to shake. A series of short, throaty, gasping sounds rattled out of her chest. Becca couldn't tell if they were laughter or sobs. Then the woman cast her head back, lips pulled wide in a corpse's grin, and cried out, *"Mothers of children!"* before she staggered into Isa's room and slammed the door.

Becca and Gilber looked at one another, dumbstruck. "What did I say?" Gilber finally managed to ask. "Did she think I was telling her more lies?" Becca only shook her head.

Isa's door opened and Van emerged. "Kethy wants me to speak with you, Gilber," he said. His face looked nigh bloodless and there were shadows between his eyes and around his mouth that would deepen to lines of care as he aged.

"What for? He didn't say anything to her that could give offense," Becca protested. "All he did was say he'd take her and her girls back home with him when he leaves Coop, if he can."

"It was an honest offer," Gilber put in. "Van, you can smooth the way for that, can't you?

Greenwoodweb's been generous to me, giving me so many souls to renew my tribe, so what's a few more?"

"A few? Do you know how many girls there were in Peony Web before it closed?" Van asked, wearing weariness like a cloak.

"Too many to come with us? So that's it. Kethy couldn't bear the thought of leaving some behind. That, else she's afraid that all of them would be a burden on the land. Oh Van, I've got to tell her she's wrong! My friends in Greenwood told me I've been promised new seed and tools to bring home besides the new blood. It's to be a gesture of goodwill from Coop to my people, part payment for past harms. When my boys aren't studying our faith with me, they're off learning ways to make the land yield richer crops. When we go back to the mountains, they'll clear new plots and show my tribe how to get more from what land we've already cleared. No one's going to hunger, no one's to be turned away. Kethy's got to know—"

He started forward, but Van blocked his way. "It doesn't matter whether there were five girls or five hundred in Peony Web," he said. "There's no hope for any of them to give your tribe new life. No more hope than there ever was for Isa."

Van laughed to see the way Gilber's jaw dropped. "What's wrong, Gilber?" he asked. "Haven't you ever seen a fool before?"

Later Becca could never remember whether she first saw the bloodstains on Van's clothing or heard Isa's screams.

Chapter Fifteen

> One stone, two stones by the sea:
> What will your pretty daughter be?
> Three stones, four stones by the tide:
> Saint or sinner, beast or bride?
> Five stones, six stones by the shore:
> Mother, monster, healer, whore?
> Seven stones beneath the water:
> Best to never have a daughter.

As soon as Becca was clear of the Flower Market, she put the wind beneath her feet and ran. She left her breath behind, caught up in the cage of Isa's screams, frozen behind Gilber's horrified eyes, fettered by the awful truths Kethy had spoken and Van had confirmed.

No, no, it's not possible, not now, not that, not after we've come so far! Denial battered at her brain, demanded entry, but was refused. The facts were too cold to be moved or even softened. *It can't be true!* But it could; it was.

Do you know what a hobay is, Gilber Livvy? Van's eyes, so empty of hope, so full of pain.

Whorebaby. Call them whorebabies. They hate the other name.

I can call them anything I choose or they choose. It won't change what they are. It won't change what they can never be.

And Kethy's voice, rising to a plaintive wail: *Mothers of children! All my little girls, harvested from the hills, brought into the city. I told myself that any life's better than none. No one counted how many babies I saved from the Lord King's cursed sword. The traders I traveled with had other things on their minds. So long as I kept the infants fed and clean and quiet, they didn't bother keeping count. That was how I could sneak so many into the city creches, let them be raised up whole, but the others—*

Hush, Kethy. Van held out his hands, willing to take her sorrow to himself, but Kethy wouldn't hush.

I was pretty then. Not pretty like Isa—I wasn't born to be a Flower Market bloom—but that was all right. The traders couldn't take one of the snap-bones with them; she'd never survive. When they wanted a woman along for their use out on long journeys, I was the one they chose. I built up my web from the outcast daughters of the steads, I filled the creches with their sons, but I couldn't save them all. And when I wasn't pretty enough for the traders to take along anymore, my saving days were done. The hills kept what the hills were given.

She looked at Gilber. *Isa was one of the last I gathered in. I was there when the meddies cut her, holding that sweet little baby to my breast same as if she'd been born mine. They cut all the girls so that they don't need to wait for once or twice a year to take on a man. Cut them so that there's always enough women for any male in this city, any time he wants.*

Flower Market girls, Gilber said, his voice as dull as his eyes. *They're the only ones get cut that way; the only ones who need to be. Not all the girls they gave me are Flower Market girls.* His face was wood.

Kethy shook her head. *Only the finest come to the Flower Market, but there's plenty of others cut the same. All the hobays.*

Whorebabies. The word rasped and broke on Gilber's lips. *You've taken everything else from them, at least give them their chosen name.*

The woman wasn't listening, deafened to all but her cadenced confession. *They took the girls I couldn't slip into the creches and they cut them. They took the boys and raised them up to wear the yellow cloth and to do the work surest to devour lives. Then they set aside the ones they wanted for the Flower Market, the pretty ones like Isa. I was there to make sure she took the drink that made her bones grow so fine. Frail as glass needles, those bones, but they did make her beautiful, like nothing human.*

Beautiful. Gilber was Kethy's echo. *Like nothing human. I guess that's what pleases you cityfolk. Nothing human can escape your walls and lead a true life.*

Esther M. Friesner

Isa's shriek made them all turn, startled. Van dashed back into her chamber, Becca with him. Isa lay drenched in sweat on a mattress on the floor. Legs like peeled white sticks were drawn up and spread wide beneath the sheet. Becca used her good hand to raise the drape and see. The scar of the old cutting had gone a deep purplish red, wet with new blood.

So that's it, Becca murmured, looking at the scar. *I wondered where it came from. I wondered why she was so slack there.* She got up and fetched her kit from an ancient chest of drawers near the door, ordered Van to fetch her some hot water. The herbs were already pounded to a fine powder; she didn't need but the one hand to mix up the draught that would ease Isa's pain. It was one of the first recipes Miss Lynn had taught her in the lost days when her future had been stead and Jamie and herbwifery. When Gilber came in to offer his help, Becca dismissed him so curtly he stared at her as if she'd turned into a stranger, but he went.

After the girl drank down Becca's brew and drifted into restless sleep, Van said, *When she told me she was carrying my child, I thought at first that she was lying. When they cut the girls, even if they do conceive there's nothing there to hold the babe inside once it's past a certain size. I don't know how it happened that this child took hold. Perhaps there was something in the way her cutting scarred over on the inside— Once I knew she wasn't lying about the baby, I started lying to myself. I thought I could get her away from here. I thought we could make a new life. I had visions of some stead welcoming us with open arms—Us! Me, a city sprat who*

*can't tell one end of a plow from the other and her a ho—
whorebaby unfit for anything but....*

Becca's belly ached. Very carefully she said, *I hear
tell how that's the way it used to be for all women.*

Smart little seedgrub. Van spoke the name without
malice, even a little tenderly. *But in those days they
didn't need to cut you for it. And if you bore a child,
they didn't take your son off to be meat for work or war,
they didn't take your daughter away and cut her too.* He
gazed at Isa. The girl's head was rolling back and forth
on her pillow, small moans escaping from lips gone
scaly dry.

That's why I hid her away, he said. *So if our baby
lives, I can sneak it into the creches like Kethy used to
do. My child won't wear yellow. My child won't be cut.
My child will be free.*

Becca noticed that he didn't speak of the possibility
that Isa too might live. At least he had let go of that
much of the old self-told lies.

She had no chance to speak of such matters further.
Isa woke up to a pain too intense to be thwarted by
Becca's simple potion. She jammed a knot of her
bedclothes into her mouth, grunting hard, but the
agony tore away the cloth and burst against the walls
of the dark little room as a red-throated scream.

Gilber came in then, Kethy with him. They
crowded around Isa on their knees until suddenly
Becca fell to one side and began to laugh helplessly.
When Van demanded to know what she found so
funny, she couldn't say it out loud. That was when
Kethy pointed out that another bout of shrieks like
that and someone outside was bound to notice.

Someone was sure to call in the Highlandweb patrols
that frequented the Flower Market. Someone would
come to see what was going on and then—

Months of secrecy, come to nothing if we don't act,
she said. *My poor baby's got to have some help for her
pain.*

I gave her the best relief I know, Becca said.

Not good enough. Kethy stroked the sweat from Isa's
brow. *She needs more.*

Please, no, I'll be— Isa's whole face spasmed, but
this time she bit back the cry. In the small, naked
voice of misery she whimpered, *I'll be quiet. I'll be
good.*

The four of them looked at one another over the
laboring girl's body. No one needed to say what they
all knew: that's Isa's pitiful promises would come to
nothing as soon as the pains came back full force.
Becca held out her bandaged hand.

*What do they have in Greenwoodweb for a webmaster's
hurt?* she asked.

That was how she happened to be running through
the city streets after dark. With only one hand to lend
if Isa's birthing reached the crisis point, she was the
one among them most easily spared for the errand.
But she wasn't going to Greenwoodweb. There was
no chance that the meddies would simply hand over
their miracle painkillers to a nobody.

They've only got limited supplies of things like that,
Van said. *They guard them, especially the compounds
against pain. They wouldn't give you what Isa needs even
if you carried a note from me. Hell, they wouldn't give
it to me without a visit from Webmaster Steven himself.*

I could go, Gilber offered. *I could find out where they keep their painkillers and take some, no one the wiser.*

No need. A smile drifted across Van's lips and faded like a shadow in the dusk. *They keep the medicine at Greenwoodweb but they don't make it there.*

Then where do they—?

Van didn't answer Gilber. He stood up and motioned for Becca to follow him into the outer room. *Now listen carefully,* he told her. *I'm going to tell you where to find Salome, but I've got nothing to hand here to let me write it down. You'll have to remember it, street for street, house for house, turn for turn. You'll also have to remember exactly what I want you to say to her when you find her. If you forget—*

I won't. She would have given him her oath on it, but he waved it away.

Swear in God's name before someone who still believes, he said. *Now go.*

She stole cautiously from Kethy's door, trod with care through the Flower Market, hugged shadows, made herself inconspicuous when there were too many people on the street for her to avoid them altogether. She wore a shabby yellow cloak with a hood over her city garb, one of Van's gifts. If any of the men stopped her, she screwed up her face just a little—enough to look unattractive, not grotesque—and gave them a lopsided smile. At that hour, the Flower Market webs were open, with scores of girls leaning out from upstairs windows. It didn't take Becca's would-be wooers more than a glance from her distorted face to the smooth masks of the webwomen before they left her be. As soon as she was out of the

Flower Market, she tore off the yellow cloak, stuffed it under her coat, and ran. She ran until she could hear the blood pounding in her ears and feel ice crystals forming inside her lungs with every breath she gulped down. Dark streets and lighted streets blurred around her like a child's stick-drawn scratchings melting in the rain. She muttered Van's directions over and over to herself as she counted off intersections and scanned buildings for the scant landmarks he'd mentioned.

At last she stood before a brightly lit building, rich and tall. Savory smells wafted from it, and the chittery, merry sounds of carefree souls. A double door painted glossy red stood at the top of a wide flight of stairs. People went up and down the steps in ones and twos and threes, their eyes aglow with contentment, laughter bubbling from their lips, entering and leaving paradise as they pleased.

Becca walked up the steps boldly, determined to barge her way in. Her courage was wasted; no one challenged her. Once inside she found herself at the top of another set of stairs—a double flight that curved down to left and right, bordered by exquisitely curlicued banisters of black iron. Both flights descended to a huge room filled with tables and chairs, glasses and bottles, food and drink, men and women.

No one stopped her as she walked down the stairs, her good hand sliding over the sleek banister. A party of older men came up four abreast and she squeezed herself to one side to let them pass. One of them gave her an appreciative smile and greeted her warmly.

She lowered her eyes, maiden-modest, and looked away. She heard the others laugh and chaff him. "Why are you wasting your time, Dick? You know that if it weren't for your webmaster and the Flower Market you wouldn't even know what a pair of titties looks like."

At the bottom of the stairway, Becca looked around. Her heart sank: There were so many faces! Some wore the traders' garb she'd first seen back at Verity Grange during harvest home, some were dressed like folk out on the street. *How am I ever going to find Salome here?* Becca's mind wailed. *And what if Van's wrong and she's not here at all?*

You'll never find her if you don't stop dithering and get a move on, came the answering thought. She pressed her lips together and waded into the crowd.

All of her determination fell by the wayside: Finding Salome turned out to be easier than finding the ground after a fall. Becca was standing in the midst of the tables, scouting around, when someone tapped her on the shoulder. "Can I help you, miss?" It was a man of about Eleazar's years, not a single strand of hair on his head. "My name is Dennis, Nearelic, Maltersweb. If you're seeking someone, I keep the club roster. I can tell you if they're here." She gave him Salome's name and was starting to add the excuse she'd dreamed up to justify this search, but he didn't stay to hear that part of it. All he said was, "Right this way."

Salome's table was over by a set of swinging doors that flapped open and closed to a steady stream of aproned whorebabies carrying trays. One glimpse of the laden platters coming from the kitchen and Becca's mouth watered. The smells alone were enough to set her stomach rumbling.

Then an abrupt, dull ache hit her below the belly and she forgot all about food and Isa and Salome. *Mary Mother, not again! I thought I'd kept tally of the days, I thought*— Her eyes darted left and right, searching for Dennis. Suddenly there was something she needed far more than the trader woman.

"Becca?" She heard Salome's voice at her back an instant before the trader woman spun her around. "It is you! I thought so. How d'you come to be here?" Salome's silvery brows lifted in speculation. "Who told you about this place?"

"Please, I—" Another low ache, a warning that had become familiar to her. "I need to speak with you, but first—it's so cold out there, and I need—"

"Oh, say no more." Salome held up one hand, grinning. "This way."

She led Becca around the edge of the room to a green door. Beyond it was a large room with a row of open-ended floor pipes with boards laid across them, an open drainway for men, and a private, curtained-off area for women's special needs. A whorebaby in a pale yellow dress stood between a table laden with small cloths and a tall hamper. When she saw Becca and Salome come in, she came forward to offer them each a cleanly laundered, neatly folded rag.

"No, thanks." Salome waved her away. "I just had to show her how to get here." She smiled at Becca. "Go on, I'll wait for you. You'll never find our table again by yourself."

Becca fidgeted, pressing her thighs together. "I can find it all right," she said. She didn't want to go into the women's booth. She didn't want Salome to see and know. The trader woman had been with her before, when the blood came, and she could count to six. *Only she won't have to count that high to make up the tally of months between then and now,* the admonishing voice came in Becca's mind. *It won't matter that she didn't catch you in your secret any of the times between: just that you don't stay clean for a sixmonth, like a normal woman.* "Please, I'm fine now. You don't have to wait for me."

"I've got nothing better to do," Salome said. And she leaned back against the wall near the hamper, arms folded.

The cramping returned, as stubborn as Salome, as unlikely to go away. Becca bit her lip, saw she had no choice, said a small prayer in her heart—*Sweet Mary Mother, cast dust in this woman's eyes! Grant she's got better things to keep track of than my affliction!*—and ducked into the curtained stall. Once inside, Becca saw that the ache had been a true harbinger. At least this place was as good and better than Carsonelic when it came to stocking all a woman in her times might need. She saw to herself and came out, putting a bold face on it, as if nothing extraordinary had happened.

She saw at once that her brash front was wasted. The trader woman regarded her keenly, those intelligent eyes clear of prayed-for dust. With a look like that on her face, there was no need for Salome to bother saying *I know what you are.*

Now the question's this, Becca's inner voice cautioned. *What's she going to do with what she knows?*

For the moment, the answer seemed to be nothing. Salome simply asked, "Feeling better now?" and when Becca nodded, she conducted the girl back to her table. It was then that Becca noticed Salome hadn't been sitting alone.

Matt's dark face looked haggard, his eyes freighted with sorrow and larger than Becca remembered. "Long time no see," he said, the words heavy and slow.

I didn't tell! I didn't tell! Solomon's ghost rose before Becca's eyes, his transparent hands clinging to the bars of the prison cell that no longer held him. She reached out to touch Matt's hand. All she said was, "I'm sorry." There was much more she wanted to say, even though she could tell there were no words mighty enough to lift so much as one particle of the grief bowing this man's heart to the ground. She kept her peace because what she had seen of Coop law had lessoned her well: *Lose your secrets, lose your life*.

Matt shrugged. "I was there. I was in the crowd of witnesses. I saw." He too had no more to say. His hands clasped the mug of strong-smelling drink before him and he emptied it by half in a single swallow. Then he said, "Law."

Salome's lips twisted up to one side. "Life," she replied, and shrugged both away. She pulled out a chair and turned to Becca. "Sit down, pretty. Tell me what brings you here."

Becca shook her head. She called to mind the precise words Van had bidden her tell the trader woman. This wasn't the place to say them, not with Matt present. *What you know gives you power over others. What others know gives them power over you. Keep all the secrets you can.* "Come with me, please," she said. "I can't— It's too loud in here to talk."

Salome chuckled. "It's precisely because it's so loud in here that we can speak freely. No one can hear any conversation apart from his own table. Don't be so nice about it: Have a seat, have a drink, join us for dinner. You won't find a better kitchen anywhere in Coop than at the traders' club." She sat down and renewed her invitation to Becca with gestures and smiles.

Becca stood firm, her good hand clutching the back of the offered chair. She had been gone too long. Isa's pains would be back, growing stronger. The frail girl would never be able to stand them without her screams bringing half of Highlandweb running to see who was being slaughtered. *Unless she dies of the pain first*, Becca thought. *Her and the babe.* The notion surprised her: She'd never before thought of an infant's death as a mercy.

She would have to speak here, and pray she could shift Van's words just enough so that Salome could understand without Matt catching wise. She glanced at him. He'd finished his drink and was summoning a whorebaby to fetch him another. The whites of his eyes were almost the color of the server's dress, except they were also shot through with red. *Wine is a mocker*... Pa's voice stirred out of memory, reading Scripture to his family on a holy day, most of them with no more knowledge of wine than of Behemoth and Leviathan. But Becca knew; Becca always questioned, always sought answers. She knew that enough drink left a man half out of his senses, numb if not happy.

Matt's far gone, she thought. *I can speak.* She took a deep breath and said, "Please come with me. Van sent me. The pain he spoke to you about in the bower is on him now. He wants your promise fulfilled or he'll forget his."

Salome shot to her feet. Her easygoing manner turned to steel and ice. "Cht!" The terse, urgent whisper for Becca's silence sounded like a flint-struck spark. Matt's head sank to the tabletop as Salome seized Becca's arm and dragged her away.

She didn't utter another sound until they were out of the club and around the corner, standing before a huge building that looked like one of the barns on Verity Grange. "What the hell were you thinking?" Salome rasped in Becca's face. "Saying *that* name in front of Matt? Didn't you hear him say he was *there* when they killed Solomon?"

"I—"

"You think he doesn't know the name of the man who was the Face of justice? Oh, that and more! He found out who called the raid that night."

"You told him?" Becca was stunned.

Salome gave her a scornful look. "Do I look like I want to cut my own throat? Matt didn't need to learn it from me. He's got his contacts. You don't make your life as a trader without knowing things. You don't keep your life without holding fast to plenty of knowledge, not when you're the kind of traders Matt and Solomon were."

"But you're part of Thirdweb, and the law—"

"I'm a trader. Every web has its traders. It doesn't matter to us what our web's main business is, so long as we take care of our own. If we do it well enough, we become too valuable to be watched or questioned, unless we grow too arrogant or our luck runs out. What happened to Solomon didn't need to happen at all. I used to ask them why they bothered going to that club when they already had each other, but they just laughed at me and said they liked the music." She looked up at the first glimmer of starlight. "Matt doesn't laugh anymore."

"You...you mean you—?" Becca's lips parted, but Salome's fingertips stopped any word from escaping.

"You mouth that triple-damned word at me, girl, and Van can drown in pain before you'll have my help. I don't care what he runs to tell Webmaster Steven about me; I can only die once. *Abomination!* I've seen enough things worthy of the word to laugh when I hear you pious-minded bastards fling it at us."

A cold twitch touched Salome's lips, barely enough to be called a smile. "Oh yes," she said slowly, her eyes weighing Becca's every reaction. "Us. Me, Matt, poor dead Solomon, all the pretty little yellow blossoms in the city gardens. Do you want to tell? You saw what will happen to us. In my case, at least I'll meet death alone. I have no one, for now. There was a quarrel, the trading season came on, I had to travel, she was no trader, only a hobay, so there was no way she could come with me—"

Regret creased itself between Salome's brows. Her eyes squeezed shut, casting out old loss. When she opened them again they were stone. "Tell that to Webmaster Steven and I'll tell him that he picked the wrong one to spy on you. Eleazar's as good a sneak as any in our web, but useless to learn a woman's true secrets. He'll only have my word for it at first, but he can afford to wait and see if it's true. One month's not too long a time for that old spider to bide. I don't know whether He'll go mad with joy over catching a freak like you or simply mad because there's no ceremony of law to tell him how to give you your death. But no fear, he'll improvise something. He's a great one for ceremonies, our webmaster. They fatten up his old bones with pride."

"Tell him, then." Becca's calm response sounded alien to her ears, as if someone else had stepped inside her skin. By rights she knew she should be shaking in fear for her life, but all she could feel was this cool, distant serenity of spirit, as if she had stepped into an empty room, white-walled, bathed in late sunlight. "If that's your choice, run and tell. But do it like that, straight out, for your own reasons. Don't threaten me. Don't dream you're safe telling me your secret because you've got mine to hold over my head. This is one time you've learned a secret that gives you no power at all."

Salome's expression slowly shifted to grudging admiration. "You're not afraid, are you? You're honestly not afraid."

"Me? I think I must be the biggest coward God ever saw fit to let live. There's so many fears riding me that I just don't have room in my soul for any more. I'm too weary for fear. Tell Webmaster Steven what you know about me and go your way after, but for now come with me. Van said you can lay your hands on the painkillers they reserve for the webmasters. We have to bring some to him now, quickly. There isn't much time."

Salome gave her a peculiar look, but said nothing. She jerked her head sideways, silently bidding Becca follow her. They entered the barnlike building. Becca gazed all around at row after row of the smallest traders' chariots, row after row of even smaller vehicles that she'd only known from books before this. Two wheels, a pair of handlebars, pedals to drive, a chain to turn the rear wheel— She remembered seeing an old picture of a girl riding a bicycle, her hair streaming out behind her, her lips drinking the wind.

The barn was guarded by at least six whorebabies, all male, all armed, all in yellow coveralls. "D-23," Salome said to one of them and he raced off, coming back with a freshly shined blue bicycle. there was a narrow wooden slat attached behind the saddle, over the rear wheel. Salome mounted, then motioned for Becca to get on behind her. She cast a critical look over one shoulder, then told the whorebaby, "Get her some pins for that skirt. If it fouls my spokes, you're the one who's going to hurt for it."

Before long, they were sailing through the night. Becca had her arms wrapped tight around Salome's waist. The streets went by too fast for her to mark them, and it was too dark for her to recognize the route. Salome made one. It was a large building built almost flush to the city wall, the streets surrounding it lit brighter than any Becca had seen until now, and swarming with heavily armed patrols of Highlandwebbers, all in glistening helmets. Becca heard Salome speak a single word to the one among them who challenged her and they were passed through.

Salome hustled Becca into the building, leaving the bicycle lying on its side near the front door. "Wait here," she said almost as soon as they were inside, shoving the girl into a little room off the main entryway. Becca lingered by the door, wondering whether or not to anticipate a trap. She hardly had time to review her choices before Salome was back, a brown metal box in her hands, two pairs of traders' coveralls slung over her arm.

"Traders go anywhere, any hour," Salome explained as Becca struggled into the alien garment. "Even females into the Flower Market," she added with a wistful smile. "I'm assuming that Van's so-called pain really belongs to that sad little girl of his. Nine months up so soon?"

"No. It's come on early."

"I expected as much. Good. Maybe the kid'll be born dead. Well, least we can do is make it easy on the mother, though I doubt she'll live long enough to thank us. Here, check out the contents." She handed the box to Becca and continued to speak while she put on her own set of coveralls: "There should be ten loaded needles—that's what the label says; I didn't get the chance to make sure. We traders are supposed to bring goods *in* to the storehouses, not take them out, but we manage. The trick's to keep our mousings small and subtle. You *do* have alcohol and clean swabs? Have you ever used needles?"

"Uh—"

"Never mind. I have. And if you don't have alcohol, we'll make do. It's not as if we're expecting her to make it. What's infection to a corpse?"

"Don't talk about Isa that way," Becca said, even though her own mind pictured the laboring girl as good as gone. For some reason it rankled her to hear another voice those thoughts.

"I won't say another word. It won't change anything, but you're free to dream."

They left the storehouse and hastened to the Flower Market. Their traders' garb gave them the free passage Salome had promised. None of the clients and none of the street patrols said or did anything to hinder them. Becca suffered a momentary pang when Salome entered the door of peony Web so boldly, without even a glance around to see whether anyone was watching. She scampered in after the trader woman, bringing the bicycle as Salome bid her and standing it against the wall.

They climbed the stairs in silence. Becca strained her ears, harking for some sound from above. She heard nothing. *Maybe Isa's dead.* And she despised herself for the relief she felt at the thought.

Kethy was waiting for them on guard, a heavy chair

leg in her hands. "It's me, Kethy, I brought the painkiller," Becca called out.

The makeshift club lowered slowly. "Who's that?" Kethy waved it at Salome.

"A friend of the family," Salome answered, deadpan.

Gilber lurched out of the inner room. His face lit up when he saw Becca. "We're lucky; your drink's let her sleep, but it's going to turn worse soon. Did you get it?"

Salome stepped forward and handed him the box. "You're the one's been living at Greenwoodweb. Seen them use needles there? Know how yourself or do you want a hand?"

"I've done it a time or two and I've watched the meddies do it more than that. Thanks." Gilber took the box and ducked back into the birthing chamber.

"Men at a birth." Kethy shook her head in wonder, let the chair leg fall. "If that doesn't beat the devil."

Salome dropped into the rump-sprung armchair and stretched her limbs. "Strange days, end of the world. Wake me when the Beast of the Apocalypse comes to call." She closed her eyes and seemed to fall into a light doze.

"That was why I laughed," Becca said softly.

"What's that?" Kethy frowned.

"Before, when we were in there with Isa. A thought hit me. Christmas. Eleazar took me to see the holiday play. I knew the words to the story—Pa read it to us every year—but I never did see it as a living picture before: the Holy Family there in the stable, waiting on the Child's birth, and then the shepherds come, and the angels, and the kings. All of them crowding 'round sweet Mary Mother, getting on their knees like any one of 'em's to be the first one to take the Infant from Her womb and be blessed with the precious blood. All of them shoulder to shoulder, and not a midwife in the lot, and all I can think of's *Merciful God, what that poor woman wouldn't give for a decent birthing stool about now!* Then in there," she nodded toward the closed door of Isa's room, "so many of us crowded 'round like we was all part of that same Christmas play, only we're praying for a death, not a birth, and there won't be any blessing to the blood that's to come. All of it so close to holy, so near to damned, so funny that I just had to laugh over it."

Without warning, Kethy dealt Becca a sharp cuff on the ear. The girl gasped. "Laugh over *that*, fool," the woman snapped. "God knows, you mean Isa well, but where your head is half the time, I just don't know. We've got no room under this roof for fancies. All we can shelter is what's here, what's now. Mark me, it won't be long before those men come busting out of there, frantic to find you. When they do, you're going to be there for Isa—all of you, no wandering thoughts. You save your crazy laughter, girl. You save it for when we're done."

At that instant, as if to give Kethy the prophet's crown of a true Deborah, Isa's door swung open and Van stood there, his face pale and wild. "It's time, Becca. Come help her. It's you she wants, not Gilber."

"My hand—"

"I'll be your other hand. Come."

Chapter Sixteen

Do you dare speak to me of an unfair judgment? I have given you my verdict. If it were anything but fair and just, it could never have left my lips. Question my judgments and you question the law. Question the law and you question all that holds us above the beasts and those men who became worse than beasts in the lost times. I have lived with the law, of the law, within the law for so long that the law is now as much a part of me as blood, bone and breath. I am the law, in its mercy and in its terror; how then do you expect me to answer to that which I already encompass? Question me and you question justice. Question justice and the only answer you can hope to have will be your death.

"Isa? Isa, I'm here." Becca clasped one of the laboring girl's hands with her good one. "How are you feeling?"

Isa managed a weak smile. "Better, now. There's no more pain. Not so much, anyhow. I can stand it." A sudden look of concern flashed across her face. "It won't hurt my baby, will it, the painkiller Gilber Livvy gave me?"

Becca didn't know the true answer to that, but she did know that sometimes truth wasn't a needful thing. "It won't harm your babe at all."

"Are you sure?" Isa persisted. Her thin hand tightened over Becca's. "When I was little, I always heard how pain's our lot when we come to give birth, all on account of Eve's sin, sure as we're born."

"We're born naked and hungry and helpless too, but I don't hear anyone insisting we accept that as our lot." She forced herself to wear a cheerful face. "Eva and Adam dwelled in the wilderness after they lost Paradise, but I don't see the Lord sending angels with fiery swords to drive us out of our houses to live in the trees. Food comes raw, and we cook it, and that's no sin. If we've found the way to hold off birthing pains, there's no need to fear God's wrath over that either."

Isa sighed and closed her eyes. "Thank you, Becca. I was afraid—" Her words stopped short. She sucked in her breath sharply. "Something..." she said, eyes wide.

Becca disengaged her hand from Isa's grip and pulled aside the sheet. She bit her lip hard in consternation at what she saw. The child was coming on early and by rights should be small, but what difference could that make when its mother was such a frail splinter of thing? She looked between Isa's legs and found the babe's head beginning to crown, corked tight. Despite how they'd cut this girl, despite how wide they'd stretched the doors of her womb, this child was still more than her body could free. Isa was panting now, whimpering, taken up with a pain too potent to be banished by all the magical elixirs of Greenwoodweb. Her belly rippled and shuddered. She let loose a shriek as she was torn apart from the inside.

"Dear God, what's going on?" Van barged into the room, Gilber close behind him. "I thought you'd seen to her pain?"

"I thought so too," Gilber said quietly. He glanced at the box of needles on the floor beside Isa's mat. "Shall I give her another?"

"Better not," Salome said from the doorway. "If you don't know the dose, you could kill her." Her face was pale, her eyes fixed on Isa. For once she didn't speak of the girl's death as inevitable. She came forward and put her arm around Van's shoulders. "Go to her. Be with her. She needs you."

Van did as Salome directed. While he knelt beside Isa and held her hands, Becca motioned for Gilber to join her. She saw how he winced at the blood. Kethy came to the door to peer in, only to have Salome herd her out again. "She's got help enough and she needs room to breathe. We'll just be in the way." She closed the door after them.

Isa's pains increased, in spite of the drug. They

came closer and closer together, lasted longer and longer until the girl's distorted body writhed in an agony that seemed without end. Becca tried to get her onto her feet, supported between Van and Gilber. There was no proper birthing stool and no item of furniture in Kethy's old web that could pass for one, so using the two men for the purpose seemed the best Becca could do.

It didn't work. Isa couldn't bear to be moved. Though Becca gave her another draught of the herbal brew, she couldn't contain her anguish. When Van and Gilber linked their bared arms behind her and beneath her so that she could squat for the birth, she howled like a soul in torment an instant before Becca heard something go *snap*. Isa's left leg folded under her, the too-delicate bones of the ankle broken. The unexpected pain heaped atop what she was already feeling was too much for the girl and she fainted.

Van laid her back on the mattress and wheeled on Becca. "You brainless stead cow! Is this the best you can do for her?" More insults spewed from his mouth as he pressed Isa's hand to his heart.

His abuse reached Becca as pure sound, free of meaning. All of her attention was concentrated on the small (but oh! not small enough) head she now saw so much more clearly between Isa's thighs.

"Shall I—?" Gilber began. His voice came to her from far away. There was only room in her mind for Isa and the baby. She shook her head briskly and waved him off. With the mother flat on her back, even one good hand might be enough to help the child from the womb. She steadied herself for what she knew was to come.

Isa's pale skin was going stark white, losing more and more color with every pulse of the pain. Isa moaned, roughly hauled back to consciousness by her pangs. Becca tore her eyes away from the infant's crowning head just long enough to order Gilber to ready all they'd need to cut the birth cord. She glanced at Van and saw him glaring at her with pure, perverse, irrational hate.

He blames me for her pain, she thought. *He'd share Isa's birthpangs if he could, but he'd be in Heaven if he could slap them onto me.*

And if there's a death here, who'll he force to share that? the little voice inside her skull whispered.

The baby didn't give her time to think of an answer. With a rending of skin and flesh and the pink-tinged peek of its mother's shattered pelvic bone, Isa's child was born. Blood flooded Becca's lap as she held the infant across her knees, clearing its nose and mouth with her good hand. Isa shook with the last departing breath of life as Becca slapped the first weak cry from her baby.

Gilber looked at Van, who still clung to Isa's damp, cooling hands. "You've got a daughter," he said. He reached across to sever and knot the cord.

Slowly, slowly Van looked away from Isa's glazing eyes. It was like having two corpses in the room, except one of them still moved. "A girl…"

"Gilber, get the swaddling cloths and have Kethy fetch a basin of clean water," Becca directed. Gilber hastened to do her bidding and soon she stood by in her blood-soaked skirt watching the webwoman wash the newborn clean.

"Here," said Kethy once the babe was tucked up tight. She offered the tiny bundle to Becca. "She wants a body's warmth. Can you hold her?"

"Won't you—?"

"Not if I can help it." The woman shook her head. "Too many memories. I held her mother just so, when we came riding back into the city from my last trip to the hills. Now there she lies. Here," she repeated, and forced Becca to hold the infant the best way she could manage. She and Gilber watched with the oldest of all fascinations as the tiny mouth rooted for Becca's breast.

Reluctantly, Becca lifted her eyes. "Van?" She spoke his name as if she feared a word said too loud would bruise him. "You come and hold her."

Van stayed where he was, at Isa's side, didn't even bother to glance at Becca or the babe. "Take her out of here," he said.

"Van, she's your daughter. If you turn from her, who'll have her? Isa—" She was about to say *Isa died to birth her*, but thought again and instead said, "Isa would have loved her for all she holds of you. Can't you love her for Isa's sake?"

Now Van did look up, his face streaked with tears, sticky with mucus, his bare arms still dappled with Isa's blood. "I will," he said. "I do. But I can't hold her; not just yet." He stroked Isa's brow, lowered the blue-tinged eyelids over the staring eyes. "Let me do

what I can for Isa first, then I'll look after our child."
He got up slowly, like an old man, and brought the
basin of water and the cloths Kethy had used to wash
the newborn. He began to clean away the bloody
tokens of his beloved's hard-fought and ultimately
lost battle.

Becca took the baby from the room, following
Kethy, sure that Gilber was following her. Then she
felt the door slam behind her and turned to see that
he had stayed behind. "But the blood—" she
protested to the silent wood.

"Ever see a birth without it?" Kethy responded
dryly.

"You don't understand. Gilber calls such things
uncleanly, blood and all. It's how he was raised."

"Huh! Well, he's a Jew. No telling how strange they
can be."

"Oh, is that it?" Salome drawled. She had flung
herself back into the armchair. "God knows, the way
he looks at you is strange enough, Becca. Here I've
been thinking it was lovesickness made him so weird,
when all the time it's only him being a Jew."

"He is *not* weird," Becca said with a little stamp of
her foot. The baby at her breast mewled and coughed,
then raised its voice into a hearty wail. None of her
efforts could hush it.

"What's wrong?" Gilber asked, opening the door.
"We can hear that child right through the wall. Van's
reached the cliff's edge: he says if anyone in the
streets outside bothers to call the patrol to
investigate, Isa's died for nothing." He came nearer

and gazed at the bundle in Becca's arms. "Kethy, you maybe know where we could find this creature some milk?"

The webwoman looked doubtful, but she shrugged and said, "I'll go see." She left the room, her footsteps echoing back up the stairway.

"Meanwhile, try this," Gilber said. He rearranged things so that Becca cradled the child in the crook of one arm and gave it a finger of her good hand to suck. The baby fussed at first, then settled down. "Good. Now I've got to get back to Van." He slipped away into the inner chamber, shutting the door firmly.

"If *that's* not weird, it'll do," Salome remarked. "A man knowing that much about women's matters isn't natural."

"Then I guess we make a good pair, him and me," Becca shot back. "I'm nothing natural either."

"And I am?" Salome laughed. "I'm more unnatural than the pair of you together. Not the reason *you* think. The reason we share, pretty. Whoever said God works with a plan should try explaining this to me: A throwback to the old days, a woman always ready for a man, and what's the use of it in *me?*"

Becca felt the baby's mouth stop moving around her finger. The infant drowsed. Softly, so as not to disturb it she whispered, "You mean...like me?"

"Every moon." Salome said it as if it were no great thing. She slung her legs over one arm of the chair, her head over the other. "Well, not *every* moon, or I'd be dead. Don't they keep watch over your stead girls after the first time you bleed?"

"Yes. We've got to pass a clean sixmonth or—"

"Well, it's no different for us here in the city. I was just like all the rest of them until I turned twenty, as far as that went. My first few years after they took me into Carsonelic as apprentice to their old trader, I had only one secret to keep. Dear Lord, I still recall my blessed wedding night, when old Webmaster Steven himself came to 'welcome' me into the family. I think he enjoyed it even less than I did, but he did his duty. Thank God it didn't bear fruit! You show you can produce babies *too* readily and that's all they'll use you for." She sighed. "I've given Carsonelic three, and only one of them the wrong sex."

"I—I didn't think there was such a thing in Coop," Becca faltered. "Where do they leave the children for the Lord King's sword?"

"Around here, the Lord King's got a knife and a fine yellow uniform, not a sword. Carsonelic will reclaim my sons from the creche when they're old enough, but not my daughter. When I had her, Webmaster Steven determined that by the time she'd be grown, Thirdweb wouldn't need any more women. I don't even know her name."

"Salome…I'm sorry."

"For what? For the way things have always been?" The trader woman sat up straight in the armchair. "At least my work keeps me out of the city or I'd have to go to the bower all that more frequently. You know, it was on one of my longer journeys that I changed. At first I thought it was an anomaly—" She saw Becca's puzzled look and added, "A fluke, something out of the ordinary that was only going to happen that one time. But I was wrong. By the time I came back to Thirdweb, months later, I knew I had so much more to fear than when I'd left. It hasn't been easy for me, keeping this secret when I'm inside the walls, but for you—! How did you manage, living on a stead? City men have to wait for their webmasters to consult the records and tell them when a free woman's ready to have them, but I hear that your men can scent a taking woman a mile off and come swarming 'round like flies. Couldn't they tell you were different?"

As little reason as she had to love the old ways, Becca grew angry to hear Salome speak of her kin as if they were something less than human. "This didn't happen to me until I left Wiserways," she gritted.

"So Gilber knows?"

"He traveled with me."

Salome's eyebrow rose in speculation. "That he did. I'm surprised he caught you in your secret. The wilderness is a pretty big place. Couldn't you steal away when you needed to look to yourself? Or do Jews have the same keen noses on them as stead men?"

"He didn't find out by catching me in my times," Becca said, the anger rising in her, the truth of things melting in its heat. "He found out by how I could take him any time we fancied."

Salome recoiled from the invisible slap. "Then there is love between you two," she said. "I didn't think— Oh well." She shrugged. "Be happy." She closed her eyes and sank into the chair.

"Salome?" Becca stole nearer, Isa's infant now

sound asleep, tiny fists clutched tight into little pink paws. "Why did you tell me?"

"Because sometimes it feels good to let a secret fly." Her eyes screwed themselves shut even tighter. "Because it's something I thought we could share together. You wouldn't repeat it any more than you'd betray the other one, and not just out of fear that I'd turn around and betray you. You're fearless and you're kind. I need a friend like that, Becca. Van's only an ally."

"What do you mean?"

"You know how often Webmaster Steven sends Van and me to the bower when the old spider *thinks* my six months have passed and I'm waiting for my times?"

Becca recalled what her brother had told her. She nodded hesitantly. "I think I heard something about how he wants you two to breed a child."

"You *think* so?" Salome teased. "If you haven't heard the most chatted-up rumor in all Thirdweb until now, you've got wooden ears! It's all those law-pickers talk of when they're not jabbering over their latest cases. The first time it happened, I was resigned to the same old routine. I got to the bower first, stripped myself bare, lay down on the bed and waited to get it over with. I was wondering whether this one was going to want me to pretend I was enjoying myself with him. Some do, some don't care. Then Van showed up. God, if you could've seen his face when he came in and found me lying there naked! I've seen lust and shyness and even once a little tenderness in a man's eyes, Heaven help him, but I never did see such a look of despair and revulsion. I didn't know what to make of it. I'm not *that* ugly, am I?"

"You're...a very beautiful woman, Salome," Becca said.

Salome grinned at her. "Nice of you to say so, pretty. Don't worry, I won't hold you to it. Anyhow, there we were, Van and me, neither one of us eager for the chore. He stood there with his back pressed to the locked door, as if he'd make a break for freedom, if he could. Finally I sat up on the bed and asked him what was the matter and he told me: He told me about Isa, how he loved her, how he didn't want any other woman, how he didn't want me, how he couldn't even *pretend* to want me." She chuckled. "That's one advantage we've always had over them. He was scared I'd run tattling to Webmaster Steven, but I swore I wouldn't. I tried to make it sound like I was reluctant to deceive the old man, but that I'd do it as a special favor for him."

Her lips formed a self-mocking smile. "Never underestimate a sharp-minded man. Once we left the bower, it didn't take Van long to see through my supposed 'favor'. He put his wits to the problem and discovered my real reason for not minding if we never bred. The next time the webmaster ordered us up there, Van told me what he knew. Not in words— he's subtle enough to pass for Webmaster Steven's begotten son, sometimes. He just came in wearing a loose jacket, reached inside, took out a handful of pretty yellow paper flowers, and spilled them into my lap."

The baby sniffled and stirred. Salome cocked her

head to study the small, red face. "Little monkey," she said. "Maybe I can get her into a creche tonight. We'll have to get her fed, first. You can't slip through the streets with a crying baby on your hands."

"I hope Kethy comes back soon," Becca said, casting an anxious glance at the door. "Wait... Do you hear something?"

Salome harked. "Yes, I think so, but it doesn't sound like—"

The words died on her lips as the approaching footsteps turned from a faint rumble to a trampling like thunder. Becca realized that Kethy alone couldn't make all that racket if she tried, but before she could speak, the door flew open and Webmaster Steven stood glaring at the women. He was backed by two tall Highlandwebbers, and Becca thought she could just make out the shapes of more men in the shadowy hall beyond.

"So this is where you've been sneaking off to," Webmaster Steven said, striding in. The doorway filled up with guards, but they didn't cross the threshold. "You too, Salome? What did you hope to gain from this escapade?"

"Something to gain from currying favor with your heir?" Salome replied, cool and unruffled as the surface of a frozen lake. "You think you're the only one who plans for the future? Go ahead, blame me for that."

A grudging smile distorted the webmaster's wrinkled face. "If you're so fond of the future, get out of here while you've still got one."

Salome didn't wait for a second invitation. She

scurried from the room, elbowed her way through the guards, and was gone. Becca could hear her racing footsteps fading down the stairway.

Webmaster Steven came nearer and plucked aside the infant's swaddlings. "What have we here?"

"My daughter, Webmaster." Van stood in the doorway of the birthing room, Gilber behind him. Pride and heartbreak warred in his voice.

The old man took a deep breath and let it out long, shaking his head that same indulgent way a mother will over a rascally child's doings. "So this is where it ends. All your promises, lies. And the woman?"

"In here." Gilber spoke up. "She's dead."

"Hm. As you might have expected, Van, if you'd been willing to consider this entire case in a rational manner. At least we've finally seen the last of your foolishness. Come home now. These gentlemen will see to cleaning up matters here." He turned on his heel and headed for the door.

Van stood stark-faced and dumbstruck, as if Webmaster Steven spoke in tongues. He walked stiffly after the old man, but when he came near Becca, Isa's child woke and began to cry. The thin, insistent sound yanked Van back into the world. He took the infant from Becca's arms and said, "I'm not going anywhere until my daughter's settled in a creche."

Webmaster Steven paused and glanced back at him. "Out of the question," he said. "What elic would take her?"

"Couldn't yours?" Becca said, stealing near to pluck

at the old man's black sleeve. "She's small, but she's hale."

Webmaster Steven peered closely into Becca's face. "You don't *look* like an idiot," he told her. "So what possesses you to talk like one?" He sniffed disdainfully and in a breath made her invisible. "Van, you've already used up all my patience. Come *along*."

He tried to go, but Becca danced into his path. "What are you saying? Do you hear yourself? A woman died to birth that child and you act like she's not even here! Van's so precious to you, why isn't his babe?"

"Becca, don't." Van took a step forward, the baby squirming and crying in his arms. Webmaster Steven made a sign with his hand and a guard silently placed himself between the old man and the young.

"Let her talk. I assure you, she can't do herself any more harm. She is under arrest and will be taken back to Thirdweb, pending trial."

"On what charge?" Van challenged. "Helping Isa? Helping me? There's no law against that and you know it. Besides, I forced her to do it! You'll have to place me under arrest too."

"It's a lucky thing for you that we're outside the justice chamber, boy," Webmaster Steven said dryly. "There *is* a law against perjury, and not even the fact that I'm grooming you to succeed me could save you from that conviction."

Van raised his voice to be heard over the baby's hungry wails and shouted, "How dare you accuse me of lying!"

"Prior evidence. In this case, though, I have enough immediate proof. If this girl was coerced into helping you, why didn't she turn to some responsible man for aid and protection? Our first duty is to shelter women, even the stranger in our midst."

"Where would she find that man?" Van argued desperately. "The only ones she knows inside the walls belong to Thirdweb. I told her that they were all afraid of me, because of what I might do to them after I became webmaster."

"Sure of that, aren't you?" The old man sounded mildly amused.

"I made it *sound* sure when I threatened her with it," Van countered. "And she believed me."

"Well then, why didn't she go to her handsome young friend over there?" Webmaster Steven gestured in Gilber's direction. "No, wait, let me guess: You'd threatened him too."

"No one threatened me," Gilber said, coming to stand with Van and the baby. "I'm here because I heard there was a need."

"A need?" The old man's eyebrows shot up. "A need for what? For one more hobay to be born? I'd think you've got more than enough of those on your hands now. Every last one of the people that Greenwoodweb's given you to restore your degenerate tribe. I wish you joy of them; you've just seen how well the women come through childbirth, if they reach it at all." He nodded toward the birthing room where Isa's corpse lay. "You might as well try breeding up a new generation by coupling with pigs." He smirked, waiting for Gilber to react to what the webmaster imagined was revelation.

Gilber's expression never changed. "Whorebabies," he said, unruffled, serene. "I know what they are, same as I know the right name to call 'em. And I'll be leading them home with me within a fortnight, unless you've got some charge to lay against me too."

"You're still going to take them?" Now Webmaster Steven was astonished, though never beyond words. "Knowing what they are? Knowing they're just a gaggle of useless mouths your tribe will have to feed?"

"We don't throw life away. And useless? Only to you. What's cut can be mended, maybe, and the men are whole."

The webmaster laughed. "Well said, Jewman! Very practical. Waste not, want not, eh? And very bold. You see, Van? She could have gone to him for help if she needed it. He's no coward."

"He's a Jew," Van countered, but the spark in his words was dying, beaten out by weariness. "She knows he's different. Rightly or not, she must have assumed he wouldn't be bound by our laws, so she wouldn't go to him for help against my threats."

"Mmm." Webmaster Steven laid a finger to his lips. "A little far-fetched, but a possible interpretation of the defendant's motive, somewhat possible. Then why didn't she ask the other city man she knew? One not subject to Thirdweb, one with nothing to fear from our alleged heir? One whose citizenship is beyond reproach, who knows his duty?"

"I don't know any other—" Becca began.

"Send him up!" Webmaster Steven called out into the shadows beyond the door, cutting off her protests. "Send him in here at once! It's past time he had his reward."

The webmaster dug into his pockets and pulled out a fistful of the same small, dimpled, red metal tokens Becca had last seen in Van's hand in the theater. Meanwhile, the guards in the outer hall stood aside and let in a man in trader's garb, the hood pulled up though not high enough to hide his face.

Matt...He must have followed Salome and me, overheard, trailed us here, and once he knew what was going on— Becca's head spun. The same man who had looked dead with wine scant hours ago in the traders' club was keen-eyed and alert. When he saw Van, he bared his teeth in a grimace too feral to be a human smile. Solomon's lover had lost his grief, burned it away in vengeance.

Webmaster Steven took Matt's hand and poured the tokens into it. "With our thanks," he said.

Matt's fingers closed around the reward automatically, but he looked neither at the webmaster nor at his sudden riches. His eyes never left Van's face. "For justice," he said, and let the tokens cascade to the floor before he left the room.

Webmaster Steven watched him go. "Strange fellow." He shrugged, then gave his attention back to Gilber. "Still, there you have it. She *did* know that man. He told me so, said he knew you too, met you on the road here. She could've found him if she wanted to, and no doubt he would have stood up in her defense against Van's threats. Judging from how he spoke of you when he came to fetch me here, Van, he doesn't like you at all. I can't imagine why. Immaterial. He's not the one on trial."

"Am I?" Gilber asked.

"You? Heavens, no! Only the girl. Go back to your people." The old man stepped aside and bowed toward the door to the stairway.

Gilber stood his ground. "If I'm free of guilt for any crime here, so is Becca."

"One case has nothing to do with the other. Van is right: There is no law to forbid you giving medical aid and comfort to a hobay, much good it did her. I was only discussing that aspect of this situation for the sake of pure argument. It's a mental exercise I enjoy, keeps me sharp between actual cases. No, that is not the charge against Becca of Wiserways."

"What is, then?"

"That is not your business. It will be made explicit at her trial." He looked at the nearest guard. "Bring her."

The man laid one hand on Becca, who flinched away. "I can walk without help."

Webmaster Steven showed a thin line of teeth. "Very well." He spoke to the guard again: "In that case, bring *her*." He indicated the baby in Van's arms.

Van clutched the child to his chest and backed away. "No. No, you won't have her." He spun around and dashed back into the inner room.

The old man clicked his tongue. "Foolish boy. There's no way out through there."

"There's a window," Gilber said, and ran after Van without waiting for anyone's leave. Becca too followed, dodging the webmaster and the guard, ignoring the commands shouted at her back for her to stop, stand, be a biddable woman.

Gilber's cry hit her full in the face as she stepped through the doorway. It was a blast of ice to turn her marrow brittle, but it melted to nothing at all the instant she saw what had evoked it, what Gilber saw.

Van kneeled by Isa's body, their baby across his lap, the slender form of the painkiller needle protruding from the soft spot of the infant's skull.

Chapter Seventeen

I've been gone too long,
Miss the land I know.
I've been gone too long,
Longing home to go.
I've been gone too long,
Need a friendly smile.
I'll be moving on,
Just a little while.

Becca walked slowly around the examination chamber, trailing her hand over each of the eight burnished bronze pulpits as she passed it. When she'd first seen this room, so near the top of Thirdweb tower, Eleazar had been her guide. He brother took special pride in pointing out what he called the ring of judgment, the gleaming metal stands where the chosen arbiters heard out their cases and handed down their rulings. There was a ninth pulpit too, but Becca didn't go near it. It stood alone, untouched and shunned, shining silver-white in the center of the ring. That was Webmaster Steven's place. He occupied it infrequently, only for cases of the highest moment. Otherwise it was taken by the Thirdwebber he appointed to represent him—a great honor, as Eleazar had explained, and preened himself visibly before his sister as he added how many times that honor had been his. Even though the silver stand had known her brother's presence more than the webmaster's, Becca couldn't look at it without seeing that cold face, those calculating eyes. She kept herself far from its taint, even to the point of avoiding its shifting shadow. Sunlight streamed in through the chamber walls, which were all windowpane. The one place in Thirdweb with a better view of Coop than this was the roof garden. Even though it would be an easy thing for a prisoner to shatter the glass walls and escape, the sole way out was straight down. More than once since her incarceration, Becca had asked herself whether that wasn't part of Webmaster Steven's plan in keeping her here rather than sending her back to the cells of Wallweb: to have this view of freedom taunt her daily, when the only real freedom she could hope for was death.

She paused in her weary circuit to glance outside. Today the city towers were sparkling brighter than they ever had in her lost vision. "What a fool I was," she murmured, and resumed her measured pace around the room.

In time, she tired of this tedious exercise and went to sit down on the bedroll that had been provided for her on the second night of her captivity. It lay spread out beside the glass wall that looked directly out toward distant Greenwoodweb. If she turned her head to the sun, she could see the smeared prints that her own nose and lips and hands had left against the gleaming surface.

Someone knocked at the door. Becca could have laughed out loud. They always knocked, and they always barged right in. Why bother knocking at all? Who was she to give these people leave or ban to enter here? It was a pretty illusion, letting a condemned prisoner dream that her word could affect anything, even trivialities like *Come in!* or *Leave me be!* The folk of Thirdweb did what they pleased. The mask of city courtesy was brave to see until you realized it was made of eggshell.

The knock came again, for a wonder, but again she paid it no mind. Tumblers clicked, a latch was raised. Bearing a tray laden with food and drink, Salome shouldered her way into the room. Someone in the corridor outside shoved the door shut behind her.

The trader woman crossed the room to set down the tray on one of the eight blue benches spaced between the bronze pulpits. Becca had spent more than sufficient time pent up to note that the layout of pulpits and benches resembled a curiously flat-edged wheel, with Webmaster Steven's high place as the hub. More than once she'd felt its full weight rolling ponderously across her spine.

"Meat today," Salome said at last, wiping her hands

on her pants. "That's a welcome change for you." She turned to look at Becca. "You don't seem to care."

"Tell me why I should."

"I know what they've been feeding you: not bread and water, but close enough. Five days in here and this is the first decent meal you get? I'd care. I'd take notice. It means something."

"Probably does." Becca leaned back, resting her cheek against the window. "I read somewhere it's tradition to give a prisoner one last good feed."

To Becca's surprise, Salome let loose a burst of laughter. "Why, you self-centered little snot. Is that the only thing that's been filling your mind all this time? What's to become of *you*? They haven't even made you stand trial, but you've decided the verdict for 'em already?"

"So what if I have? I know what I know. It can only fall out one way."

Salome came to stand over Becca. Cocking her head to one side she remarked, "You sound sure of that. Have you heard anything specific? Has your brother been here?"

"Eleazar? No. No one else either, except the—" She jerked her face away from the cold, cold glass. She'd been about to say *except the girl who brings my food and cleans my chamber pot*. A frown knit her brows. "What are you doing here, playing whorebaby? Where's—?"

"Then who died and left you to sit in judgment?" Salome talked over Becca's questions as if they'd never been asked. "Who left you to stand *here*?" She strode across the floor to slap one hand on the slanted top of the nearest bronze pulpit. "You don't even know what law you've broken; how can you be so sure of the penalty?"

Becca scowled. "Don't treat me like I'm stupid. I told you: I know what I know. I've gone counter to Webmaster Steven's will. Is there really any other law around here that matters?"

Salome lifted one brow. "You might be surprised." Without waiting for an invitation, she walked right up to Becca and flopped herself down beside her on the bedroll. "Little girl, you can't just lie here, expecting to die."

"What do you care?"

"Call it a sib's interest. There's no blood bond between us, but we've got our pact, you and I, made in the highest currency this city knows."

"If you mean secrets, what of it?" Becca countered, rounding her back over close-hugged knees. "Yours will soon be safe enough."

Salome rolled her eyes, exasperated. "Damn it, the way you're talking I think you'll be disappointed if they *don't* kill you." She heaved herself back to her feet and folded her arms. "Since you asked, I'll tell you: Webmaster Steven was ready to have your life the same night he hauled you in here. And yes, he could've done that. Who'd miss you? Who'd miss you that could do one damn thing to stop him, I mean? The fact you're still alive right now means you won't be looking down the Lord King's sword unless you go seeking it."

"Then what will become of me?" Becca asked. "He won't just set me free." Remembrance of the Wallweb prison made her shudder. "I'd almost rather see the edge of the sword than be locked away."

"Almost?" Salome echoed, twisting the word into a jest. "I'm happy to hear that. It means there's some life-spark left in you. Your brother will be glad of it too."

Becca pressed her face into her knees and mumbled, "My brother wishes he'd never seen my face inside city walls."

"Doesn't it get boring for you, knowing all the answers?" Salome inquired lightly. "Your brother's the one who arranged things so I could take that kitchen ho—whorebaby's place and bring you news. He wants you to feel easy in your mind, to know your life's safe. He'd've come to tell you so himself, but how would that look, the webmaster's fair-haired boy—after Van, of course—fraternizing with a dangerous criminal?" She smirked.

"Salome…" Becca's voice softened; she reached up to tug gently at the trader woman's belt. "Would you take a message to him when you leave me? Give him—give Eleazar my love, and tell him that I'm grateful."

"*Sisterly* gratitude, though, right?" Salome held up one finger like an admonishing teacher and recited: "'Good boundaries make safe steads.' That's an old saying they taught us in creche school." She saw Becca's angry blush and laughed once more. "If you don't know my ways by now, when will you, pretty? Listen: There's more that Eleazar wants you to know. You're going to have visitors. They'll be here as soon as they're done with their own meal downstairs, so I can't linger long. Try to act relieved when they tell you your life's been saved, will you? Webmaster Steven doesn't like anyone spoiling his surprises."

"He's coming here?" The words prickled with loathing over Becca's tongue. "Himself? Why not just send someone?"

Salome offered Becca a hand up. When they stood eye-to-eye she replied, "That's all the information your brother could gather. Don't go whining for more. Keep your mind sharp while the old man's here and maybe you'll learn something that could save a few lives that *aren't* yours."

"You mean Gilber? Is he all right? Was he locked away too?"

One corner of Salome's mouth turned down. She shook her head. "You really do love him. I keep thinking that maybe—Ha! Don't worry, Becca, he's fine. The beloved of Greenwoodweb; they'd keep him here if they could. I'm not talking about him. I mean the children."

The children? For three heartbeats, maybe four, Becca stood staring stupidly at Salome. *What children does she*—? "Virgie!" The name was a gasp, the realization a slap in the face. Becca grabbed Salome's hands desperately tight. "What have you heard? What do you know?"

"Nothing you can't figure out for yourself. What do we always do when we've got extra mouths and no web to take them? Really, Becca, don't tell me you still think this city's some sort of magical island that never knew the hungering times, the old chaos, the wars! We just hide our bones better, that's all.

Out of sight, out of mind. There are even some people who pretend that whorebabies don't exist and that the Flower Market girls serve willingly because they enjoy it. I'm sure we could even find a few who'll tell you that every pretty little girl in yellow *asked* to be cut that way."

"No." Becca squeezed her eyes shut and brought steepled fingers to her lips, turning blind denial into prayer. "Not Virgie, not her sibs, not the children from Mark's stead, no, no, *no*!"

"Oh yes." Salome's tone had lost every vestige of her old easy mockery. "Maybe if they'd come from common steads, the webmasters might have found one of them bright enough, special enough to set aside for the future, but after the time they spent in that hellhole—? If the Greenwoodwebbers didn't chatter, the Highlandwebbers did. The whole city knows. Every trader I met spoke about nothing else for days after they were brought in. No web would risk adopting one of them. If those children escaped the Lord King's sword on their old steads, they won't outrun the city's blade."

Becca opened her eyes, turned her face toward Greenwoodweb. "Gilber has to know," she said. "You've got to tell him. He can take them away with him when he and his new tribefolk leave Coop. Virgie'll rejoice; that child's half in love with him already."

"At her age?" Salome let all her skepticism show. "She's barely old enough for solid food!"

"She's old enough for more than that. Or she will be, soon enough. I've seen sibs of mine scarce older than her who were woman-grown. If that girl doesn't come into changes before a sixmonth's sped—" Becca sighed. "And she's worshipped Gilber from the first. Could be she'll grow into a fine bride for him, in time." She seized Salome by the shoulders and demanded, "Promise me you'll tell him to take Virgie and the rest away."

Salome brought clasped hands up and out in a smooth, sweeping motion that broke Becca's hold in less than a breath. "I can promise I'll tell him, but I can't promise it'll do any good."

"It will do *something*," Becca maintained. "Gilber will see to that."

"Oh, of course he will," Salome drawled. "We all know he's a nine-days' wonder." She lowered her eyes. "They'll be here soon. I'd better go." And it didn't take much more than that to see her gone.

Becca stumbled over to the bench where Salome had left her tray. She sat astraddle while she ate and drank, but she tasted nothing and her eyes might as well have been closed for all they saw. She had almost finished and was sitting there, staring off into the distance, when the chamber door opened a second time. This time her callers didn't bother to knock.

"Good afternoon, Becca," said Webmaster Steven. He entered the room followed by Van and Eleazar. Both of the younger men walked with heads bent, eyes downcast. They reminded Becca of herself and her female sibs when they'd gone maiden-modest among grangefolk at harvest home. The webmaster made straight for his pulpit, feet guided by the force of habit. Thin fingers grasped the silver lectern. He smiled and said, "I've brought you good news. You're going home."

Nothing Salome had said had prepared Becca for those words. She gaped at the old man leering down at her.

"What? Too overjoyed to spare me a word of thanks? Well, no matter, I'm not the one who deserves it, though when you're able, you might thank Van, there. Justice couldn't hope for a better servant. His plea on your behalf helped me see that I was about to make a grievous error of judgment." The webmaster's gaunt face plumped up with smugness. "You see, my first assessment of your case left me no alternative but to condemn you to death. A woman raising up her hand against her natural lord, and for the commission of such a vicious act—! You might as well have killed him as blinded him; the penalty's the same."

"Blinded..." Becca repeated numbly. There was a rushing sound in her ears; Webmaster Steven was speaking in tongues. She forced herself to understand what he was saying. "Adonijah. What's he got to do with—?"

"Tsk, what a question. Poor child. I wonder if it wouldn't be kinder to send you over to Bell at Greenwoodweb for a while, before returning you to Wiserways? But I know nothing of stead law: Madness might be a mitigating circumstance when they try you." He sighed. "I'd spare Van to be your advocate, if I knew for a fact they'd allow him to speak for you. He presented your case so eloquently before me that you owe him your life. It would be a shame if your stead laws revoke it, but what can we do? The steads are our partners, not our subjects; we don't interfere in their ways."

Not by much, Becca thought. A red mist was drifting over her eyes. She wondered if she had the speed to leap out and knock Webmaster Steven to the floor, the strength to snap his neck before Van or Eleazar could stop her. *Not that Van would even try to stop me, but Eleazar... The Lord only knows.* He was speaking again—it was clear how dearly he loved to hear the sound of his own voice—but his words slipped away from her. Only at last did she hear:

"—save the husband must judge his wife."

"What?" she demanded. "What did you say?"

The old man looked at her as if she were a very clever beast. "I said that Van's studies into stead law told him that it is illegal for anyone but the duly recognized alph to rule in matters of assault or attempted murder, even if the attack is against himself. I believe the exact quote he dug out of the library was *None save the land's lord must judge his land's children, none save the father must judge his son, none save the husband must judge his wife.*"

A mad grin broke over Becca's face. "Then you can't send me back to Wiserways for judgment!" she cried. "Adonijah's not my husband, he took me against my will, he's *nothing* to me!"

Webmaster Steven's thin lips pursed tight. "He is the alph of Wiserways. If he took you to his bed, you're his wife."

"You don't know one damn thing about stead law; you said so yourself," Becca shot back, defiance lifting her heart. "That doesn't make me his wife any more than the kiss or the sign espouses me to any man I meet at harvest home. Any road, he's *not* alph of Wiserways, not by a long measure. What became of my case, the case I brought against him? All this time I've bided here in Coop, I thought you were sifting out the evidence I gave that he took my home by deceit and treachery. Where's the law to back that, stead or city? Alph comes after alph by *honest* striving—that's what we're taught, that's what's been the way since we fought ourselves back to order out of the hungering times. If we let the alph's place fall to cheats and tricksters, why honor lore or law at all? You'd do well to honor both, webmaster: They're all that hold up your sorry bones. Without 'em, your words are chaff and you're no more than a miserable old man."

The webmaster's half-bunched fist cracked across Becca's face in a backhanded blow that sent her reeling. She tasted salt and felt with her tongue where teeth had torn up the inside of her cheek. Eleazar was behind her, his arms supporting her. "That was stupid," he murmured in her ear.

Webmaster Steven's face was so bleached with rage it looked frost-killed. "You can't become a stead problem fast enough to suit me," he rasped. "Preach law to *me*, will you? If you were a man, I'd laugh in your face at such ignorance."

"If you were man, so would I," Becca countered, dabbing the blood from her mouth on the back of her hand, wiping it away on her skirt.

The old man started for her, but Van stepped

between them. He cast a pleading glance at Becca. She thought she would drown in his grieving eyes. *All he's lost...* she thought, and that fragment was enough to silence her.

"Sir, she's been locked up here so long, not knowing what's to become of her..." Van's hand closed over the old man's. "Anyone'd be on edge, lash out without thinking. She's going to stand trial on her home ground for worse than insolence; forgive her and let her go."

The webmaster's eyes rested on Van's upturned face; his stern look softened. "Let her admit her error and I'll grant your petition."

Van stepped away from the silver pulpit, took Becca's hand in his own. "Say you're sorry," he implored. "Say you were wrong."

Becca jerked her hand from his gentle grasp, shrugged off her brother. Head high, she met the webmaster's flinty gaze and said, "You know the law better—I'll admit that freely."

He waited for her to say more. When she stayed silent he said, "You want me to accept *that* as your apology?"

"Not by some," she replied. "I was bred up proper; I'm not too proud to beg pardon. But Van wants me to say I was wrong, wrong in all things. How can I say that in this room, before a man of law, and not be lying?"

"Meaning that *I* am the one in error?" Webmaster Steven seemed amused by the possibility. "How?"

"By naming me Adonijah's wife when I'm nothing nigh it. What does the law say makes a wife?" she demanded. "Just the having of her body? Then Isa was Van's bride as much as I'm Adonijah's." She saw the high color flare on the old man's cheeks and spoke on, faster, before he could cut her off. "If there's no calling on rightful blessing and a woman's will to make a marriage, then we're no different from the rogue bands. If it's rape says who claims me, then I'm Adonijah's bride. But if you need consent and consecration as well, then I'm Gilber Livvy's and no other's. Lord God be my witness, he's loved and protected and stood by as my help all this way, all this time. If I raised my hand against him, not Adonijah, kill me for it. A woman can't have save one husband, and Gilber Livvy's mine."

The webmaster's fingers tightened around the edge of the pulpit. "Is this true?"

"You heard me swear it so," she affirmed.

"If that's the case, sir, we can't send her back to Wiserways." Van spoke low, urgently in the webmaster's ear. "If she's not the alph's wife, and she's escaped his jurisdiction, the laws governing sanctuary say—"

"Will *all* of you dare to teach me my business?" Webmaster Steven roared. "I've forgotten more statutes than you'll ever know!" His eyes snaked left and right, stabbing at Van and Eleazar. "The question of this girl's marital status puts another face on things. I want an investigation."

"But webmaster, Gilber Livvy's a Jew!" Eleazar protested. "How could she possibly be wed to—?"

The old man's hand was still quick to slap unwelcome words away. He glowered at Eleazar's

reddening cheek and said, "There is no law forbidding
it, just as there is no law forbidding her from growing
wings and flying to the moon. Why rule against the
unthinkable? Still, there it is." He gave Becca a look
heavy with revulsion, then said to the other men,
"Come."

After they had gone, Becca let her legs give way
beneath her. Seated on the bare, cold floor of the
examination chamber, she ran her hands through
tangled hair that craved the attentions of a comb and
let a dozen whirling thoughts assault her mind.

*Mary Mother, what possessed me? What devil laid hold
of my tongue? I haven't bought anyone's salvation with
that outburst. If that old husk does acknowledge that I'm
Gilber's bride, it won't help me and it might harm him.
And if the webmaster rules otherwise, I'm still bound for
Wiserways and "justice." He never intended to consider
my case against Adonijah at all.*

Without looking, she flung her arms back to get
some support from the bench behind her. One elbow
knocked over her abandoned dinner tray. Becca
watched horrified as it clanged and clattered to the
floor, scattering the last few morsels of her meal. *Lord
forgive me, good food wasted—!* The pang of blame
struck her natural as breathing. She scrambled to
hands and knees, stuffing the scraps into her mouth,
though her innards rebelled. A lurch of the stomach
and she gave up those scavenged bits and all that
she'd eaten before. She huddled over the mess,
shivering, while the shadows of the pulpits reached
out bony fingers for her and the night came on.

She was still crumpled into a wrung rag of sorryness

when she heard the chamber door click open for the third time. "Becca?" A whisper reached her through the dark. She lifted her teary face to see the figures of two men backlit in the doorway. A hand scrabbled over the dial beside the doorjamb and the lights came on. Van stood there blinking in the brightness, and behind him—

"*Gilber!*" She didn't know if she'd made his name into cry of delight or a sob of despair. All she knew was that he was with her, his arms around her, his hand wrapped in a soft cloth to clean away the sickness from her garb and face.

"You've made a good mess of yourself, love," he said, his smile as false as his cheery tone. The truth was in his eyes, sad and loving. He made her stand up and looked her over, shaking his head. "Can you get her some fresh clothes, Van?" he called back over one shoulder.

"Maybe afterward, when I make my report to Webmaster Steven." Van sounded about as lively as a stone. "How long is it supposed to take?"

"Not much," Gilber replied.

"How long is *what* supposed to take?" Becca asked. She'd gained strength from just the sight of him. "Gilber, what are you doing here? You're not a prisoner too?"

"I'm free as can be, with my heart locked away," he said, and never the hint of a jest in those words. "I'm here thanks to him." He nodded at Van.

Van avoided Becca's inquiring look. "He's here because I persuaded Webmaster Steven that it was the simplest way around the law. He wants you out of the city, Becca. I never knew him to want anything so much in my life. Anything," he repeated bitterly.

"I thought he wanted me dead."

"Same thing. If you die here, there'll be talk. If you die back on your stead, no one here ever need hear or say a word about it."

"Funny, a man that powerful, afraid of a little gossip," Gilber remarked.

"There's no such thing as a *little* gossip when it touches the high," Van said. "A webmaster's not an alph: He doesn't win or hold his place by fighting another man for it. He gets it because he's seen to be the best man for the post, and he gets to pass it on to his chosen successor only if he keeps his reputation clean. A master can rule his web any way he likes, provided he keeps up the appearance of unprejudiced service to the city. He can be lord of his own private kingdom, as long as no one catches sight of his crown."

Becca saw the way of things. "Once people get to talking, they can get to thinking. Once they get to thinking, the can get to taking a long, close look at a man's business. Webmaster Steven likes to keep busy tongues and prying eyes turned away from him when he can."

Van nodded. "He likes things quiet and tidy."

"Does he?" Gilber said. "Then he did a sorry job of it when you and Isa—" He paused, not wanting to touch a wound that still ran red.

Van closed his eyes and drew in a jagged breath. "Go away, Gilber," he said. "Get out of this city as soon as you can, you and your whorebabies, run fast, run far. You were there to see his ruthlessness and remember it, you and Becca both, but you can escape with your skin."

"Is that it, Van?" Becca asked. "Is that why he wants me dead? Because of what I saw that day? But there must've been well over a dozen guards there as well. Does he want all of them dead and gone too?"

"Highlandwebbers born and raised within the walls," Van said. "Bred up to dread the power of the law and the lawmaster until it's part of their nightmares. They'd sooner swallow their tongues than turn them against him, and he knows it. But you! What can he make of you? Whoever heard of a steadborn girl trekking all this way to lodge a complaint against her alph? In his eyes, you're nothing natural."

"In *his* eyes…" Becca said under her breath.

Van didn't hear; he went on. "He can't depend on your fear to keep you silent; just your death. If he can arrange for it to happen discreetly, he'll have his heart's desire. But he *will* have it, and under the law. Always under the law."

Gilber pulled her closer to him. "That's how I come to be here this night, angel: in the name of heart's desire." He cupped her face in his hands and with agonizing precision he pronounced: "Behold, you are divorced from me according to the law of Moses and Israel!"

Chapter Eighteen

So then the wife, she says to her man,
(Trying to throw him off the scent of how
things was, like, him just back after all that
time away and all) " 'Course he's yours!
Can't you see he's got your face and your
hair? Ain't you got eyes?"
And the husband says to his wife, "Sure,
I got eyes. But I got fingers, too, and I
know how to count to nine!"

The tip of a soft-shod foot nudged Becca gently awake in the predawn dark. "The first daylight shift's coming on any minute," said Eleazar. "Vester owes me enough to turn a blind eye for now, but the next one up's Kenyon. He's only an apprentice, keen to show his devotion to Third. We can't bully or buy him off. You'd better get things moving."

Becca rubbed her eyes and sat up, the sheet falling away from her body. She heard her brother exclaim, "Jesus Christ, woman!" and saw him whirl away. That brought her to full, shamefaced wakefulness. She pulled up the sheet to cover her shame and reached out to nudge the man who slept beside her.

"Gilber, love, it's time you're away."

Gilber Livvy went from sleeping to fully woke in less time than it took Becca to loose a yawn. The dawn light was starting to well up out of the sea, pink and yellow, flame and gold bleeding away the dying night. It seeped in rapidly through the clear glass walls of the examination chamber, making Gilber and Eleazar look like spirits stealing their way back into flesh. Gilber was on his feet, dressed in his Greenwoodweb clothes, shirt and trousers stitched together all of a piece. He smiled at Eleazar. "I'm good as gone. Just give me a little time alone with her for farewells, then you can see me on my way."

Eleazar shook his head. "You go out with the same escort who brought you in, and you wait until Van calls for you. Vester owes me, but not enough to let me waltz out of here with a man he didn't see come in." He held a small bundle to his chest, pale green cloth that matched Gilber's outfit. "Take it. This shouldn't be found here." When Gilber accepted the crumpled jumpsuit, Eleazar added, "Don't take long." Then he was gone.

Gilber let the clothing fall, pulled Becca to him, and pressed his lips to her tangled hair. "You be brave," he said. "Brave like you know how to be. We'll find a way through this wilderness too."

Becca gave a little sigh of contentment against his chest. "I'm not the one needs bravery. Gilber, swear to me by your shabbit that you'll get those children free!"

"Good as done, angel; better. Think these cityfolk won't be glad to have me volunteer to take more extra mouths off their account? My new tribe and me, we're supposed to leave the gates tomorrow or next day, so we can get some distance between us and the city before shabbit comes on. That'll be more than enough time to clear Virgie and her kin for joining us." A stray thought darkened his face. "Heaven grant those little ones have the strength for a long march."

"They will." Becca was set against believing any other possibility. "They're stead. When you're stead, you do what needs done or you're gleanings."

Gilber's rough hand stroked her cheek tenderly. "A child shouldn't have to live that way."

"Then you give them a different way to live when you reach your folk in the mountains."

"*We'll* give them that way," Gilber corrected her. "I'm going to get my new tribe off into the wastelands, then double back for you."

"Gilber, no! How'll you ever get back into the city? You know how it is at the gates. The best you can hope for's to be sent packing. Don't make me think of the worst." She hugged him tight, her bare skin rasping against cloth and buttons. "Mary Mother watch over your going and God be thanked for what we've had tonight. There's not a day left me but I'll spend it blessing poor Van for this last gift."

Gilber forced her head up, made her look him in the eye. He had a hard look on him that could lesson a stone in stubbornness. "Don't you talk of it that way; it *wasn't* our last time together! I'm only sorry it was our first in so long. Heaven forgive me for having kept you off, but I'm seven kinds of fool and I hope you'll forgive me for that. I looked at you and all I could see was miracle. I thought a man could only come nigh a miracle with prayer, not love." He shook his head over his own past folly. "Didn't Moses' wife live with miracles and still love her man?"

Becca smiled at him. "If it took you divorcing me to bring you back into my bed, I'm grateful for it, even if it does make me a harlot in your eyes."

Gilber wasn't smiling at all. "I said those words with Van as witness because that was the price of my being brought to you. Webmaster Steven wanted all things swept clean so that he could hand you over to your stead, no strings attached." A wayward hint of bitter mirth touched his eyes. "And no husbands either. But what I said was gabble; it means nothing under our law. You're still my bride, Becca, you're still my wife, and it'll take death itself to end what makes us one."

"Does Van know he witnessed nonsense?"

"Does he care?" Gilber shrugged. "He was the one who came to the old scavenger with the idea of fetching me here to divorce you. He told me 'Just say anything to her that sounds authentic, something I can run back to repeat to Webmaster Steven.'" The memory of sweetness melted his straight-set lips into a half smile. "That was how he contrived to leave us alone. And later on he used his authority to send your guard away so Eleazar could put on these clothes—" He toed the castoff jumpsuit. "—and pretend he was me, leaving Thirdweb tower, just in case of prying eyes. Your brother can go stealthy, when he likes; he'd make a fine hunter."

"Then how will you get out of here now?" Becca demanded. "A man can't leave the same place twice."

"No fear, love, these guards aren't Highlandweb. They're just Thirdweb men who've been called up to do what their master bids 'em, while you're captive here. And they're none too thrilled about it, believe me. They see it like an insult to their true training in the law; they're only standing guard with one eye and a resentful heart. Van studied how it was with 'em since the day you were brought here, and he says one watchman doesn't trade talk with the next. Once their portion of guard duty's done, they do their best to put it from their mind, act like it never happened."

As if he'd heard his name, Van opened the chamber door and stuck his head in. "Come *on*, Gilber. Vester's just gone off and Kenyon's on his way. We've got to get you out of here *now*." Then his eyes focused on Becca and he swallowed hard.

She whisked up her sheet into a makeshift gown and hurried barefoot across the floor to embrace him. "Oh Van, what you've given us—!"

"Nothing," he muttered. "Thank me when you've

got a real debt owing." He pushed her aside and dragged Gilber away with him, not even giving him the chance to retrieve Eleazar's disguise.

She heard their voices just outside the door, greeting the new guard. Van did most of the talking. He spun a fine tale of how he'd been compelled to bring the Jewman in to the prisoner at Webmaster Steven's behest. It was all true, except for the *when* of it. If apprentice Kenyon had any misgivings, Van quickly soothed them away with a gush of praise and heavy hints concerning the wisdom of not questioning the man destined to inherit the webmaster's five silver flowers.

Becca began to dress for the day only after she caught the sound of the guard checking the lock's security, the familiar click of tumblers covering the echo of retreating footsteps. There were fresh clothes awaiting her, also thanks to Van, who had cleared away her sick-stained blouse and skirt as if he were the lowliest whorebaby. "Could've saved himself the trouble," she murmured, looking down at the Greenwoodweb jumpsuit that had been left behind in Van's haste to get Gilber gone. "That looks comfortable enough." She was just folding it to hide under her bedroll when someone knocked at the door.

"Just a minute!" she called, cramming the jumpsuit away all anyhow. A sleeve stuck out but she had no time to tuck it up. She barely had the time to pull her new dress over her head before the door opened and a brawny young man with hair the same red gold as the sunrise poked a long nose around the edge. He saw her standing there, half in and half out of her dress, some of her small-clothes showing, and grinned sheepishly, a wooden comb in his outstretched hand.

"Van said to give you this," he said, his voice rising up and stopping just this side of an awkward squeak. It sounded more than odd coming from such a powerfully built body. "Sorry to trouble you." No matter how man-grown he looked in body, his youth was still painful clear to see.

Young... She didn't know how the idea came to her. It struck her in an instant, bursting from her brow like the half-formed child of an impatient womb. She cast a glance at the telltale sleeve of the jumpsuit trailing out from under her bedroll and made up her mind then and there, for good or ill.

"You're more than welcome, sir," she said, stepping forward to take the comb from him, all brazenness in her eyes. Back home the girls had been well lessoned in a proper woman's place, how best to show any man undying gratitude for all he'd done to feed and shelter them. The practice sessions with the wooden phallus, all its sections duly marked and numbered, were only part of it. Just because some of the younger men were shy was no reason for a dutiful woman to turn from her obligations. "And I'm more than grateful."

Becca's hand reached for the comb, but her fingertips alit instead on the soft skin of the lad's upturned wrist. She traced the path of blue-green veins lightly, with a delicate, teasing touch that called up bright color to his face. She gave him no time for more than a single gasp before her hands darted out to cup his face and bring it to hers in a breathless kiss. Touch and go, touch and go, her tongue was a tiny arrow all aflame at the sensitive corners of his mouth. She felt his pulse leap high as she stroked the invisible line than ran behind ear and jaw, down the sides of his neck.

The wooden comb clattered to the floor. She ignored it, pressing her breasts to him, drawing him back into the chamber with her step by step. She would wager her own life that none of the Flower Market girls bothered much with the refinements stead women had passed down through the years. But then, a Flower Market girl's place in life was set firm, a stead woman lived or died by how well she pleased her alph. Kenyon held onto enough presence of mind to grope behind him and slam the door, but she heard no click.

He'd never close us off from sight if that door latched of itself, she thought, letting her fingers loose the buttons of his collar. *He'd be a fool to risk getting locked in the garden, no matter how sweet the fruit. Whatever he fancies this means—whether I've gone mad with confinement or crazy in love with him on sight—he's protecting himself. Thinks he'll take what's offered and be back to his post before anyone comes along to see. Thinks he's got a man's strength to back him, and he does—he'd be worthy to strive as alph onstead. Thinks whatever he thinks of steadwomen—whispered, wanton, ignorant tales to make a young cityman sweat and breathe hard—but knows we're only women after all. He knows that even the meanest man can do what he likes with a woman. Oh, they don't take fools into Thirdweb!*

She pushed away from him, laughing deep in her throat, and pulled off her dress before beckoning him back to her arms. Her hands wandered over his body more boldly now, undoing every fastening they found, plucking aside his shirt and opening his trousers as she sank to her knees. "Your strength has brought me sanctuary, your kindness has fed me, your honor vouchsafed me salvation," she recited, the rote words every decent stead woman spoke before offering a man comfort. "I would show you thanks and gratitude." She smiled up at him sideways, a fox's grin, and then, so he couldn't mistake what was being offered him, she let him know a little of the kiss and the sign.

He gasped with pleasure and surprise. He sounded almost like a stead maiden, the first time the old wives explained her duties concerning men. He was very young. Becca had guessed that Flower Market girls who owned more skills at pleasuring a man than merely letting him take them were reserved for elders, for webmasters, for men of higher standing in their elics than this Thirdweb apprentice.

It didn't take him long to catch on, to seize with both hands the gift she offered. He let her know that he'd have more of the kiss, and she set herself to bring him to the very gates of Paradise.

But there were spikes atop the gate, spikes sharp as Becca's snapping teeth, wicked as the nails of the hand she drove up into the lad's groin at the same time. He gaped in shock, sucking in air for a shriek of agony loud enough to rouse all Thirdweb tower and bring them running. She was up and at him before the last of that breath rushed into his lungs, one hand clamped to his mouth, the other a fist to drive hard into his temple. He fell, and she fell with him, fists and elbows, feet and knees striking the cry from his lips and the light from his eyes.

She left him stretched out full length in the shadow of Webmaster Steven's silver pulpit, his breath coming shallow, his eyes a thin line of white showing between his lashes. She stripped off her dress and scrambled into the pale green jumpsuit, always with a wary eye on Kenyon. When she was clad for her going, she used her teeth to tear her bedding to strips, then bound and gagged him. Only then did she think to search his clothing for anything that might prove useful in her flight.

She had little luck: Her guard was unarmed. Why should he be, when he was only standing ward over one slight girl barely into her womanhood? She recovered the comb and yanked it fiercely through her tangled hair. It wouldn't do for a woman of Greenwoodweb to be seen passing through the city streets so unkempt; folk would pause to look and wonder. Handfuls of hair were torn out by the roots, but at last she had it neat. She anchored it to the back of her head with the selfsame comb, opened the door, and took back her freedom.

The stairwell was deserted for the first three storeys she descended. Once she heard footsteps coming up, and she ducked out onto a floor, hugging the wall until the people passed. She went as fast as she could and still keep her downward flight as hushed as might be. A little luck was with her: At that early hour most of Thirdweb's elics would be gathered in their dining rooms having breakfast, if they were stirring at all.

And how long before the girl comes up to bring me my breakfast and finds that unlucky boy? Becca wondered. She dearly wished she'd paid more mind to the comings and goings of the Thirdweb whorebabies who'd served her, noticed whether their tasks had hewed to a fixed hour or happened at random times. *You're just as good as Coopfolk at turning them invisible, she thought grimly. Well, it's likely that no whorebaby's spared to serve a prisoner until all the honest members of Thirdweb've been fed. I've got some small measure of time safe.* She made herself believe that. It was what sustained her until she reached the ground floor and stole out of Thirdweb tower, into the street. If she didn't hang onto that scrap of certainty, she knew she'd bolt and run.

She couldn't run; running drew eyes. She strolled away from Thirdweb tower, never looking back, Lot's wife turned mindful of heaven's warning. The city streets swallowed her fast enough. The path to Greenwoodweb was familiar ground, soon covered. It was bitter cold. She missed her coat, though the jumpsuit was made of heavy fabric that took the edge off the weather. If she adopted a brisk pace, she would look natural enough: a meddie who'd been called away on some emergency in too much haste to bring a proper jacket. She walked boldly into the first building she reached, found a stairway, and followed it as far down as it went.

She found herself in the dim maze of tunnels through which Gilber had led her to the tower where his new tribe bided. She'd been sure to fix her eyes on the tower itself while she was still in the city streets, and even underground she thought she had a good idea of where it lay.

Can't be too hard to find, she thought, pure faith strengthening her resolve. *Any road, I've got to find it, no choice about it at all, or I might as well lay down and die right here.* A white pipe directly over her head let out a gurgle loud enough to spook her, but she recovered herself quickly and set out after the tower.

It wasn't as simple as she'd prayed. She'd marked the direction of the tower in a straight path from where she was, but there were no straight paths under Greenwoodweb; the tunnels didn't cooperate with her theories. They hit dead ends when she wanted them to go dead on. They made her double back and choose a second route, then a third, then a fourth. They persisted in looking alike, with no more than a darkening or lightening of paint or pipes to distinguish one from another.

Her legs began to weary. She fled the infrequent stairwells like a littlesinger fleeing the shadow of the nest-devouring scythe. The rumblings and hissings of the pipes took on the sound of human voices, and she fled these too, pressing herself into dark corners, stumbling into passageways where no light came at all. Her old fear of dying in the dark stole out to set its talons to her throat, companion to the burning thirst already lodged there. She'd frozen in the city streets, now she broiled beneath them. Sweat soaked her every limb, and her breath was a raspy sobbing in her ears.

Her mother's spirit rose up in her mind. Hattie's imagined presence clanged like the tongue of a great brazen bell. *This is the just reward for your perversity, Becca! This is what you reap for tearing down what's holy and raising your voice against what's so!*

Tired and hopelessly turned around in the passageways, Becca found a space of clear wall, leaned her back against it, and sank to her haunches. Resting her head on her knees, she wept quietly, wondering whether Webmaster Steven's Highlandweb hounds would find her here before she died.

At length the tears left her. *You're a sorry woman, Becca of Wiserways,* she chided herself. *Salome had it right, taking you down for all this self-pity when there's others in dearer need. Now you get yourself on your feet and the next stairway you find, you climb it back to the surface and you start for the tower fresh!*

She raised her face to take a deep breath before heeding her own orders. Something in the air tickled her nostrils peculiar. She sniffed some, then more avidly. *Stew, I'd say. Could be I'm near the Greenwoodweb cookhouse or...*

She got to her feet, propping one hand hard against the wall, and began to follow the trail of scent. In the warm, stagnant tunnel air its pungent track was unmistakable. After only a couple of wrong turnings, it brought her to the foot of a familiar set of steps. Becca stuck her head into the stairwell and harked. This time there was no confusing the sound of human voices high above with the noise of steam and water pipes. She uttered a thankful cry and clambered up the stairs.

Near the top, she almost fell into the arms of the three whorebabies who were heading down. She recognized one of them as Yemina, once of the Flower Market. The yellow-veiled girl stared down at Becca as if she saw a restless ghost, then breathed, "Oh, lady!" and fell to one knee on the steps. Her fingers clutched a small object hanging from a length of cord around her neck. Before Becca could say a word or steal a glimpse of what it was Yemina grasped so tight, the girl whipped a frowning face onto her companions and rapped out, "Where's your brains, Cassius? Where's your worship, Ger? Don't you remember Rev Livvy's teachings? Don't you know her when you see her? You don't deserve to have her blessing!"

The other two wanted no second telling. Their hands grabbed for the pendants they too wore, and they bent their bodies low, though it was an awkward thing to do on a stairway. "Your blessing, lady," Cassius muttered.

"My blessing?" It came from Becca's lips as a question, but the three whorebabies heard it otherwise. They lifted beaming faces to her and held out the pendants around their necks. The orbs of crudely beaten gray metal had almost no sheen, but a wisp of white cloth escaping from Yemina's charm looked bright as a candle flame in the stairwell shadows.

Becca reached her hand up, wanting to touch one of the pendants, to bring it closer to her eyes for a better look. The whorebabies nearly shoved one another down the steps, each overcome by zeal to

make sure Becca's touch was for his charm first.
While they jostled for place, Ger's foot caught in the
hem of Yemina's dress. He slid down the stairs with
a yelp of alarm that turned into a horrified shout
when he bowled Becca off her feet. Together they
rolled down most of the flight, coming to a halt
where the stairs turned a corner.

Becca's head spun, but she'd taken no grave hurt.
She sat there blinking, Ger's scrawny body sprawled
across her lap. His left fist was closed tight around
his pendant and even half stunned as he was he
managed to gasp out, "Your blessing, lady!"

Then the stairwell filled with faces. A yellow river
came rushing down to sweep Ger off Becca's body and
haul her to her feet. Angry shouts mingled with fresh
pleas for her blessing, along with the sound of slaps
and harder blows. And over it all at last came Gilber
Livvy's voice, crying peace. Becca rested against the
stairwell wall, still catching her breath, feeling the
ache of a few newly blooming bruises, watching as
Gilber waded through the mass of scowling
whorebabies. The knot surrounding Ger gave him the
most trouble. They were pummeling the poor boy and
he wasn't even trying to fend off their blows.

"What's this? What do you think you're doing?"
Gilber demanded. "Haven't I taught you better than
that? Isn't it enough that every man's hand's raised
against you out there, but you have to hurt each
other?"

"But Rev Livvy, he did a terrible thing!" Cassius'
voice was shrill with indignation. "He struck the
lady!"

"The lady?" Gilber's brows came together in puzzlement, then rose slowly, slowly, as Yemina shyly touched his arm and turned his gaze toward Becca.

"Hello, Gilber," she said, her voice all a-quaver, and stretched out her hands to welcome him as if she'd done no more than come home from the fields at dusk.

Chapter Nineteen

*So when Gideon came to meet his
enemies, he hadn't many soldiers in his
ranks, but he had brains. He gave them
torches and he gave them orders to fill the
night with clamor enough for an army three
times their size. Didn't they! Oh I'll say so!
And I don't know how many of them felt
they was playing the fool or how many
stopped to question their alph's doings, but
I do know this: It worked. Spooked off
Gideon's enemies fine. He was plenty
smart, was Gideon, for a Jew.*

They raced through the city like a wind with
nightmare under its wings. They cast aside the garb
that Greenwoodweb had provided for their new lives

in Gilber's tribe and put on their yellow clothes again, all of them, melting into the city, trickling into all the places they needed to go, like water seeping into the earth. Their instructions were as clear and simple as they were vital: *Go back to your old places. All of you steal food. Those of you who can, steal weapons. Meet in the great barn of Greenwoodweb by eleven, no later, or be left behind. Do whatever's needful to claim us our caravan. If you are caught, die before you betray the lady.*

Becca stood by the tower window and saw them emerge from the different buildings singly and in their twos and threes. She watched them scatter to the four quarters of the city and shook her head in sorrow. *What have they made of me?* The thought left her heartsick. Every one of those yellow-garbed little figures down there wore a gray metal ball tucked inside shirt or dress, and each of those pendants contained a scrap of cloth stained with a woman's blood.

"Mine, lady!" Becca could still hear Yemina's proud declaration. "Mine, *though we've agreed to let it stand for yours. Rev Livvy told us how it is for you. He called you miracle; we knew you for a portent. To have the bloodsign on you every time the moon changes! To be able to take a man whenever you like and not need to be cut for it! To bear daughters like you, and for them to bear more until the knife's stilled forever!"* The girl pressed Becca's trembling hands to her brow. "Bless *my blood by your power and take it for your own."*

What could I say? Becca agonized. *How could I dare say anything that might take away their hope? Oh Gilber, what have you done? Taken up these throwaway children, offered them escape when escape's their sole salvation, taught them to hang my face for a mask on all their worship—*

—made you a god? A small presence, razor keen, pricked its way into her mind. In other times, another life, she would have mistaken it for Satan's worm in her brain, or for the sting of madness. She knew herself better now. *Not Gilber's, that blasphemous lessoning. You know better than that. All the time he's been gathering up his new tribe, all the time he's been helping them, teaching them, gaining their trust, he's also been talking to them like human beings. Human beings trade stories, natural as breathing. He must've told them about you so they could gain hope. Hope's what they hunger for. A miracle's just a hope writ large. What happens to you every moon, he likely told them that tale to give them hope that things can change, anything can change. Anything from when a woman bleeds to how a whorebaby lives. You're no god; not unless your own pride tries to make you one. Then I promise you, Gilber Livvy'd be the first to tear your altar down. His scroll and your Scriptures share this much, at least: No other gods before Me!*

No god... What am I, then, for those poor children?

A sign, a symbol, a talisman. That's what they've made of you, and what can Gilber do to stop them? For souls who've only had misery lifelong, sometimes a symbol before their eyes seems more powerful than any god in a far gone heaven.

But to be willing to die for me... She closed her eyes.

Her head echoed with the clamor of the whorebabies taking the oath Niv created and made them all swear to before setting out on their various missions.

Her other voice sought to soothe her: *All roads are paved with bone. They believe that now their deaths mean more than just another whorebaby body to clear away. If you take back that hope of honor, they'll find their deaths at last, any road. You who shun the dark, will you take away their only spark of fire?*

She opened her eyes once more and gazed down. There were no more yellow-clad figures emerging from any of the Greenwoodweb buildings. Gilber's hands rested on her shoulders, lending her strength, then tightened to pull her back into the room.

"No more time," he said. He hustled her down the stairway, and the few whorebabies who'd stayed behind in the tower room pressed themselves as near to her as they dared. If Becca glanced to left or right or over one shoulder she saw a face transfigured by the bliss of worship.

A spark of fire or a holocaust? she wondered. *I'm no god, and if they follow Gilber's true teachings they can't see me as one. But I'm no monster either, no freak. I am different, but I am as God made me. If my blood answers to a different hour, that is the gift of God. If I turn from it, if I flee it, if I don't use it, then my sin will fill ten thousand Prayerful Hills with the bones of the innocent. The Lord King in all his bloody glory will be as nothing next to me.*

She broke away from Gilber, moving faster, taking the lead. "Hurry," she whispered. "We have to fetch the children."

When they were down in the tunnels, she ceded her place to him willingly. He knew his way well, taking each turn swift and sure. She followed, pulling the collar of her dress tighter around her neck, trying to make it close up proper; it wouldn't. The borrowed garment belonged to one of the whorebabies still with them, a girl called Portia whose bosom was almost as flat as a boy's. Becca longed for her castoff jumpsuit but knew it was no use yearning after what she couldn't have—not yet, any road. Portia was the only female whorebaby who hadn't been sent off into the city, the only one who could spare Becca the yellow-dyed clothing she needed to get through this alive.

They swarmed up a stair, Gilber still in the lead. He carried his rifle openly. In the pocket of the coarse apron covering her skirt, Becca's reclaimed gun made an awkward weight. It slammed into her thigh with every step she climbed, every stride she took. It called up fresh pain from the bruises she'd gathered falling down the stairs with Ger, but every blow held a strange comfort for her. *No more*, she thought. *No more lying helpless in their hands, no more being chaff blown by every city-bred word. I've got a word of my own to say, and they'd do well to heed it!*

They reached the ward where Virgie and her sibs were kept without incident. "They'll be in their rooms with their breakfast trays," Gilber whispered down the ranks. He'd dwelled so long in Greenwoodweb that he knew its hourly turnings by heart.

No time, no time, no time! The words sounded a knell inside her head. Morning was still a new thing, noon needed to see them all out the city gates and away. They'd lashed together plans made of desperation and necessity and more than a little prayer. The faster they acted on them, the less chance they had to think through whether they had a hope of succeeding at all.

Gilber instructed his people to divide into smaller groups, two to stand watch by the stairs, two to resume their old whorebaby posts behind cleaning carts, one in green to play the meddie's part and accompany him and Becca into the children's rooms.

Brave in Becca's hastily donned jumpsuit, little Portia hugged a sheaf of important-looking papers to her chest and put on a solemn face. The jumpsuit sagged and swam on her, despite a borrowed belt and some hastily done basting stitches, but it would take the powers of hell itself to deter that girl from serving out her part. She did just as Gilber had lessoned her, striding into Virgie's room and announcing in her deepest voice, "Well, children, you're to come along with us for some tests now," just in case some idle-minded passerby in the hall might notice them and eavesdrop.

The man already in the room with Virgie and five other girl-children was no passerby. He was seated on the edge of a bed, taking a smear of blood from a weeping child's finger. Becca saw that he wore the sign of an aide, the embroidered Greenwoodweb tree over his heart supported by two golden hands. He half rose when he saw the three of them barge in. "What the—?" His eyes said more than that, fairly shouted that he knew a false meddie when he saw one and that he wouldn't be shy about calling for help.

"No you don't," Gilber said softly, leveling his gun at the man's chest. He never took his eyes off the aide while he instructed Portia to bind the man and Becca to prepare the children. They left him tied up and stowed with the chamber pots under one of the ward beds, clad only in his small-clothes. His shirt and trousers, jacket and shoes were all plundered to clothe the children, along with their blankets.

Becca gave silent thanks to sweet Mary Mother that they encountered no more trouble as they gathered up the others. It joyed her to see how fit and hale their stay in Greenwoodweb had left the refugees from Mark's unlucky stead. Then she saw their little feet. Some were shod in flimsy slippers, some were bare. Virgie was the only one with decent shoes, and those too big for her, stolen from the captive aide.

The great barn of Greenwoodweb holds many chariots, she thought. *God grant us the luck or help us muster the strength to capture one, at least. Elsewise, if we've got to bring these babes with us afoot, especially the littlest ones—* Her heart ached at the chance of it. *How will they survive the trek awaiting them?*

If we live to start the trek at all.

They shepherded the children back down into the tunnels, Becca and Gilber and Portia. The two whorebabies who'd been standing watch while they reaped the ward floor had gone off to join the two who'd taken the cleaning carts. Before long all four came rushing back, their arms laden. Three of them carried piles of neatly folded, freshly laundered uniforms, some yellow, some green. The fourth, a young man named Felix, grinned wide enough to split his sallow cheeks when he upended the coarse sack on his back and a hail of shoes fell to the ground.

"Stuff 'em with rags to fit," he suggested as Virgie and the others rummaged through them.

Gilber patted him on the back and looked proud. "How'd you do that? How'd you find them?"

Felix tried to stretch his smile even wider. "While that bunch was cleaning out the linen closets, I grabbed me a mop and went into the meddies' lounge. They got showers there, and there's a whole shift just come off duty. How many people you know shower with their shoes on?"

They got the children clothed all anyhow in the stolen uniforms, good enough to keep off some of the cold. Gilber looked them over and sighed, then said, "Once we're clear of the city, needn't take the same road home that brought us here. We can swing north or south, whichever way we could maybe find a stead that doesn't know us, do something to get these babies more warmth to wear."

"Don't call us babies!" Virgie spoke up, proud, and her feelings were echoed by a number of the older children.

"I only mean the *real* babies," Gilber soothed, and won her smile.

"Better find a stead with no trade ties here," little Portia said. "All the others are going to know us, all right. Word's going to get out as soon as we do."

"You think they'll post a reward for us?" Felix sounded ready to panic.

"It's not you they'd be after," Becca said. "Once they had me, they'd let the rest of you go."

Felix's face lost its little-boy look of fright in an instant. "Only way they'll have you is over my dead body," he said. "And if you come asking help of any stead, lady, they better give it or they'll have to answer to us!"

"Oh, they'll give us an answer, Felix." Portia's words carried the weight of harsh lessoning, cruelly learned lifelong. "It won't be anything but *no*. Anything we get from them, we'd have to steal or fight for. We don't even know if the others will scare us up any weapons. Maybe you were planning on using sticks and stones? I can't even do that." She pulled back the sleeve of her jumpsuit to show a forearm that looked slender and fragile as a glass wand, the delicate bones that marked the born whorebaby girl. "One blow and I'm finished."

"I thought the steads were free," Gilber said. "Does the city own them?"

He spoke to Becca, but again it was Portia who answered. "Might as well; they do in all but name. None of this city's steads would dare help us: They'd risk being cut off from all future aid, outcast from their grange, left on their own and called fair game. Any other stead with a taste for taking on more land could try to conquer them and no one inside the walls would even blink."

Becca cringed at the thought of such a happening. Her sire had seen to it that his children were well lessoned in the mistakes of the past. It taught them to be properly grateful for present wisdom.

Becca knew that there'd been wars in the olden days, in the years when steads and granges and cities were just starting to drag themselves into the light after the chaos of the hungering times. Wars over land, wars over water, wars over anything one stead had that another might covet. Sometimes the wars brought back the worst of the lost ages. Then the cities mustered their power, offered their wonders to the steads provided that the steads would accept their judgments. The steads that first agreed to the trade alliances soon owned better seed, better livestock, better tools for sowing and reaping.

The other steads saw this, envied it, and made haste to pledge themselves as well. The cities welcomed them all, negotiating among themselves over a fair distribution of influence. They never meant to rule the steads, they said; that was for the alphs to do. They were only there to mend fences, mind borders, and cultivate peace.

"Then we'll just have to find a stead that *will* help us, and that'll lose nothing by it," Becca declared. "And if that's beyond us, we'll make our way to the mountains on our own."

"Bless you, lady, if you say it, it'll be so." Portia clasped Becca's hands and bowed over them.

"Nothing will be so unless we move," Gilber said. "I can't tell the hour down here, but it wouldn't hurt if we got over to the great barn now. The sooner we lay hands on something to ride, the less I'll worry over the little ones."

Once more he took the lead, walking briskly through the tunnels. Virgie fell into step behind him just as if they were still crossing the wilderness. The other children filed after her, eyes wide and mouths tight shut. They clung to one another hard enough to snap finger bones and kept jerking their heads this way and that every third step, seeking demons in the shadows.

Poor babies, Mary Mother take you under her veil, Becca thought. *Every home you've ever known, torn from you. When we're through this trial, you'll have a place to bide that no one's going to take from you, I swear it.*

She took a place at the very end of their parade, ready to help any stragglers. Little Portia was there beside her, bringing up the rear. As they marched along, Becca couldn't help pondering one thing, and at last she asked the girl outright: "How'd you come to know so much about law dealings between Coop and stead?"

"How?" The girl stared at her, perplexed, as if she'd just been whisked from her feet and plopped down in the middle of the examination chamber. "My lady, I worked in Thirdweb all my life, Carsonelic mostly; I overheard enough law talk to learn by. I'm not stupid."

" 'Course you're not," Becca said, half to herself. Her voice was calm, but her thoughts were frantic. *Thirdweb! Carsonelic! She was probably there when I first came. Skinny little arms like that, she couldn't do enough hard work to suit 'em, so they sent her off to join Gilber's tribe and no loss. I must've seen her a dozen* times before that, but I don't remember. She's a whorebaby. Who ever sees a whorebaby?

She swallowed her shame and smiled as she patted Portia's shoulder, commending her for how well she'd played her part back up on the children's ward. The little woman's bliss over such simple praise was more than Becca could bear. *She thinks I've laid the moon in her lap when all I'm doing is salving my conscience. I'm her lady, I'm the lady for her and for all of them. She'd die for me without asking why and I can't even recall her face. Merciful Lord, shield us all from what I might become!* She made some excuse and scurried up to the front of the line to walk beside Gilber.

They didn't go much farther before the piped and plastered tunnel walls gave way to smooth, featureless passageways lined with dark green metal closets. Two walls of locked doors flanked them and the strong smell of fuel made Becca wrinkle her nose. The echo of machines at work wafted up the corridor, a muted growling of gears and pistons heard over the sound of shouting human voices. They reached the end of the passageway and stepped out into the great barn of Greenwoodweb.

There were bodies bleeding on the oil-slicked ground, bodies in yellow, bodies in green. Blue-white light from glow globes bigger than any Becca had yet seen turned all the space beneath them to a place of stark, razor-slashed planes of brightness and shadow. Something whistled past her ear, someone cried out behind her. She turned her head and saw one of the whorebabies, a pinch-faced man named Ozias, his arm pierced by a green-spined fleche. She looked back and saw Gilber raise his rifle to his shoulder with a hunter's cold concentration and fire. The report echoed and reechoed in the confines of the tunnel mouth, numbing her ears, and the reek of a spent shot assaulted her nostrils. None of this was real. It was happening too quickly to be real. She stood there staring while Gilber fired again and again.

"Lady, get down." Felix was grabbing her arm, pulling her back into the passageway. She saw Virgie and the children lying flat to the floor and for an instant she imagined that they were all dead, cut down by city magic in some sort of Coop winnowing called up by Webmaster Steven for her sins. Then she heard one of the littlest ones crying and saw Virgie crawl over to comfort him. She sighed with relief.

"Damn it, I told you get *down!*"

Becca was shoved farther back into the tunnel and forced to her knees. They scraped raw against the rough cement floor. The pain snapped her back into full command of her senses. She looked up and saw Felix standing over her with his face dead gray and a look in his eyes that begged God for a swift death.

"Heaven forgive me, what'd I do?" he groaned, covering his face and shrinking down small. Becca cast her arms over him, tried to say something, but he shrugged her off violently and wailed, "I've laid hard hands on you! I've cursed you! I'm as good as dead!"

Becca pressed her lips together and gave the stripling a healthy shake. "Stop that!" she ordered. "You saved my fool life, *that's* what you did! *I* was

the one good as dead, standing there like a mooncalf.
Now you snap out of it and be useful. Your kin need
you, Rev Livvy needs you, God witness I need you,
and not like this! Or will you let me face them
alone?" And she drew the gun from her apron pocket
to let him know she meant to join the battle.

His eyes were dripping tears when they met hers,
but he'd lost his fear. "Lady, you're my strength.
Name me your right hand and you'll see how well I
serve you."

She touched his head and spoke a hasty blessing
because she didn't know what else she could do and
still save his mind. He grabbed her hands and pressed
them to the amulet around his neck, then leaped up
and dashed for the mouth of the tunnel where Gilber
now knelt and continued to fire his rifle. He made
the great barn of Greenwoodweb echo with his battle
yell before a sprinkling of bright-winged fleches
brought him down.

His death tore across Becca's eyes. She snapped out
orders to the remaining whorebabies in the tunnel:
"Stay where you are! Protect the children!"

"Don't need to tell me twice," Ozias muttered,
nursing his wound.

Gun in hand, Becca crept forward to crouch by
Gilber. The bloody bodies on the ground had stunned
her, but now she was fully alert, able to take in all
that was happening beyond the passageway.
Whorebabies in their yellow garb were swarming over
the orderly rows of meddie transports, using their
stolen weapons to fight off the uniformed guards.

They weren't common city troops—Gilber had

often told her how Greenwoodweb was a city unto itself, with no need for Highlandwebbers to ward its property. ("Keep to yourself, keep all your secrets safe, that's how they reason it," he'd said.) The whorebabies had the guards outnumbered, but the guards had Gilber's tribe out-armed. Becca heard soft explosions of air come from weapons that looked much like Gilber's rifle, saw blowpipes launch a fresh volley of fleches. Every time a guard fell, the nimbler whorebabies would dart in to snatch his weapon away. Sometimes they came away with the prize, sometimes they fell too.

But those who lived to carry new weapons to their comrades soon outnumbered those who fell. Their cry was "For the lady!" and the look in their eyes had room for only victory or death. The Greenwood guards saw this and quailed. Slowly, inexorably, the fight was turning against them. They didn't care to wait for it to reach a natural end. One man among them barked the order for retreat; no one bided long enough to hear the last of his words. They pounded up the ramp that led from the great barn into the streets of the city.

Gilber straightened up to watch them flee. "They'll rouse Highlandweb, if no one's done it yet," he said. "We've got to get out of here now." He made for the largest of the transports, its motor already running.

Becca trotted after him, trying not to count the numbers of their dead as she passed. He hailed a crowd of whorebabies clustered around the big transport, two of them already up top at the controls.

Foul smoke puffed from its underbelly, and the chuffing of its engine filled the air.

"Get this loaded and we're gone," he said. He cast his eyes across the great barn and singled out a second transport of nearly the same size, then pronounced, "That one too."

The whorebabies exchanged worried looks. "Rev Livvy," said the young man at the transport controls, "I'm the only one left alive who knows how to drive one of these things."

Before Gilber could say anything, Becca pushed her way to the fore and clambered up the transport's side hand over hand. The whorebabies made room for her at once, giving her free rein to examine the controls. It didn't take her long to announce, "On stead, my sire sometimes let me drive the big machines at planting and tending time. This one doesn't look so different. Load up!"

"Becca, get down from there!" Gilber called. "Do you think we want you out in the open like that, a fine, clear target? No way you're going to ride this anywhere but safe inside."

"How safe will it be if we've just got the one driver and they pick him off?" she countered. "Better some of us have a chance of freedom than none. Any road, you don't expect all of us to fit into one chariot, do you?"

"Those who don't fit inside will come afoot." Gilber didn't sound pleased with his sole alternative, but he did sound determined.

"And die afoot! I won't have it." She stood up atop the transport and turned her face to the massed whorebabies below. "I am the lady and I say I will take you out of the city with me all together or not at all!"

The cheer that went up nearly knocked Gilber backward. He scowled and started up the transport after Becca, but Niv leaped up to grab one of the climbing rungs and bar his way.

"You're our teacher and our father, but we follow her," he said.

Gilber's hand tightened around his rifle. "If you don't step aside, Niv—" he began.

A rumble like oncoming thunder drowned out the rest of his threat. Down the ramp trundled the biggest transport Becca had yet seen. It was painted the dull brown of roadway dust and it lumbered along on earth-devouring treads. The driver rode up on top of the tanker, secure in a riveted steel box with slits for air and sight. Engine still a-growl, the monstrous transport lurched to a stop. A panel in its side dropped open by degrees.

The small hatch ceiling of the driver's compartment clanged open and a close-hooded head popped out.

"Well?" Salome demanded. "What are you waiting for? Come on!"

And like her echo made flesh, Van stuck his head around the edge of the open panel and cried, "Come on!"

Chapter Twenty

Come ye down to stable town,
Lords and ladies all.
Blest is she, the pure Marie,
By the Spirit's call.
Humble maid, be not afraid;
Men shall praise your name.
Meek and mild, you bear the Child
Cleanses us from blame.
Blest the womb as blest the tomb,
Blest the risen Son.
Heaven win whose life was in
Stable town begun.
Come ye down to stable town,
Lords and ladies all.
Sweet Marie, salvation be
From false Eva's fall!

It was dark and hot and there was no air to breathe. The smell was foul beyond her power to describe. Bodies pressed in on her from all sides. If she lost her footing they would tumble down on top of her and crush the breath of life from her. The floor shook and lurched. Vomit climbed her throat, searing it with acid. She fought it down and braced her legs wider, groping blindly for something, anything to hold herself steady.

Then the shaking underfoot came faster, and a roaring filled her ears. Somewhere in the dark a child was screaming in pure terror, mindless and shrill. The floor shook more violently, then lurched. A tumble of bodies rammed into her. She struggled to stay upright, but they were too many, too heavy. She went down, their bulk like iron weights on her chest. Her right arm bent back at a crazy angle before it snapped just as if she'd been a twig-limbed female whorebaby. Her pain filled the dark with flaming bursts of red and her shriek tore at the metal walls surrounding her.

A louder shriek raked away her pitiful cry, the shriek of metal tearing itself open against stone. Suddenly there was light, white and blinding, and gust after gust of flesh-killing cold. The whole world had gone white, though the pain from her shattered arm continued to paint over her sight with a trail of blood. Helmeted men in uniform came rushing in out of the whiteness. Some carried guns, some air-poppers, some the slender blowpipes that fired fleches. The stench was gone, and the heat, but the screams came from all around her.

She saw one man dragging Virgie away into the whiteness. Becca tried to move, tried to cry out for help or mercy. The bodies holding her down had vanished. She propped herself up on her good arm and called Virgie's name until her throat was a raw ruination.

A hand dug into her shoulder and flung her onto her back. She looked up into more whiteness falling silently from a leaden sky until a man's face loomed between her and the slowly drifting flakes. Though he wore a thick bandage over his eyes, she knew him. Her tongue tried to shape his name and God turned it to wood in her mouth. Adonijah straddled her broken body. He held a fleche in either hand, their long steel points shining. He smiled and jabbed them into her eyes.

Becca woke up gasping, half drowned by the hideous dream, without the breath to scream. She hugged herself, desperate for something to cling to, and rocked back and forth in her blankets. The campfire blazed high, but it gave her no warmth. She looked to the right, where Gilber always slept, but his place was empty. She saw the prints of his shod feet leading off across the snow into the night.

His turn to stand watch, she thought, pulling the blankets even tighter to her body. *That, or else he's taken another scouting party off to forage. He never tells me where he's going or when or what for; he just goes. The tribe's his first care now; as it must be.* She sighed and tilted her head back, seeking sight of the stars. Their steady light was a comfort to her on these clear nights, even if they no longer brought her miraculous visions.

Glory be to God for all His miracles, her heart prayed. *For those we call by that sacred name and those we haven't got the wit to name so; for water turned to wine and just for water, pure and sweet; for the great sea that's split by a man's word and for the great sea no man's word can touch.* She found a measure of comfort in her own soul-sayings. She sat there awhile, drinking peace from the stars.

The last of the nightmare ebbed from her body, leaving behind only a little shudder at the bone. All around her, the new tribe of Gilber Livvy slept peaceably. There were a few other campfires scattered around and crude screens, blankets and tarps, set up here and there to break the wind's breath. When Salome came driving her tanker into the heart of Greenwoodweb, she hadn't let them leave before she showed them that those rows of metal doors lining the tunnel were really storeplaces, brimful of necessary things. It had been the trader woman's doing likewise to fetch three small tents in her transport, shelter for those too frail to brave the open air but not frail enough to merit a sleeping place inside the tanker itself.

Heaven bless her, Becca thought, turning her eyes to where the tanker bulked huge against the night sky, the distant hills. Salome never slept anywhere but inside the tanker, along with Virgie and the children. No one could question her strength, yet neither could they question her right to sleep within the shelter of her life-saving gift to them all. Calm but wakeful, Becca decided it wouldn't do any harm if she were to wander over in that direction some. Might be she'd find another sleepless soul and share a bit of human chat. The stars set her mind at ease, but left her lonely.

She left her campfire and headed for the tanker, keeping herself within the several circles of firelight whenever she could. Every fire had its designated watcher, vigilant to spy out any unwelcome strangers the ranging guards might miss. Most times these watchers were women, whorebabies too snap-boned to risk on the marches 'round the bounds of the camp. All they had to do was feed the fire, sit tight, look keen, and sound the alarm if need be; a job even an older child could do, and often did. It made them feel useful, true sibs of the first family most of them had ever known.

Becca didn't want to cause needless trouble by being mistaken for a prowler. She walked within the light and took care to make some small noise in her throat so the watchers would note her and not fear. They smiled when they saw her, and their hands homed to the pendants at their throats. She waved to them and saw how they pressed the little metal orbs to their lips in answer for a blessing they imagined she'd given.

She walked on. The thin layer of snow on the ground crunched crisply under her shoes. Out here in the lands between steads it didn't seem to have fallen so thick as in the city. She stooped to scoop up a handful and watched its silvery crystal beauty unmake itself in the heat of her palm. "I never thought I'd live to see this," she breathed over the melting snow, and her frosty whisper traced its own small ladder of angels up to heaven.

"Like nothing I've ever seen either," said Salome. She stepped out of the darkness just beyond the firelight and smiled to see Becca's momentary startlement. She laid a finger to her lips and jerked her head sideways, bidding Becca come with her. They walked some way off, around to the far side of the tanker, so that they could talk without chance of waking the sleepers.

Salome leaned back against the cold metal flank of the machine and took a deep breath, letting it out deliberately in little puffs of cloud. She had one of the tribe's too-few coats by right of having brought a dozen of its mates along, but Becca had the feeling that Salome reveled in the cold, clean air of the open places. Only when she tired of the pastime did she turn to Becca and say, "You seem to spend more time on the march by night than by day. That dream again?"

"I think it's getting better," Becca answered. "I didn't even scream this time."

"It's not getting better; you're getting used to it," Salome corrected her. Her eyes softened with sympathy. "Look, Becca, you're not the only one who's been having dreams about our escape. All of you shut up inside the tanker together, crowded in all anyhow in the dark, nothing to see but plenty of scary things to hear and worse to imagine—" She folded her arms and shook her head. "I can only guess what you all must've been thinking when I rammed our way out Rivergate, smack through the old grating. It probably sounded like the end of the world!" She reached up to pat the deep gougings that now ran the length of the tanker's armored body, a beloved war-horse's battle scars. "If this old lady'd been a little wider in the beam, we'd never have made it."

"The end of the world..." Becca murmured. She tucked her hands under her armpits for warmth. "Pa used to read us Revelation, all the signs and portents of the world's end, blood and fire and locusts and monsters...but not snow. If I could set pen to paper, I'd write that in, how there'd be heavy snows come down to let us know that Judgment was at hand. Snow clings to the ice mountains; it doesn't come down to the city's shore and fall so thick."

Salome chuckled. "That was a sight to remember, wasn't it? I don't know what stuck in my mind more, seeing the snow come down *ploof*! like a big white blanket or seeing the expressions on your faces when we could finally open the door and let you all out."

"From now on when I pray to sweet Mary Mother, I'm going to see her mantle white instead of blue," Becca said. "That snowfall was a miracle, pure and simple."

"I don't know if I'd go that far," Salome said. "It was extraordinary, I'll give you that much, something unheard-of for ages, but there've been snows like that before—I've read of those times. I'd guess it's been twenty generations and more since it happened, but it *happened*. No miracle to that."

"It is so a miracle," Becca maintained. "Like Moses at the Red Sea, with Pharaoh's chariots after him.

It's the reason they didn't come after us from the city."

"Is that so?" Salome raised one brow. "You sound like you've convinced yourself, anyhow."

"I'd like you to tell me what other explanation we've got. If the sight of that snowfall didn't put the fear of God between them and us, why haven't they come hot on our trail? Lord knows the snow's left them our tracks plain to see."

"Mmmm, that's so." The trader woman lounged there awhile, tapping a finger to her lips in thought, then shrugged it all away. "Fine, call it a miracle. I should know better than to argue with one of heaven's own."

"Salome!" Becca's indignation just made her laugh. "Are you going to throw that in my face?"

"Throw what? A little scrap of bloodstained cloth? It's not even your blood, you say, but they claim the thought's what counts. The whorebabies who were wounded at Greenwoodweb say that a touch of the lady's holy amulet speeds the healing! Now *that's* a miracle." She chuckled.

Becca wasn't amused. "I'm not to blame for what Gilber's new tribe's made of me."

"Oh, I'm not blaming you for anything; I'm glad of it! For the first time in my life, I feel like there's half a chance for me to breathe free. Do you want to hear a *real* miracle? When I was up there alone at the tanker controls, the instant before I crashed that thing through Rivergate, I felt the weight of a million secrets lift themselves from my shoulders and blow away. It used to be that when I left the city on a trading mission, I'd feel them lighten, but they never really left, they just hovered at my shoulder until I came back through the city gates; then they all came home. This time they're gone. I'm clean of them."

Becca looked at Salome as if she had spoken in tongues. "You mean you're going to tell folks about— about what you are?"

"No, I'm not going to outright *tell*; not unless it comes up in the conversation. But if it does, I'm not going to hide it."

"Oh, Salome, I don't know if that's wise...."

She leaned closer to Becca. "Wise or not, that's what I'll do. It's only a matter of time before they learn I'm like you. What do you think they'll do then? Set me up as their second lady or believe that maybe you blessed me enough to change me?"

Becca wasn't smiling. "You know that's not the part I mean."

"Ohhh. *That*." Salome nodded. "Good little steadgirls don't talk about such things, they just pick up the nearest stone. After all you've seen, is that the only way you can think of me? As an abomination in the sight of your God?"

Becca flung her arms around Salome and hugged her fiercely. "You know that's not so! You are who you are, no more an abomination than any of us. We owe you our lives, Salome." She relaxed her embrace and looked the woman in the eyes. "But I'm not the world. I don't know what Gilber'd make of you, or the tribe itself."

"Even the outcast need someone worse outcast than they, hm?" Salome stepped out of Becca's hold.

"Lower than the lowest of the low, a scapegoat. They can't feel human without someone they can point out as less than human. Well, don't worry: They won't find that in me. Nothing's going to happen when I tell them all my secrets. Not a thing, if the *lady* speaks for me. And you will, Becca. I know you will." Her breath was coming in thin threads of steam, a visible marker for her rising heartbeat. "Or will you teach them a new way to root out abomination from their midst? Will you tell your faithful that the blood they worship's no good unless it's freshened up with mine? With anyone like me, or Solomon, or that bastard Matt, or even poor Van?"

"*Van?*" Becca gaped, and the cold air rushed into her mouth.

"You mean you didn't know?"

"But—but Isa—"

"Isa's dead, child, and Webmaster Steven's living. I wish you could've heard the whispers that ran through Thirdweb when he brought Van back. It didn't take long after that for everyone to know what was going on between them. Not that anybody'd say a word—too terrified of the old worm for that. But you were locked away; how could you hear anything?"

"Webmaster Steven and Van," Becca repeated to herself, stunned. She stared at Salome. "Then why's he here with us? Why didn't he stay in Thirdweb? Why'd he run off?"

"Well, maybe I misspoke a little," she admitted. "Poor dead Solomon and Matt and me and Van, some of us are as God made us and some owe it all to man. Van does, though he's not exactly grateful for *that* particular gift. He never wanted it, but Webmaster Steven forced him to take it anyway."

"Webmaster Steven forced—?" Becca saw Salome nod. "Why did Van let him? The old man's not above *all* the law. Why didn't he call out, bring a charge, go to my brother—?"

"That's not something I could tell you," Salome replied. "All I know is you're not the only one who came away with nightmares. Van hasn't gotten used to his yet. He always wakes up screaming. It got so bad that he stopped sleeping in the tanker. He's volunteered to walk patrol almost every night, all night, just to be able to sleep by day, only Gilber refuses him. He thinks Van only does it so he can avoid the marches. Look, I can't guess what more there is to tell you. If you're that curious, ask him yourself." She jerked her thumb toward the front of the tanker.

Becca started forward, pausing to look back after she'd gone only a few paces. "Aren't you coming with me?"

"You don't need a chaperone, little girl," Salome replied. "And I don't need to face tomorrow half asleep. I'm going back to bed." She turned her back on Becca and disappeared around the other end of the tanker.

Becca found Van wrapped in his bedroll under the teeth of the tanker's tread. From a distance he seemed to be asleep, but when she stole nearer she saw the glitter of wide open eyes. He propped himself up on one elbow when he heard her coming nigh. "Who's there?"

"Just me." She found a space to sit down on the blanket by his feet and took it without waiting for leave. "Salome says you're nightmare-ridden."

She could hear the sound of his teeth clenching before he answered, "Salome talks too fucking much."

She leaned forward and laid her hand over his. "I was hoping I could bring you some comfort. I haven't lost my bad dreams yet either. They come back almost every night the same: We're fleeing the city, only we never make it. The tanker tears open, the Highlandwebbers come pouring in, and then—" She choked on saying more, stopped herself before she could speak of the nightmare's final image. Her mother Hattie sometimes taught that to name the devil was to summon him. She wouldn't run that risk with Adonijah.

"Is that all Salome told you?" he asked. "That I've got bad dreams."

"Well…no." Becca lowered her eyes. "She told me about what—what happened to you. What Webmaster Steven— I'm guessing that's what's been haunting your nights."

He drew his hand away, but slowly, like it was a thing he was compelled to do against his will. "Becca, can you imagine a man so strong he can have anything he wants, so old that all he hungers for is something new, so cold he doesn't care what he does to get it? He took everything I ever cherished in my life because he thought it was the only way to reach me. It didn't make any difference how long it took. It didn't even matter when his first desire died and it all became no more than game. He still had to win it." A deep sigh shuddered out of him. "And one day, he won. I can still see the look on his face when I agreed to do what he wanted. That's what I dream of every night. That's the sight that makes me wake up screaming."

"Oh, Van..." Becca put her arms around him, held him close. When he tried to push her away, she refused to concede, until finally he slumped against her like an exhausted child. "You know, I've heard tell there's a way to turn an evil dream," she said softly.

"Did it work for yours?"

"Yes...no...some, I guess. Some dreams hang stronger than others. Any road, my dreams aren't yours; isn't it worth a try?"

"I suppose." He sat upright. "What is it?"

"You tell yourself waking that the thing you fear most in your dream's far gone, long gone. There's miles between you and it, and you're the one who's put them there. It's lost all power to affright you any more. Then you fix your mind on something blessed and seek it when you sleep."

"I've tried that cure," Van told her. "It's only made it worse. It makes the bad dream longer. I take the vision with me, I stand it like a shield between his leering face and me, and I tell him *You can't touch me anymore! She won't let you!*" He covered his eyes. "That's when he laughs and shows me my vision standing with a wire noose around her neck at the cliff's edge, and he holds the wire's end."

"She—?"

He was on his knees, his hands knotted in her

sleep-tousled hair. "Oh Becca, why do you think I told him yes when all I wanted was to die? He said he'd kill you otherwise. He said it was up to me, whether he tried you and condemned you then and there or whether he hunted up some legal excuse to spare you. I couldn't let him hurt you. After all you'd done for me, for Isa, for our baby—" Tears rose in his eyes, spilled down his cheeks. His voice rose to a heartsick wail. "Oh God, I couldn't carry another ghost! There's too many on me now!"

"Hush, hush, you're going to wake the children." Becca gathered him back into her embrace, eased him gently down, took his head and laid it to her bosom. She stroked his hair and kissed it the way she'd sometimes brushed her lips over her baby sister's sweet head. He sobbed and shook against her, his hands clawing for something human and loving to anchor him back to the world. She shifted slightly, and when she felt his fingers steal through to cup her breast she didn't push him away. "Hush," she said, over and over again. "Hush."

✖ ✖

The tanker devoured the miles that took Gilber Livvy's tribe farther and farther from the city, nearer and nearer to their beckoning mountain home. Salome was a seasoned traveler; she knew the lay of the land and the alliances binding every stead between the coast and the mountains. The steads knew her too. Once Becca donned one of the trader woman's spare suits and accompanied her into Sheaf

Stead. Salome presented her as a likely apprentice, keen to learn the job.

Sheaf Stead's alph received them royally on the steps of the big farmhouse. "Lord knows what's brought you out our way this time of year. Then again—" He cast a chary eye over the snow-laden fields. "—This hasn't been a year like others."

"Isn't that a fact?" Salome returned pleasantly. Patting Becca on the back she added, "I couldn't think of a better time to give this girl some experience, let her try her hand at making a deal or two. Better now than at harvest home when there's something big for you to cheat me out of, eh, Gavin?" Becca marveled to see the two of them share a laugh just as if they'd both been men together.

With a little prompting from Salome, Becca managed to trade several bags of city-bred milo seed for as much motor fuel as the two women could carry away with them. "Let me send my sons to bear that for you," Gavin offered.

Salome shook her head and whispered something in the alph's ear. His dark face flushed and he said no more about it, except to bark an order for his sons to keep well away from the women.

The stead children clustered around Salome looking hangdog. One of them, bolder than rest, went right up to her and demanded, "Why didn't you bring your wagon up to the house this time? I want a ride!"

Salome pinched the boy's cheek and replied, "This time I'm riding a big one, child, a monster with four clawed paws to tear apart the earth. It's too big to come up your roads without devouring them, and maybe you with 'em, so we left it beyond your daddy's fields and came here on foot."

"Huh! *I'm* not afraid of your monster," the boy shot back. "It tries eating up my daddy's fields and I'll make it spit 'em right out! I'll teach it manners! I'll—"

The alph's hand came down in a lazy arc and swatted the boy against the wall of the house. "Learn some manners yourself before you go teaching them," Gavin instructed his child. Becca felt her hands clench, but she stood still and said nothing.

When the two women were walking back down the stead road, lugging the heavy fuel cans, she finally spoke up. "What did you say to that man to make him call off his sons?"

"Just that you were a taking woman," Salome replied as if it were no great thing.

"And he believed you? But when a woman's taking, a man can tell! A stead man, any road."

"Yes, when it's a stead woman. But we city women are different. Didn't you know that?"

Becca saw the mischief sparking in Salome's eyes. "Why, you liar!" she exclaimed with admiration.

"It worked, didn't it? And a lot simpler than having a pair of Gavin's boys come discover our camp. I doubt they'd believe I'd taken on *that* many apprentices." They laughed.

That was how it went for them, rolling over roads that could take the tanker's span and over open country elsewhere. Salome knew where to go for fuel or food. Sometimes she took Becca with her on her trading jaunts, sometimes Van, and sometimes she went alone.

Once she returned from a solitary expedition with a young steadwoman at her side. "This is Dalis. She's an old friend of mine," was all she said. The steadwoman said nothing and no one questioned her, not even Gilber. She traveled with them for two days, during which Salome moved out of the tanker and took back one of the tents. On the third day, Dalis was gone, and Becca saw Salome weeping as she took her things out of the tent and threw them back into the tanker.

There were ten big sacks of city-bred seed stowed away in the tanker. Becca never came to ask how Salome had managed to lay hands on them. She knew that the trader woman and Van had acted on the spur of the moment, the instant word hit Thirdweb of what she'd done to poor Kenyon. Neither one could bear the weight of the city anymore, neither cared if they died trying to get away.

"I've always been practical," Salome had told her. "Van was all set to dash after you—where else would you head but to Gilber?—but I made him come with me first to Trader's Hall, gear up and get the tanker. I lied and he loaded. If we did escape the city whole, I damn well wasn't going to starve to death in the wilderness after! There's nothing like seed when you want to travel light and trade keen. Steadfolk think that if you plant anything from the city, it'll grow tall as the rooftops overnight. Well, it might not be *that* good, but it's good enough to buy us what we need."

They traveled on. The whorebabies who were fit for the march walked in the tanker's wake or paced it, the wounded and the weak rode inside with the smaller children. Virgie and the older ones insisted on marching most of the day, but there were times they chose to climb up the tanker's flanks, spread blankets over the cold, flat expanse of metal, and make a glorious progress. Gilber allowed this only when the lay of the land was flat enough so there'd be no danger of them sliding off. The children put on solemn faces and promised to behave, but soon they were horsing around just like kids who'd never walked through darkness or felt the breath of death on their necks. They sang and shouted and sometimes one of them would slip off the top of the tanker on purpose. The whorebabies watched in awe and envy as the sturdy-boned victim—strutting proud to be the momentary focus of all eyes—walked away from the incident with a few bruises and maybe a sprained ankle at most.

When shabbit came, Gilber and his tribe kept it after the ways he'd taught them back in the tower at Greenwoodweb. Becca and Salome and Van and all the stead children save Virgie camped apart on those days. If there were any fires kindled then it was only because they were the ones who fetched the wood, built the hearth, and struck the sparks. When the sun first went down to begin the holy time, they huddled together and harked to the strange songs rising up from Gilber and his chosen kindred, the alien chanting that he told them was prayer.

Sometimes at a lull in the singing, Gilber would come over to let them know they were welcome to join if they liked, but they never did. He smiled and shrugged, wrapped up in the arms of his shabbit bride, and left them. One time, Virgie started after him, but then one of her sibs whimpered and she rushed back to comfort the little one. She'd grown to worship Gilber as her hero long ago, but like him she'd come to learn the difference between worship and love.

When shabbit came, there was only Becca and Salome and Van to stand watch over the whole camp and pray their own prayers that the children didn't let the campfires go out. It was on a shabbit watch that Becca suddenly came awake to how many shabbits had passed since they'd left the city. A woman on the march might miscount days, but never shabbits. She reckoned up the tally twice, then stood there atop the little hillside and stared unseeing at the stars.

Another shabbit passed. The land began to put on a familiar face. One day Becca recognized the fields and buildings of Grange in the distance. Her chest turned tight with ugly memories, but the tribe passed it by without incident.

"Don't you fear, love," Gilber told her, his encircling arm her sanctuary. "Our best route home doesn't even come within hollering distance of your old place. If any of your steadfolk do see us from their watch posts, we'll be too far off for them to trouble over."

"And Hallow?" Becca asked. "Can we make Hallow Stead without rousing attention? My little sister Shifra must be grown out of all knowledge by now." She smiled fondly.

"Hallow Stead…" Gilber echoed, the name trailing

off as if there were something on his mind he didn't want to say.

"We could go there quiet," Becca said. "Just you and me, leave the others far off. Or else maybe Salome could—"

"It's not *how* we'd do it that worries me," Gilber said.

"Then what does? Is Hallow so far out of our way? I'm all turned around with travel; I don't know where it lies, but— Is Hallow too *dangerous* to draw nigh, is that it?"

Gilber sighed. "Hallow's a strong roof and warm blankets and a good fire against this hard time of year. Hallow's food we maybe couldn't provide for a baby on the road. I'm longing to see that infant back in your arms again as much as you, but for now, Hallow is Shifra's best haven."

"Ah." It was only a little sound Becca made. She understood how right Gilber was, but that didn't shield her heart from breaking and it didn't stop a fresh concern from preying on her mind.

About a day's march later, she asked, "It's not far from Wiserways to the mountains, is it?" Becca's question was a plea and a hope.

"Well, I'd be lying if I said so," Gilber replied. "But we'll make it all right. Why? That eager to have my kin meet my bride?" He hugged her.

She said nothing, but in her soul she wondered how many months' travel it would take to bring her to her new home, and what would happen when… She bridled her thoughts. Some things were best set aside until you *had* to speak of them.

The snow was nearly gone and a hard chill set its edge into the air. Gilber parleyed Salome into making another trading foray to bring back a coat for Becca. Becca overheard and took a stand in front of Salome.

"That's Makepeace," she said, tasting gall in the name of Adonijah's former home. "Don't set foot on that cursed ground."

"I can take care of myself, Becca," Salome said meaningfully. She had one of the smaller blowpipes at her belt and a good supply of fleches. "Gilber says you've been shivering like a leaf this past week; you need something warmer to wear and I'll get it for you."

"I don't want it that bad. Don't go to Makepeace Stead. If Zacharias is still alph there, you'll be treating with the devil's own sire."

"You think that scares me?" Salome reached two fingers into her jumpsuit and pulled out one of the gray metal pendants the whorebabies wore. "Nothing can touch me while I wear the protection of the *lady*," she said, and burst into mocking laughter.

Becca wasn't laughing. She glared at Salome for a bit, then turned on her heel and stalked off, leaving her still laughing. But later on, when Salome set out on the road to Makepeace, she found her way blocked by a corps of armed male whorebabies, Becca at their back, arms folded, eyes bright.

"What the hell is this?" Salome demanded. "Get out of my way!"

"The lady says you're not to go there," said one, and before Salome could utter another word, they closed in on her and bore her back to camp. Her curses filled the air and brought Gilber Livvy running.

When he heard what had happened, he stood there puzzling awhile, then said, "Well, if she's *that* set against a coat, no sense forcing her."

Salome shrugged off the whorebabies' restraining hands and snarled, "I wouldn't fetch her a coat now if she were neck-deep in ice. Let her freeze." She stomped off, but later that evening she came sidling up to Becca and said, "That was pretty slick, what you pulled on me."

Becca brushed aside the compliment. "It seemed like a pretty harmless way to see how far they *would* obey me. Better if I learn that I'm their lady in more than name by setting them against you than against a real enemy."

"You expecting to meet with a real enemy?"

"I don't know. Still no sign of hunters from the city, but even so—I'll feel more settled in my mind when we see Gilber's mountains." She gave Salome an apologetic look and added, "I'm pleased you don't bear me any ill will over it."

"Me? No, I agree with Gilber: You feel that strongly about freezing, go freeze with my blessing."

True to his word, Gilber led them roundabout the fields of Wiserways. They caught sight of the hands on watch, but they kept enough distance to pass unmolested. They never had so much as a glimpse of the stead buildings. A day's march west of Wiserways they made camp in scrub land none of the Grange steads cared to claim. Not much grew there—a hard and scanty harvest for their campfires—but as Becca set out her bedroll, she breathed easy for the first time in days.

That night, about two hours after the watch had been posted and the tribe lay sleeping, a shout from one of the guards roused everyone. Becca sat up just in time to see Gilber already on his feet, hurrying to meet Alban as the young man came striding into camp, dragging a stranger by the wrist. It was only when he brought his captive well into the light of the niggardly campfire that Becca saw first that it was a girl and second that she was no stranger.

She crept from her blankets while Gilber fired questions at Alban and Alban did his best to hold onto his prize. The girl was exhausted; she kept slumping to the ground and Alban kept yanking her back to her feet, calling her a spy and doing all he could to make sure everyone within earshot knew what a wonderful thing he'd done in capturing her.

Becca stepped in and undid Alban's grasp. If he had any objections, he swallowed them after one hard look from his lady. The girl staggered back, but didn't fall. Becca moved forward slowly, offering no threat, to take the girl's face in her hands and stare at her until the truth could no longer be denied.

"Rusha?"

"*Becca!*" With a wild cry, Becca's sib collapsed into her arms.

Chapter Twenty-One

The sword of the Lord, and of Gideon.

Gilber was waiting for her outside the tent when she finally emerged around midnight. "How is she?" he asked.

Becca didn't answer at first. She wiped blood from her hands with a rag and tried to recall whether there was a stream running somewhere near. She'd never had the need to know the lay of the land west of Wiserways. Now she wished she owned the knowledge. It would take oceans of clean, running water to wash away the sickness she felt from the skin to the bones.

"She's burning up with fever," she finally said. "And the baby's gone. I did what I could to stop the bleeding." She placed herself in the circle of Gilber's arms before she found the strength to say more: "She thought we were a trading party, but she said she'd have come running after us even if we'd been a rogue band. She was crazy to get away. That babe she lost— Oh God, how am I going to tell her?— that babe was Adonijah's get. He rooted it in her the night he killed our pa."

"Could be she won't take the news too hard, then," Gilber offered.

Becca shook her head. "She clung to that babe as the one good thing to come out of so much hatefulness. It was what gave all her suffering a good cause, helped her bear the memories. She told me so. That's why she risked her life, running away to save it."

"You mean Adonijah wants it—wanted it dead?" Gilber's fingers tightened on Becca's shoulders and back.

Another negative shake of the head. "Adonijah wouldn't have any say in the matter. His six months' grace as new alph of Wiserways will soon be done, and then any man can challenge him for the stead. He's blind, Gilber, blind by my hand; how could he hope to win any challenge? And once the old alph's dead, the new one does all he can to wipe out all trace of his seed: a winnowing of the youngest, the innocent, the ones too small or too unlucky to run away and hide until the red time's past."

"But her child wouldn't even be born when that happens," Gilber said.

"Then the new alph will wait until it is and see to

it then, or else if he's real impatient—" She bit her lower lip, remembering how Pa's embittered wife Thalie had gladly drunk down the stead-crone's potion that was the scouring of her fruitful womb. Thalie'd come to hate Pa when his sacred manlore called for the death of her child Susanna. Through no fault of her own, the little girl had violated the harvest law that banned females from the fields. Fond Thalie thought that her husband's love for her would let him make an exception in Susanna's case; she was wrong. She never forgave him, and when Adonijah killed him and took Wiserways she was eager to cast out the dead alph's last rooted seed, joyful to welcome his slayer to her bed.

"Well, I guess all that's settled now," Gilber said, glancing back at the tent. "Poor child. I'll send someone to see to the infant's burial and I'll brew her up something to bring down the fever."

"It'll want more than your bark brew to help her," Becca said. "She's too weak to travel, she's lost too much blood, and we haven't got the medical supplies to tend her proper."

"What can we do, then? She can't travel with us, you say, but we can't stay here. The nearest stead's Wiserways. Do you *want* to show your face there?"

"No. Never again," Becca said, and meant it. "But maybe we could send her back with Salome. Salome could have one of the other girls go along, spin her usual tale of how she's come winter trading to give her apprentice practice at the game, and Rusha stumbled into their camp."

Gilber thought it over. "It's worked before, and it'd get her safe home. But what about the babe she lost? She won't be punished for that?"

"God's will isn't reason for punishment," Becca told him. He was satisfied with that and gave her his blessing to hunt up Salome and carry out the plan come morning.

Gilber went off to find someone to bury the babe, a task forbidden him, a priest's son. Becca went back into the tent where Rusha lay. She settled herself down beside her sib's bedroll and laid a hand on Rusha's fiery brow. Some rags soaked in a bowl of water nearby. She wrung one out and draped it over the girl's forehead. By the light of the small clay lamp she gazed at Rusha's face, so very white, the blue smudges underneath her eyes darkening like a twilight sky.

I didn't tell him everything, Rusha, Becca thought. *What's one more secret between us? He doesn't know all there is to know of stead ways, so he assumes if I don't point out something as remarkable, it's common practice with us. Could be he thinks we let our women go wandering at will, that no one at Wiserways would question how you came to be so far from your bed at this time of night. Bring you back now, openly, and even if you won't be punished for losing the babe, you'll still pay the price for haring off. And Miss Lynn will pay it too.*

She plucked the cloth from Rusha's brow; it was still damp, but so hot she imagined it steaming in her hand. She wrung out a fresh one and tenderly washed the girl's pale face. She could still hear her sib's terrified chatter when she first came back to her senses, the fever-ravings she'd uttered while Becca worked uselessly to keep her infant from coming into the world so soon:

"Miss Lynn came on her rounds to see us. All the talk onstead was how there was a trading party passing through our—I knew I had to get away. I made it my turn with her last—late, sundown already past but I begged her—room back of the house—mine, now, Adonijah said—brought her tea, put something—Gram Phila gave me a sleep powder when I told her I couldn't— put it in Miss Lynn's—the window was—Oh God, oh God, don't let them kill my baby!"

How long had the stead-crone's sleeping powder lasted? Becca didn't know that anymore than she could tell whether anyone had bothered to look into Rusha's room yet and discovered what the desperate girl had done. If so, it would be too late for Miss Lynn already; she'd be held to blame for Rusha's flight. But if not—

I know the lay of Wiserways. If we can slip Rusha back into the house, me and Salome together, might be no one's yet noticed she's gone. Miss Lynn can tend her. As for the babe— She freshened up another cloth to cool the fever and with all the bitterness in her heart she murmured, "God's will be done."

❧ ❧

"I think she's bleeding again," Salome whispered, shifting the small, blanketed form in her arms. The women hugged the shadows of an outbuilding, their eyes fixed on the open window at the back of the big house. A light burned low in the room beyond. Becca stood on tiptoe and thought she saw a shape slumped over in a straight-backed chair inside.

"We're not back before time, then," Becca responded. She stooped for a moment to roll the cuffs of her borrowed trousers more securely. "I'm going to climb in the window first, then you hand her through to me."

Salome glanced this way and that. For the first time since she'd known Salome, Becca saw her skittish. "You sure? If we rouse the house, we rouse the stead, and I don't think they'll buy my story about running a winter trade with *this* in my arms." She leaned Rusha's weight against the side of the building. The girl's light body had been a shared burden all the way from the camp to the main cluster of stead buildings, but from that point on Salome had insisted on carrying her alone.

"We've been under Mary's mantle so far," Becca told her. "She'll shelter us through this." She started for the house.

"From your lips, straight to heaven," Salome said. She stepped away from the wall. The spot where she'd rested Rusha's body showed a small daub of red.

Becca reached the open window and looked in. Yes, there was someone in the chair, a shawl over her head, an herbwife's kit at her feet, an empty cup on the table beside her. She was breathing slow and regular, deep in slumber. Becca smiled and said a silent thanksgiving. They could have Rusha back in her bed and be away before dawn light caught them. She brought one knee up to the windowsill.

Light froze her there, and an angry cry from Salome. She whirled around to meet the eyes of a score of Highlandwebbers. Full half their number held tubes that shot beams of brilliance right into Becca's face, painting the whole side of the house with a false dawn. In the ruthless light, Becca saw Salome hugging Rusha to her like an infant, the girl's blanket slowly soaking through with blood.

"Well, that's one of them," said Webmaster Steven. He stepped to the fore from between two Highlandwebbers and looked straight at Salome. "Which is one more than I'd hoped for. Thank you, Becca." He flicked a faint smile in her direction. "I knew *you'd* come, but to bring Salome too—! Just what I wanted. You must be a mind reader."

He returned his full attention to Salome. "I think we'll start the charges with grand larceny. That is, I think the *traders* will do that. Theft is a capital crime among your brethren, correct? One of the disadvantages of belonging to a guild with its own independent department of justice. Still, favors are owed; I *might* be able to convince them to let Thirdweb try you. That way we can limit the penalty to a term of imprisonment. You should still be able to breed a few more children for us after you've served your time. You do breed such lovely children, my dear."

"How did you get here?" Salome snarled. "You didn't track us; we would've known."

"The best reason not to track you directly," Webmaster Steven replied. "You would have turned to face us somewhere near the city and made a stand…and a scandal. I've had enough of those. You would have been overcome, of course, but there would've been talk about the incident back home. This way I can avoid all that. We knew where you were headed, we knew the route you'd most likely take, and we knew we could outdistance you. Wiserways lay along that path, which turned out to be quite a stroke of luck for us. We simply circled around and waited. All very discreet."

Becca stepped forward, a burning in her belly. "She was your lure; Rusha."

"What a bright thing it is," the old man said.

"What did you do to make her lie to me like that? What did you promise her? That she could keep her baby after Adonijah was dead?"

"Don't you *dare* speak so ill-omened of him!" A long-unheard voice shrilled out indignantly behind Becca. She turned and saw Thalie at the window, the shawl still over her head. "You little harlot, now you'll get your rightful pay!"

There was a stirring beyond the area lit by the wondrous glow tubes. The folk of Wiserways came creeping and crowding around behind the city troops. Some of them had brought lanterns, homely golden lights that took back only small nibbles of the dark.

Her eyes now used to the dazzle, Becca could make out familiar faces: the stead hands who'd passed from Paul's reign to Adonijah's, the sibs who'd seen her grow, Gram Phila's girl Martha, Pa's surviving wives, and the complement of creatures Adonijah'd brought with him when he came to challenge Pa. They were weasely things, these sorry shanks of men, too weak to come to much on their old steads, but sly enough to scuttle under Adonijah's wings and rise with him, loyal while it paid them to be loyal, gobbling up his crumbs. It turned her guts to look at them.

Adonijah…he was there too. She knew he would be, though until the instant she set eyes on him again she'd cherished the impossible hope that somehow the earth had opened wide beneath his cursed feet to swallow him. Just as they had done for Webmaster Steven, two more of the Highlandwebbers drew apart to let him pass. His sightless eyes were covered by a thin strip of blue cloth and he walked into the light guided by Becca's sib Orissa.

Thalie vanished from the window and came scurrying out of the house to push Orissa aside and take her place at Adonijah's elbow. "Let me do it," she begged. "Let me be the one to take her sight the way she took yours. An eye for an eye!"

Adonijah clucked his tongue. "Now, now, Thalie, such harsh talk! The prodigal has returned, we should rejoice. What's all this about blinding her? That won't do. Hello, Becca," he added. "Welcome home. Your rightful place is waiting for you. I've decided to forgive you for your crimes and take you back as my well-beloved wife. I'm going to make it my sole purpose in life to get a child on you, a child I'll take under my own hand. I hope you'll have an easy birth. I want you to keep your life as much as I want you to keep your eyes. If not, how will you ever see how I raise your baby? I love you so much, I've decided to spare you the drudgery of brat-tending. I'll do it all, just me and your child from the very day it's born. I have so many things planned for the little one, it will take years to do them all." The cloying sweetness in his voice jellied Becca's spine.

"You won't live to do it!" she defied him. "As soon as your six-months' grace is done, another man will come and—"

"Years," said Webmaster Steven. "Six *years'* grace now, by special degree of Coop authority for valuable favors rendered by the alph of Wiserways." His lips twitched over the fine jest of it all. "The necessary documents are already on their way to Grange and Coop."

"Favors..." Becca repeated.

"The recovery of two fugitives, Salome and Van," the old man elaborated. "We would trade the Jewman your life for theirs."

"Gilber wouldn't soil himself on such a trade," Becca cried. "He'd never be fool enough to trust you!"

"Why not? We'd keep our word: Your life for theirs, I said. Your life, not your body; that he can't have. Here you are and here you'll stay in your proper place as wife to Adonijah of Wiserways." He smirked. "Small enough thanks for what he's done. It was Adonijah's idea to use the girl as bait. Frankly, I doubted it would work, but I stand corrected."

"It worked because she's stupid," Thalie spat out. "Stupid like Rusha."

"Be fair, Thalie," Adonijah chided. "Rusha wasn't *stupid*; she just didn't know any better. A visit from all these fine Coopfolk! Wouldn't that turn any girl's head? Why wouldn't she believe they'd come for only the best of reasons? They even brought a city healer with them, a miracle worker! If she let the man examine her, did she have a choice? I told her to submit. And if he did anything different than Miss Lynn, by the time she felt the pain it was too late." Again his voice dripped with false sympathy. "Poor girl, that fever's been on her for days. She could hardly tell dreams from waking. Whatever she said when she found you, she didn't know it was lies."

"And I'll bet she never knew who planted those lies in her poor spinning head either," Salome said. She moved Rusha's body in her arms. The girl's blanket fell open, drooped over Salome's hands. Becca saw many faces in the crowd turn to ash at the sight of how badly Rusha had bled.

"Does it matter?" Webmaster Steven's bland expression never altered. "She fulfilled her purpose, that's all that counts. There's no need for her to suffer any more." He plucked a small, silvery tube from his belt, set it to his lips, and blew once, hard. A tiny metal point flew through the air and lodged in Rusha's cheek. The girl flinched, then her breath stopped. Webmaster Steven looked pleased with himself. "Never say I don't show mercy."

Salome dropped Rusha's body like a half-filled sack of seed and threw herself at the webmaster. A knife glittered in her hand, hidden until this by the drape of the dead girl's blanket. The webmaster staggered back, toppled under the force of the woman's attack. Almost to a man, the Highlandwebbers dropped their glow tubes, raised their weapons to fire—

—and didn't.

They're afraid they'll hit him, Becca realized, blinking her eyes in the newly returned dark. *They don't know what to do. They're all looking at—* And suddenly she saw the gift that had been placed within her reach. Before the last flicker of that thought went through her mind she was running headlong at the nearest city guard.

He never saw her coming; his eyes were fixed on the tangle of old man and wild woman rolling at his feet. He was one of the few who still held a glow tube in one hand, a rifle in the other, and he was futilely trying to keep the beam of light focused on Webmaster Steven and Salome. He might have heard Adonijah's angry demands for someone to tell him what was going on, he might have heard Thalie's furious shouts for the stead hands to close in and pull the bitch off, he might have heard Webmaster Steven's gasped orders for his troops to shoot, shoot, shoot anyhow, what were they waiting for? In the end it didn't matter what he heard.

There was a loud crack as Becca's heel slammed into his leg just below the kneecap. He screamed and fell sideways, his glow tube rolling away, his helmet flying. Before he hit the ground she linked her hands into a single fist and brought it down with all her strength at the base of his skull. His rifle was hers, and she had no qualms about where to aim it or whether to fire. She tucked it to her shoulder and brought its muzzle up. She thought she heard the voice of Gram Phila's strange girl Martha cheering her name.

This time, Adonijah, she thought. *This time I won't miss.*

But Thalie saw what was happening and dragged Adonijah back into the crowd. The city guards heard the curses she shouted at Becca, turned from the melee at their feet to a target that stood fair and clear. Becca saw their eyes find her despite the dwindled light and wondered whether she'd be able to take down any of them before they got her. She adjusted her aim and pulled the trigger.

The shot deafened her, echoing through her head as the force of the recoil rammed her shoulder. A volley of shots erupted. A guard spun around, dropping his rifle, clutching his upper arm. Another guard doubled over onto the frozen earth. A third shrieked as a steel-tipped fleche sank its snout into his neck.

Shouts came from all sides, the blaze of torches from everywhere at once. Steadfolk scattered, women wailing, men thickening the dark with their curses. Lanternlight streamed away. Another Highland-webber fell, a startled look on his face. Death had taken him by surprise.

Becca saw complete astonishment on the faces of Webmaster Steven's troops as the torchlight flooded over young men in yellow aiming air-poppers and a few gleaned rifles, girls in yellow with blowpipes to their lips, and all that fantastic army of freed whorebabies crying out with each spare breath they drew, "For the lady! For the lady!"

The Highlandwebbers were retreating in confusion.

If any of them had ever seen hobays attack, it had only been in nightmares. Their world was ending around them and they fled before they were buried in the wreckage. Becca dropped to her haunches and crouched in a thicket of shadow, watching them run. She heard Van's voice shouting "Becca! Becca!" but she couldn't tell from which direction it came.

Then she saw him standing over Salome, trying to haul her off Webmaster Steven's body. The old man's face was a latticework of slashes, but he was still alive. Salome was swearing at Van, calling him a hundred foul names, but he held tight to her wrist. The webmaster threw himself on his belly and crawled away quicker than any creature with only two legs.

"Van!" Becca stood up and waved her rifle overhead.

Van's face broke into a triumphant smile when he saw her. "There she is!" he shouted. "We've found her! She's safe! Fall back, in the lady's name!"

She thought that the sheer volume of the whorebabies' victory cheer would shatter every glazed window in Wiserways.

Chapter Twenty-Two

*And Esau said to Jacob, "Feed me, I
pray thee, with that same red pottage, for I
am faint."*
*And Jacob said to Esau, "Give me this
day your sons."*

Becca sat beside Salome in the cab atop the tanker
while she warmed up the engine. If she peered out
through the view-slits, she could see the tribe
clearing away the last vestiges of their camp. The
only thing they'd left behind to mark their stay was
a tiny mound of fresh-turned earth over the place
where Rusha's baby lay.

"You'll have to forgive him sometime," Becca said,
still studying the bustle of breaking camp.

"Sure, after he explains what the *hell* he thought

he was doing," Salome said. "How can he want that old bastard to live after all he's suffered from him? He must be crazy."

Becca shrugged and turned to her. "Maybe he's already carrying enough ghosts."

Salome gave her a quizzical look. "If you're going to go crazy on me too, at least wait until we reach the mountains."

"The mountains…I wonder how long it'll take?"

"Is that all you ever ask? Every time you're with Gilber, I overhear you posing the same question. It's not as if we're heading for paradise. It's a hard life there, as he's not shy to tell us. What's your hurry?"

"I just want to get there and settle in to plain living again. I've been uprooted for too long. I need to find my place in the world."

"Oh really?" A silvery brow rose, assaying the real worth of Becca's words. "Don't you mean your nest? Or maybe your nursery?" Her know-all grin and Becca's eyes widened at about the same rate before she chuckled and said, "I *thought* I was getting a little lonely doing washdays on the road. Thank God I had my privacy when the time came each month, but as for you—" She made a face. "I don't know what I thought. That maybe you were snipping up your bandages as relics for the faithful instead of washing them clean? But we didn't come away with so much cloth to spare."

"I might've gone back to the ways of other women," Becca said, cheeks hot. "Did you ever think of *that* chance?"

"*Did* you go back?"

"No."

Salome eased her hold on the throttle. The tanker engine subsided from a great roar to a comfortable purr. "Gilber doesn't know, does he?" she asked.

"Not yet."

"I figured as much. If he did know, he wouldn't let you out of his sight. You'd never have been able to sneak off the way we did last night."

Becca wrapped her arms around herself. "It would've been better if we hadn't." Her voice caught. "My poor, unhappy little Rusha…"

Salome reached out to pat her hand. "After what they did to her, I doubt she'd have lived. At least now they know we're not just a helpless gaggle of hobays— Don't give me that look; I'm just saying what *they* call us."

"'Us'?" Becca echoed, surprised.

"What's wrong with saying *us*?" Salome challenged. "Aren't we all together in this now? Aren't we as much one people as any stead?"

Becca fished up the bits of a shy smile. "I guess we are."

"I'll say!" Salome loved to win her point. "And we showed them we can fight. They won't bother us again." She cocked her head as if listening to some oddity in the engine noise and casually added, "So when are you going to tell him?"

"Back to that?" Becca sighed and rolled her eyes. "I don't *know*."

"You do beat all, do you at least know *that*? You

know he'll be ecstatic with the news, and as for the tribe—! What an obliging lady you are, bringing them their very own messiah, and so soon."

"Stop it, Salome," Becca said. "Just stop it. Can't you see that's why I haven't said anything? If I tell Gilber, it'll be no time at all before the rest of them hear of it. I don't want them to know. I want to birth a baby, not a miracle."

"*That* choice, my dear, may not be yours to make," she said.

"Becca! Becca, where are you?" Gilber's call from below reached the tanker cab even over the sound of the engine. Becca popped the hatch and climbed out, then came down by the rungs.

"Here I am," she said, running to meet him. "What is it? Are we ready to go?" She looked around and saw the side panel of the tanker still lowered, Virgie and her sibs still hard at work stowing gear. They wouldn't be ready to move for a while yet. "Why did you call me?"

Gilber looked grim. "There's someone to see you."

Becca knew she must look like a sorry coward, so much foreboding in her heart that it couldn't help but show plain on her face. "Who? Not Adonijah?"

"Not him. Not exactly." Before she could question him, he motioned with his hand and a group of six armed whorebabies, male and female, formed up around them. "Come on. You'll be safe."

Surrounded by her devoted people, Becca walked with a hard pit of dread sprouting thorny tendrils in her belly. They marched up to the road that led to the grain fields, the selfsame path that branched off to bring a body to Makepeace Stead. In a sheltered spot where a few skinny oak saplings struggled to grow, Becca's mother Hattie waited.

She wore no coat, no jacket, not even a shawl to keep off the cold, and when the wind blew down between the low hills it wrapped her long dress tight around her legs, proof that she had only the one layer of skirt between her flesh and the bitter season. She stood hugging herself against the cold, her hair so heavily streaked with gray that for a moment, at a distance, Becca mistook her for Gram Phila. It had been months since she'd last laid eyes on her mother, but the woman's appearance made it seem like years.

"Becca?" Hattie raised her head, lips chapped and trembling.

"What do you want?" Becca asked, colder and more distant than any winter star. Not even the sight of how low her mother had fallen in rank among the stead wives could touch Becca's heart. There was no power on earth capable of letting her forget how Hattie had begged her to betray the hiding place of her infant sister, Shifra. Paul's lastborn child, her life should have been forfeit to the new alph. Adonijah made it clear to Hattie that Shifra's death was the price of her life, but Becca had hidden the babe too well. It didn't matter to Hattie that Becca and Shifra both were the children of her womb; when begging wouldn't force an answer from Becca's lips, she'd beaten her, with as little success. The bruises were long gone, the memories were forever.

"I have a message for you from Adonijah," Hattie said.

"Keep it. He's got nothing to say I need to hear. We're leaving." She turned on her heel and started away.

"Becca, no!" Hattie threw herself after her daughter, work-worn hands clawing the air. One of the male whorebabies placed himself between them, held the older woman off with his rifle, snatched from a fallen Highlandwebber only the night before. He'd never owned such a weapon, likely didn't know how to fire it, but he knew enough to use it like a quarterstaff, batting Becca's mother aside. She huddled on the dank ground, arms outstretched, still crying, "Becca, come back! You have to hear! You have to know! Lord King have mercy on the little ones else, for Adonijah won't!"

Becca stopped and looked back. "What are you talking about?"

There were tears running down Hattie's seamed cheeks. "Come see. God have mercy, Adonijah ordered me to tell you what he's done, but that's no good; you wouldn't believe me. Hardly a soul on stead believes it. Come. Please come. I'd spare your eyes the horror if I could, but there's no way around it: You've got to see." She started up the road. She moved slowly and with pain.

Becca stayed where she was, Gilber at her back, her guards around her. "Did you raise a fool, Hattie? I'm not going anywhere with you."

"With me or without, it's all one. Go to the Lord King's hillside, Becca. Go and see what waits there, desecrating holy ground. There'll be a vengeance to pay for it, a judgment on Adonijah that I pray I live to witness. God curse the day I ever raised my voice or my hand in his service, for he's the devil's own." She walked on, and never looked back at her daughter's face.

"Well?" Gilber asked. "Will you?"

Becca stood watching her mother's crabbed form getting farther and farther away. "Whatever else she is, she's a proper steadwoman. For her to speak out so against her natural lord and master— He's done something inhuman, Gilber. Adonijah's raised up an abomination worse than any that Scripture law condemns. I have to go see what it is."

"If you go, you go with the tribe," Gilber said, his hand a welcome weight on her shoulder. "And you don't go close. Please."

"That's just how I'd have it," she replied. "That hillside— You know how little I want to see the place again, but I think—I think I'd best. With the tribe. With our people."

They came at their lady's summons. They would have all attended her, but Van counseled caution and Becca agreed. "It doesn't make sense to risk us all," she said.

"A third of our folk to stay here and mind things," Gilber directed. "A third to come with Becca, and a third to bide within earshot, ready to come help us in case there's treachery."

"That's a safe wager, if Adonijah's hand's in it," Becca said, tight-lipped. "We'll go to the Lord King's hillside, but no nearer than it takes for us to see what's there."

The morning sun shone bright out of a sky blown

clean of clouds. The hillside where the unwanted children of neighboring steads were left to the Lord King Herod's mercy could be seen from a good way off. The wind blew from that quarter, bearing with it the sound of weeping. Becca turned to stone in her tracks at the sound, so long banished from her life, never from her mind.

"We're with you," Van said in her ear, his arm around her. "Don't be afraid."

"You don't need to go," Gilber said, at her other side. "We'll scout it out, tell you what we find."

She put out her hands and clasped both of them by the wrist. "I do need to go. I can. Listen—" She held her breath, harking to the tearful sounds on the wind. "Does that sound like an infant's cry?"

Van said nothing, willfully deaf to any such sound. Becca could understand: The last babe's cry he'd heard had been his newborn daughter's. But Gilber said, "It sounds too strong for that, and I hear more than one voice in it."

They went on. The Lord King's hillside was bathed in sunlight, its flanks bestrewn with all the castoff blankets and baskets, the shattered clay arks and tattered swaddlings of the infants who'd been left there to await the Lord King's grace. Becca's eyes were keen, and she cursed them for it, because even at this distance they let her see the scattered bits of bone among the refuse of so many abandoned lives. Not all the steads who shared that hill were as scrupulous as Wiserways when it came to taking back the husks of the Lord King's harvest.

Again she was a child of Wiserways, sitting at her

mother's feet, hearing Hattie tell her the wonder-tale of how the Lord King Herod saved the infant Christ from dying for want of bread. *There was famine in the land, and too many useless mouths born to eat what little bread there was. The holy Child was born as subject to all the perils of the flesh as any common babe. How could He grow to save sinful mankind by His sacrifice on the cross if He died of hunger in His infancy? All this was revealed to the Lord King Herod, by the grace of God. And so the Lord King took up his sword, and consecrated it to God, and closed the mouths of the children that would have devoured the holy Child's bread, but by his mercy he opened their eyes to Paradise.*

Useless mouths...useless mouths... It was an alph's calling to determine which mouths were useless, and when. His word gave life or death. But it was a sin to kill an infant whose only wrong was being born female when the stead's future already owned enough breeders or male when there were already enough strong field hands growing up ahead of him. So they were given to the hillside, the useless mouths of many steads, and sometimes it happened that one stead's castoff was another's treasure. An alph who couldn't beget enough daughters in his bed found them on the hillside, and one who abandoned daughters there, reaped sons.

They stood among the bones and the baskets, Adonijah and the children. The alph of Wiserways turned his sightless eyes to the sun, a look of eager anticipation on his face. His wife Thalie was beside him, holding his arm tight, as if feared someone would try to wrest him from her. They were attended by a score of the strongest stead hands Wiserways could bring. Of these, ten were ranged on the downslope of the hill, and each held fast to a child and a knife. The children were no older than ten, no younger than four, boys and girls who had survived the winnowing when Adonijah came to power. Now they squirmed or thrashed or sagged in their captors' grips, all with as little effect.

Thalie was the first to see Becca's party approach. "There they are!" she cried, tugging at Adonijah's arm. "They're coming!"

"Becca?" Adonijah called into the wind. "Are you there, Becca?"

Gilber stepped in front of Becca before she could reply. "She's here and we're here with her," he answered. "What's the meaning of this, Adonijah?"

"Becca's tame Jew," Adonijah said softly, but still loud enough for the words to carry. "Do you really want to know what this means? It's a parting gift for the bride you stole from me. Oh, Webmaster Steven told me everything, how she says she's your wife, not mine! He claims that's no longer true, that you said some sort of gobbledegook over her that set her free, but I don't believe it. She fucks sweet, Jewman; I ought to know. I can't see any man giving that up so easily."

For the first time, Becca heard Gilber Livvy speak words foul enough to leave ground barren. Adonijah only laughed.

"Why are you angry? She's yours now. Take her away, if you like. If she'll go. Because the moment my men tell me she's set foot off Wiserways land, these children die."

"*No!*" Becca's anguished cry caught the wind and slapped into the faces of the men who held the knives. "Don't be a fool, Adonijah! You'll cut your own throat for spite. You bought yourself six years of life from the city; live them! If you do this, you're a dead man. All Wiserways will rise against you."

"Shut up, whore!" Thalie screeched, her face distorted with hate. "If I had my hands on you—"

"Hush, woman," Adonijah said *uwuSoₕn¹ uuw du0* speak. It only shows her ignorance. Do you hear that, Becca? You can rave all you like about how Wiserways will cast me off; I *am* Wiserways. While I'm alph, these lives are mine."

"Is he right, Becca?" Gilber murmured for her ears alone. "Is that the law?"

"I don't know. Manlore's mostly secret, and law's spoken only when the alph deems there's cause." Her eyes filled with the children. She fought to hold herself strong, not to show Adonijah he'd weakened her to tears. Boldly she called out, "What will you take for them, Adonijah? What's the price of their safety?"

His smile uncoiled itself like a well-fed serpent. "I thought you knew, Becca."

"The only life I can hand over to you is mine," she said. She heard Gilber and Van both gasp her name in protest, and from the corner of her eye she saw the horrified faces of her guards, but she spoke on: "You can't have the two that the Coopman wants."

Adonijah snorted. "He can look after his own business from now on. I got what I wanted from him, and I earned it in good faith; it's not my fault his troops scattered. They're all back at the house now, still shivering from fright for all I know. They're the ones who let him down, not me. Your life is the only one I want."

"Will you swear to that?"

"I promise you—"

"I don't want your promises. I don't trust them or you. If you and I reach any agreement, I want you to swear a holy oath before witnesses that you'll keep your part of the bargain."

Adonijah's smile iced over. "*You* want?"

"Yes, *I* want." His scorn kindled a spark in her that flared white hot, hardening her fear to anger in the blaze. "Did Thalie tell you what she saw last night, Adonijah? An army came into Wiserways; *my* army. I'm not alone anymore."

"Then why bargain with me at all?" he sneered. "If you command so many willing to die for you, why not lead them back into Wiserways and take it for your own? Or does their obedience have limits?"

"I don't think it does," Becca replied quietly. "Maybe that's why I won't order them to fight unless there's no other choice. It's nothing you'd understand."

"Nothing worth my while trying to," he said. "All right, Becca, I'll give you your oath. Thalie!"

She paused only long enough to shoot a venomous look at Becca, then answered, "Here I am."

"Go back to the house and fetch a copy of Scripture. I'll swear on that, if it'll suit *her*."

Becca said nothing, but Thalie raised her voice to object: "I won't leave you here alone! She's a snake; she'll have her outlaws rush the hill as soon as—"

"By the time they reach me, it'll be over ten dead bodies," he said as easily as if he were speaking of the weather. "Go quickly."

Thalie did as her lord commanded. Becca saw her disappear over the crest of the hillside, heading back for Wiserways. "Do you think she'll bring what he asked?" Van whispered. "Or has she gone to stir up more of them to arms?"

"No telling," Becca murmured back. She wet her lips. "Good thing we heeded you, Van. We may be glad of having our own help just a shout away."

"They won't let you do this, Becca, not our people," Gilber said. "*I* won't let you. Surrender yourself to Adonijah? He's slippery as a melon seed. He'll swear a hundred oaths and do what he likes after."

"Not an oath like this." Becca was adamant. "Not one sworn on something holy, with witnesses. You don't know stead ways, Gilber. An alph makes a promise and doesn't keep it, folk think less of him but don't do much because they fear his strength. An alph makes a sacred vow and breaks it, he's lost his soul. The stead that bends to such a man's accursed. Their own souls are forfeit, chaff in the wind. No matter if that alph's a second Samson, they'll all rise up against him sooner than risk that."

"I wish I had your faith, Becca. I haven't the strength to test mine against your life."

"You can't." She squeezed his hand. "It is my life."

Thalie came back. *How did she do that so fast?* Becca marveled. *The house lies too far off for her to have run all the way there and—*

Then she saw that Thalie hadn't brought a copy of Scripture. The woman had fetched something else for her husband to swear his oath over, something that many souls would call a far holier relic than words in a book. She climbed the slope and took Adonijah's hand. "Here," she said, laying it over the curve of a baby's skull.

Adonijah flinched as his fingers discovered the gift his wife had brought him, but only at first. Then his hand closed over the small knob of bone and his teeth flashed. "You've done very well, Thalie," he said. "If I'm to give my word, Becca should give hers too. This will be a better binding on her than Scripture, seeing how much of God's holy word she's already scorned. But this—!" He held the skull up to the sun, exulting.

"The first child of Wiserways ever to know the Lord King's mercy," Thalie intoned so that all present might hear and bear witness. "I brought it from its niche in Prayerful Hill. There's no other relic on all Wiserways carries half the power of this."

Adonijah turned the little skull in his hand, then said, "Then by this token I swear that if Becca of Wiserways consents to give herself up to me, no child of this stead will be harmed." With that, he pressed his lips to the gleaming ridge of bone rimming the skull's right socket. "Now take it to her, Thalie, and let her pledge her word that she's mine."

Thalie took the relic from him and padded down the slope. Gilber and Van stepped forward to bar her way, but Becca motioned them aside. Thalie's eyes were raw with contempt as she offered up the skull to Becca's hands and said, "An oath for an oath. Even a whore's word should be binding, given on this."

Becca let that pass. She cupped the skull tenderly and gazed into the empty eye sockets. Every curve and indentation of the relic held its own promise of perfection, of miracle.

I was the first, came the whisper in her head. She stiffened when she heard it. *I was the first they left to cry my life away alone. No one knows my name, nor the name of the man who bragged of my begetting and my birth, but who let me pass into the shadows. He said it was God's will, and that any who stood against it were accursed. He spoke of the Lord King's precious sword, and the paradise awaiting me. The only paradise I wanted was my mother's breast. Better if I'd never known the light, to have it torn from me one shred of breath at a time, alone on the hillside, waiting for a miracle that didn't come.*

I was the first, but not the last. How many more, Becca? How many more?

A darkness rose up out of the black holes in the ancient bone, a blood-dark anger than poured into her heart, casting all sense away. Once more she was a girl standing her vigil at Prayerful Hill, her Sixmonth passed clean, her woman's place on Wiserways awaiting her. They came to her there, the little voices. Some stridently called out the names of Wiserways women living, some feebly wailed the

names of mothers long dead. But always the voices
rose up to shake Becca's soul with a single cry: *How
many more? How many more?*

Their sorrow echoed louder than summer thunder,
cut her off from everything but the sound of their
helplessness, their despair. She was only dimly aware
of Thalie's shrill voice trying to penetrate, to reach
her and drag her back into the here and now. She
thought she felt the steadwoman lay hands on her,
but stronger hands brushed Thalie's grasp aside. The
ten children on the hillside were only a single grain
in the harvest of countless years. Pity for the lives
already lost, fear for the lives now in the balance, all
burned away to a black core of fury in her womb
against the power that gave creatures like Adonijah
full say over who lived and who died.

The rage mounted to her brain, seized possession
of her eyes, and painted them with the blazing light
of prophecy. She held the skull to heaven and
shouted, "I swear by this relic, before these witnesses,
that I will kill you with my own strength, Adonijah,
sooner than let you have power over my life or the
life of any other soul of Wiserways!" And she kissed
the fleshless cheekbone with a mother's love.

A muttering went up from every side. The stead
men who served their alph goggled at her so
awestruck that one of the older children managed to
slither from her captor's grasp and run away. The man
gave chase, dogged by Thalie's screeched curses.
Thalie snatched the skull from Becca's hands and
rushed back to Adonijah's side.

He was silent for a time. When he spoke again,

every word had the weight of an iron shackle. "You never were one to measure the wisdom of your words before you said them, were you, girl?"

"I know what I said," she replied, a chill wind buffeting her cheeks scarlet.

"And do you also know the penalty for a wife who defies her husband?"

"I'll go to my death before I'll let you call me your wife. But enforce that penalty if you can, Adonijah," she said, calm as the full moon's face. "Kill me by your own hand, if you dare to try. Or are you afraid?"

"He's not afraid of *you*, bitch!" Thalie shouted. "But he's not stupid, either. He's a good alph; his stead needs him alive! He knows better than to risk his life against that pack of scurriers you run with."

"Gilber Livvy's tribe has no part in this quarrel," Becca told her. "The oath was mine; I made it of my own free will. None of my people will interfere if I forbid it."

"Becca—" Gilber grabbed her arm, his eyes pleading with her to unsay so much.

She uncurled his fingers from her flesh and met his gaze, steady in her mind, set in her spirit. "If I bend to him, the children die. If I turn from him and leave with you, the children die. There's too many bones in Prayerful Hill put there by those who did it just because they could. It's got to come to an end, Gilber, either one I make or one I can't live to see."

"I won't allow it."

"Don't make me stand against you, too. They're your new tribe, but I'm their lady. Don't force them to choose where their souls' allegiance lies."

"What's wrong, Jewman?" Adonijah's scornful call rang out through the thin, clear air. "Can't you make the brat mind either? Maybe she's more than just another female. Maybe she's an evil omen, a sign to remind all decent folk to keep alert against the doings of the devil. There were women enough like her and plenty in the years that brought the hungering times!"

"Kill her!" Thalie shouted. "Kill her before God takes His vengeance on us for letting her live!" Spurred by her wild words, some of Adonijah's men started down the hill. The whorebabies moved forward to form a protective wall around Becca, guns and blowpipes and air-poppers coming up to choose their targets. The stead men saw the weaponry they faced and hesitated while Thalie reviled them without mercy for cowardice.

One of them turned to scowl at the ranting woman. "Coward, am I? The alph makes the stead. If Paul was still alive, I'd fight against a hundred scrawny scraps like them, devil take what kind of arms they bear! At least with Paul we'd know we fought for something true. But what the hell are we fighting for here? So he can pay her back for his lost eyes? Why wasn't he man enough to save 'em from her in the first place? Damn it, I say *let* Becca keep the oath she swore, if she can! If a man can't save his skin from a little bit of a girl like that, that's the *real* sign from God, and it don't take half an eye to see what it means!"

"God damn you, Hanoch, you dare talk of *eyes*?" Thalie stooped to pick up a rock from the hillside.

"Just you get near enough to me and I'll give you what that witch gave my Adonijah, only I won't need any sorceries to do it! Then see how easy you prate about *eyes*."

"She's right," said another steadman. "Even a kid like Becca could take down a blind man. Some oath!"

"*Silence!*" Adonijah's bellow stilled every voice. He turned his sightless face in the direction from which Becca's voice had last come. "Is that your final word to me, Becca? A challenge?"

"A challenge, Adonijah," Becca replied. "One I'll meet with honor. That's more than you did when you killed my pa."

"Look who's preaching honor!" he exclaimed, shaking with silent laughter. "A runaway whore who's fucked an army into following her! A Jewman's bitch with two good eyes to aid her! All right, I'll take your challenge. But only if *I* set the terms and the bounds of our fight."

"What terms?" Becca asked, her throat tightening. "What bounds? What weapons?"

"Weapons? I'll carry none. Hand to hand, so that you can keep true to the letter of your vow. You ought to keep true to *something*. With your own strength, you said. That suits me. But in a place where your eyes won't serve you any better than mine, and somewhere neither one of us can escape until the other's dead. Those are the terms. I've said my say, take or it leave it. Yes, leave it and walk away from a sacred oath that turned to shit on your tongue!"

Becca closed her eyes, willing all her anger back into its proper place. She would not give him even this small taste of satisfaction, to see that he'd riled her with his jibes. "Where will you have it be, Adonijah?" she asked calmly. "And when?"

"This sunset," he replied, his answer as smooth as her asking. "At Prayerful Hill."

Chapter Twenty-Three

I repeat, Webmaster Steven, we cannot spare the manpower to pursue this matter further. The offshore experiment is in crisis and requires all our attention, all our resources. It's not as if we lack the force to destroy them utterly, should they become a problem. But failing that circumstance, we see no reason to disrupt more vital programs at this time.

We will examine your motives later, if any complaints from the affected agricultural unit arise. It will be a very thorough examination, be assured of that.

As for the unfortunate incident at Greenwoodweb, the less said, the better. Most people are under the mistaken though suitable impression that it was the result of

*lax security in Bell ward, the work of
escaped lunatics. Naturally we are doing
what we can to promote this impression.
What suits us, survives, whether it's a
rumor or a man.*

Virgie stuck her head inside the tent flap. "Becca?"

"Come on in, Virgie," Becca called from the shadows.

The girl obeyed, feeling her way in the dark until her groping hand found Becca's foot. "I brought you a bite to eat." She settled herself on a thin blanket and shivered off the cold. "I'll be glad when we're gone from here," she said, handing Becca a piece of flatbread that smelled of sour butter.

Becca only sighed.

"Eat up," Virgie directed. "It's the scrapings of the crock Salome bartered for last place we camped. Smells funny, but it's still good."

"I'm not hungry."

"You ought to eat, with what's waiting for you." The girl sounded just like a settled steadwoman, a mother many times over. "I know plenty of our people'd be grateful to have something good to soften their bread."

"Give it to them, then," Becca said, handing it back. The two lapsed into silence.

"Why won't you speak with him?" Virgie asked at last.

"Gilber Livvy? We've got nothing to say."

"He's got plenty to say," Virgie corrected her. "He's

been saying it all through the camp, to anyone that'll hear. Van's been helping him, two tongues wagging the same way."

"I don't have to guess what they're saying," Becca said. She sounded tired, though she'd made it a point to retire to this hastily pitched tent and sleep away the remainder of daylight. She knew she'd be wanting all her strength, and lately there were times she felt more than naturally weary. "They don't want me to fight Adonijah. They've been trying to sway the tribe to keep me from it, isn't that so?"

"Um." It would've cost the girl nothing to agree with Becca, yet she kept mum. Virgie could hold more secrets than a stone, when she was minded, but she couldn't feign as if she had no secrets to hold. Becca's eyes were used to the darkness. She could just make out the girl's face, lips tight shut, eyes giving away nothing. No one held their looks and words so closed-off unless they had more than a little to hide.

"What are they doing, Virgie?" she asked. No answer. "What've they got planned?"

Instead of a straight answer, the girl blurted out questions of her own: "If you die, will our folk really attack the stead? All of 'em? There's not enough of us to win—not enough who know how to use the weapons they've picked up, anyhow. Only reason they could save you and Salome that night was 'cause Gilber threw 'em at the stead like Gideon, all noise and fire and confusion to make those city troops bolt. But the Coopfolk, they're still here." A sob of fear caught in the girl's throat. "If we attack, they'll come to back the steadfolk. It could turn against us too easy. What'll be then? What'll they do to my sibs, if no one's left to guard 'em? What'll become of Gilber Livvy's first tribe in the mountains, waiting on help that never comes?"

"Virgie, honey…" She tried to put her arms around the girl, to offer her a little comfort. Virgie flailed her gesture away, her breath coming short and rough.

"You can't do it, Becca! Gilber Livvy's right; it'd be the end for all of us. Anything he does to stop you is right. So what if Adonijah kills those brats? Better leave 'em die now than later, living with him for alph. They're not your people anymore; we are!"

"My people…" She shook her head. "Where's the kindred blood to bind us? I was born on this stead. Those are my sibs that Adonijah means to kill."

"You think it's just blood that binds?" Virgie spoke with all the contempt that a young girl could muster.

"That's just it, Virgie; I don't," Becca replied. "There's threads of blood and threads of heart, threads of happenstance and threads of spirit tying me off a dozen different ways. All I can do is look to what my soul tells me to do. If I sat back and calculated matters, you and your sibs'd still be buried in poor Mark's burrow, the little ones raised up in evil ways."

"That wasn't our fault." Virgie turned sullen, defensive. "If we'd've stayed on our old steads, the new alph'd take our blood to the winnowing. And when we joined with Mark, what we ate under his roof—" She swallowed hard over the bitter memory. "We did what we had to do to live."

"I know, child." This time when Becca reached out

her hand to touch Virgie, the girl didn't bat it away. "I'm not blaming you for it. It's what we all did, times past: What we had to do. *Anything* we had to do. It's hard to just lie down and die rather than do some awful thing to survive. A body wants to live. We say that we'll find time to heal our soul of the body's sins after, but for now we *live*, any price. That's human. And when the sins we do turn too ugly for us to bear looking at ourselves after, we stop calling them sins. We give them godly names to wear. That's human too."

Virgie began to sob in earnest, crumpled up in Becca's arms. "I should've saved my sibs from that! I should bear their sins on my soul!"

"Hush, love," Becca whispered. "Hush, little one. Let God name what's sin. Let sweet Mary Mother spread Her mantle over you and bring you peace. Our Father and our Mother both can't cast aside the children, can't leave us wailing in the dark. And how can I turn my back on the children, any children, when it lies in my hand to save them? Or at least to try."

Virgie sniffled and wiped her nose on the back of her hand. "You want to do that, you best not eat that bread I brought you. I saw Van go off, come back from somewhere with a poke of powder. He and Gilber Livvy was talking and I heard what they had to say about it. It's to make a body sleep."

"I sleep and they spirit me off," Becca concluded. "I wonder how Van came by such a thing?"

Virgie shrugged. "I don't know. I can't say I saw them sprinkle it in the butter crock, but I got that bread from Van's own hands. He told me make sure you ate. I don't know what I'm gonna tell him now."

"I'll do the telling." Becca stroked the girl's hair. "You did the right thing, Virgie." She stood up as much as she was able, inside the little tent. "What's the hour?"

"Sunset's coming on."

"Then I guess I'd better be on my way." She pushed aside the tent flap and stepped outside.

She had time to draw two breaths of the chilly air before they were on her, a host of the whorebabies. Frantic questions assailed her, countless hands held up a trembling sea of gray metal charms for her blessing. Becca found herself surrounded, then borne ahead in the midst of her people. They swept her along like twig on a floodtide to where the tanker stood, its engine silent. The side panel was down and many lights made the interior bright. The mob urged her up the ramp to where Gilber, Van and Salome stood grimly waiting.

"What *is* all this?" Becca demanded as soon as the crowd ebbed enough for her to stand free of it.

"*This* is what we've been coping with ever since you issued that crack-brained challenge," Salome shot back. Both women spoke low, guarding their words from the eager ears of the massed whorebabies. "The minute you came back to camp and ducked into that tent, it's been like this. The whispers went like wildfire through the camp."

"Some of those whispers had help," Becca said, looking narrowly at Van and Gilber.

"The change of orders didn't help calm things down either."

"What change?"

"What *change?*" Van echoed. "Nothing much. Just to do a full about-face, dig back into a camp we were bundling up to leave."

"And I suppose it'd calm them if you loaded me into this thing like I was a meal sack, and we all rode away?" Becca countered.

"I *said* you should've brought her the food." Van wheeled on Gilber. "*You* could've gotten her to eat. That stupid kid couldn't—"

"It wasn't right," Gilber said, almost like he was convincing himself of it. "Just not right. The whole plan had a funny smell. What made you think you could trust anything that came from his hands?"

"Look, I told the old bastard that the sleeping powder was for *me*. You think he'd actually give me something that'd harm—?"

Before Becca could break in to question either one of them, she felt Salome seize her wrist. "Look at them, Becca," she whispered, nodding ever so slightly at the eager faces turned toward the tanker. "Smile for them. They think you're going to give a speech. They expect you're going to announce a fresh change of plans. It's going to be a short, simple thing you'll say: You won't be going out to fight the steadman after all."

"I'm not saying anything of the kind, Salome," Becca murmured. "I'm going to meet Adonijah when I said I would, and when. I swore to it."

"Then look at them again, Becca." Salome's voice hardly rose above a hiss, but her sweeping gesture was clear: The whorebabies would have to be blind as Adonijah to miss knowing that she and their lady were talking about them. "One last look. You're going alone, but you're taking their lives with you, every one. Your death's theirs."

Becca stared at her as if she'd lost her mind. She searched Salome's face, hoping to find the usual telltale glint of mockery her eyes. None was there. When Salome spoke on, she spoke words plain and inescapable as the grave. "If you were just one idiot girl running after the fool killer, I'd say let you run. But you stopped being just one girl months ago. You're risking more than your life. *Look* at them I say. What do you think it's going to mean to them if you lose?"

"You can't go, Becca," Van put in. "You're all they believe in. You're the first thing to hold their faith."

Becca looked out at the faces spread out over the campground. "Oh no," she breathed. "You're talking crazy, like they've turned me into some sort of—"

"God?" Van finished for her.

"They can't," she maintained, shaking her head as if that would shake away the unthinkable. "They can't. Gilber, tell him he's wrong."

"It's true, Becca," Gilber said sadly. "Near as I can tell, it's true. It's beyond my control now. All I've tried to teach them of my tribe's ways, it's nothing to them next to you. They mouthed my words because it was their way out of the city. They do their best to follow our beliefs out of gratitude, but it didn't take gratitude for them to put their souls in your hands."

"For what?" Becca implored. "Can one of you tell me for what?" Her voice began to rise. Salome and the rest silently urged her to hush, all in vain. Below, the crowd of whorebabies clustered nearer, harking to every word that was said. "Because I bleed every moon? Because I'm a taking woman any time? What about it? That's how it used to be for all of us once, times long gone. That's how it might've been before this, if there wasn't murder every time a girl's body showed the signs of going back to the old ways. I'm just lucky I passed a clean Sixmonth before this change showed itself in me."

"Lucky?" Salome repeated. "Luck's made more gods than a thousand miracles."

"Becca, hark to me," Gilber pleaded. "Come away with us now; there's no shame in it. Don't give up your life for nothing. Let them—" He choked over words he didn't want to say. "Let them keep their god."

Becca looked at him long and steady. She could feel the burden of every single pair of eyes in all the encampment resting on her. She could feel the shadows stretching out their dark hands for her as the sun declined. And always in her ear, her head, her heart, she heard the constant sound of one lone infant wailing its life away on the cold hillside.

She turned from Gilber and Van and Salome to face the people. "What have you done?" she cried. "What have you made of me?"

A murmur of confusion ran through the crowd.

Head bent to head as the whorebabies whispered together. Becca saw the smiles of bland worship change to frowns of puzzlement.

"I'm not your god," she said, spreading her hands. "I'm no one's god. I can't hold any soul but my own, or any life. But I *will* hold that life! I was raised on this stead. I was milkfed with the lore that all I was and all I ever could be wasn't for me to say. I said different. I put teeth behind my saying so. They came to force me back into my place, but I didn't bend to it. Now you want to do the same to me. Chains of iron or chains of flowers, I won't wear them, any road. I won this life of mine too dear. I made my vow to fight Adonijah of my own free will. Any who tries to keep me from it stands with him and all he is, no matter how loud they say they love me." She bowed her head and said just loud enough for some of them to hear, "If you love me, let me be."

She walked slowly down the ramp and they parted their ranks to let her pass. She thought she heard Gilber Livvy call out her name one last time, but she held her eyes to the path. As she walked on, she saw the whorebabies looking at her with pity, with anger, with the bewilderment of children cast unready into the world, with the stone-faced resentment of the cheated, and sometimes—even yet—with love.

When she reached the road that would take her to Prayerful Hill, she heard a hastening sound behind her. She turned and saw Gilber followed by four men and two women of his new tribe jogging to overtake her. He carried his rifle, they clutched blowpipes. She went on guard, ready to fight them if that was what it took, but when he reached her he said, "However you choose to stand against him, you're not going into the midst of your enemy's camp alone."

Hattie was waiting for them on the road. The older steadwoman looked her daughter over from soles to crown, saying nothing. Becca wondered what her mother must think, to see her come dressed so unwomanly, in borrowed shirt and trousers, a second shirt cast over all instead of the jacket she lacked. But there was no life in Hattie's eyes, no flash of the old righteous wrath against all things other than ageless stead lore. The older woman pressed her lips together and blinked red-rimmed eyes as a fresh shudder of chill rippled over her scant-clad body.

"I'm sent to meet you, Becca," she said. "They've prepared the place. When you and he step inside, a wooden panel goes down to block the entry. There you'll be left until—until—" Tears swam to the surface of her eyes, spilled down her cheeks. She clapped work-worn hands to her face and sobbed, "Forgive me, Becca! Oh my baby, if Prayerful Hill swallows your bones too, I don't know how I'll bear it! Don't go into that dark place without forgiving me!"

Becca gazed at her mother, and a sliver of pity no wider than an infant's nail-paring opened a way into her heart. She tried to draw the ice back over it, and failed. *She is what she was raised to be. She never turned her eyes to anything but what they taught her. And she was afraid for her life. The things we do then— Not all of us are steel.*

She took the older woman into her arms and

pressed her cheek to the gray and wispy hair. "I forgive you. And if I live, if it's in my power, I'll seek out Shifra's forgiveness for you too."

"Shifra's—?" Hattie's hand trembled as she brought it to her mouth to smother a cry. Her eyes swarmed with a thousand questions she would have asked about her vanished lastborn child, but Becca only shook her head.

"It's almost sunset," she said. She took off her warm overshirt and settled it on Hattie's shoulders. She wouldn't need it once she reached the hill.

Adonijah stood before the opening of Prayerful Hill, Thalie at his side. Above them, on the brow of the mound where winter-killed grasses rattled and hissed in the wind, a troop of four Highlandwebbers manned a thick slab of planking, ready to let it slip down over the entryway at a word. Four others waited to shove it snugly into place. Stones and poles were there for the bracing. If they thought anything about this job of theirs, their faces gave nothing away.

Webmaster Steven came from behind the poised wooden panel and looked down at Becca with an expression of mixed surprise and speculation. "So Van didn't get you to take the sleeping powder after all."

"*Is* that what it was?" Becca replied.

The webmaster's hearty laugh was cut short by a wince of pain. He touched one of the bandages on his face gingerly, then passed his fingertips more lightly over a cut too shallow to demand binding. One sleeve of his jacket hung empty, the garment draped like a cape over his thickly wrapped left arm.

Salome had left him many tokens to remember her by.

"Did you think it was poison?" he asked lightly. "If it were, how long do you imagine it would take for your mob of savages to find out where it came from? No, I intend to return home alive. Besides, Van was so proud of his little sham, pretending the powder was for him, me pretending to believe him. It took a good deal of courage for him to come to me like that, secretly; courage or lunacy. What if he decided to add some realism to the role and took a dose of the stuff I gave him? He's a fool, and fools die soon enough on their own. I don't need to ensure his death. Or yours."

The jacket slipped from his shoulder. As he readjusted it he added, "You're of no further interest to me, Becca. If your alph kills you or if you kill him, it's seedgrub business. The same goes for Van and Salome; I'm done with them. I believe I'll miss her more than him, if truth be told. She was a fine trader, a pretty good breeder, a useful woman. As for Van—" A delicate shrug, so as not to disturb the jacket a second time. "I thought he had the brains to make a worthy heir. I should have seen the flaw in him earlier, but when one pins one's hopes so tightly on another human being, one tends to nurture certain blind spots. I'm thankful I finally woke up and cut my losses."

"You could've spared a lot of people a lot of hurt if you'd woken sooner," Becca said.

"Hmmm." Webmaster Steven's reply barely

acknowledged that she'd spoken at all. He looked down at Thalie and Adonijah and asked, "Is there going to be some sort of ritual first or can we get this started? My people and I have a considerable journey to begin tomorrow. We'd like to get some rest."

"You'll have it." Adonijah tilted his head back, sharp teeth showing. "No need for you to lose a night's sleep. I'm ready to enter the hill when she is, but no one has to stand vigil. Open it again come dawn. You'll be sure to find things decided by then."

Webmaster Steven chuckled. "You want *us* to open it? I expect dawn to find us well on the homeward road. Send me word of the results, if you insist. I suppose the girl's brother will want to know."

As Adonijah had said, there was no ritual. A little bickering between Gilber and Thalie was all that marked the entry into Prayerful Hill. Before she'd allow her alph to step over the threshold, Adonijah's wife raised a fuss, demanding Becca strip off her clothes to prove she'd hidden no weapons on her person, and Gilber refused such shame in Becca's name.

"Shame?" Thalie mimicked his protest. "Shame touching *her*? She doesn't know the meaning of it."

"Oh, for the love of—!" Impatient to bury them and be gone, Webmaster Steven snapped out a command to his men: "Search the two of them and get it over with." Becca's face flamed as a Highlandwebber's hands wandered purposefully over her body.

"No concealed weapons on her."

"None on him."

"Rustic honor," Webmaster Steven commented dryly. "What a privilege to witness it."

Becca sought Gilber's hand and pressed it between both of hers. Her lips parted, and she drew breath to bid him goodbye, but fear of saying anything ill-omened left her silent. She kissed him once, and he responded so fiercely that she grew afraid that he might never let her go.

But he did release her, though the anguish she saw in his eyes tore her heart. She glanced in Adonijah's direction and saw the alph likewise taking leave of his wife. Thalie's face burned like a blade in the forge when she finally stepped back and let him go.

There was a single clay lamp burning inside the hill. Becca recalled it from the time her sib Tom had been sent to stand vigil with the bones. It seemed like centuries had rolled over the world since then.

A groaning, grating noise came from behind her. The planked slab was being lowered into place, scraping over the stone facings that flanked the entryway. The last of the outside light was cut off. She was alone with Adonijah in the tomb of the innocents.

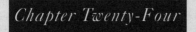

Chapter Twenty-Four

Yet they are thy people and thy inheritance.

"Are you there, Becca?" Adonijah stood with his back to the wall of skulls, his hand hovering over the flickering wick of the vigil light. Becca couldn't tell whether he was mocking her or not. Somehow it no longer mattered whether Adonijah's words were laced with scorn or given in all sincerity. The time to weigh words was past.

"I'm here," she said. The bones were all around her. They gave back every word she uttered in an echo heavy with the coppery scent of faded blood. She could feel their power, and it filled her with a dread of touching them, even by accident. Solid steadlore taught that it was only sorrow for an unwed girl to touch the bones of Prayerful Hill.

But I'm no longer a virgin girl, Becca thought, her eyes passing over the walls packed tight with memory. She recalled all her old fears: the dread of those small spirits, too soon dispossessed of life, lingering near the bones they'd left behind. The steadwives whispered how a single touch of a living hand might wake the souls of the Lord King's chosen ones. Then what could prevent their leaping from dead bone to living flesh? What could keep them from stealing into a waiting womb to grasp a second chance to walk the daylight?

—And when that girl's first babe's planted in her, there's two souls striving to lay claim to it. No womb can hold such a battle. Her babe's true soul's cast out, the other lingers, even if the rightful infant's body's brought forth too soon. The child of Prayerful Hill just waits for a second planting, and a third, and more. Poor girl! She'll never bear a living babe. Or if she does, it'll be a misbirth, monstrous, proof of her sin, because her touch on a dead babe's bone called back a soul to earth that rightly should've rested in paradise.

"You're quiet, Becca," Adonijah said. "Are you planning to sneak up on me?"

"I'm here," she repeated. She knew it made her sound mindless, but she was only half-hearing his words. Other voices stole into her mind, whispers like sand sifting down. "I'm—I'm at prayer."

Adonijah gave a low, grunting laugh. "Still the good girl. Make your peace with God now. I won't try and stop you. Just do me one favor: Give me an *amen* to go on, by way of warning. It'd be shameful if you used prayer to cover over you creeping in for the kill."

"I won't do anything so low, Adonijah."

"Still proud, too. I hear what you're not saying better'n I hear what you speak! *You* won't do anything so low as something *I'd* do. No, Becca, take off the saint's white robe; it's no more yours than mine. I confess my sins: I took this stead from your sire by any means I could. There's some would call it low fighting, deceit, treachery, but it damn well *worked*. When it was done, I was as much alph of Wiserways as any of the old fools who took this stead by the strength of their arms."

"A cur barks and frights a lion over a cliff, that doesn't make that cur a lion," Becca said.

"And a bitch in heat shows her tail to a Jewman," Adonijah replied. "She takes that sorry bastard by the balls and leads him where she wants him to go, but *she's* not getting what she wants by treachery, oh no! *She's* pure as if the holy water's just run off her brow!" His face contracted into a horrible grimace of rage. "He shot me down so you could come and steal my sight. Without him by you that night, I'd've—"

"You'd've done nothing," Becca said, wrapping herself in the calm of certainty. "You were too busy running for your life. From me, Adonijah. You were running away from *me*."

He snorted. "From the gun you stole, you witch, that's what I ran from. Like any man of sense would run! But you don't have that gun in here with you now, and you don't have your pet Jewman neither. Your pride brought you to this. Your high head and

your stiff neck let you think you're a match for a man.
Well, let me tell you, you make your prayers and you
make 'em fast, because in a little while my fingers
are gonna snuff this light, and then my hands are
gonna find that stiff neck of yours and teach it how
to bend until it snaps in two."

"Why don't you just put it out now?" Becca asked.

Adonijah's wrathful look relaxed into an
unnaturally wide grin. "There's no hurry. The longer
I bide, the less time I'll need to sit in here with just
your corpse for company. 'Sides, this is your last sight
of the world. I wouldn't want you to join me in the
darkness without something this fine to remember."
And he flung back one hand to let the fingers ripple
down a row of little skulls.

Becca gasped at the irreverent gesture. The Lord
King's chosen babes gave their souls to paradise, but
their hallowed bones came home to rest. Women
birthed the babies, men birthed the bones, taking up
the lifeless bodies of the hillside and seething them
pure of flesh and blood, picking apart the bones and
laying each kind with each in the niches and hollows
of Prayerful Hill. The smallest, finest bones of all
were placed in wide-mouthed urns of stone, but the
larger kind were placed with their fellows. Time
nibbled at the bones, changed their hue, sometimes
snapped those below with the weight of those above.
The layers of earth that men had heaped up over the
true foundation of Prayerful Hill would shift now and
again as the leavings of former generations shuddered
back into dust.

There was one exception: the skulls; so many, so

small, so old. Theirs was the place of most holiness, most honor, and when time took its tithing from them, the men of Wiserways would come with plaster to repair the loss. They filled the wall at Adonijah's back with their silence, and nothing showed in the hollows of their eyes but eternity.

Without thinking, Becca placed her hands over her quickened womb and murmured a woman's prayer. It was one she'd heard many times on her mother's lips when Hattie went big-bellied with Shifra. It called out for Mary Mother to take up her heaven-blue mantle and shelter the unborn child beneath it. It was a common prayer that every steadwoman knew.

Adonijah knew it too. He harked to the soft words pouring from Becca's mouth and he smiled, nodding. And then, with no warning, his fingers nipped the flame from the lampwick well before Becca brought it to the last *amen*.

She couldn't help but give a little cry of shock at the sudden dark. It left her lips one moment and Adonijah rammed into her the next. He crushed her to the earth under the full weight of his body. Beyond all reason, her eyes strained against the blackness, starving to see the face she fought. There was only the dark, flat against her sight.

His left hand scrabbled up her arm, seized her right. She struggled to catch her breath and inhaled his, hot and sour. She bunched her left hand into a fist and jabbed it at his face. She heard a faint crunching sound, then his curse, and smelled his blood before it spattered her cheek.

Then she felt something glide across her chest.

Instinctively her free hand followed its track and found the fabric of her shirt sliced cleanly open. "You—!" she began, all agape.

"A virtuous woman, who can find?" he whispered. Another pass of the blade, so tiny, so keen, opened Becca's sleeve to the hill's icy air. "Or one with Thalie's wit, to give her loving husband so much more than just a kiss in parting?"

Becca moaned, the sole protest left her in this place. Adonijah still had her pinned down. She tried to jerk her knee up between his legs, but he overlay her too heavily for that. There was no light; but memories needed none. Once more she lay helpless, powerless beneath him, only this time it was her life he meant to take.

Not just mine.

She whipped her head to the side and brought her teeth together on the wrist holding down her right hand. He screeched and loosed his hold. She fisted up both hands and clapped them against the sides of his head, trying for the temples. One struck true, the other hit the bone behind. He slashed at her with the blade his wife had slipped into his hand. It was so well honed that it licked her flesh open without pain. Blood streamed down her arm.

She linked her hands together and with a sweeping motion knocked him sideways. He rolled only a little from her body, but she seized on that small respite, putting her own strength to his motion, tumbling him off to the side. She scrambled to her feet, gasping for breath.

It had grown very hot inside the hill, and very

silent. Hark how she might, she couldn't hear any sound but her own labored breath. *He can hear that too*, she thought, and strove to force it shallow and quiet. She took a tentative step backward. Her shoe leather creaked loud enough to be a thunderclap.

She thought she heard a sound. Then something whooshed through the air past her head and hit the wall with a clatter of loosened bones. A second object flew after, this one striking her in the chest. Unhurt, she stooped to seek it: a shoe. Adonijah had been quick to take a lesson from her example. He now padded barefoot over the holy ground, with nothing to give away his movements.

Her pulsing heart filled her ears with the blood's rapid, frantic throbbing. She thought she sensed a thread of cool air seeping across her cheek, stealing into Prayerful Hill through the cracks that the sealing door must have all around it. *If it were day, there'd be a bit of light come in that way too*, she thought. But night was all there was, and no hope of dawn for many hours.

Adonijah made a sudden rush at her. Even barefoot, his feet thudded against the frozen earth. She heard and threw herself to one side, praying that blind choice would save her. His empty hand grazed her back. She scurried away on hands and knees from his wild gropings until she could spring back to her feet. She put out her hands to support her trembling body.

Bone rested under her hand. She jerked it away, unable to suppress the little whimper of horror that rose to her lips. Her reaction had a price: Adonijah lashed out with his blade and caught a fresh taste of her blood.

Now he'd wounded both her arms, though the second hurt wasn't much more than a scratch. The other, though, bled freely, stickiness puddling into her cupped hand. The first numbing shock was gone; the blade's track beat with pain. In the darkness, Becca saw dainty spirals of violet and yellow light begin to spin before her eyes. She bit her lip hard, blinked them off, and sidestepped nimbly away from the spot where Adonijah's cursed luck had let him find her.

Her hands glided over bones, shin and thigh; not truly long, but long enough when held against their brothers. They seemed to go on forever as she sidled past. She tried to recall what her hands would encounter once they reached the neighboring niche. She knew that no matter how foolish it would be, if her fingers blundered into the place of the skulls, she would fill Prayerful Hill with a madwoman's screams.

Her knee barked against something heavy. She stumbled forward, taking down the obstacle with her as she fell. Smoothly hewn rock, round and cool, scraped against her wounds. Tiny bones clattered as the dust of their stone cradle wafted up to choke the one who'd dared disturb their rest. On her belly over the tumbled urn, Becca coughed and sneezed loud enough to make the hill shake.

He threw himself at the sound, stabbing ahead with the blade. It clacked against the urn's stone side. She pushed herself backward with her feet, kicking wildly. The dark had sapped her, mind and spirit. All the old lessonings she'd had at the hands of Gram Phila's Martha winked away, all the hours she'd spent learning how to fight were gone. Despair took her. Countless small ghosts fluttered up on the freed clouds of bones become dust, their infant voices clamoring to be heard.

They flowed into her ears, her eyes, her mouth, her belly. The dark heart of Prayerful Hill became the vigil night of years past, when she'd first heard the voices, when she'd first let slip the measured order of her life. *Becca, Becca, what have you done?* came the wailing in her head. *You've gone running after death when you might've held to life. If only you'd have kept your proper place, you'd be wrapped warm in your bed tonight, your womb fruitful by your lawful husband, an honored wife of Wiserways. Instead you're locked up amid the bones, your own blood to drink, your babe never to be born! Oh child, the devil's in you! What have you done?*

Her hand slapped hard against the bones, her flesh tingling with their inescapable reality. Her fingers closed around a single one of their countless number. She yanked it free, slammed it into the wall, heard it splinter. The harsh sound drove out the voices. She put her face to the dark, a storm-battered traveler choosing to confront the wind. "Adonijah!" she shouted defiantly, and the echoes rang with the name.

He came at her in full fury, bowling her over backward. Even as they fell together, she met his onslaught with one arm before her to bar the

downstroke of the blade and the other jabbing up
with all the strength left in her, bone piercing flesh,
bone drinking blood, bone grating against bone. Her
knuckles met his jaw as the full length of the
shattered thigh bone entered his skull. She heard him
scream for only an instant before her head struck one
of the stone facings framing the hill's entryway.
Darkness swallowed darkness.

⧓⧓

It astonished her, how easily the great wooden door
fell away. It toppled from its place at the lightest
touch of her hand as she stepped out into the living
world. There were still a few stars visible in a paling
sky. The moon was gone. No one was there to greet
her: No one expected the hillside to open before
dawn, from within. For the longest time she only
stood on the threshold of Prayerful Hill, tasting the
sweetness of breath. Then she went back inside to
tend to her hurts.

When she emerged a second time, her arms
throbbed beneath the bandages she'd torn for herself
from Adonijah's clothing. She'd bound up the worst
of her wounds with the cloth he'd once used to cover
his ruined eyes. If she tried to close her hand, her
fingers stuck together with her own drying blood
mixed with his. She wished for water. There was a
fearful aching in her womb, as though a hand had
cupped it and was slowing squeezing it dry.

Some thoughts didn't bear the thinking. She

banished them by forcing others into their place. "I have to go home," she told the stars. She started up the road.

She hadn't gone far when she heard it, the sound of an infant's cry. It was a reedy, weary sound. She shook her head, trying to dislodge the illusion. It clung to her ears, refusing to be cast away, until she understood it was a true thing.

The baby lay at the very summit of the hill, wrapped up in a single blanket, its gaping lips tinged blue. Whichever stead had cast it out was mastered by an alph who fancied himself a thrifty husbandman. Not even an old basket or the shell of a broken pot had been spared to house the child until the Lord King might show it mercy. Becca knelt down and took the chilled scrap of life to her bosom. An icy cheek nuzzled through the slashed fabric of her shirt, seeking warmth and milk. Though Becca's breasts were swollen, they had nothing yet to give. Still, for the abandoned child the sham of feeding was enough to leave it content for a time.

Becca stood up and looked into the lightening eastern sky. A woman could see much from so high up, and hear much too. She thought she saw the open space before the great house at Wiserways, and the stolen tanker there with all her people—stead and city and wilderness—gathered around it. She knew that she was given to seeings, that distance demanded that this be another vision, and a false one besides. "They're probably waiting for me in the camp, Gilber and the others," she told the babe. Still, when she walked down the hill, she set her feet on the steadbound road.

And they were there, just as she'd foreseen them, Gilber and all their tribe. Some drowsed, most stood on guard around the tanker, a few were taken up in chary conversation with steadmen likewise made to stand watch. The open space teemed with people. From the great house, the wives of Wiserways Stead leaned out of windows or clustered on the porch, their children with them. She knew they'd seen her when she heard Thalie shriek as if the Last Days had come upon them and when she saw Gilber's face light up brighter than the breaking dawn.

He ran to meet her; she walked past without a word. She caught just a glimpse of how his face changed when he saw the infant in her arms. She heard the whispers and the words of wonderment all around her, but she walked apart from these. Somewhere in the distance an engine was rumbling to life: Webmaster Steven and his city troops had kept their word to be gone before daybreak. She turned her eyes to the looming shape of the tanker.

While the people murmured at her back and the word *miracle* seemed to ride on every breath, she scaled the tanker's side. She knew that the real miracle was that she could climb the iron rungs with only one arm free, the other cradling the child, neither whole.

Salome was waiting for her at the top, her face unreadable. She helped Becca up, then took herself down by the rungs without a word. Her belly knotting with a dull ache, Becca stepped to the very edge and looked down.

Then she took the drowsing infant from her arm and tore away the rag of blanket swaddling it. Holding the child in both her hands, she raised it toward the daybreak. High, higher still she lifted up her offering to the sky. The sudden cold startled the babe to full wakefulness. Every living soul of Wiserways was witness to the clear baptismal light washing over the trembling newborn limbs. Even the dead seemed like to rise at the sound of the baby's lusty, furious cries. All the people saw, awestruck at what they could only name miracle.

The child still struggled in the light as Becca cried, "People of Wiserways, you know me! I was Rebecca, daughter of Paul, Hattie's child. I was Rebecca, once one of your own, still your own, but made more than that by the will of heaven! I have passed through the wilderness, I have been to the gates of the city, and I've come back now from the very bones of this stead! Will you have what I bring you? Will you open your hearts to a new way, a new judgment, a cleansing for your lives and for your souls?"

She lowered the child to her milkless breast. The little mouth closed greedily around her nipple and all at once Becca's pain dropped away from her. She raised her head and shouted out at the distant city, "*In God's name, I am Rebecca, alph of Wiserways Stead!*"

"In God's name!" all the people answered, coming to their knees, faces drinking in the light.

Esther M . Friesner

In God's name! came the echo that shook to the roots of the world.

The End

Esther M. Friesner

Esther Friesner was educated at Vassar College, and went on to Yale University, where within five years she was awarded an M.A. and Ph.D. in Spanish. She taught Spanish at Yale for a number of years before going on to become a full-time author of fantasy and science fiction. She has published twenty-two novels so far.

Ms. Friesner won the Romantic Times award for Best New Fantasy Writer in 1986 and the Skylark Award in 1994. Her short story "All Vows" took second place in the Asimov's SF Magazine Readers' Poll for 1993 and was a finalist for the Nebula in 1994. In 1996, she won the Nebula award for Best Short Story for "Death and the Librarian" and her story "A Birthday" was nominated for a Hugo award. Her *Star Trek: Deep Space Nine* novel, *Warchild*, made the *USA TODAY* Bestseller list.

She lives in Connecticut with her husband, two children, two rambunctious cats, and a fluctuating population of hamsters.

The following is an excerpt from
children of the dusk,
the forthcoming final volume in the
madagascar manifesto trilogy.

Nosy Mangabéy

Grasshoppers blackened the moon.

The Malagasy laughed delightedly and pointed what was left of his fist at the predawn sky. Abandoning his guardianship of the limestone crypt, he shrugged off the ragged clay-colored loincloth. By the fading light of the stars, of glowworms, and of the last embers of the coconut husk fire, he began a sinuous dance of triumph. He moved around the moss and ivy covered totems that dotted the area, carelessly swatting at the mosquitoes and the rain flies that heralded a tropical rain. When he tired of the dance, he removed a liana from one of the totems, wove it into a garland, and placed it on top of his grisly red and salt-and-pepper head like a crown.

He ran his misshapen fingers down the totem. Miniature zebu horns topped an arabesque of curling leaves and carved lemurs balanced on one another's backs, looking outward with huge, whorled eyes.

The grasshoppers moved away from the huge egg yolk tropical moon, away from the Zana-Malata who grinned a toothless grin. *"Minihana!"* he shrieked. "Eat!" He opened the gaping pink hole where his nose and mouth should have been, pushed his tongue outward in the manner of an iguana, and drew a stream of glowworms into his throat.

He exhaled a burst of fire and chuckled at his own cleverness. Soon, he thought, it would be time for *lambda*, the dressing of the dead, and only he knew who waited inside the crypt. He and the tree frogs and the glowworms. Meanwhile, he could wait. Here, in isolation, time meant nothing to him—any more than it did to those who were buried in the *valavato*.

He moved around the moss- and ivy-covered totems that dotted the area. At his feet, a *Dô* snake slithered away, carrying with it the soul of one of the dead who haunted the burial ground. Behind him, five short, black men, eyes painted with white and black tar circles, bodies pulsating with a luminous white substance, appeared out of the rim of trees, cavorted a moment, and disappeared.

As if it, too, knew that changes were imminent, the rain forest chorus stopped. When only the bats sang *a cappella* in the damp tropical air, the fox-lynxes raised their long faces to watch him. The aye-ayes and the larger lemurs fled, the oxlike zebu sauntered down the hill, bells clanking hollowly and dewlaps swaying beneath their chins.

The Zana-Malata stayed where he was, listening to the voices of the dead. Chief of all he surveyed, he stared down at the crescent coral reef three hundred feet below the burial ground. On the horizon, his keen eyes discerned the lights of a ship moving toward him. He glanced at the moon hanging over the horizon.

It was beginning. The ghosts were returning to Nosy Mangabéy, his island where the dead dreamed.

•

In no mood to encounter anyone, Erich skirted the meadow and the Zana-Malata's hut by taking a trail through the jungle on the steeper, northwest side of the saddle formed by the island's two hills.

He began to climb.

After about half an hour, his interest gave way to fatigue as his calves and thighs started to feel the strain of the climb. If this was to become his hill, his refuge from the problems of Hempel and Miriam and the Jews, there would have to be a wider path. And, he thought wryly, he had better rid himself of the thirty-one-year-old city-boy weakness that had developed in his muscles since the demands of rank and family had curtailed his daily workouts. He would take Miriam's advice, he decided, ignoring the spirit in which it had been given. He would fashion himself a javelin and use that and daily walks up this hill to get into shape.

He put his arm back, took several long strides which carried him through the last of the trees and onto the top of the hill, and threw an imaginary javelin. The action felt good.

Very good indeed.

He leaned against a heavily sculpted totem and saw that there were more than two dozen of them, each bearing the skull of an ox. At the crest of the hill stood a stone menhir—what looked like a three-sided rock house dug into the hillside. The roof was a huge stone slab overgrown with moss. At the northwest corner stood a larger totem. It, too, bore the skull of an ox, this time crowned with a woven liana garland.

He examined it up close. He could make out miniature zebu horns, curling leaves, carved lemurs standing on top of one another's backs and looking outward with enormous eyes.

He put out his hand to touch the totem, and quickly withdrew it as the thought occurred to him that the syphilitic had probably forged the path and woven the garland. Automatically, he turned full circle to make sure that the hideous black man wasn't standing somewhere watching him. Assured that he was alone, he forced himself to relax.

He had only been on the island for two days, yet he felt oddly at home.

If only...

He looked down at the area he had chosen for the base camp. The encampment, was roughly the size of a soccer field. The far corner had been set aside for the Jews, some of whom were still at work emplacing the tall posts of an eastern sentry tower. Others, barehanded, strung barbed concertina wire across the fences they had just completed. As for electrifying the fences—which Hempel was trying to insist upon—there were other, more urgent uses for the generator when they got it up and running. First and foremost, it had to be used for lighting the compound at night, and for pumping water into the water tank if the rain couldn't keep it full.

Yes, Erich thought, he could be happy here, if only Taurus were not taking the climate so hard, and if only he could avoid conflict between his trainers and Hempel's men, and the major's syphilitic friend, and...

Putting the question of Miriam and Solomon aside to examine later, along with his assessment of Hempel's true motives in accepting this assignment, he looked across the meadow at the trainers, exercising their animals while Taurus lay helpless in the medical tent.

Maybe he could use the seaplane for escape once it was ready. Take the dogs and the baby, and let the rest rot. From what Perón had told him, Buenos Aires seethed with women beside whom Miriam was a dishrag.

Yet despite his desire to leave, the island seemed to speak to him in tongues he understood. It was his, in a way the Rathenau estate could never have been.

•

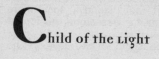

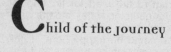
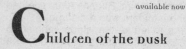

In *child of the light,* world war I draws to an end, a communist revolt brings gunfire to the Berlin's tree-lined avenues, and economic disaster looms threateningly. In this penetrating look at the birth of Nazi Germany, three friends come of age in a rapidly changing world: a Jew, a catholic, and the girl they both love.

This moving story of love, friendship, and survival presents a bold and powerful look at a painful chapter in history. Follow the three friends as they grow up and begin to follow their destined paths, as one joins the SS regime, another becomes a fugitive, and the third is caught between them.

Child of the journey continues the chronicle of the three friends as they struggle to find reconciliation between hate and compassion. As the war rages on, the survival of one depends on betrayal of another.

Children of the Dusk concludes the tulmultuous journey of the three friends. Taking the story thousands of miles from Germany, friend is pitted against friend as a once hypothetical plan is put into action: to create a Jewish homeland on the African island of Madagascar.